FIREFOX DOWN!

FIREFOX DOWN!

CRAIG THOMAS

BANTAM BOOKS
TORONTO · NEW YORK · LONDON · SYDNEY · AUCKLAND

FIREFOX DOWN!

Bantam Hardcover edition / October 1983
2nd printing . . . October 1983
Bantam rack-size edition / October 1984

Grateful acknowledgment is made for permission to quote from copyrighted material:

From "Fire and Ice" from *The Poetry of Robert Frost* edited by Edward Connery Lathem. Copyright 1923, © 1969 by Holt, Rinehart and Winston. Copyright 1951 by Robert Frost. Reprinted by permission of Holt, Rinehart and Winston, Publishers.

Four lines from "Hawk Roosting" from *New Selected Poems* by Ted Hughes. Copyright © 1959 by Ted Hughes. Reprinted by permission Harper & Row, Publishers, Inc.

Library of Congress Cataloging in Publication Data

Thomas, Craig.
  Firefox down!
  I. Title.
PR6070.H56FS   1983   823'.914   83-90654

ISBN 0-553-24305-5

Bantam Books are published by Bantam Books, Inc. Its trademark, consisting of the words "Bantam Books" and the portrayal of a rooster, is Registered in the United States Patent and Trademark Office and in other countries. Marca Registrada. Bantam Books, Inc., 666 Fifth Avenue, New York, New York 10103.

PRINTED IN THE UNITED STATES OF AMERICA

H   0 9 8 7 6 5 4 3 2 1

for

CLINT EASTWOOD

—pilot of the Firefox

ACKNOWLEDGMENTS

My thanks, especially on this occasion, to my wife, Jill, for her editing of the manuscript, and for bullying and cajoling me through the writing process! Thanks, too, to T.R. Jones, for acting as my technical adviser.

AUTHOR'S NOTE

One of the perils of writing a sequel, especially to a novel which I originally completed early in 1975, is the very passage of time. The present novel takes up the story of Mitchell Gant and the Mig-31 at precisely the point where its predecessor left them. One of the principal characters of the earlier novel was Yuri Andropov, then Chairman of the Soviet intelligence service and secret police, the KGB. Events have overtaken me, since that gentleman is now, following the demise of Leonid Brezhnev, the leader of the Soviet Union. For the sake of continuity, I have had to keep him in his former job. However, I shall always think of him, in company, no doubt, with millions of Soviet citizens, as the head of the most powerful and repressive secret police force the modern world has ever experienced.

FIREFOX DOWN!

PART ONE
THE PILOT

I think I know enough of hate
To say that for destruction ice
Is also great
And would suffice.

—Robert Frost
Fire and Ice

1 / **DOWN**

Beginning . . .

The Firefox crossed the Norwegian coast 80,000 feet above the Tanafjord. The on-board computer issued instructions to the autopilot for the first predetermined change of course. The aircraft banked. Mitchell Gant watched the curve of the earth far below him tilt and then reassert itself. Above him, the sky darkened almost to black. It was empty. He was entirely alone.

Beginning to relax . . .

The shower of turning, bright, sun-caught metal leaves, falling out of the tumult of smoke that a moment earlier had been the second Firefox, returned to flash upon a screen at the back of his mind. A white ball of flame, then erupting, boiling black smoke, then the spiraling, falling pieces, then the empty clean sky.

Nausea diminishing, almost gone. Hands almost not shaking now as they rested on his thighs. Left cheek's tic—he waited, counting the seconds—still now.

He had done it. He had won. He was able to form the thoughts with calm, precise, satisfying clarity. He had done it. He had won. And, like an undercurrent, he admitted another idea—he was still alive.

The Firefox banked once more, the scimitar-edge of the earth's surface tilted again, then leveled. The aircraft had begun its complex zigzag across Finland, en route to its rendezvous with the commercial flight from Stockholm to Heathrow. In the infrared shadow of the airliner, he would be hidden as he crossed the North Sea to RAF Scampton, where Aubrey the Englishman would be waiting for him with Charlie Buckholz from the CIA. Two men whose orders had placed him in continual danger for the past three days. Two men who had given him . . . ? He let the thought go. He didn't owe them. They owed him.

The congratulations . . . he wanted those. The unconcealable smiles and gestures of satisfaction, even of surprise and relief. They owed him all of those.

The other faces came back, then, as if to lessen and spoil the moment. Baranovich, Pavel, Semelovsky, Kreshin—Fenton's broken face on the wet embankment of the Moskva river. All of them dead. All of them willingly dead, except for Fenton, simply to put him in physical conjunction with the Firefox. *This* . . .

His hands smoothed the controls, like the hands of a man buying his first new car and expressing his awed sense of ownership. He touched the instrument panel in front of him, he read the Machmeter—Mach 0.9. His speed would remain below Mach 1. He had no wish to trail a betraying sonic boom across Finland. The altimeter displayed 60,000 feet. The Firefox was dropping slowly towards its rendezvous altitude through the dark-blue empty sky.

He didn't want to entertain the faces, and they slipped from his mind. It was all becoming unreal; hard to understand that it was no more than three days since he had arrived at Moscow's Cheremetievo airport disguised as Orton, the Canadian businessman and suspected drug-trafficker.

Increasingly, there was only *now*, this moment. He owned the moment as he owned the aircraft. The Firefox was his. In perhaps less than two hours he would have to surrender it to others—to men who could never, in a million years, fly it. It would be examined, tested, dismantled, reduced to a hollow shell; finally shipped in crates in the belly of a Hercules across the Atlantic. But now, it was his airplane. In two hours, also, he would begin his own decline, his return to the anonymity, the emptiness, of what he had been before Buckholz had resurrected him.

He wanted to cry out against it, for his sake, for the sake of the airplane. Instead, he squashed the thought like a beetle. Not now, not yet—

In the mirror, the sky was dark blue behind him. The cloud layer was far below him. The curve of the earth fell away on either side of the aircraft. He was utterly detached from the globe beneath. A stream of sparkling diamonds rushed away like the tail of a comet behind the Firefox, like the wake of a swan he had once seen lifting from a lake at evening. Sparkling water . . .

The aircraft's nose eased round a few degrees as the Firefox automatically altered course once more. The stream of diamond droplets altered with it. Tinkerbell, he thought, remembering the darkened movie theatre in Clarkeville and the petulant sprite with her Disney trail of gleaming dust. His mother, if she knew his father had been drinking, always gave him money for the movies saved from her meager housekeeping, though there was rarely the extra for popcorn. By the time the main feature ended, his father might have fallen into a drunken sleep, and it would be safe to go home.

And then he knew. His heart and stomach seemed stunned by a physical blow. Fuel droplets, escaping into the thin cold atmosphere. A broken necklace of fuel droplets—

Frantically he flicked switches, read the gauges and flow meters, made the calculations with a frozen, horrified sense of urgency. Before he had noticed, before it had dawned on him, the tanks were almost dry. He gripped the control column, but did not move it. It helped to still his shaking hands and forearms. He guessed what must have happened. The fuselage and the tanks had been punctured during the dogfight. Either that or the second Firefox had ruptured one of the fuel lines with cannon fire. Even one of the falling metal leaves from the exploding aircraft might have done it.

He knew that he would never make landfall in England.

Perhaps not even in Norway. A safe landing . . . ? Perhaps nowhere. The calculations were horrifyingly simple. At his present speed, he had less than twenty-five minutes' flying time left. Much less, because of the fuel he was still losing. The rate of loss he could not accurately measure. He could not stop it. Twenty-five minutes? As little as ten?

The cloud layer seemed a long, long way beneath him. The Firefox would drop towards and through it into a frozen wilderness. At first, the clouds would be light, gauzy, slipping past the cockpit like curtains brushed aside. Then the light would go. Greyness would thicken until he broke through to the snow that lay beneath. Trees would rush endlessly beneath the Firefox's belly as it glided on empty tanks. Finally, the airplane would run out of supporting air, as if it had gained weight, and the trees would brush against its flanks and belly. They would snap at first, then their strength in succession and combination would snap the wings, and pull the Firefox into the ground.

By that time, he would have ejected. In order to die of frostbite and exposure. He would freeze to death in Finnish Lapland. All this he knew, and despite his fierce grip on the control column, his forearms quivered. His body felt weak, helpless. And filled with a self-accusation that burned him. *He should have checked*. After the dogfight he should have checked—! He had been caught like a rookie pilot on his first solo flight.

His mistake had killed him. He was almost out of fuel, despite the mockery with which the two huge Turmansky turbojets behind him continued to roar as violently as ever. The noise was like their own, last protest—

52,000 feet.

What? Where?

He couldn't land the Firefox in neutral Finland, that had been made clear to him from the beginning. Never, under any circumstances. Nor Sweden, because of the same neutrality. There was only Norway. But where? Bardufoss was far to the northwest by now, and he was well south of Kirkenes. Both of those airfields were effectively closed to him by distance.

Oslo was hundreds of miles ahead of him still.

Did he have more than twenty minutes left? He could not believe he did.

The Firefox's nose nudged around as the aircraft altered course once more, mockingly obedient to its computer instructions. A chicken with its head cut off, still running.

What—?

He glanced down at the map strapped to his knee. He released the control column with his right hand, stilled its quivering, and estimated distances. Kirkenes was less than ten miles from the Soviet border with Norway. Bardufoss was perhaps another hundred miles further from his present position, but it was a NATO base.

How—?

Climb.

Climb, he thought, climb, climb. The sweat ran freely down his arms and sides. His whole body arched in a sigh of relief. His facemask was misty when he finally exhaled. Zoom climb. As he had done before, before he found the ice floe and the American submarine with its priceless cargo of fuel. Climb.

He hesitated for no more than a moment, then switched off the autopilot and canceled the on-board computer's instructions. Once more, Gant controlled the Firefox. Out over the Arctic Ocean, ignorant of the location and nature of the rendezvous, he had had to glide on over the sea, slowly dropping towards it, the Arctic ice cap white on his horizon. Now he knew the distances; he could calculate the length of his glide. He would make it.

He moved the control column and the Firefox banked, altering course for Bardufoss airfield. Altitude: 49,000 feet. He pulled back on the column and eased the throttles forward, wincing as he did so; he recalculated. Seventeen minutes' flying time left to him. The engines roared steadily. He lifted the nose further. The sky was dark blue almost deepening to black ahead of him. And empty. Gant felt competence return, an almost-calm. Every panic was shorter now. He came out of his helplessness more and more quickly each time. He would make it—

The aircraft began to climb. He had to assume virtually empty tanks by the time he reached Bardufoss. To glide the whole distance, he would require an altitude of more than one hundred and thirty thousand feet. Once he reached the required altitude, he would set up the engines for maximum range. Then all that remained to him was to fly until the engines failed through lack of fuel. Bardufoss was—he tapped at the tiny keyboard of the inertial navigator display, summoning a distance-to-target read-out. Almost at once, the dark-green screen declared in glowing red that Bardufoss was 224.6 miles away. He calculated his best speed to be two hundred and sixty knots. Even if the engines suddenly cut at 132,000 feet, gliding at that speed he would make it all the way.

He watched, edgy as a feeding bird, as the altimeter needle ascended through the fifties, then the sixties—seventy-two, seventy-four thousand. The sky darkened; deep purple-blue. Almost outer space. Eighty. He listened to the Turmansky engines. They roared steadily, healthily. Eighty-four, eighty-six . . .

Come on, *come on—*

His left hand twitched on the throttles, and he had to restrain himself from pushing them forward. It was an illusion. His speed was O.K., all he needed to reach the required altitude.

98,000 feet. Purple-black above and ahead and around. The curve of the earth was evident even in the mirror. One-zero-nine.

The engine note remained steady, comforting. Not quite empty. One hundred and twenty thousand. Almost there, almost . . .

He pulled back the throttles, retaining only sufficient power to keep the generators functioning. He almost heard the thin, upper-atmosphere slipstream outside the cockpit. The Firefox quivered in its flow as he began his glide.

Yes. He'd make it now. They'd need the new Arrestor Barrier at Bardufoss to help him brake. He'd have no reverse thrust by the time he arrived. The last of the fuel was trailing behind him now in a thin crystal stream.

It didn't matter.

Then a warning noise bleeped in his headset. He saw that two bright blips of light had appeared on his passive radar screen. Two aircraft, climbing very fast towards him. The power used in the zoom climb must have betrayed his position to infrared. Two jets, small and fast enough to be nothing else but high-level interceptors. The closest one was already through 95,000 feet and still climbing at more than Mach 2.

Foxbats. Had to be. Mig-25s. And if they were Foxbat-Fs,

they had a high enough ceiling to reach him. Two of them. Closing.

He could see them now, far below him. Gleaming.

The read-out confirmed contact time at six seconds.

The windows in the fuselage of the Tupolev Tu-144, the Russian version of the Concorde, were very small, no larger than tiny, oblong portholes. Nevertheless, Soviet Air Force General Med Vladimirov could see, in the clear, windy afternoon sunlight, the crumpled, terrified figure of KGB Colonel Kontarsky being escorted from the main security building towards the small MiL helicopter which would return him to Moscow. In the moment of the destruction of the second prototype Firefox, KGB Chairman Andropov had remembered the subordinate who had failed, and given the order for his transfer to the Lubyanka prison. His dismissive, final tone had been as casual as the whisking away of a noisy insect. Watching the defeated and fearful Kontarsky climbing into the interior of the green helicopter, Vladimirov witnessed an image of his own future; bleak, filled with disgrace and insult, and short.

He turned reluctantly to look back into the cigar-shaped room that was the Soviet War Command Center. The map table was unlit and featureless. Already a box of matches, a packet of cigarettes, a full ashtray, and an untidy sheaf of decoded signals had invested the smooth grey surface. It was a piece of equipment for which there was no further use. The personnel of the command center remained at their posts, seated before consoles, encoders, avionics displays, computer terminals. Motionless. Air Marshal Kutuzov leaned his elbows on the map table. Beside him the Soviet First Secretary of the Party stood at attention, strong hands clasped together behind his back, pinching the coattail of his grey suit into creases. His head was lifted to the low, curving ceiling of the room, cocked slightly on one side. He listened, as if to music.

The only sound in the room loud enough to mask the hum of radios and encoding consoles, was Tretsov's voice. The First Secretary had ordered the tapes of Tretsov's last moments to be replayed, almost as if he could edit them, alter their message, create victory rather than defeat. Despite himself, Vladimirov listened as Tretsov died in playback. The command center was hot. He was certain of it. It was not himself nor the rush of anticipations through him, it was the ambient temperature. The air conditioning must have failed. He was hot.

"I'm behind him . . . I'm on his tail . . . careful, careful . . . he's doing nothing, he's given up . . ." It was the excitement of a boy regaling his parents with the highlights of a school football match in which he had scored the final, winning goal. "Nothing . . . he's beaten and he knows it . . ." Caution, *caution*, Vladimirov's thoughts repeated. He had silently yelled the thought the instant he heard the tone of delight in the young test pilot's voice. The boy thought he had a kill, had already counted Gant a dead man, had begun to see the hero's reception . . . *caution!* Even had he shouted the word into the microphone, it would have been too late. Tretsov would have been dead before he heard him. *Caution.* "I've got—"

That had been the end of it. A crackle of static and then silence. Total and continuing, leaking from the receiver as palpably as sound. Tretsov had not known Gant, had not understood him. And the American had fooled him. He had triggered the tail decoy, in all probability, and one of Tretsov's huge air intakes had greedily swallowed the incandescent ball.

"I've got—" the tape repeated. Not quite the end. Only the moment when Vladimirov had known it was the end. He'd sensed the change of tone before the last words. "Oh *God*—!" the tape shrieked, making Vladimirov wince once more, hunch into himself. The static scratched like the painful noise of fingernails drawn slowly down a pane of glass, and then the silence began leaking into the hot command center once more.

Oh *God*—!

"Switch it off—switch it off!" Vladimirov snapped in a high, strained voice. "Damn, do you want to *revel* in it? The boy's *dead!*"

The First Secretary turned slowly to face Vladimirov. His large, square face seemed pinched into narrowness. His wide nostrils were white with anger, his eyes heavily lidded.

"A communications failure," he announced. Even Andropov beyond him seemed surprised and perplexed.

"No," Vladimirov announced tiredly, shaking his head. "The boy is dead. The second Firefox no longer exists."

"How do you *know* that?" Vladimirov could sense the

large hands clenching tightly behind the First Secretary's back.

"Because I know the American. Tretsov was . . . too eager. Gant probably killed him by using the tail decoy."

"What?"

"Tretsov's aircraft *ate* a ball of fire and exploded! Couldn't you hear the horror in his voice? There was nothing he could do about it!"

A moment of silence. Andropov's features, especially the pale eyes behind the gold-rimmed spectacles, advised caution, even apology. Don't be foolish, don't anger him now, the Chairman's expression warned. Vladimirov understood, but his anger would not allow him to comply with his knowledge that the man in the grey suit outranked all the uniforms, the medal ribbons, the shoulder boards denoting high rank. The First Secretary, the Soviet leader, controlled this situation. Even though he was bereft of answers, the politician's power was absolute, even now. Then, in a calm, steely voice, the First Secretary said:

"And you, General Vladimirov? What can *you* do about it?"

Behind the Russian leader, the shoulders of a young radio operator were stiff with tension. The back of the man's neck and his ears were red. In the distance Vladimirov heard the helicopter bearing the arrested Kontarsky lift into the midday sky and drone away from Bilyarsk. Vladimirov was aware of the awesome, complete power he had held until a few moments before, and which had disappeared with the second Firefox, and then he moved swiftly to the dull surface of the map table, his hands sweeping the ashtray, the matches, the batch of signals onto the floor. Cigarette butts spilled near the First Secretary's shining black shoes, and the ashtray rolled beneath the chair of an encoding console operator, who flinched.

"Give me North Cape and Norway—quickly!" he snapped. The operator of the map table's computer terminal was galvanized into frantic typing at his keyboard. The dull grey faded, the blue of the sea, the green and brown of a country— Norway—glowed, flickered, then resolved into sharpness. The operator typed in the dispositions of aircraft and ships and submarines without instruction. The First Secretary and the Chairman of the KGB both remained aloof from the map.

Vladimirov noted the positions of the missile cruiser

Riga, the Red Banner Northern Fleet hunter-killer submarines, the "Wolfpack" squadrons aloft. They remained concentrated in the area west of North Cape.

Where? he asked himself. Where now? He's refueled . . . all he needs is friendly airspace.

The long backbone of Norway stretched from top to bottom of the map, a twisted spine of mountains. Like the Urals, Vladimirov thought. He used the Urals to mask his exit—would he use the mountains again? Perhaps—

"Any reports?" he snapped. He could not be blind again, rush at this . . . "Any visual sightings, infrared?"

"No, sir."

"Nothing, Comrade General."

"No."

The chorus was infinitely depressing. However, as he glanced up, it seemed to satisfy Andropov in particular. The KGB's failure to protect the prototype Firefox was well in the past; forgotten, avoidable now. Vladimirov had volunteered himself as the ultimate scapegoat.

"Very well." Kutuzov's watery old eyes warned him. Expressed something akin to pity, too, and admiration for Vladimirov's recklessness. But he could not prevent himself. This contest was as real and immediate as if he were flying a third Firefox himself against the American. He would not surrender. He was challenged, by perhaps the best pilot he had ever encountered, to fulfill his reputation as the Soviet Air Force's greatest and most innovative strategist. Gant had declared the terms of the encounter, and Vladimirov had accepted them.

He was on the point of suggesting incursions into Norwegian airspace. His voice hesitated just as his hand hovered above the spine of Norway glowing beneath the surface of the map table. And perhaps the hesitation saved him—or at least prolonged his authority.

"Something, sir . . ." one of the operators murmured, turning in his chair, one hand clutching the earpiece of his headset. His face wore a bright sheen of delight. Vladimirov sensed that the game had begun again. "Yes, sir. Visual contact. *Visual contact!*" It was the eager, breathless announcement of a miracle. The operator nodded as he listened to the report they could not hear. His right hand scribbled furiously on a pad.

"Cabin speaker!" Vladimirov snapped. The operator flicked

a switch. Words poured from the loudspeaker overhead, a brilliant, excited bird-chatter. The First Secretary's eyes flicked towards the speaker. Heads lifted slowly, like a choir about to sing. Vladimirov suppressed a grin of almost savage pleasure.

There was surprise, too, of course. And gratitude. He had hesitated for a moment, and the moment had proven fateful. He would have said Norway—even now the country lay under his gaze and his hands like a betrayal—and it would have been an error. Gant was over Finland; neutral innocent Finland. At 130,000 feet. And he'd been picked up visually and trailed by two Mig-25 Foxbats, at high altitude themselves. Now he had climbed almost to his maximum ceiling. Why was he at such an extreme altitude? Contact time a matter of seconds . . . orders required . . . Vladimirov blessed the young map operator who had typed in new instructions. The twisted spine of Norway disappeared. The land mass fattened, blurred, then resolved. Finland, Swedish Lapland, and northern Norway occupied the area of the map table. Now, what orders—?

His eyes met the steady, expectant, even amused gaze of the First Secretary. Everyone in the room understood the narrowness of his escape from an irredeemable blunder. Andropov was smiling thinly, in mocking appreciation.

"Sir!"

"Yes?" he answered hoarsely.

"An AWACS Tupolev has picked up the two Foxbats. We—"

"Bleed in the present position. Quickly!"

Then he waited. Contact time diminishing, split-seconds now . . . Gant still climbing but he must have seen them by now . . . orders required . . . engage? *What was that?*

"Repeat that!" the First Secretary ordered before Vladimirov could utter the same words. The order was transmitted, and the voice of the Foxbat pilot repeated the information. Fuel droplets—a thin stream of fuel! Gant had a serious fuel leak. He had climbed to that extreme altitude in order to stretch his fuel, and to be able to glide when the fuel ran out. Just as he must have done to find the submarine and the ice floe. "Engage!"

"No!" Vladimirov shouted. The First Secretary glared at him, his mouth twisted with venom. He took a single step towards the map table. The positions of the two Mig-25s glowed as a single bright white star on the face of Finnish

Lapland. Vladimirov's cupped hand stroked towards the pin-point of light and beyond it into Russia. "No," he repeated. "We can bring him back! We can bring him back! Don't you see?"

"Explain. Hold that order." The two men faced each other across the surface of the map. The colors of sea and land shone palely on their features, mottling them blue and brown and green. "Explain."

Vladimirov's hands waved and chopped over the glowing surface of Lapland. Then his right forefinger stabbed at the white star that represented the two Mig-25s.

"There," he said. "They are two seconds away." The First Secretary's face was expressionless as Vladimirov looked up for an instant. Then the Soviet General, one lock of silver hair falling across his intently creased high forehead, spoke directly to the map table. "It's already beginning. They'll peel away and return without a definite order. They're good pilots. *They have to be,* he thought, to be in their squadron: the aircraft are advanced Foxbat-Fs, the next best thing to the Foxfire itself. "The *border* is *here*." The finger stabbed again and again, as if an ant on the surface of the table persisted in maintaining life. "Less than a hundred miles. Minutes of flying time at the most. They can *shepherd* him!" He looked up once more. Puzzlement. The Russian leader's thoughts were seconds behind his own. "Look: they can do this with him . . ." Once more, his hand swept across the map, ushering the white star towards the red border, away from dotted blue lakes to more dotted blue lakes—Soviet lakes. For a split-second, Vladimirov remembered reading Solzhenitsyn's short story of the lake guarded by barbed wire that represented his country, then he shook his head and dismissed the image. His voice was unchanged as he continued. "It will take clever flying, but I'm certain it can be done. Once he's across the border, then he can be brought down. He's almost out of fuel, I'm sure of that. He will have to land. We can shepherd him straight into an airfield . . . one of ours."

He looked up. The First Secretary was, for the moment, dazzled. He nodded eagerly. Vladimirov listened. Over the speaker, the leading pilot of the two Foxbats was reporting the peel-off and the encroaching return. Contact time: four seconds.

"Shepherd—repeat, *shepherd*," he snapped. A remote mike had been patched in. They could hear him direct. "You know the procedure. It's ninety miles and no more to the border. Bring him home!" He grinned as the second of hesitation passed and the leading pilot acknowledged with a chuckle in his voice. Then he studied the map before ordering: "Patch me into *all* forward border squadron commanders—all of them. And to flight leaders of 'Wolfpack' squadrons already in the air. Every commander and flight leader who can give me a Foxbat-F." He looked up at the Russian leader—beyond his shoulder the light glinted from Andropov's glasses but Vladimirov ignored any warning they might be transmitting—and smiled confidently. "We'll put up everything we have that can reach that altitude," he announced. "The American will feel like the last settler left alive inside the circle of the wagon train!"

The First Secretary seemed to remember the old cowboy-and-Indian films which, as the child of a prominent Party member, he would have been privileged to see, and laughed.

Vladimirov looked down at the map once more, and breathed deeply. It would take constant dialogue with the two pilots, instantaneous communications, if he was to supervise the recapture of the Mig-31. But he could do it, yes. It would take perhaps eight or ten minutes flying for any other Migs to reach Gant. The two Foxbats would be working alone—but they would be sufficient, he assured himself. No other aircraft could achieve that altitude except another Foxbat-F. And there were only the two of them in the area. The map, with its clearly marked border and the slow-moving white dot of the routine Early Warning Tupolev Tu-126 "Moss" aircraft travelling southwards along its snaking line, confirmed his optimism.

For a moment, as the two Foxbats had peeled away from the Firefox at more than Mach 1.5, the single white dot that represented them had become a double sun. Now, the separate lights had once more become a single white star.

They had come sweeping up towards him, then past and above. He had loosed neither of the remaining advanced Anab missiles, slung one beneath each wing; suppressing the mental command to fire with a certain, decisive violence of reaction. The two Foxbats had broken their unity, peeling away in opposite directions and dropping down from the purple-blue towards the globe below like exhausted shuttlecocks. Then, finally, they had begun to climb again, almost touching wings as if joining hands. Aiming at him like darts. Contact time: four seconds. Their speed was slower now, as if they had been advised to the utmost caution. Gant was fiercely aware once more of the two remaining air-to-air missiles. Two Migs, both advanced Foxbat-Fs. Two missiles. Fuel—critical.

Unlike the Foxbats, he had the fuel neither to fight nor to run. He had to wait, just as he suspected the two Russian pilots were themselves waiting for orders.

They bobbed up to port and starboard of him like corks on the surface of invisible water, slightly above him at 125,000 feet and hanging, like him, apparently suspended from the purple-blackness above. On his screen they had converged to a single glow and at the extreme edge the dot of the slow-moving AWACS plane patrolling the Soviet-Finnish border continued its flight. He had been aware of it when he began his climb, and had smiled in the secure knowledge that he was invisible to it. Now, however, it could see the two Foxbats. His position was known—to everyone.

The fear passed quickly, surprising him by its feeble hold; delighting him, too. He accepted his role. He had to wait until they attacked. 122,000 feet. His slow flight northwest had begun, but now he would not be allowed to continue. His hand gripped the throttle levers, but he did not move them either backward or forward. Slowly, as if tired, the Firefox continued to descend.

He looked to port and starboard. The two Foxbats were sliding gently in towards him. Each of the pilots was engaged in a visual scan. By now they knew he had only two missiles. By now, they knew he had a fuel leak, and they would have guessed at the reason for his altitude. They would be confident. Orders and decisions would be crackling and bleeping in their headsets. Not long now. Gant armed the weapons systems, switched on the firing circuits, calculated his remaining flying time. He knew he would have to use the engines, use *all* his remaining fuel, to escape the Foxbats.

The Foxbat to starboard, no more than two hundred yards from him, was now in sharp profile. Gant waited, beginning to sweat, his mind coldly clear. The Foxbat loomed on his right, and yawed slightly towards him. Cannon fire flashed ahead of him as the Russian plane slid across and

below the level of the cockpit sill and he lost sight of it . . .
he flung the Firefox to port—

Flickers of flame at the wingtips from the cannon, the
Foxbat in profile, the savage lurch of the sky, a glimpse of the
port Foxbat maintaining its course, then he was below it and
leveling out, watching the radar. Two dots. He watched the
mirror, the radar, the sky ahead of him, the mirror, the
radar, the sky . . .

Bobbing corks. They were on either side of him again as
he flew level, the distant dot of the AWACS Tupolev now in
the corner of his screen, ahead of him.

He glanced to port and starboard. He could see the
pilots. He watched them as they watched him. He understood what they had witnessed. He'd dropped away from the
cannon fire rather than dived. He had confirmed his fear of
empty tanks as clearly as if he had spoken to them.

Port, starboard, port, starboard . . . Gant's head flicked
from side to side. With each movement, his eyes glanced
across the instrument panel, registering the dials and screens
minutely as if they were small, precise physical sensations on
his skin or at his fingertips. He waited for movement. Between them, he knew himself to be safe from their AA-6
missiles. They were too close to one another to be certain of
hitting only him. It would be when one of them dropped
away suddenly that the other would launch a missile.

Yet they remained level.

Ninety-nine thousand now. They'd followed his slow
descent, exactly paralleling his course. He could try to stretch
them, exceed their ceiling, yet knew he would not . . . he
had calculated that he dare not afford the fuel. 95,000 feet,
still descending . . . They remained with him, long slim
bodies dropping from the darkening arch of the sky above.
Twenty miles above the earth.

94,000 feet . . . three-fifty . . . three . . .

The port Foxbat-F slid towards him like a huge animal
turning lazily to crush him, enlarging alongside and over him,
its shadow falling across the cockpit, across the instruments,
the sunlight gleaming from its closing flank—

He saw the black visor of the pilot's helmet, and understood the man's hand signals. He was being ordered to follow
the Soviet fighter and to land inside Russia. Alter course . . .
follow me . . . land, the hand signals read. Gant watched the
pilot's turned head. He waved acceptance, his body tensing

as he did so. Had he delayed sufficiently? Would his acceptance appear genuine?

He waited.

Then the Foxbat banked to its left and began a shallow descent. Gant saw it gradually accelerate. The second Foxbat remained to starboard of him, as if wary of some trick. He dipped the nose of the Firefox, following the Russian aircraft. Then he gave the command. The port wing quivered and he saw the flame at the tail of the Anab missile as it sprang ahead of him. It dropped away with terrible quickness, pursuing the descending Foxbat. Its trail quivered like the tail of an eager dog as it sought and found the heat emissions from the Foxbat and locked onto them. Gant banked fiercely to prevent the second Foxbat maneuvering behind him. He glimpsed the engines of the descending Foxbat flare and the plane flick up and away, standing on its tail. The speed of the tactic shook loose the trailing missile. The aircraft was already perhaps three miles from the Firefox. The missile continued its now-wavering course downwards. It would run out of fuel thousands of feet from the ground.

Gant pulled back on the control column and eased the throttles forward, beginning to climb again. He had, he realized, committed himself. He could not, with the slightest certainty of success, complete his flight to Norway. But he would not be shepherded back to Russia.

The Foxbat was closing again, its white dot moving back swiftly towards the center of his screen. The second Foxbat had done no more than remain with him, exactly duplicating his fierce bank and levelling out, popping up again to starboard and beginning to climb with him. It remained apparently passive, as if its companion had, like a child, run to play and was now returning to a complacent parent. Evidently, neither pilot had orders to fire, to destroy. Unless, no doubt, he failed to comply with their instructions, or attempted to elude them.

Bobbing cork, and the second Foxbat-F had already turned, closed up and resumed its position on his port wing. 115,000 feet—

The AWACS plane was on the Soviet side of the border. The border was less than seventeen miles away. He understood what they were doing. He had run between them, cautiously and yet with as little choice as a sheep between two dogs. He was almost back in the Soviet Union. He pulled back on the throttles and leveled out, then pushed the control column gently forward, dipping the nose of the Firefox. Like mirror-images, though silver not black, the two Foxbats dipped their noses in unison, beginning to descend with him.

Fifteen miles . . .

108,000 feet . . .

The two Foxbats were like slim, dangerous silver fish swimming downwards with him. Once again, he imagined he could hear the noise of the slipstream against the canopy, much as if he had been hang-gliding. The wingtip of the starboard Foxbat wobbled, reinforcing the impression of fragility, of slow-motion—of powerlessness.

He flung the Firefox into a tight roll, the globe and sky exchanging places with wrenching suddenness, and slowed the aircraft. When the horizon reestablished itself, he was behind and only slightly to starboard of one of the Foxbats. He glanced around—

The port Foxbat had imitated his roll and drop in speed. He saw it gleam in his rear mirror. He was boxed again, and fear surfaced for a moment as he realized he had made himself a sitting target. Then the Russian aircraft drew level again to starboard. The pilot waved, as if they had been practicing for an air display.

Twelve miles . . .

97,000 feet. Cloud lay like a carpet far below; the air was perceptibly bluer. Eleven-and-a-half miles to target. The AWACS plane was still maintaining its border patrol, passing slowly across his screen. Nothing else showed on the screen, but Gant knew that the border squadrons would be waiting only for the order to scramble. Once airborne, they would be only minutes away. When they came they would buzz around him like flies, hemming him in.

The port Foxbat banked slightly, slipping across the intervening space, casting its shadow on the cockpit of the Firefox. He watched it settle into a position directly over him, no more than a hundred feet above. As they dropped lower, the Foxbat increased the rate of its descent, pressing as palpably as a flatiron towards him. He increased his own rate of descent, cursing but impotent.

Clever. Good pilots. Armed with eight AA-6 missiles.

Nine miles—80,000 feet.

The three aircraft slid downwards . . . seconds passed . . . 70,000 feet . . . seconds passed . . . seven miles . . .

Clever, the mind behind it, the orders being issued, Gant thought, and the silence of his cockpit pressed upon him like the form of the Russian fighter above. *UHF—*

He switched on the UHF set, his fingers hesitating until he recognized the button for the search facility. A red dot stuttered and flashed, then steadied as the search was completed.

A voice, speaking in Russian, crackled in his ears. Gant pressed the lock-on button. It was one of the two Foxbat pilots replying to an instruction. Gant smiled. It was one of the most secret tactical channels with variable frequencies used by the Soviet Air Force. The red dot stuttered as the frequency altered, perhaps two or three times a second. But the signal was constant.

"Bring him lower," he heard; the voice of the man in Bilyarsk who controlled the situation. "Bring him right down."

The order was acknowledged. Gant watched the form of the Foxbat above him as it inclined its nose more steeply, its speed exactly matched to his own. He dipped the nose of the Firefox obediently, preserving the distance between the two fuselages. Then the Russian aircraft slipped sideways, as if moved by no more than the airflow over it, and dropped suddenly towards him. At the same moment, his headset crackling with the voices of the two Foxbat pilots, the starboard Foxbat bobbed higher and sideways towards him, banking slightly. Then it, too, settled down towards him, as if the air were too thin to support its weight.

The two Russian fighters lowered gently, inexorably, towards his wingtips, as though applying pressure to snap them off. He waggled the wings, as if warding them off, wiping flies away. The headset gabbled at him, most of the Russian too quick and distorted for him to understand. They were attempting to break his nerve.

Four miles—61,000 feet . . .

Then he heard the order, over the same frequency: "Scramble designated squadrons."

From the western margin of the Kola Peninsula, where the latest Mig interceptors were based, was no more than a few minutes' flying time at top speed. They had fuel to squander, literally squander.

He had run out of time, almost run out of distance. Two miles. He must be over the border by now, in Russia.

The two Foxbats pressed down upon him. Altitude now

49,000 feet. The three aircraft were in what might have been termed a dive. The two Russian pilots had tilted him forward and down, throwing the Firefox over a cliff of air towards the clouds beneath.

Dive—

Gant thrust the control column forward, then rammed the throttles forward almost to the detent and reheat. The Firefox leapt at the cloud layer, the huge Turmansky jets roaring. He saw the two Foxbats accelerate behind him, closing the gap he had opened. He opened the airbrakes, jolting the aircraft, then flung the Firefox into a roll and pull-through, suddenly changing the direction in which he was moving. It avoided the optimum firing position he had given them on his tail, and increased the time lag between them. He closed the airbrakes and pushed the throttles open as he came out of the pull-through. In his mirror, two abandoned stars gleamed and winked. On his screen, the white dot moved away from him. He forced his left hand to keep the throttles wide open. The silver trail of droplets sprayed out into a mist behind him. The white dot on the screen steadied, altered course by going through his own maneuver, and then began to struggle to regain the center of the screen. His headset babbled in Russian, from the pilots and from Bilyarsk.

He jabbed the airbrakes out again, slowing with wrenching suddenness, rolled and pulled through, closed the brakes, and opened the throttles again. Once more, the two Foxbats were left further behind and away from his tail. He felt the suit around him resist the pressure of the G-forces. He was now traveling directly west, across the neutrality of Finland towards Norway. How much distance the tanks would still give him he did not know because he had no idea how quickly he was losing fuel in that sparkling, dazzling spray of diamonds behind him. But any distance between the Firefox and the border with Russia was good and right and necessary.

The Foxbats altered course, and closed once more. Airbrakes, roll, pull-through, close brakes, throttles. He whirled like a falling sycamore pod once again.

30,000 feet . . . twenty-five . . . twenty, nineteen . . . the figures unrolled on the altimeter. The white dot that was the two Foxbats still in close formation was steady in the lower half of his screen. No more than a mile away . . .

14,000, and the sun disappeared and he was blind, the

grey cloud slipping past as if his speed were tearing it like rags, but it was still thick enough to exclude the light. 10,000 feet . . .

Eight, seven, six—

He used the airbrakes and closed the throttles. He pulled back on the column. The Firefox began to level out.

Four . . . three . . . two-point-seven, two-five. The white dot split into two tiny stars, and both moved nearer the center of the screen. The headset babbled. Bilyarsk ordered the border squadrons at top speed to the last visual sighting, before he entered the cloud.

Cloud, *cloud*—

The Proximity Warning began to bleep again as the Foxbats closed.

1500 feet, the glimpse of a somber, snow-covered landscape, an horizon of low white hills, a uniformly grey sky now above him—he pulled back on the column, and nosed the Firefox back into the cloud. The world contracted, wrapping its shreds tightly around the cockpit. He slowed almost to stalling speed, feeling the adrenalin and nerves and fear and sweat catch up with his decisions. He breathed quickly and heavily enough to begin to cloud the facemask of his helmet. There was a heavy dew of sweat on his brow. The two white dots hurried towards the center of his screen, blind but somehow confident. They would pass within a mile of him, to starboard of his present flight path. Other, new dots had appeared at the edge of the screen, like spectators spilling onto a soccer field. He demanded a range-to-target readout for the approaching squadrons. Then he altered the request—time-to-target. Two minutes seven-point-four, the computer read-out supplied. Then the distance between the two Foxbats increased, and Gant realized that one of them was retreating again above the cloud layer; a tactic designed to catch him by surprise if he suddenly increased altitude. He would pop out of the cloud into bright betraying sunlight, within missile range. He grinned.

He banked the Firefox, moving to intercept the other Foxbat as it continued to rush through the cloud layer. He armed the only remaining Anab missile, and waited. He canceled the read-out, replacing it with information on the closing Foxbat. Range-to-target—two miles, one-point-nine, one-point-seven . . . He activated the thought-guidance systems on the console to his left.

He would have to be right. Optimum moment. The Anabs that had been replaced by the submarine crew on the ice floe were not equipped with a steering system linked to his thought-control capability. They were an earlier model, captured from a Foxbat in Syria. He had to rely on judgement, on selecting the exact moment. He could not guide the missile once he launched it.

Point-nine . . . point-eight-seven, six, five . . . six, *fire*. He formed the command precisely, in Russian, and felt the Anab drop, then flick forward. It was an orange glow in the cloud, then it disappeared. He watched the screen, the infra-red glow of the missile's exhaust slipping across the small gap of screen between himself and the Foxbat. The Russian fighter, blind in the cloud, continued to descend like a white meteorite, nothing showing on his radar.

Then the white dot suddenly altered course. The pilot's headset had yelled a warning. The orange dot encroached, neared, sidled towards . . . The white dot accelerated, changed course, dipped and weaved. The orange dot, like a faithful dog, ran behind, accelerated, sniffing the radar and other electronic emissions from the Foxbat, closed, closed, dodged with the white dot, closed closed—

A brief flare on the screen, and then there remained only the white dots of the second Foxbat above the clouds, the slow-moving AWACS plane, and the more distant inter-ceptors at the edge of the screen. Gant banked the Firefox, easing the throttles forward as he settled on his new heading, and began running west. Altitude 3,000 feet, speed 270 knots, fuel nonexistent.

The crowd of white dots rushed towards the center of the radar screen, towards the now-fading flare that had a moment before been an aircraft and a pilot. The cloud slipped past him, seemingly lighter and thinner.

He tensed himself for the first visual sighting when he ran out of the cloud.

The ministry car had left the M1 north of Leicester, and they had used the A46 through Newark and Lincoln to reach Scampton by lunchtime. Flat land beneath a cloud-strewn sky, the three honey-colored towers of Lincoln Cathedral overlooking the red-roofed city, and then they were on a minor road between clipped, weather-strained hedges before arriving at the Guard Room of the RAF station.

Kenneth Aubrey had been voluble during the journey, excited as a child on an annual holiday. To the two Americans, Buckholz and Curtin, he was tiresome in his complete and impenetrable pleasure at the success of the Firefox operation. Their passes were inspected by the guard, and then they were directed towards the C.O.'s office.

Group Captain Bradnum was on the steps of the main administration building, two stories of red brick, and he hurried to the car as it came to a halt. Aubrey almost bounced out of the rear seat to shake his hand, his smile bordering on something as vulgar and uninhibited as a grin. Bradnum's heavy features reflected the expression he saw on Aubrey's lips. It was all right. Everything was all right.

"Well, Group Captain?" Aubrey asked archly. Buckholz and Curtin left the car with less speed and more dignity, yet with as much pleasurable anticipation.

"He must be safe by now," Bradnum replied.

Aubrey glanced at his watch. "The British Airways flight from Stockholm leaves in thirty minutes, I see. I presume Gant's going to be on time—mm, Charles?" He turned to Buckholz, who shrugged, then nodded. "Oh, my apologies, Group Captain—Charles Buckholz of the CIA, and Captain Eugene Curtin of the USN Office of Naval Intelligence . . ." Hands were shaken. When the formalities were over, Aubrey said: "You said he must be safe by now. Why? Has anything happened?"

Bradnum's face was lugubrious. "The Nimrod—at your request—was monitoring Gant's advised flight path . . ."

"Yes, yes," Aubrey snapped impatiently. "What of it?"

"Only minutes ago there was nothing in the area except a Russian AWACS plane on the Soviet side of the border with Finland."

"And—?"

"Now there are two Foxbat interceptors in that airspace—and a great deal of coded signal traffic, and—" Bradnum shrugged. His mirroring of Aubrey's smile had been unwarranted, a moment away from the truth. "Eastoe in the Nimrod claims they were climbing very fast, very positively . . ."

"On an interception course?"

"They're close enough to spit at the Firefox," Eastoe said."

"Why weren't we told this?" Buckholz demanded heavily.

"It happened only minutes ago."

"And in those minutes?"

"Eastoe's reported a great deal of maneuvering . . ."

Aubrey turned away, facing south across the still-wet runways. Beyond the hangars and other buildings, beyond the flagpole and the perimeter fence, a sudden gleam of sunlight displayed the distant towers of Lincoln cathedral on its perch of limestone. Then the towers were dulled as the watery sun disappeared behind a swiftly moving cloud. He turned back to Bradnum.

The noise of an RAF Vulcan taking off seemed a mocking, unnecessary intrusion into the tense silence.

"I know Eastoe—what's his best guess?" Aubrey asked quietly. "He would have one and he would have offered it, asked or no."

Bradnum nodded. "They've been in the tightest formation and descending very slowly for two minutes or more. He thinks the Firefox is there, too. It's too deliberate to be for no reason."

Aubrey snapped his fingers in an inadequate expression of anger and urgency.

"We must talk to Eastoe," he said, addressing Buckholz. "At once. From your Ops Room, Group Captain. Lead on, if you please."

At the edge of eyesight, another shaft of sunlight warmly lit the distant cathedral towers. Aubrey shivered with the cold of the wind.

"What now? What now?" the First Secretary demanded. The Tupolev Tu-144 was cruising at 50,000 feet, almost a hundred miles of the journey from Bilyarsk to Moscow already accomplished.

Vladimirov leaned heavily on the other side of the map table, his eyes focused upon the dark-haired wrists that protruded from beneath the Russian leader's shirt cuffs. Grey hairs, too . . .

The report from the surviving Foxbat confirmed that visual contact with the Firefox had been lost. Gant was hidden somewhere in the twelve or thirteen thousand feet of the cloud layer. On low power, an infrared trace would be difficult to establish, almost impossible to pinpoint and attack.

Because attack would be the next order. Vladimirov knew that. For him the game was up. Deluded by the apparent passivity of the American and the success of his two Foxbat pilots, Vladimirov had fatally delayed the order to the border squadrons on the Kola Peninsula to scramble. Now, he was once more blind, the Firefox's anti-radar concealing the American. Neither the surviving Foxbat nor the AWACS Tupolev "Moss" could detect his presence.

Vladimirov's own future remained difficult to envisage. His pride was hurt. He had lost to the American once again, and he could not forgive himself. The anger of others failed to interest him.

Eventually, he looked up at the Russian leader. The man's face was dark with habitual anger, habitual power. Threat. The image of the bully. Yet the stupid man had no ideas of his own—had no *conception*—!

The scatter of luminous blips representing the scrambled interceptors, mainly Mig-25s and swing-wing Mig-27 Floggers, moved across the bright map towards the border with Finland. Other dots scurried southeastward from the west of North Cape, their contact time still six minutes away. Although no more than a futile gesture, the AWACS Tupolev had changed course to patrol the hundred miles or so of border which contained the point at which Gant would have crossed—*had crossed*, he reminded himself—into Russia. The single remaining Foxbat's white dot buzzed and twisted in tight little circles on the map, like an insect dying.

"In two minutes we will have eighteen, even twenty-four aircraft in the area," Vladimirov said calmly. "Visual contact will be reestablished."

The First Secretary sneered, then compressed his lips above his clenched jaw. When he spoke, all he said was: "And what will you do if and when he is sighted?"

"I—await your orders, Comrade First Secretary . . ." Vladimirov announced in a quiet, restrained voice. Behind the Russian leader, Air Marshal Kutuzov nodded with the wisdom and cowardice of great age, paining Vladimirov by his assent. Andropov smiled thinly, and flicked a little nod in the direction of the general. The gesture acknowledged the acquisition of good sense, proper caution; the priority of survival. The First Secretary appeared suspicious, then mollified.

"Very well." He leant more closely over the surface of the map, the colors of the projected land mottling his features.

It was a parody of knowledge, aping the strategist. The First Secretary had been a Political Commissar during the Great Patriotic War. His reputation suggested, even in the sanitized, history-book version now current, that he had killed many more Russians than he had Nazis. No, no, Vladimirov warned himself, stilling the angry tremor of his hands. You've begun it—play it out. "Very well," the First Secretary repeated. "We—will wait, until our forces are in the area." He looked to Vladimirov for approval, and the general nodded perfunctorily.

Masterly, Vladimirov announced silently and with irony. Quite masterly. Aloud, he said: "Contact time of closest squadrons—one minute. Warn them to concentrate on infrared search. Blanket the area. Gant is virtually weaponless, and out of fuel." Even to himself, his optimism sounded remarkably hollow. It appeared, however, to satisfy Andropov and the First Secretary.

The room was filled with the crackles and bleeps of exchanged communications. The Kola squadron flight leaders, the surviving Foxbat pilot, the AWACS captain. An energizing electronic chatter. Easy to picture them, translate the moving dots into planes and men and tactics and search patterns. His fingers circled the area where the Foxbat had been destroyed by Gant's last missile. In there, he's in there . . .

The First Secretary's impatience was evidently growing. To do nothing, to abdicate the display of power, was anathema to him. Vladimirov suspected that the impotence of inactivity had determined the Russian leader's order for the Tupolev to return to Moscow. The physical location of the War Command Center was a matter of indifference to Vladimirov. The First Secretary studied the map, he glanced from face to face, he listened to the reports. He watched the red second hand of the largest of the room's many clocks moving like a spider leg around the white face. He watched time pass without the search locating the Mig-31. One minute . . . a minute-and-a-half . . . two minutes . . . three . . . Vladimirov controlled his features, controlled his sense of rising body temperature.

Gant was out of fuel—he should be hugging the ground— the weather satellite shows broken cloud, he can't run around inside the cloud forever—he should be hugging the ground, making a run . . . when would the American's nerve break, when would he run for cover, skimming across Finland like a flat stone before his engines sighed and surrendered?

Four minutes . . . four-and-a-half . . . five . . . six . . .

Then: "Got him! He's run out of cloud!" The operator had increased the volume so that the Foxbat pilot's ringing, boyish voice was audible above the cheer in the command center. "He's at zero feet and traveling subsonic, perhaps four hundred knots, no more. I'm going down!" Then, more formally, he added: "What are your orders, Comrade General?"

"His exact position and heading!" Vladimirov snapped, then to the room at large: "Alert the search to home in on the Mig-25—repeat speed and altitude just—"

"Give the order to attack!" the First Secretary announced, glaring at Vladimirov. "No more games—no *strategy*! Tell them to destroy the Mig-31 on sight!"

Ground clutter, ground clutter, clutter, ground clutter, his mind kept repeating as the Firefox leapt at the landscape at an altitude of less than a hundred feet, the automatic pilot and the terrain-following radar preserving it from the snow-softened folds and contours of Finnish Lapland. Invisible, invisible, he chanted almost as a prayer. The clutter of images from the landscape would mask the Firefox from any searching eyes—other than those of the Mig-25F still on his tail, less than two miles behind him.

Two pilots with no more to do than choose the moment for the kill; to select, savor, review, revise, reselect the optimum moment. Two pilots—one with four AA-6 missiles, the other with cannon fire and empty tanks. Effectively, he and the pilot of the Foxbat were alone, skimming across the surface of Finnish Lapland. The squadrons of searching Migs above them were rendered doubly blind—the anti-radar protected him, the ground clutter masked his pursuer from assistance. The pilot of the Foxbat was transmitting a stream of positional fixes to his newly arrived colleagues, but he was offering old news, history. The Firefox flicked, twisted, whipped through the landscape at four hundred knots—a butterfly that refused to be pinned to the card.

Until it ran out of fuel, finally . . .

The threat had hung over him for so long—perhaps fifteen minutes' flying time since he had first noticed his fuel state—that he had begun to disbelieve the gauges. They claimed he could have as much as six minutes' flying time left at his present speed. Yet each evasive maneuver squandered fuel, and even more fuel streamed away behind him. And he still could not shake the pursuing Foxbat. It followed him indefatigably. Over his headset, Gant heard the frantic but assured reports of his pursuer. There was a gap of time to be traversed, the optimum moment for the kill still lay in the future, but there was no doubt of the outcome.

He'd heard, too, the strong voice that had first addressed him after the takeoff from Bilyarsk. The Soviet First Secretary. This time, he had heard it snapping orders, not addressed to him but to every particle of the pursuit. *Kill, eliminate, obliterate. Destroy the Mig-31.* The First Secretary's voice had cut across that of the strategist, the man who had weighed and watched and planned and guessed. The gambler. The man who, if Gant could outwit him, offered the chance of escape. He had pride and self-confidence and he believed he would win. Therein lay the potential for error, for opening the wrong door for just long enough for Gant to take his chance. But the Soviet leader's voice expressed only power, accepted only certainties. He wished to end the game—now.

Landscape, suddenly rushing at him with a new ferocity. Mountains, hills, ridges, folds. Lake Inari, the sacred lake of the Lapps, had been no more than a brief glimpse of ice blocks, ice sheets, snowbound wooded silent islets and the occasional glimmer of windows in sudden and disappearing villages. Now the land creased and folded as if to baffle the terrain-following radar, confuse his eyesight. The Firefox bucked, nose up, then dipped again over the brow of a snow-covered hillock. Gant's stomach settled, and the pressure suit relaxed its reassuring grip on his frame. Snow flew and boiled in the wake of the Firefox, flung up by the passage of his slipstream across the treetops. It made the rear mirror blind, but he knew that his pursuer remained behind him. Waiting for the moment to launch one of his four AA-6 missiles. The Foxbat would be carrying two infrared homing missiles, and two which homed on radar. The rocket motors of the missiles were capable of propelling them at speeds far in excess of the Mach 3 that was the Mig-25's top speed. Gant knew that with full tanks he might have outrun a launched missile; but not now. He would have to wait. The range of the missiles was perhaps twelve miles. His pursuer, clear on

his rearward-looking radar sensor, was less than two miles
behind him.

Gant's course was northwest, towards the nearest point
of the Norwegian border.

Wait . . .

It was all he could do. The two Turmanskys continued
to roar but, at ground level, he was wasting the last of his
fuel . . .

Wait . . .

Two narrow frozen lakes, smooth-surfaced, then white-
clad forest, then the narrow valley of a frozen river. Snow
flew and rumbled down behind him from the sides of the
steep, knife-cut valley. He watched the rearward screen. He
was traveling in a straight line, it was a moment of calm in
the violent changes of course demanded by the landscape.

Optimum moment . . . ?

A dot detached itself from the pursuing Foxbat, which
had entered the valley. There was nothing in the mirror but
rolling clouds of snow. Out of that would spring—

The AA-6 missile leapt up towards the center of his
screen, homing on his exhaust heat. A tenth of a second, a
fifth, a quarter . . . Gant's hands were still on the throttles.
The right thumb had already armed the tail-decoy system.
His left hand twitched on the throttle levers. The missile
moved dementedly, like a virulently poisoned insect, coming
at him at perhaps more than Mach 4. He hesitated . . .
point-seven of a second, point-eight . . . point-nine—

He released the tail-decoy. Almost immediately, it ignited and the snow was a dazzling, torn-apart curtain, hurting
his eyes. Then it brightened further, and he felt the shock
wave of the explosion overtake him and shudder through the
airframe. His teeth chattered. There was nothing on the
radar except the pursuing Foxbat, which had broken to port
to avoid the debris and had then dropped back into the
narrow valley. It was already accelerating, too. Less than a
mile and closing.

A hillock ahead. Without conscious thought Gant canceled the automatic pilot and terrain-following radar. He
banked the Firefox to starboard, slowing his speed as he did
so. The pursuing Foxbat swung left of the long, white, whale-
backed hillock, and Gant knew that the pilot had made an
error. He anticipated catching Gant broadside-on, an unmis-
sable target for cannon fire or another missile. But, if he

hadn't slowed down enough, however . . . Gant had time to form the thought in the second he was hidden from the Foxbat, and then he realized that the valley was a closed one. He would have to lift over the ridge, exposing the Firefox's flank to attack—he'd made the mistake, not the Russian. The hillock had tricked him. The valley wall rose in front of him. He pulled back on the control column, sweating with new fear.

The Foxbat leapt the ridge a split-second ahead of him, its pilot similarly surprised by the valley wall ahead, his speed no more than a few mph faster than that of the Firefox.

But he was there. For a moment, he was there—!

Gant banked savagely and pulled tighter, then fired. The Foxbat, caught like an athlete halfway through a jump, seemed to hold, even stagger in the air. As Gant closed on the silver shape, he continued firing. The cannon shells raked through the cockpit and down the spine of the fuselage.

Gant passed beneath the Foxbat, buffeted by its slipstream as it continued to climb. There was a minor explosion— Gant saw it as he pulled round to attack once more—and the cowling of the port engine was breaking up. The Foxbat lurched, staggered, but continued to climb. Gant followed, overtaking it as it reached the apex of some already dictated parabola. He could see the pilot dead in the cockpit, beneath the cracked and starred canopy. The nose tilted, began to drop . . .

The Foxbat stalled at 5,000 feet, dropping back towards the ground with as little weight and independence as a leaf. Gant glanced at his radar. The white dots of searching Migs were scattered across it like crumbs from a meal untidily eaten. Fire was streaming from the Foxbat's port engine. In a matter of seconds, the aircraft would explode—

And he would explode along with it . . .

He grinned. He would disappear. The Foxbat was spinning towards a hillside where it would bury itself in deep snow. He spiraled down, following it. It was a second from impact, and burning like a torch. He loosed a tail-decoy, and it ignited, glowing on his infrared screen, to be matched then surpassed by the explosion of the Foxbat at the base of the hill behind him.

Two fireballs in close succession. Two kills.

The cockpit was silent, except for the jabbering Russian

as Bilyarsk and the search squadrons tried to raise the dead
Foxbat pilot. He switched off the UHF set. It *was* silent.

Christ—

Then it happened. The sudden sense of the Firefox
slowing that he had dreaded. His rpm was falling rapidly. In
his headphones, he could hear the chatter of the auto-igniters.
Altitude 4,000 feet, fuel nonexistent . . .

He could see the snowbound landscape beneath. He had
no more than minutes in which to decide to eject or to land.
Then the engines caught for a moment as the pumps dredged
the last of the fuel from the tanks. He pulled back on the
column. He needed all the altitude he could muster. Three
seconds later the engines died again, the rpm dropped, the
gauges presented zero readings. The engines were silent,
empty. Again, he had to decide—eject or try to land . . . ?

He wouldn't eject, he told himself. Not now, not after
everything that had happened.

He banked the Firefox over the wilderness beneath the
grey sky, searching for a runway that did not exist.

"AWACS Tupolev reports losing all trace, Comrade
General."

"We can't raise the pilot, sir. He's not answering."

"No infrared trace after the two explosions, sir."

Two explosions, Vladimirov thought, and immediately
found himself trapped in the Byzantine labyrinth of his own
qualifications and guesses and instincts. It was a maze which
was inescapable every time he appeared to be presented with
evidence that the American had died, that the Firefox had
been destroyed. And again now, when it seemed certain that
the second Foxbat, itself shot down, had caused an explosion
aboard the Mig-31, he doubted. He hesitated, he would not
look up from the map table, he would not listen to the First
Secretary's gruff sense of relief.

And yet, he could no longer express his doubts. He had
learned that much diplomacy. He had learned silence.

"Very well," he replied to the now-finished chorus of
reports, still without looking up. "Very well. Institute a reconnaissance search for wreckage of the two aircraft—and possible survivors . . ." He looked up into the First Secretary's
face and at Andropov behind the Soviet leader. "Just to make
certain," he added. "Routine." He hated the apologetic tone

in his voice. This new role did not suit him, but it was the only one which offered itself. He had, at last, begun to consider his own future. "It should not offend our friends, the Finns—if they ever discover our overflights."

The Soviet leader laughed. "Come, Vladimirov—the game is over. And to you, yes, it was only a game? Played with the most expensive toys?" His hand slapped the general's shoulder and Vladimirov steeled himself not to wince at the contact. Kutuzov appeared tired and relieved. The operators began to relax. The cabin speaker had been switched off.

Nothing, Vladimirov told himself without hope of conviction, nothing . . . There is nothing there now except wreckage. The American is dead.

"Chairman Andropov—some drinks, surely?" the Soviet leader instructed. Andropov smiled and moved to summon a steward. "No, no. We'll leave this crowded room. Come, some comfortable chairs and good drink before we land—mm?"

"Yes, of course, First Secretary," Vladimirov murmured, following the Soviet leader out of the War Command Center into a narrow, deceptively spacious lounge filled with well-upholstered, deep chairs, a television screen, a bar. Already, drinks were being poured . . .

Kutuzov appeared at his elbow and whispered: "You've shown good sense, Med—at last." His voice was a dry whisper. He'd been operated on, successfully, for cancer of the throat some years before. "It's over now."

"Do you think so?" Vladimirov asked in an urgent whisper. "Do you?"

Kutuzov indicated Andropov and the First Secretary, backs to them, already at the bar. "It would be foolish—monumentally stupid—for you to think otherwise at this moment," he whispered. Then he smiled. "Come on, drink with them, listen to them—and remember to *smile!*"

"It was—such a beautiful aircraft," Vladimirov announced abstractedly. "And the American showed us how good it really was."

"Perhaps they'll build us some more—but don't count on it." Kutuzov's laughter clogged and grated in his throat. The First Secretary offered them vodka.

"Come," he said. "A toast."

* * *

Two frozen lakes . . . Silence except for the clicking of the automatic ignition with no fuel with which to work. Gant switched it off. Silence. Two frozen lakes, lying roughly north-south, one larger and more elongated than the other, both surrounded by birch and conifer forest. Snowbound, isolated, uninhabited country in the north of Finnish Lapland.

Little more, according to the map on his knee, than forty miles from the border with the Soviet Union. His escape from the Foxbat had taken him further north than he had wished and turned him unnoticed back towards Russia.

Silence. Wind. Out of time.

He was gliding, the heavy airframe wobbling and quivering in the stormy airflow. Altitude, 2,500 feet. The lakes moved slowly southwards behind him. He banked sharply and glided towards them once again.

He would not eject, would not . . . He'd come this far. The airplane stayed in one piece.

2,000 feet. The larger of the two lakes was perhaps more than one mile long—long enough to be a runway. The second lake was fatter, rounder, and he would have to land diagonally across it to be certain of stopping the Firefox with room to spare. There appeared to be a lot of surface snow which would effectively slow the aircraft. It would have to be the larger lake.

Pretend it's the floe, he told himself. Just pretend it's the floe. At the end of March, the ice should be thick enough, it should bear the weight of the airframe.

It didn't matter. It was the only available alternative to a crash-landing, or to an ejection which would leave the Firefox to plough into the ground and break up once it ran out of supporting air. He would not let that happen. Instead, he would land the airplane, and wait. When he was certain the search for him had been called off, he could communicate with Bardufoss or Kirkenes—Kirkenes was much the closer—and they could drop him fuel. He checked that the airbrakes were in and the booster pumps off. All the trims he set to zero. He tugged at his straps, checking their security.

He could make it. The conifers grew down to the southern neck of the narrow lake and stretched out drunkenly over it—he could see that clearly—and if he could get in close enough to the frozen shore, he would be sheltered from any chance visual sighting. Excitement coursed through him. He could do it. He could preserve the Firefox.

Altitude, 1,000 feet. He had only the one chance.

He nudged the rudder and the Firefox swung as lazily and surely through the chill grey air as a great bird. He lowered the undercarriage as he leveled, and operated the flaps. Four hundred feet, well above the trees which rushed beneath the aircraft's belly. The lake joggled in his vision ahead of the plane's nose. Two hundred feet and out over the ice. He'd got it right. The Firefox sagged now, on full flap, dropping with frightening swiftness, and the wheels skimmed the surface snow for a moment, then dug into it, flinging up a great wake around and behind him. He gripped the control column fiercely, keeping the nose steady. The nosewheel touched, dug in, and Gant saw the surface snow ahead rushing towards him, beneath him. The Firefox began to slow, began to stroll, then walk . . .

The Firefox rolled gently towards the southern neck of the lake, towards the frozen stream that either fed or drained the lake in summer. His speed slowed quickly—too quickly? The aircraft seemed to no more than crawl towards the overhanging shelter of the trees. Would he make it? It had to reach the cover of the trees . . .

It was enough. The airplane had sufficient speed to move in close to the bank at the very end of the lake, where it narrowed almost to a point at its conjunction with the frozen stream. Low-hanging branches deposited their weight of snow on the cockpit canopy as he slowed to a final stop. Branches scraped along the fuselage. The nosewheel stopped just short of the bank.

He'd done it. The Firefox was hidden. In one piece, and safely hidden. He breathed deeply. Then he raised the cockpit canopy. Cold air rushed in, chilling him to the bone, making his teeth chatter uncontrollably. He grinned at the drop in his body temperature. He disconnected his oxygen supply, the radio and thought-guidance leads to his helmet; he unlocked his leg restraints, and his seat straps. He removed the helmet and, as he stood up in the cockpit, he began to laugh.

Yes, the trees hid almost everything. One wing tip and the tail assembly were still exposed, but the shape of the aircraft was altered, destroyed by camouflage. The sky was heavy with snow. A fall would hide the signs of his landing. It would be all right.

The Firefox lurched, as if the starboard landing gear had

snapped. Gant clung to the side of the cockpit to steady himself, his ears filled with a terrible, strained cracking noise. He dropped the helmet he had just removed.

A black, crooked line, like a tree growing in hideous fast-motion, moved away across the ice. Branches grew from it. The Firefox lurched again, this time to port, and settled unsurely. Other black trees grew out across the ice around and behind him.

Horrified, he looked over the fuselage. He could see water behind the starboard wing, water behind and in front of the port wing. Water beyond the tail. Huge jagged plates and slabs of ice bobbed and rubbed one another around the Firefox, which now floated on its belly, buoyed up for the moment by the empty fuel tanks in the wings and fuselage. Gant knew that as soon as the engine inlets and tail pipes filled, the aircraft would sink steadily into the lake.

2 / DEEPER

The tail of the Firefox slid deeper into the water as the tailpipes and inlets flooded and the undercarriage sought the pebbled floor of the lake where it sloped steeply from the bank. The nose of the aircraft jutted into the lower branches of the nearest firs but it, too, was slowly sinking. Gant did not understand. The ice was thin and weak at the neck of the lake, even though the stream that provided the lake's outlet was evidently frozen between its banks. Everything was frozen—yet the Firefox was sinking.

He felt panic mount, rising like a thermometer. He could not control it because he had used all his reserves of energy and self-control to reach the lake with the aircraft intact, and this disaster had struck at the moment of his release, his greatest relief. The panic rose in waves through him, and his hands gripped the side of the cockpit, numb with the pressure he exerted; a mad, dazed ship's captain waiting for the end.

Floor of the lake steep—draining water leaving a pocket of air under the ice, making it thin—engine weight will roll her back into the lake, further out—she'll drown, drown . . .

The jagged plates of ice touched, rubbed, moved apart. He could easily make it to the shore, even though the overhead branches were already out of reach. It was the airplane, the Firefox—

There was nothing he could do. His frame shuddered with tension and futility. He was weary, and his limbs seemed very heavy. He had nothing left. Water lapped up the fuselage, moving higher very slowly—the branches over the cockpit were now over the up-jutting nose. The huge weight of the engines and the airframe was slowly dragging the Firefox deeper and further out into the lake. The long nose section thrust from the water like the snout of a creature that had breached the flimsy ice.

The cracks had stopped. They branched perhaps fifty or sixty yards out into the lake behind the aircraft. The loose plates of ice had floated away from the fuselage to gather like a motiveless crowd where the ice remained deceptively firm. To his left, the snow-covered shore of the lake was still within jumping distance.

Gant climbed onto the lip of the cockpit, poising himself, his hands gripping the edge of the cockpit tightly. He looked back down at the still-lit instruments, the fallen helmet, the pilot's couch . . .

The Firefox lurched backwards, out from beneath the shelter of the trees, the water lapping up the fuselage. Now, it was little more than a foot from the edge of the cockpit; another movement, and the first icy ripples would spill into it—fusing, shorting, damaging everything. The panic in his stomach and chest would not subside. There was no nightmare of Vietnam, not in this cold, not with the smoky grey shoreline and the omnipresence of snow. But he was as bereft of purpose as if he were suffering one of his bouts of paralysis.

The aircraft was steady now, tilting backwards on the sloping bed of the lake. Perhaps only for seconds . . . The water was ten inches from the lip of the cockpit . . . the

tail was half-submerged, the huge engines already underwater . . .

He dropped, in his apelike crouch, back into the cockpit,
his hands nerveless and numb as he tried to make them
operate small, delicate switches and buttons. Thought-
guidance— shut down . . . come on . . . weapons systems—
shut down . . . radio, radar, autopilot, ECM systems—shut
down . . . His hands seemed warmer now, no longer lumps
at the ends of his arms but active, moving with a trained,
automatic precision and speed. In seconds, he shut down the
aircraft—killing it, rendering it lifeless. Then he climbed over
the lip of the cockpit. He was still wearing his parachute.
Clipped to his life jacket were his inflatable dinghy and his
survival pack. Icy water touched his heel, and he withdrew
his foot. Awkwardly, he moved over the cockpit sill, his toes
feeling clumsily for the spring-loaded steps. When he found
them, and balanced himself, he pulled out the cockpit canopy
hand crank from its compartment below the cockpit sill. He
cranked down the canopy until it closed tightly. Then he
closed the manual, exterior locks.

A moment of pain, of acute failure, and then he poised
and leapt. He landed in soft snow, paining his hand on a
buried tree root, rolling over and scrabbling for a hold on
frozen grass and icy rocks beneath the snow. His survival
pack and the dinghy lay beneath him. Snow filled his mouth
and eyes, even his ears, though they were still alive to the
terrible scraping lurch that meant the Firefox was moving
further out, further under the surface.

Yes. He turned to look. The water had reached the
cockpit—thank God he'd remembered to close and lock it—
and the nose pointed to the grey sky at a more acute angle
than before. He drew his knees up to his chest—the cold of
the snow seeping through the pressure suit and the thin
underclothing beneath—and dropped his head. He could not
move. He felt it was like waiting by a deathbed—but not his
father's, for that had been an impatient wait with release and
the throwing off of hatred at the end of that tunnel.

It would be no more than a minute now—

He laughed; high and crazy. The noise was like the call
of a rook in the thick cold air. He could not prevent it; a
cackle of survival and defeat. *He'd certainly hidden the Firefox,
hidden it good—*

He could not stop the laughter. Tears rolled down his

blanched, cold cheeks, down the creases of his pained face. He cackled like a madman. *He'd really, really hidden it—*

Another grating lurch—some part of him remained surprised that the undercarriage had withstood the pressure upon it—and he looked up to see the cockpit now half-submerged, the water lapping towards the nose of the Firefox.

And the laughter stopped.

The locked and shut down aircraft was twenty yards from him, the black nose jutting, the cockpit half-submerged. Everything—*everything* electronic, every means of communication, was locked beneath the canopy, locked inside the airframe. Radio, radio, *radio* . . .

Gant swallowed, savagely wiped his mouth. The aircraft was steady again, one of the wheels, perhaps, halted against the chock of a boulder or sunk in softer mud. Tantalizingly steady—

There was nothing—

"Nothing, dammit!" he exploded, banging his clenched fists on his thighs. A bird replied in a hoarse voice from one of the trees. "Nothing—!" He could do nothing. He couldn't sit in the Firefox until help came, he couldn't dismantle the radio and rescue it, he couldn't . . . couldn't, couldn't—

Strangely, he heard the voice of Aubrey then. The soft, self-deprecating, insinuating tones. His final briefing, the fake transistor radio that was a homing receiver which had saved his life, listening as it had done for signals from "Mother One," the submarine that had refueled the Firefox. It was attached by a single adhesive strip to one corner of the instrument panel.

Receiver—?

Transmitter, too . . . Aubrey had been reluctant to mention it, hovered over the words like a choosily feeding pet until he had uttered them. *In case of some*—final *emergency, my dear fellow . . . not likely, of course . . . but, it has an emergency signal facility if you*—*have to . . . you understand?*

Gant was on his feet, still nodding at the remembered words as he had nodded when he first heard them. Aubrey didn't want to mention crashing, injury, death, but Gant had understood.

And he had left it in the cockpit!

He slipped and scrambled down the steep bank. He unclipped his survival pack, his parachute harness, the dinghy. The dinghy—! A fringe of ice cracked beneath his weight, and he slid into the icy water. He cried out with shock. He stepped back—pebbles and larger boulders on the bed of the lake, so he moved carefully—and the water retreated. He dragged the dinghy towards him, and inflated it. It boiled and enlarged and groaned, then bobbed on the water. His teeth chattered, his whole body shuddered. A bird croaked, as if in mockery. The nose of the Firefox tilted upwards like a snub, a dismissal of his frantic efforts. He climbed into the dinghy, and paddled furiously towards the aircraft. His head bobbed up at every frantic stroke to study the unmoving nose of the plane. His body temperature continued to drop. His heartbeat raced with tension, with the sense of time lost and almost run out, with the fight to keep the blood warm and circulating.

His hand touched the fuselage, and he withdrew it as if shocked, in case the pressure of fingertips might be enough to thrust it beneath the water. He juggled and bumped the dinghy slowly along the fuselage until it was beneath the cockpit tilted crazily high above him. His hands felt for the spring-loaded steps up the side of the fuselage.

Felt, fumbled, found . . . He tested his chilly weight against the strength in his arms, and then heaved his body out of the dinghy, feet scrabbling—careful, don't kick, don't struggle—until they, too, discovered toeholds. He hung there for a moment, sensing the steadiness of the airframe. It was holding. He began climbing, hand over hand, feet following with exaggerated caution, slipping more than once.

Lip of the cockpit, smoothness of the canopy . . .

He rested, aware of the airframe now as a seesaw. He waited for it to move. It remained still. The water covered the rear section of the canopy. Water would spill into the cockpit when he opened it. It wouldn't have to matter.

Left-hand side of the instrument panel. He unlocked the canopy, then cranked it slowly open. Water gurgled into the cockpit, splashing down instruments, becoming a pool in the well of the pilot's couch. He eased the canopy open sufficiently to insert his gloved hands, and scrabbled blindly, leaning forward, touching along the instrument panel, across dials and read-outs and displays and buttons and switches, until he felt the edge of the homing device. Like a black cigarette case, slightly larger than that, same shape . . .

He tugged at it. The adhesive held it. With both hands he heaved and it detached itself from the panel. With a chilly, sodden, shivering triumph, he drew it out and clutched it against his side, hugging it to him like a prize. Still the airframe remained motionless, rock-steady. He began to crank down the canopy once more.

The Firefox shuddered, and the entire airframe lurched away from him towards deeper water. The huge tailplanes sank almost to their tips. The Firefox continued to slide away. With the instinct to preserve himself and the aircraft, he cranked more furiously and grabbed with his other hand at the handhold just below the edge of the cockpit. A tremor ran through him as he heard the homing device slide down the fuselage with a clatter, then drop. He cranked furiously, closing the canopy. He dropped the cranking handle then, in order to hang on with both hands. He knew the Firefox was going under . . .

He would float away. He looked around frantically for the homing device, and for the dinghy, already ten yards away. Surely he had heard the impact of the plastic on ice, not the slight splash of its falling into the water—but he could not locate it. The water mounted the canopy towards him. The airframe was steadily rolling backwards now. It would stop only when the slope of the lake bed leveled. The water was only inches away—he would float off.

He released the grip of his right hand, then made to move his left. He unclenched his fingers from the handhold, and tried to move his arm. Water touched his fingers, embraced his thighs. The canopy was almost submerged, the nose was sinking. The tips of the tailplanes were still visible, the leading edges of the wings protruded from the dark water. He could not move his left arm.

He had trapped the sleeve of the pressure suit in the canopy when he cranked it shut. Without the cranking handle he could not open it again. As the water reached his waist, he tugged frantically, attempting with all his strength to rip the suit.

Clinging to the canopy of the Firefox, he began to slip beneath the water with the airframe. Waist, chest, neck, mouth. He could not free his sleeve . . .

Above the noise of his blood and breathing, he again heard the bird croak mockingly. Then he disappeared beneath the water.

*   *   *

"There were *two* explosions—two *distinct* explosions . . . you're certain of that?"

Aubrey waited. The underground Operations Room of RAF Scampton had shrunk to a microphone, two revolving tape reels, and the console and its operator controlling the high-speed, scrambled communications between himself and the captain of an AWACS Nimrod aircraft over the Norwegian Finnmark. Beyond the glass, down on the main floor of the room, Buckholz and Curtin stood beside the huge plot table, staring at the model that represented the Nimrod. Buckholz wore a headset clamped on his short, grey hair. His shoulders were stiff with the tension generated by the transmission and reception delays of Aubrey's conversation.

The tapes rolled swiftly, halted, rewound, then Aubrey heard Squadron Leader Eastoe's voice, mechanical and distant, but clear.

"There were two, almost in the same spot, but distinct. A small time and distance gap. At . . ." A slight pause while Eastoe consulted something, then: "Sixty-nine-forty North, twenty-seven-fifty East. That's no more than twenty-two nautical miles from the nearest point on the Soviet border— about the same from the Norwegian side . . ."

Eastoe seemed to have paused once more, rather than to have concluded his message. Aubrey lifted his head. Someone pushed a futuristic model into position on the plot table. It was old-fashioned—on one wall of the Operations Room was a fiber-optic, computer-operated plot map where aircraft, ships and missiles were registered by moving lights—and yet Aubrey found the plot table comfortingly familiar. It had a wartime association. It was out of date, superannuated. He could see, quite clearly, that Gant was deemed by Eastoe to have met his death in a narrow neck of Finland between the Soviet Union and Norway. The model of the Firefox, placed in position, was in the nature of a memorial. Curtin and Buckholz gazed fixedly at the table—except for a brief upward glance by the senior CIA officer. His face was grim. Aubrey, almost furtively and in shame, lowered his head to the tape reels and the microphone. Eastoe had not added to his statement.

"You conclude that one of the Mig-25s was successful?" he snapped. The tapes spun, then waited. Spun again, rewound, played.

"Yes," Eastoe replied. Aubrey watched Buckholz's shoulders hunch, shrug. Curtin's face was abstracted. The naval officer seemed fascinated by the small black model of the Firefox. The plotters near them hovered like deferential servants, or like the policeman bringing news of a road accident. "They tried to shepherd him, he shook them off, took out the first of them—the second must have pursued at ground level, and they got each other. We couldn't see the Mig-31, of course, so we don't know whether it was damaged earlier. Since the explosions, nothing. The area's filling up with Migs now, but their activity suggests they can't locate anything." Eastoe's voice paused, then: "Mr. Aubrey—what do you want me to do?"

Aubrey rubbed his chin vigorously, as if conjuring the answer from a lamp. The tape reels waited for him to speak. Alongside him, the staff of the Operations Room sat behind their consoles and radios and radars and screens. The plotters hovered. The huge wall map gleamed with moving lights. The walls of the Ops Room displayed other maps crowded with pins and scribbled legends, colored tapes. Blackboards revealed information regarding the serviceability of aircraft. Large meteorological maps were heavily marked, garlanded with satellite weather photographs. A long row of pale blue headsets, together with a single red telephone, stretched away on either side of him. A multiplicity of technical devices were at his disposal. He dragged his hands through the hair above his ears. His fingers touched at the back of his head. He heard old bones and muscles crack and stretch reluctantly. He replaced his hands in his lap, hunching forward. He did not know what to say to Eastoe. He did not know how to begin to use the people and equipment that lay at his disposal.

Not once, not once . . . his thoughts murmured hesitantly. Not once, not once—

Until now, he answered himself. Until now. Not once had he doubted, truly doubted, not once had he thought the game lost, the aircraft or the pilot lost . . .

Until now.

Now he believed it. It had been forced upon him. Gant was dead, the aircraft scattered over the landscape like sooty dots on the carpet of snow. Nothing, nothing left of it.

Despair was an unfamiliar companion. A sometime acquaintance, away elsewhere for long periods; older and leaner at each unexpected return. Yet it was despair Aubrey felt. He had failed. The whole operation had failed. Delicate, complex, devious—brilliant and his own, it had failed. Aubrey's despair dressed in a sober suit and carried a briefcase. It was an entirely professional emotion, and bottomless.

He saw an image, then, of civilian air disasters. Newsreel film. Flight recorders being searched for by the experts who did not concern themselves with the search for the living and the dead. Black boxes. Cockpit voice recorders, flight recorders. The secrets of the dead.

In his mind, he could see a recent piece of newsfilm. The joggling camera registering the walking legs of a man and the two heavy, black, flame-scarred boxes he carried, one on either side of him. Walking legs, black boxes—

He rubbed his eyes. Voice-activated, the tape reels moved.

"Remain on-station, Eastoe," he ordered, his voice clearing and strengthening as he spoke. "Fly up and down that piece of border until you hear something!"

A pause. Eastoe's reply returned, was rewound, then became audible. "Please repeat, Mr. Aubrey."

Aubrey slapped his forehead. He had not explained. "I wish to be certain," he said. Buckholz, one hand holding the earphone of his headset, looked up towards the glass-fronted gallery where Aubrey was sitting. "If the aircraft has crashed or been destroyed, then there may be nothing. If Gant is alive—if the aircraft is still intact—then you may pick up a signal from his homing device. You have the equipment to activate and receive it."

After a little while, during which Aubrey felt hot and the small sense of excitement that hope had brought deserted him, he turned pale and felt foolish like a gauche new entrant to an ancient and dignified club. Foolish—must try it—foolish, though . . .

"Roger, Mr. Aubrey. If he's there, we'll find him."

"Yes," Aubrey replied abstractedly, unconcerned that the word and its tone would be transmitted. The console operator turned to him. Aubrey flapped his hand dismissively, staring at his lap. Gant was dead. The Firefox was in pieces.

"The AWACS Tupolev is watching us watching him," Eastoe announced. Aubrey hardly heard his voice. "He'll be listening for the same thing. Could he pick up a signal?"

"I hope not," Aubrey murmured in a moment of uncalculated honesty that was full of doubt and foreboding.

*   *   *

The shock of the icy water which engulfed him almost made him open his mouth to scream, to expel the lungful of air he had snatched as his face was dragged into the water. His chest seemed too full, inflated under pressure from within. If only he could expel the air, make his body more empty, smaller, the cold would be less intense, less painful. He forced himself to retain the air.

Even a few feet beneath the surface, the water was lightless because of the disturbed silt, as if the ice had closed over the Firefox as soon as it sank. The noise of the undercarriage moving down the steeply sloping bed of the lake, was magnified and distorted into a prolonged groan. The Firefox dragged him by the sleeve deeper beneath the water. His body banged against the metal of the nose as he bobbed and attempted to float. His body's buoyancy tugged at the trapped sleeve of his pressure suit, turning him almost in a cartwheel, twisting him, slamming him down on his back against the fuselage, then scraping him along the nose of the aircraft.

His lungs seemed fuller. He knew he was beginning to drown. There seemed a simple solution, but he believed it was lightheadedness that suggested the idea. He was trapped. He tried to reach his left arm with his right hand. The Firefox continued to roll, and he could not tell whether it was beginning to level out and slow down. He could not reach his trapped sleeve. Without purchase, he could not apply any force to the feeble grip of his right hand on the material of the suit. His hands were numb, anyway, fingers crooked like claws, frozen.

Weariness, and the knowledge that survival and escape had been snatched from him, curtailed his ability to think, to move, to even desire anything. His chest hurt with retained air. His head swirled like the dark water. Just as around him the disturbed mud drifted back towards the bed of the lake, his body sagged down to straddle the nose of the Firefox.

The napalm of his nightmare lit the scene. Freezing and numb though he was, his body still felt hot, burning. From within the bamboo cage in which he had been imprisoned, he witnessed his rescue; the attack upon the Vietcong detachment and their hidden village. He saw the little girl with the sadly wise face running, and he saw her dissolve in the gout of napalm dropped near her. He saw all the others burn like matchsticks, like trees in a forest set alight. He felt himself burn. He was one of them—he *was* them . . .

The nightmare claimed him. He struggled against it, but his body seemed to have no conception of water and drowning, only of his recurrent dream, only of the napalm. The water around him seemed redly lit by its flare. Every one of the gooks had burned, the little girl had burned. He had remained untouched physically, safe in his abandoned bamboo cage. Ever since, horror and guilt had caused him to burn, melt, dissolve with the Vietnamese; with the little girl, in her place . . .

His hand embraced his left thigh. He noticed the touch, the clawlike grip. The crablike scrabbling, the tugging at a snap-studded flap. His mind was detached and separate from his right hand. His left hand was feelingless, somewhere above him, against the canopy of the cockpit. His lungs were bursting . . .

He could see only the red burning color of the water as his right hand closed thumb and forefinger upon the flap on his thigh. Gant did not understand. The flap pulled slowly open like a hesitant mouth. He did not know what his right hand expected. He wanted, more than anything to empty his lungs, more even than to stop the nightmare because this time he was going to die inside it. His right hand closed on something and withdrew it from the pocket. It felt hard.

The little girl's body, right at the center of the mass of golden-red fire, dissolved . . . he was on the point of opening his mouth to scream . . . and something detached itself— straw hat or head he had never known, had never dared to look—he wanted only to scream . . .

His right hand brought up the hard object, close to his face. His right hand needed the evidence, the use of his eyes. But his eyes did not work, dazzled by the light of the flames. Where his hand was, where the object was, it was dark. Thin gleam—? He could not focus. His head swirled. The flames lessened. His right hand continued to act, reaching forward, ahead of him into the place where the numbing, icy cold seemed to be coming from, where it had already swallowed his left hand, left arm. He tried to watch, to understand—

Empty your lungs, he told himself. *Look*—

See—

He saw the dinghy knife trailing its safety cord which his right hand had withdrawn from its sheath, he saw it hack at his left hand, left arm, so that he wanted it to stop. Feeling returned to his left arm as it cringed in anticipation of a wound. Then the sleeve was torn, sliced open, and he expected blood but there was none and his arm drifted down towards him, to be clenched against his stomach, its torn sleeve freed from the canopy.

Feebly, he kicked with numb feet, drained and leaden legs. His face was uplifted, but everything seemed dark. He kicked again, leaving the napalm fire behind him now, afraid at that moment that it was already too late, that he was blacking out and would open his mouth, letting the bubbles dribble out as his body slackened . . .

He felt his boots scrabbling on the metal of the Firefox's nose, and pushed upwards. It was only a matter of feet, but in time it seemed endless, because there were gaps of inky, swirling black between his attempts to count.

One, one-two. Black. Two-two-two. Black. One-two . . .
Black—
Grey—
Black—
Then light.

He roared as he expelled the air, felt his lungs painfully deflate, then draw in cold new air which hurt and made him cough. He swallowed water. His cold arms and legs wouldn't tread water. Breathe . . .

Inhale—hold—exhale . . . inhale-hold-exhale . . . sweeter now. The air tasted. It was sweet, cold, pure. His body hung on the surface of the water, exhausted, as if threatening to slip back beneath it. Life . . . jacket . . .

His hands fumbled on his chest, dabbling there uselessly, it seemed, for whole minutes.

Then the life jacket inflated, bobbing him unresistingly onto his back, holding up his hanging, useless, numb legs, pushing his arms out into a crucifix, keeping his chin out of the icy water. He breathed air gently, savoring it, pushing at the water with gentle movements.

A long time later, it seemed, his feet dragged gratingly against the pebbles of the shore. He was almost sitting in the water. He tried to stand up, could not, fell on his side—the life jacket turning his face to the grey sky at once—and then turned wearily onto all fours and crawled the last feet to the steep, snow-covered bank.

And rested, shuddering with cold, hands and feet and knees still in the water, reminded of warmth and function by the sharp pebbles beneath them. The dinghy knife was still in his right hand, sticking up out of the water.

When his hands began to pain him with their freezing numbness, and his feet were dead from the cold, he clambered upright, and stood, rocking with exhaustion, gauging the height of the steep bank of the lake and his ability to ascend it. He succeeded in climbing by dragging his body behind his arms up the slope, digging the dinghy knife deep into the frozen soil and heaving against it, digging it in again further up, heaving his body up to its level. It took him ten minutes; the bank at that point was a steep slope perhaps twelve feet high. He lay, when he had inched over the lip of the slope to the bole of the first fir tree, exhausted, panting, his eyes hardly able to focus. For one thing alone he was thankful. He had left the napalm of his nightmare down there behind him, in the lake with the Mig-31.

Later, he ate chocolate. Later still, when feeling had returned to his hands, he was able to rub life into the rest of his body. The pressure suit was stiffening as it slowly dried. Later, he inspected the area of water at the neck of the lake, realizing that his panicky guess had been near the truth. The stream that acted as the lake's outlet was indeed now frozen. But it must have gone on draining the lake before it, too, froze. The draining water had left an air pocket which had kept the ice thin, dangerous. Later still, after the noise of a low-flying, searching Mig had faded east of the lake, he realized that he should put some distance between himself and the site of the forced landing. The ice would knit again, form like a cataract over the eye of water the airplane's weight had opened. The Firefox would be totally hidden by the following dawn. Already, the short Arctic day was beginning to fade.

He had the dinghy knife, the survival pack, his parachute, and the standard-issue Makarov officer's pistol and two spare magazines. He had no extra clothing, and his body was chilled to the bone. The dinghy had drifted out into the lake, like a marker to indicate the airplane's position. He drew the Makarov, hesitated, steadied his aim, and fired twice. The noise was deafening. Birds protested with cold voices. Slowly the dinghy deflated, began to sink. Gant sighed with relief. No trace.

He was alive. Standard procedure dictated that he remain near the aircraft. In this case, he dare not. If they searched for him—when they failed to find any signs of wreckage they could attribute to the Firefox—then they must not find him near the plane. He had to head . . . northwest, try to make some indentation on the daunting twenty miles or more between his position and the Norwegian border. He had to blindly hope that it was not only the Russians who would be searching for him . . .

The homing device. The transmitter—

In a new moment of panic, he looked around sightlessly. It was nowhere to be seen.

Had he—? Had it been switched to transmit? He could remember every movement of his right hand as it sought the dinghy knife and then his trapped sleeve. Now, he had to recall every moment of the few when the slim black plastic case was cradled in his left hand, against his body. Had he done it, automatically? Had he switched it on?

His memory fumbled, struggled with the effort of recalling automatic responses, mere reflex actions.

Yes, he decided. Yes, he had switched it on. His eyes scanned the ice. The remains of the dinghy had disappeared. He walked clumsily, slowly along the bank—even for the transmitter, he would not allow himself to step onto the treacherous sheet of ice on the lake—searching for what would be no more than a black dot. He did not find it. The landscape was nothing more than black and grey and white.

Finally, he concluded that the transmitter had sunk to the bottom of the lake. If it had dropped onto ice—he was certain he remembered that kind of sound when it fell—it must have slipped off when the ice had been moved or distressed by the underwater eddies created by the moving bulk of the Firefox. It was lost.

Now, distance was his only imperative. He could not stay near the transmitter, near the lake. If he was found, it needed to be miles from here.

His body failed him for a moment, daunted by the prospect of movement, of travel; of survival.

He looked northwards up the lake to where the heavy, crowded trees were little more distinct than a dark, carbon smudge made by someone sketching the scene. The ice was a smooth sheet. He was on the western shore of the lake. He checked his compass and the map he unstrapped from his thigh. In its clear plastic, it had remained dry during his immersion. The pressure suit was achingly cold.

He looked in the direction he must travel, towards Norway. Conifers crowding to the water's edge, low hills beyond them. He heard the mocking dissuasion of large, unseen birds. He looked down at the water, still like setting jelly, its temperature dropping. The Firefox was undetectable, invisible. It had to be enough to satisfy him; drive him on.

He picked up his parachute and buckled on the harness. He clipped the survival pack to his now deflated life jacket, and adjusted its weight for comfort. Then he turned away from the lake and entered the trees.

Air Marshal Kutuzov glanced towards the other end of the compartment and the door which led to the small private office the First Secretary used when aboard the Tupolev. Evidently, the Soviet leader and the Chairman of the KGB intended remaining there for the rest of the flight. Kutuzov glanced at his heavy gold watch. Twenty minutes to the military airfield southeast of Moscow. He cleared his throat, patting Vladimirov's leg as he spoke. "Med, I think you have secured the succession for yourself." The old man tapped the shoulder boards on his own uniform. His pale, rheumy eyes twinkled, and he nodded vigorously. "You're learning. And in time—just in time . . ." It was evident that Kutuzov was philosophically drunk.

Vladimirov stared at his own small glass. How many drinks—? They'd been drinking for less than half an hour. No one gets drunk more quickly than a Russian. What was he drinking to? The American's death? The excessive, almost manic bonhomie of the First Secretary, the cold, glinting appraisals of the still-sober Andropov—both had ceased to irritate or impinge. The vodka had distanced them. He had managed to drown reason and insight like two wasps at the bottom of his glass. Their stings pulled out.

He glanced towards the door of the War Command Center, then at the door to the First Secretary's office. The Soviet leader had been summoned to the telephone to deal with the diplomatic niceties of airspace intrusions.

Through the vodka, the sense of self-contempt was returning. Vladimirov warned himself against it. And, as if his companion sensed the threatened change of mood, he patted Vladimirov's hand and said: "Be sensible—continue to be sensible, General Vladimirov." The formality of the address was intentional. Vladimirov shook his head in what was a gesture of agreement rather than protest. The alcohol stirred in his head like a solid mass lurching across an empty space.

"I know it—I know it," he murmured. "It's much better to be—oh, what? Nothing? Perhaps not. Better to be sensible." As he moved his hands angrily, vodka slopped from his glass onto the shining toes of his knee-boots. He watched the oily droplets flow like mercury across the polish. "I know it."

He stared again at the door to the War Command Center. Through it officers had appeared periodically in the past half hour to make their negative, comforting reports. They were like something added to the vodka, doubly calming. Wreckage photographed, pictures being returned for examination; search planes reporting no distress signals, no electronic emissions, no survivors.

Soon, it would be no more than a matter of experts examining the photographs of the wreckage to confirm that the Firefox and the Mig-25F were destroyed at the same moment in the same area. Then later the Finns would give permission for crash investigators and a recovery party to examine the site and bring the wreckage home. Black boxes would be removed, bodies wrapped in plastic sacks and brought back. End. Over. Finished.

The First Secretary had canceled all overflights of the crash area before taking his call from the Finnish President. All intrusions of foreign airspace could be apologized for because now they had ceased.

"I am offering you no more than a lesson in survival," Kutuzov announced. It was the slurred voice of the vodka. "Because I want *you* to command the air force. *You.*" He was patting Vladimirov's knee slowly and heavily to emphasize each word.

"I know that, old friend," Vladimirov replied, nodding. Even to himself, his words sounded indistinct. He mocked himself silently, reproaching and ridiculing himself as bitterly as he could. He swallowed what little remained in his glass. His stomach surged. "I've accepted. I—am a member of the team . . ." He smiled, his lips forming the expression imprecisely. "*How* long before we land?" he added with sudden exasperation.

"Patience. You are now a courtier. You will get used to waiting. It is a talent."

"Courtier . . ." Vladimirov murmured.

"Another drink?"

"No, old friend. I wouldn't be able to keep it down."

"No Russian can. We get drunk too quickly."

"Do you blame us?"

"No."

The two men stared into their empty glasses. Vladimirov lifted his to reflect the overhead light. He could see the last oily smear in the glass, see the smudges made by his lips and fingerprints. Then he stood up, swaying slightly, tall, grey-haired, drunk, but evidently, so evidently, an officer of distinction. As if he saw his form reflected in a mirror, he mocked his appearance. An impressive outward show, even when he was drunk. Hollow man . . . hollow man.

A young officer opened the door from the War Command Center. Vladimirov whirled almost too quickly to face him. In his hand he carried a message pad.

Hollow man . . .

Stop it—

It was impossible to drown the wasps, then.

"What is it?" he snapped, his tongue furry, his eyes glistening. The rest of himself retreated somewhere, to wait for a more opportune moment.

"It's the Tupolev, sir—the aircraft commander, Major Antonov. This . . . I don't think he can understand it."

Vladimirov snatched the pad, plucking his half-glasses from his top pocket, wobbling them onto his ears. Sobriety nudged him, having returned from its short absence. Antonov would not be the pilot of the Tupolev AWACS aircraft, but the political officer who theoretically commanded the crew. He was a member of GLAVPUR, the armed forces' political directorate. However, he might still be competent aircrew, even though he was on the Tupolev "Moss" because it flew near all kinds of hostile borders across which its crew might be tempted to take it—*liberating* it and themselves in the process. So, Antonov . . .

At first, Vladimirov did not understand the report. A frequency-agile signal, intermittent; they'd picked it up once or twice, got a line on it—the first fix—but not a second clear fix which would give them the exact position. They only knew the signal emanated somewhere along a straight line, a point not near the crash site.

Finally, the request for orders; the passing of the buck. Vladimirov waved the young officer out of his path and stepped into the War Command Center. Immediately, he sensed the familiar and the desired. Yes, it was a clean, well-lit place. It was comfortable here, at the center; the uniformed center.

He would have been criminally stupid, he reflected as he crossed the room, to have thrown all this away—and why, and for what? Because the Soviet leader was a boor and a thug? Because the Chairman of the KGB was a psychotic? Because he loathed their company and their intellectual inferiority? Those would have been his reasons; pride and snobbery. Caste.

A clean, well-lit, comfortable place. His place. It would have been criminal to throw it away.

"Put me through to Antonov—over the cabin speaker," he announced calmly, soberly. A moment later, he was given the signal to proceed. "Major Antonov, this mysterious signal of yours—what do you suppose it is?"

"Yes, Comrade General," he heard the distant, crackling voice begin, "we don't know what to make of it—any of us."

"When did you first pick it up?"

"Fifteen minutes ago. But we lost it—then found it on a different frequency. The third time, only five minutes ago, we managed to get a line on it, but we haven't been able to pick it up since." The tone was apologetic, but it managed to include the entire crew of the Tupolev in any consequent blame.

"Find it again, Major. I beg of you."

"Yes, Comrade General.

Frequency-agile: a signals or communications emission, but without a message or code. What was the source? A somehow-still-operating piece of clever electronics thrown far from the crash site? How far though, this source was too far . . . Some Finnish ground installation not on the maps? Unlikely. There had been no Personal Survival Beacon signals from either pilot, so Gant and the Foxbat pilot were both dead. Neither of them had ejected in time.

Personal Survival Beacon—*Beacon*—secure signal . . . he *remembered*, secrecy when all the pilot would want was the loudest scream across the widest band. Because of the Mig-31 project, there was secrecy surrounding the aircraft, the pilots, the ground crews, the instruments, the pressure suits . . . the obsessiveness of the Soviet state, how many times it had enraged him!

The P.S.B. for Firefox test pilots was frequency-agile

and intermittent, to ensure that only those instructed how to listen would ever hear . . . and Gant was wearing dead Voskov's pressure suit!

"It's *Gant!*" he roared. Shoulders and heads twitched with shock. Vladimirov beat his fists against his thighs. "He's *alive!* He's been alive all the *time! You!*" he barked at the officer who had brought him the scribbled transcript of Antonov's message. "Get me the details of the frequency code for the P.S.B. in a Firefox pressure suit—get it now!" He hurried to the door. Turning, he added: "Transmit it to Antonov as soon as you have it. And tell Antonov he *must* find that signal again and obtain an exact fix. No excuses!"

He went through the door, slamming it behind him, already knowing, without careful analysis, what must be done. The First Secretary and Andropov were emerging into the hospitality room at that moment. Immediately, Vladimirov pointed his long forefinger at Andropov as at a recalcitrant and untrustworthy subordinate.

"I want your Border Guards, Comrade Chairman!" he snapped. "I want a helicopter patrol, three ships, ready to cross into Finland immediately. Gant's been alive all the time!"

The contents of the survival pack from the Firefox were spread around him at the foot of the fir tree. His eyes were gritty with tiredness, and refused to focus for any length of time. Tension and weariness produced bouts of violent yawning. His body shivered almost constantly now, with cold and reaction. He had escaped. He had walked perhaps a little more than three miles in a northwesterly direction, keeping to the cover of the forest. He wanted only to sleep now. The pressure suit creaked and groaned as it froze into stiff, awkward sheets and folds around his body. His toes and fingers were numb. He had to sleep.

He would repack the survival kit except for the sleeping bag, which lay like an orange-and-blue brick near his left knee. If he got into it, perhaps only for an hour . . . surely he could afford the time, he hadn't heard the noise of a searching aircraft for perhaps twenty minutes now.

He had to sleep. He could not form ideas, make plans. He could not stay awake. There was good overhead cover here. The sleeping bag, tight around him, would eventually warm him, restore the circulation. He would be able to continue, if only he slept now.

A white Arctic hare watched him from the other side of the fir tree. Its nose twitched as it assessed the intruder. Gant watched it dully, head hanging forward, staring at the small, still animal from beneath his furrowed brow. Even to hold the white hare in focus against the snow required vast concentration.

Automatically, the Makarov pistol came out of its holster, took aim, and fired once. The noise was deafening, frightening in the silence to which he had become totally accustomed. It seemed to invite pursuit, create lurid images of capture. The hare leapt backwards with the force of the 9mm bullet at such close range, its powerful back legs flicking up. Then it lay on its side. A small stain spread from beneath its fur, darkly red. It would supplement the rich cake, the chocolate and biscuits in the rations of the survival pack. He was tiredly, exaggeratedly saddened by the killing of the hare, and as soon as he entertained the emotion it became self-pity; he was utterly weary. He could not, now, gather up, skin, cook the hare.

He began shivering again. Furiously, as if to punish himself, he rubbed his hands on his arms, trying to warm himself. Or scrape away from his skin some guilt or paralysis that clung to it.

An object. Hard. Inside one of the pockets. Left arm. He unzipped the pocket, and withdrew a small orange cylinder. He recognised it at once. His P.S.B., his distress signal transmitter.

He stared at it, unbelievingly. He had forgotten it, hadn't even attempted to locate it. It would have been activated—without the shadow of a doubt it would have been activated and begun transmitting—the moment it was immersed in the waters of the lake. He looked up at the sky, wildly. Nothing. The search had been called off—

Then he remembered the white dot of the Tupolev AWACS airplane as he had seen it on his screen.

The transmitter in his cupped hand undoubtedly had the power to beam a signal the thirty or more miles of distance and the 40,000 feet of altitude to the Tupolev. They must have heard it. They knew he was alive, where he was—

Panic removed weariness with a rush of adrenalin. He stood up, swayed, then dropped the P.S.B. He stamped on it, grinding it out of shape, puncturing the skin, smashing the transistors and wiring within. Killing it. The hare lay beyond the distress he had made in the snow, unmoving. He knelt again, scooping the scattered items back into the survival pack. The brick of his as-yet-unfolded sleeping bag, the folded .22 rifle and its half-dozen rounds, the chocolate and biscuits, the compressed rations, the solid tablet stove.

He glanced at the hare.

He dragged a plastic bag from the pack, scooped up the hare with apologetically gentle hands, and thrust it into the bag, then the package into the survival pack. As he stood up, he kicked fresh snow over the small, darkening smudge of blood.

His tracks would not show because he had been beneath the forest roof for the greater part of his journey. Eventually, he would have to sleep, but now he must strike in a more northerly direction. He slipped the harness of the pack over his shoulders, wearily assuming a fully upright posture when he had done so. He swayed with tiredness. He looked at his watch. Darkness was still as much as two hours away. Two hours, then, before he could rest.

He groaned aloud. The noise disturbed, yet magnified the silence of the forest. He studied the map. Ahead of him a country of patchy forest, narrow valleys, dotted lakes. Like Alaska.

He hefted the pack's weight to comfort, shivered with cold and anticipation, listened to the brooding, continuous silence, and turned to face northwards.

He began to walk.

Squadron Leader Alan Eastoe turned the AWACS Nimrod in a slow arc as he completed the southerly leg of his patrol at 25,000 feet above the road which straggled across the Norwegian Finnmark from the Tanafjord to the small town of Karasjok. The road marked the border between Norway and Finland. The aircraft was above the cloud layer as it once more headed northeast, following the wriggling line of the unseen road.

It had been almost two hours since they had reported what Eastoe suspected had been the pursuit and destruction of the unseen Mig-31. He had immediately been ordered by Aubrey to remain on-station and to begin this idiotic patrol in the ridiculous hope of either picking up a signal from Gant's

P.S.B.—and they hadn't done that because Gant was dead—or evoking some response from a piece of sophisticated gadgetry that must have been destroyed with the Firefox.

Yet Aubrey needed to be convinced. Thus, they had to keep on attempting to make the Firefox's homing device emit a simple carrier wave on which they could take a bearing. According to Farnborough, the homing device would be capable of responding to their pulsed radio signal for at least eighteen hours. Eastoe did not believe they would ever pick up the carrier wave. No one but an uninformed civilian like Aubrey would have expected to do so. There wasn't a ghost in the machine. The Firefox was just—dead.

Eastoe yawned and adjusted his tinted glasses on the bridge of his nose. At their altitude, the sunlight still gleamed from the surface of the cloud layer below, even though below the clouds it would be getting dark.

"Christ, Terry," he murmured, looking towards his copilot, tossing his head in dismissal, "bugger this for a ball of chalk. The poor sod's dead—and I'm sorry he's dead—and the plane's a write-off, and I'm sorry about that because I'd like to have seen it, just the once . . . *But*—!"

The copilot shook his head, smiling. "You've worked with Aubrey before, skipper . . ." he began.

"Worked *for*, Terry—worked *for* Aubrey. There's all the difference in the world. He's never bloody convinced. I can see him in the Garden, swearing blind the risen Christ *is* only the gardener!" Eastoe laughed, despite his exasperation. He heard a crewman's chuckle in his earphones. "Come on, then, he'd say—just one or perhaps two miracles to prove you are who you say you are—no, perhaps *three* miracles will suffice. Silly old sod!"

"Why worry? In half an hour we'll have to go off-station to refuel at Bardufoss. He won't order us up again tonight, surely?"

"Don't bet on it," Eastoe grumbled.

Except for their voices, the flight deck of the Nimrod was almost silent. As in all its endurance flying, the aircraft was using only two of its four engines. It was, in every way, a routine, empty day's flight. Yet exasperating to Eastoe—sad, too, because the Yank had almost got away with it, he'd almost pulled it off. Something had gone wrong—damage during the earlier dogfight when the second Mig-31 had been destroyed, probably—and he'd been caught on the hop and finished off. Poor bugger.

"Anything at all, John?" he asked, almost wailing into his microphone, addressing himself to the tactical navigator seated before his displays in the first of the major compartments aft of the flight deck. "What's that bloody stupid Russian doing?"

"Who—pissed-off Pyotr in the Tupolev?"

"That's the one."

"He's running up and down his bit of the border, doing just what we're doing, skipper. He's having about as much luck, by the look of it. No changes of heading, except when he comes to the end of a leg. He's now at—"

"I don't want a bloody fix on him, for Christ's sake! Is there nothing else?"

"Nothing. Not even a Finnish fighter. Keeping their heads down on orders from Helsinki, I should think. Anyway, they've been proven right. Ignore the problem and it'll go away. No Migs anywhere over Finnish airspace. They've gone home for tea."

"They've got their snaps of the wreckage. They'll be analyzing those. Perhaps we should have . . . ?"

"We're approaching optimum distance from the point of the explosions," the routine navigator offered like a grinning tempter. "Are you thinking of having a look, skipper?"

"I'm numb with boredom, but I'm not stupid," Eastoe replied. Why bother? Aubrey would have arranged something with Finnish Intelligence, or an American satellite. If he'd wanted proof of the crash from photographs, he'd have asked for them. Why bother? The same silent answer would be forthcoming. There was nothing to find. The captain of the Tupolev knew that's all there was just as surely as he did himself.

And then, the thought popped into his head. Why not? The Russians had been encroaching into Finnish airspace all afternoon. What if—?

The colder thought was—

We could be out of range of the bloody homing device. They might have already triggered the carrier wave, but they could be out of range by ten miles, or even a mile, if it was transmitting on very low power.

If he changed course, then the Tupolev would assume he'd found something. But, if he photographed the crash site at low level, then the bluff might work—and the snaps would be useful, more useful than tooling up and down the border.

"Anything, John?"

"Nothing, skipper."

Eastoe glanced at his copilot. "Everybody stay alert. I'm just taking a little shortcut here—a little corner off the map. I'd like some souvenir snaps. O.K.?"

The copilot watched Eastoe, then remarked: "You really do like working for these cloak-and-dagger sods, don't you? Deeds of bloody derring-do. When are you going to grow up?"

"Like you?" Eastoe was grinning. "Beats routine patrol. Who'll ever know? Who'll ever make a fuss? We can have our own snaps of the wreckage, and a closer listen for that bloody carrier wave—then, I promise, we'll go home."

"Three or four minutes in Finnish airspace doesn't constitute the crime of the century, Terry," the tactical navigator offered.

"Bob?"

"Yes, skipper?" the routine navigator replied.

"Give me a course for the crash site."

"Roger, skipper."

Eastoe grinned. "Blame me at the court-martial, Terry," he offered.

"You bet."

Eastoe nudged the alteration of course through the rudder. The Nimrod's blunt head swung to starboard. The cloud layer beneath the aircraft was devoid of nationality. Simple, Eastoe thought, feeling the tension stiffening in his frame as they crossed into Finnish airspace.

"Twenty-four kilometers from the crash site—right on course."

"No transmission, skipper."

"ETA fifteen seconds."

Eastoe dipped the Nimrod's nose. "I'm taking her down slowly to avoid creating *any* suspicion—then we'll turn and come back over the crash site. Everyone ready with their Brownies, please."

The cloud layer rose up to meet the nose of the Nimrod, almost touching it.

"That's it!"

"Christ, what—?"

"The carrier wave. We're locked on now, transmission steady. It's her all right!"

"I'll alter course for the fix."

The clouds slid around the Nimrod, darkening the flight deck.

"No, it's almost due south of us now. I've got the line . . . first fix, skipper. Just keep on course. Don't alter a bloody thing."

"South?" Eastoe remarked, genuinely surprised. "Not at the crash site. Christ, then he didn't go down . . . ?"

"Wait till you find the distance. It could have been thrown upwards of a mile," the copilot offered.

"Jeremiah. Come on, John . . ."

"Give me time, skipper. Fifty, fifty-one, two, three . . ."

"Do it now. I'll come back for another run if you need it," Eastoe ordered impatiently.

"Right. Got it." Eastoe hummed tunelessly in the silence. His ears buzzed with anticipation. The tactical navigator would now be drawing his lines on the map, out towards the point where they would intersect and establish the precise position of the homing device. Then they'd know how far away it was—exactly *where* it was.

"It's almost forty kilometers south of us. On what looks like a lake—or *in* a lake."

"His P.S.B.—anything?"

"Nothing."

"If he's in the plane, he'd have it working. So, where the hell is he?"

Gant awoke. Some part of his mind became immediately and completely alert, but he sensed the rest of himself, his thought-processes, his whole personality, struggling to throw off the deep sleep into which he had fallen the moment he climbed into the sleeping bag. Something had woken him—something . . .

He groaned, then clamped his hand over his mouth. Something, something that could already be as close as the Arctic hare had been when he had shot it—

His hand scrabbled within the sleeping bag, emerging with the Makarov pistol. It was almost completely dark. He could see little more than the glimmer of the snow, the boles of the nearest small trees, like fence-posts. He listened, the remainder of his mind and senses becoming alert, shaking off sleep.

He pressed the cold barrel of the Makarov against his face, leaning against the gun as if for support.

Distantly he could hear the noise of helicopter rotors, the whisper that had penetrated his sleep. He had no doubt that the sound was approaching from the east and moving in his direction. Russians. Lights, troops, even dogs . . .

He kicked the sleeping bag from his legs and began to fold it untidily then thrust it into the survival pack. He hoisted the harness, slipping it over his shoulders even as he began running.

3 / **IN FLIGHT**

"There!" Aubrey announced when he located the coded map reference Eastoe had supplied, his finger tapping at the large-scale map of Finland, which lapped down over the edges of the foldaway table. "There—in a lake, gentlemen. In a *lake!*" There was a note of triumph in his voice.

"The lake would have been frozen—that's why he might have thought he could land safely," Buckholz speculated quietly, tugging at his lower lip and glancing towards Curtin for confirmation. The USN officer nodded.

"He must have gone straight through—otherwise the Russians would have spotted the Firefox," Curtin murmured, his brow furrowed. It was evident he was considering Gant's chances of survival.

"Agreed. But it's there."

"The homing device is there," Giles Pyott offered. He was still wearing his uniform greatcoat, his brown gloves were held in his right hand. They tapped at the map in a soft rhythm. "But what else, mm? My guess would be wreckage. Gant must have ejected."

"Then why is there no trace of Gant's P.S.B.?" Curtin asked gloomily. "Where is he, Colonel Pyott, if he's alive?"

"Mm. Tricky."

"Maybe he switched it off—or destroyed it," Buckholz suggested. "He wouldn't want to get himself picked up by the other side. They're a lot closer than we are, and there are a hell of a lot more of them." Despite the offer of such qualified optimism, Buckholz shook his head. "But, maybe he isn't alive. We have to face that possibility."

"But the Firefox—!" Aubrey protested impatiently.

"It could be in two pieces, two hundred, or two million," Curtin answered him. Aubrey's face wrinkled in irritation. "This location is twenty miles from the point where the Foxbat impacted," Curtin continued. "That was up here . . ." He, in turn, tapped the map. It was as if the contoured sheet had become a talisman for them as they gathered around it. Pyott's military cap rested over northern Norway, his gloves now beside it, fingers reaching into the Barents Sea.

"So, it was damaged," Buckholz said. "Maybe on fire— twenty miles is nothing. There's no hope down that road, my friends."

"We really must *know*!" Aubrey snapped in utter exasperation. "We must have a *look*!" As he uttered the words, he was staring up into Pyott's face, like a child expecting assured parental activity. Giles Pyott smiled thinly.

"Kenneth, my dear chap, let's take this one step at a time. In the ten minutes since I got here from M.O.D., I've completely taken over his flying station from the poor Group Captain, all in the name of this project of yours . . . what else would you have me do?"

"Eastoe must overfly—"

"The lake? What about diplomatic noises from the Finns?" Giles Pyott drew a folding chair to him, flicked it open with a movement of his wrist, and sat down. He placed his hands on his thighs, and waited. Three more chairs were lifted from a dozen or more stacked against one wall of the Scampton Ops Room, and arranged in a semicircle in front of Pyott. Aubrey seemed content, for the moment, to become the soldier's subordinate. Buckholz was surprised, until he realized that Aubrey was simply playing a waiting game. He expected to be able to manipulate Pyott, if the colonel from M.O.D's StratAn Intelligence Committee was given the impression of command, of superior authority.

As if he read the American's thoughts, Pyott smiled and said: "You're flattering me with your undivided attention, Kenneth . . . nevertheless, there are things to be done." Pyott's eyes roamed the Ops Room. His curled forefinger now rubbed at his small auburn-grey moustache. Scampton was, to all intents and purposes, at their disposal. But, what to do with its resources? Where to begin? "I agree that Eastoe might make a single overflight. I wonder, however, whether photographs will give us enough information? It's getting pretty dark up there by now." Aubrey's face, Pyott noticed, wore an intense, abstracted air, like that of a child furiously engaged in building a sandcastle in utter ignorance of the behavior of tides. Aubrey was preparing himself to bully, to plead—to ignore the diplomatic in favor of the covert. And yet, his priorities might be the only really important ones in this case . . .

"We need someone to take a really close look," Aubrey remarked quietly.

"Mm. Director Buckholz—Charles—what is your honest feeling? What do we have up there, at this moment?"

"I side with your Squadron Leader Eastoe, Colonel. Gant was picked up visually, pursued, and shot down. We've got wreckage up there, is my best guess." Pyott turned to Curtin who merely nodded in support.

"I'm not disinclined to agree with you . . ." Aubrey made an impatient noise, but remained silent. Pyott continued: "You all know the delicate political situation. Finland agreed— largely because of personal links between Kenneth and the DG of Finnish Intelligence—to this covert overflight by the Mig-31, if its capture was successful. Perhaps they know, or suspect, what has happened. I would expect them to take a very negative line . . . unless you, Charles, can convince your government, as I must convince mine, that pressure should be brought to bear?" Pyott shrugged. "I am suggesting that we hold our fire until we are ordered to proceed by our respective governments. In other words, you and I, Charles, must be very convincing. Now, are we prepared to say, hands on hearts, that the Firefox might still be intact and the pilot alive?" He paused, looked at each of them intently. Almost willing them to answer, Aubrey felt. Then he added: "Well? Time to consider, gentlemen?"

"Not for me," Aubrey declared firmly. "It may very well be true. I, for one, must know for certain." Aubrey glared at Charles Buckholz. "Charles?"

"I don't know—look, you could be right. I hope to God you are. But—it just doesn't look that way to us."

"Will you say that it does—just for the moment?"

"I don't know . . ."

"We can't just write the whole thing off, Charles—!" Aubrey cried, standing up. His chair collapsed behind him, making a disproportionate noise in the Ops Room. "There has been too much expenditure of planning, time, and lives involved. You must want to be certain, surely? The Russians will want to be, and we may already be behind them in a race we didn't even know we'd entered!"

Buckholz's face was puzzled and a little fearful as he looked up at Aubrey, bent intently over him like a bully. "I—" he began, but Aubrey seized upon his hesitation.

"Once they've seen the pictures they took of the crash site, they'll find the Firefox's remains are missing. We know the plane isn't there. Once they know—and they may know it already—they'll be looking for it. And, if it is intact . . ." He left the threat unelaborated.

Pyott stroked his moustache. "I think Kenneth has a point, Charles," he murmured.

"Maybe," Buckholz replied reluctantly.

Curtin was nodding. "I think we have to, Mr. Buckholz— we have to follow this thing through."

Buckholz shrugged heavily. "Very well. For the moment, I'll lie my head off to Washington. And you'll do the same for London, uh?"

Pyott nodded. "We will."

"We must get our political masters to order us to go ahead," Aubrey instructed in a dark, Machiavellian voice, his face at first somber but breaking into a mischievous smile as he finished speaking.

"O.K."

"Let's not waste time. There are secure telephones in the Briefing Room. You can call Grosvenor Square at once,

Charles. We'll wait until you've finished your call before we make ours."

Buckholz felt himself dismissed, but not slighted. He motioned to Curtin. "Come on, Gene—let's agree on our story before anyone makes a call."

The two Americans disappeared into the Briefing Room, the door of which led off the main Ops Room. Giles Pyott and Aubrey watched it close behind them.

"Can we do it?" Aubrey asked quickly.

Instead of answering, Pyott stood up and moved to the huge plot table in the center of the underground room. He brooded over the models and tapes and markings on its surface. "Damn bad show," he murmured, turning to Aubrey, who now stood alongside him. The crash site was represented on the plot table by a model of a Mig-25 and the black, futuristic model of the Mig-31. In deadly, fatal conjunction. Deliberately, Aubrey picked up one of the cuelike rods the plotters used to alter the position of symbols on the table. Awkwardly, he reached out with it and shunted the model of the Firefox southwards, letting it come to rest on the blue spot of a lake. For a moment, Aubrey's movements reminded Pyott of a short, bald croupier.

"There!" he said with intense triumph.

"You're convinced it's in one piece?"

"I'm not convinced it's in a million pieces, Giles—besides, we could still learn a great deal from whatever is left of it—from Gant, were he alive. To know, we must have someone *under* the ice, so to speak."

Pyott rubbed his moustache with a quicker, stronger rhythm. When he faced Aubrey again, he said: "I know what you want of me, Kenneth. There are some people who would suit, up in the Varangerfjord at the moment. Some of our Special Boat Service marines . . . practicing landing on an enemy coast from a hunter-killer submarine, that sort of training. Routine stuff. Under the supervision of an old friend of yours—Major Alan Waterford of 22 SAS. Perhaps that seems like the workings of an auspicious fate to you, mm?"

"Can we—?"

Pyott shook his head. "Not until we have clearance—a direct *order* to do something. Washington and Number Ten must give that order. You know that, Kenneth."

"Unfortunately, yes."

"The Finns gave us permission for the covert overflight

of their country, and certain reluctant backup facilities. They are unlikely, without pressure from our masters, to involve themselves any further in this affair. I must argue, from StratAn's point of view, you from that of SIS. JIC and the Chiefs of Staff will, in all likelihood, have to persuade Number Ten to continue with the affair. It really depends on Washington's attitude."

Pyott's attention moved from Aubrey to an approaching RAF officer. He had come quickly down the metal steps from the glass-fronted gallery which contained the communications equipment. All that could be seen from the floor of the Ops Room was a row of bent heads. The Pilot Officer hurried towards them.

"Mr. Aubrey—Colonel Pyott, I think you'd better come quickly. Squadron Leader Eastoe wants to speak to Mr. Aubrey urgently."

"What is it?"

"I don't know, sir—the Squadron Leader just said it was very urgent and to get you to the mike at once."

Pyott strode after the RAF officer as soon as the young man turned away. Aubrey scuttled after them both, his eye glancing across a litter of paper cups, bent backs in blue uniform shirts, scribbled blackboards and weather charts, before he concentrated his gaze on the metal steps as he clattered up them behind Pyott. Eastoe was waiting for him behind the glass, pausing on tape for a scrambled spit of sound that would be Aubrey's speeded-up reply.

Aubrey thrust past Pyott and said to the operator: "Play it for me."

"Mr. Aubrey had better be told at once," Eastoe began, "even through the ground clutter and the intermittent snow, we're picking up signs of helicopter activity, moving west and southwest. Our best guess is three of them, and they're troop-carriers. They're not interested in our lake, as far as we can tell—their course would take them northwest of it. Our ETA for the lake is four minutes two. If you want us to go, that is. Over."

The tape stopped. Aubrey rubbed his cheeks furiously. It couldn't be—they couldn't have picked up the carrier wave from the homing device, only Eastoe could do that aboard the Nimrod . . . What, then?

"Eastoe—keep track of them if you can. Do whatever you have to . . ." He merely glanced up at Pyott, whose face was impassive. Aubrey hesitated for a moment, then said firmly: "I'm ordering you to overfly the lake—deceive them as to your object—and obtain the best photographic record you can under the circumstances. And, when you've done that, I want you to take a look at those helicopters. I want to know what they're doing—dammit!" The tape continued to run. Aubrey finally added: "Good luck. Over and out." Only then did he return his gaze to Pyott, whose face was gloomy. His eyes were glazed and inward-looking. Evidently, he was weighing the consequences of Aubrey's precipitation. "I had to," Aubrey explained. "Things are beginning to outrun us. I had to have better information, whatever the fuss."

"I agree," Pyott said. "Even though I don't much like it. Well, we'd better talk to JIC and the Chiefs of Staff—I may have to get down there myself . . ." He crossed to the door of the communications gallery, then turned to Aubrey. "I do hope our American friends are obtaining the most hopeful noises from their President, Kenneth—for all our sakes."

The icicles were like transparent, colorless gloves worn over the dead twigs of the bush behind which Gant crouched. Below him, the noise and movement belonged to a wild hunt: an image of his own pursuit, probably no more than a mile behind him now.

He had heard the noise of dogs. The helicopters—three, he was almost certain—had cast about for signs of him, often appearing as they drove westwards above him or close to one of his hiding places. It was as if they knew his position, and were herding him ahead of or between them. He knew one of the helicopters was west or northwest of him now, its troops probably working back towards him . . .

Towards this village, too, this collection of wooden huts below him, beyond which a group of Lapps were penning reindeer. One short, brightly clothed man was dragged on his stomach behind a galloping bull reindeer, his hands still gripping the lasso. He disappeared within a flurry of hooves and upflung snow, then rolled clear. The images seemed almost to come from within him, as they stirred memory. A rodeo, but now performed by a people as alien to him as the Vietnamese. Short, olive-skinned, some dressed traditionally even to the long-bobbled woolen caps and heelless shoes, others affecting blue denims and sheepskin jackets.

Alien. People he did not know, whose language he did not speak, therefore could not trust. Reindeer barked and hooted. Men whisked among them like matadors. Great snouted heads tossed. The sight of the roundup chilled him. He had followed the noises, stumbling upon the village, and had become rapt by a sense of the familiar. Then this parody of something American so far north of the Arctic Circle had quickly alienated him.

Torches flickered, lamps gleamed. The lights of a truck and the headlight of a motorized sledge were focused on the corral. Shadows galloped and tossed in the beams. They would be finishing soon, when darkness came. Gant could smell cooking. The Russians, too, would be here soon. It was time for him to move.

He climbed into a stooping crouch. The flying suit creaked with ice. His body was stiff and slow. He needed something warm to wear; a jacket or cloak or tunic, it did not matter. He would steal whatever he found.

In his right hand he held the folding .22 rifle, loaded with the single bullet it would hold. He had buried his parachute, but still wore his life jacket because he needed its harness to hold his survival pack. The Makarov pistol was close to hand. He moved cautiously down the slope towards the nearest wooden huts. Behind the buildings, the noises of the roundup subsided, becoming no more than a confused babble and a drumming through the frozen earth. He hurried to the wall of the hut, pressing himself against it, reclaiming his breath before moving slowly along the wall to the steamy window from which a flickering lamplight spilled onto the snow. The black holes of his descending footprints were visible in the light. He listened. He could hear nothing except the sounds of the roundup. The Russians could be no more than half a mile behind him now. He shivered with a new awareness of the cold. He had to be warm. He would not be able to spend the night moving unless he was dressed more warmly.

He stood on tiptoe, looking into the long, low room. A huge black stove in the center, bright rugs scattered, armchairs, a plain wooden table, places laid upon it. Time—

He listened for the noise of helicopters, but heard nothing. He tested the window. Locked. He moved around the angle of the wall towards what he assumed was the rear of the hut. One window locked, another, another . . .

He eased it open. The smell of cooking was strong. There was no one in the small kitchen. On an old cooker, a huge pot was simmering. The smell was coming from it. Meat. Hot meat in some kind of stew. He dragged his leg tiredly over the sill, sat astride for a moment—where was the cook?—then dropped into the room, dragging the rifle from his shoulder, aiming it towards the door into the main room. He could hear someone now, moving about, the noises of cutlery quite distinct and recognizable. He sidled across the kitchen towards the stove, moving with exaggerated stealth. There was a ladle in the pot. He reached out with his left hand, eyes still on the doorway, and touched the ladle, then removed it, tasting the stew like a chef. The meat flavor was strong—reindeer, he presumed—but his stomach craved it. He leaned heavily, his head against a clouded mirror, watching the doorway, the ladle moving as silently as he could manage from the pot to his mouth—pot to mouth, pot to mouth . . .

He swallowed greedily again and again, his stomach churning with the sudden, gulped feast. The warmth of it burned through him. He shivered. A pool of melted snow from his boots spread around him.

Then she returned to the kitchen. Small, olive-skinned, a pear-shaped face with a black, surprised little round hole opening in the middle of it as she saw him and understood the rifle. Dark hair, plump figure. Check shirt and denims; again, the familiar—the log-cabin imagery—surprised him for a moment. Then he motioned her into the kitchen with the barrel of the rifle. She came slowly, silently.

"I—mean you no harm," Gant said slowly. "No—harm. Do you understand?"

"Yes," she replied, staring at the rifle. Its barrel dropped as an expression of Gant's surprise.

"You speak English?"

"A little. I—was taught. Who are you?" She studied his flying suit, her face screwed into lines and folds as if she were trying to remember a similar costume.

"My airplane—it crashed."

"Oh." Her face showed she had identified his clothing.

"I—I'm sorry about the food . . ." He gestured towards the stove. His stomach rumbled. The woman almost smiled. "I—I'll leave you . . ."

"Why?"

"I have to."

"We—can help you."

Gant shook his head furiously. "You can't get involved in this," he said.

She moved closer. Evidently, the man represented no real threat to her, despite his intrusion into her home. "Why not? We have a radio." She gestured towards the doorway.

"Christ, radio—" he blurted.

"Yes . . . where are you from—the Finnmark?" Her English improved; rusty with disuse, it was now working again. She indicated her mouth, then pointed at him. His accent . . .

"Yes. But, how long?"

"Long?"

"Will they come now, at once?" She shook her head. "Then no radio. I must go now. I—" He decided to ask rather than demand. "I need something warm—to wear—?" She nodded.

"My husband—he will take you on the sledge, when he returns, or tomorrow, to the main road, perhaps." Not alien, somehow familiar and expected. He was warm at last. Tears of weariness and response pricked at his eyes. The promises of aid in the strange, halting English numbed him as certainly as the cold outside.

Could he—? No. No risks . . .

Quarter of a mile, no more than that now.

"Clothes," he said heavily.

The beam of the searchlight from the descending helicopter swept over the room, fuzzily gleaming for a moment through the steam-clouded window. Then it was gone, bouncing off the slope before it finally disappeared and all that remained was the racket of the rotors. Gant listened. Only one, still time . . .

"Clothes!" he snapped, his voice ugly. She did not, however, react as if she feared him. She nodded.

"Who are they?"

"Russians."

She spat, suddenly and surprisingly. It was the reflex, racial memory of a once-real hatred. She snapped: "We are 'Skolt' Lapps—we live here now since we lost our homes in Petsamo. Petsamo belongs to *them* now, since the war. Russians—!"

The rotors roared, then began to wind down. Gant pressed

himself against the wall, and squinted through the steam on the window. The rotors died. He heard no dogs, but the noises from the roundup had ceased. Two minutes—?

He glanced around the room. The woman had gone. He panicked, but as he moved, she reentered the doorway, holding a heavy check jacket and a pair of thick trousers. And walking boots.

"These—I hope they fit you."

He bundled them under his arm, fingers locked inside the boots to hold them. She moved to the outside door. He stared at the puddle that marked his presence, the one or two half-footprints on the polished floorboards. Smiling, she tilted the pot on the stove. Stew sloshed onto the floor. Then she beckoned him.

Cold threatened from the door.

He dropped his bundle, pulled on the jacket for disguise and warmth, then collected the trousers and boots and rifle. He could hear voices, almost conversational in volume and tone, but he could not hear dogs. On the doorstep, he nodded to her. She touched his shoulder, her expression already settling to a kind of passivity. She was preparing her face.

"They are pretending to be Finns," she whispered. "But their accents are bad. Go now. That way." She pointed back up the slope. He saw the deep black holes of his descent of the slope. She pushed him ahead of her. "I went for a walk, looking for the dog," she said.

He turned to thank her, but she merely shook her head. "Go," she instructed. "The Finnmark is twenty miles away."

He was already climbing the slope, urgency driving out the sense of who had given him the jacket and the clothes he carried under his arm. He was primarily aware of his right hand once more and the rifle it held.

He turned back once, at the crest of the slope, near the bush which had earlier concealed him. The door to the hut was closed. Probably, the woman had begun to be afraid now, to physically shake with reaction, as much at his presence as that of the Russians. Now, she would be deciding she should not have helped him, that her home had been broken into, invaded.

The roundup had ended. Reindeer stamped and shuffled. The MiL helicopter sat like a squat beetle, rotors still, near the corrals. A group of men were talking. Dark clothing and white Arctic camouflage.

Three, four—six . . .

Spreading out, searching. There seemed no resistance from the Lapps. Perhaps they believed the fiction that the soldiers were Finns. He turned his back on the village and trudged into the trees.

Twenty miles, she had said. Twenty.

It was a huge distance, almost huge enough to be a void, something uncrossable.

Vladimirov turned from the window of the Tupolev as Dmitri Priabin entered the War Command Center ahead of the First Secretary. The young man's face was elated, yet he also appeared to be recovering from a bout of nausea. There was a bright sheen of sweat on his forehead, and his neck was pink above the collar of his uniform. Vladimirov knew, with an inward, cold amusement, that the young officer had survived, that the collar and shoulder insignia of the uniform would soon be changed. Now, they denoted Priabin as a lieutenant. What next? Captain Priabin, or the dizzy heights of a colonelcy—? It appeared that the young man's former superior, Kontarsky, was to bear the burden of failure entirely alone. Priabin had first identified Gant, probably by accident more than design, and almost in time to stop him. He had earned the reprieve of promotion.

He had arrived expecting to suffer, and had been rewarded. Vladimirov did not envy him anything except his youth as he hurriedly exited from the room. Then he turned his back on the First Secretary and looked down at the tarmac, where an imposing queue of black limousines was drawn up. Priabin went down the passenger steps and climbed into the back of one of the cars. It drove off towards the administration buildings and the perimeter fence. Presumably, Priabin had some woman to impress with his narrow escape, his unexpected promotion. Vladimirov returned his attention to the War Command Center.

The Soviet leader had donned his overcoat. His fur hat rested like a pet in one of his gloved hands. His face was stern. He had paused only to listen to the latest report from the commander of the KGB Border Guard units they had despatched into Finnish Lapland. As the voice from the cabin speaker proceeded with the report, the First Secretary nodded occasionally.

Vladimirov watched Andropov. There was a faint gleam of perspiration on his shaven upper lip. Responsibility had passed to himself, as well as to Vladimirov. It was an uneasy and temporary alliance that the air force general did not welcome or trust.

The high-speed transmissions from the command helicopter were received by the AWACS Tupolev, then retransmitted to Moscow. In the War Command Center, they were played back at normal speed. Vladimirov could not rid himself of the analogy of some obscure sporting commentary. He listened through the caution, through the wanting-to-please, wanting-to-succeed, and tried to assess how close they were to the American.

For he was there. The parachute had been found by one of the dogs, tracks had been followed, a village might, or might not, have given him shelter, clothing, food. He was heading in a northwesterly direction, towards the closest outjutting of the Norwegian frontier. He was, they guessed, less than twenty miles from his objective. The hunters had a night and part of a day, no more.

The transmission ended with a request for orders. Immediately, the First Secretary looked at Andropov and at Vladimirov, and then, having fixed each of them with a blunt, unwavering stare, merely nodded. Men sprang to renewed attention as he exited from the compartment. They heard his high shoes ring on the frosty metal of the passenger ladder. Vladimirov resisted the impulse to turn his head, and continued to watch Andropov. Suddenly, the Chairman of the KGB gestured him to follow, into the recreation suite.

"Tell the commander to hold for instructions," Vladimirov snapped, following Andropov. He closed the compartment door behind him. Andropov was pouring himself a whisky at the bar.

"Drink?" he asked.

"No, thank you."

Andropov gulped some of the liquor as he turned on Vladimirov. "Well?" he demanded. "What now?"

"From your people?"

"*Our* people!" Andropov snapped.

"I'd forgotten—our people."

"What about this Nimrod aircraft in the area?"

"It must have picked up the helicopters. Obviously, they also wish to know what happened."

"And will they have units like ours in the area too?"

Vladimirov shook his head. "I doubt that. Unfortunately, we have been unable to help giving something of the game away. We need him quickly now. The Nimrod was very low—presumably it collected photographs, which will be analyzed. That gives us time. I think enough time."

"Damned forest!" Andropov erupted.

"I agree. It makes things more difficult. We know he was with the Lapps—but he stole food and clothing, no more. He wasn't hiding there. He cannot be more than a mile ahead of our people—once again, they must put down men ahead of his probable track."

"Yes, yes, of course they must—!" Andropov drank the remainder of the whisky, and studied the glass. Vladimirov saw his gaze stray to the bottle on the bar, but he made no move towards it. "Where is the plane, Vladimirov? There's not enough wreckage in those photographs . . . you and I know that, even though the experts will take hours to decide the same thing." Spots of pink glowed on the Chairman's high cheekbones. "We *know* it isn't there— so, where is it? Eh, where is it, this priceless white elephant of ours? We know he didn't eject because of the parachute they found—he landed that plane, Vladimirov. Do you realize that?"

Vladimirov nodded. "Yes. I do. But I do not know where. Only he can tell us that. Had he been one of our pilots, or had it been an American aircraft, he would have stayed near it. In this case, he has been trying to open up the distance between himself and the Mig-31. The British Nimrod, too, wonders where the aircraft is, no doubt. Only Gant knows."

"Then we must have him!"

"We will. His time is running out."

"I wish I could be certain of that."

"Your men are following his tracks, Comrade Chairman! What more do you want? Their footsteps are planted in his. In an hour, perhaps two, he will be ours." Vladimirov smiled. "Then we will both be off the hook, mm?"

Andropov merely glowered in reply. He pondered for a time, then said: "Couldn't we track back along his journey?"

"Perhaps. But, had it been me, I would have changed direction a dozen times. And, by now, his tracks will have gone, and his scent will have grown cold. Don't worry—Gant has the answer. Soon you will be able to ask him for that answer—personally."

"There's no doubt about these photographs," Buckholz protested vigorously, his finger tapping the glistening enlargements that lay scattered on the plot table of the Scampton Ops Room. "You use dogs to sniff for explosives—unlikely—or you use them to hunt men. Those are dogs—KGB Border Guard dogs." His large, blunt-fingered hands spread the enlargements in a new pattern, as if he were dealing cards or flinging down items of evidence. "These troops are in Arctic camouflage, but they're not military. These MiL Mi-4s are what the Border Guard favors for personnel and equipment transport. And they don't have any markings at all . . . just the way the Border Guard operates. No, Colonel, what else do you need to see before you make up your mind?"

"Charles," Pyott began defensively, "I realize that Washington is very keen to get on with this job, but—"

"You have to get your government off its butt, Colonel! Time is running out for Gant, and for us."

Aubrey, as a distraction, picked up a sheaf of the photographs that had been transmitted over the wireprint from Eastoe's Nimrod. They were all pale, shining with the ghostly light of the advanced infrared cameras that had produced them. Men almost in negative in the very last of the daylight and the ensuing darkness.

He looked at the prints of the lake. Broken ice near the neck of the lake, but very little of it. A small, shrinking patch of black water. Yet the Firefox had to be underneath the water, beneath the healing ice. The remaining pictures, of the wreckage at the point of explosion, were uninteresting. Aubrey, without study and without expert advice, knew that nothing of the Mig-31 lay there.

Pyott glanced at Aubrey. "Number Ten is being very reluctant over this, Kenneth," he began, seeking an ally.

"Because the Cabinet Defense Committee has always pooh-poohed the Firefox, I wonder? Andrew Gresham isn't bullying them any more, I suppose?" He turned to Buckholz. "Is the President applying the right amount of pressure, Charles?" Buckholz nodded. "Everyone would like to walk away, except for Washington."

"The usual restrictions, of course, Kenneth—if you're caught, we'll deny everything."

"We work with those every day—they're not important. It's *doing* something—and quickly—that *is* important." He stared meaningfully at Pyott, who held up his hands, wrists pressed together to represent unseen bonds. "Tied they may be, Giles—but *really*!"

"What can I do?" Pyott asked softly.

"Look at them!" Aubrey returned, his hand flapping towards the scattered enlargements. "Gant may be alive—he knows where the body is buried, as do we. If they get to him, *they* will know! We must at least establish what is beneath the ice—*before* we decide our response." He looked at Buckholz, and shook his head. "I don't think there's anything we can do for poor Gant—I can't order military units into the area."

"I know that. So will he. He knows he's on his own."

Aubrey nodded lugubriously, plucking at his lower lip. Then, as suddenly and superficially as a child, his mood changed. He turned on Pyott and said, in an intense whisper, almost hunching over the enlargements on the plot table: "You already have Waterford standing by with a four-man unit at Kirkenes. Their diving equipment is loaded onto a Royal Norwegian Air Force Lynx helicopter. You have the agreement of Commander, Allied Forces Northern Norway, for this flight under the guise of a search-and-rescue mission . . . Giles, *please* make up your mind to act—!"

"I have other people to please apart from yourself, SIS, or even the CIA . . ." Pyott began, then clamped his lips tightly shut. He shook his head. "Unofficially, JIC wishes something done—so do the Chiefs of Staff, but Cabinet opinion is against any exacerbation of the situation. They'll settle for the loss of the two—the *only two*—production prototypes of the Firefox. The expert reasoning is that the Bilyarsk project will have been put back by at least two, even three years by what has happened. The Russians may even scrap the whole hideously expensive project . . ."

"And if the Firefox is *intact*? And the Russians ask their friendly neighbors, the Finns, for their toy back?" Aubrey demanded with withering irony, his face red with frustration. His hands were clenched at his sides.

"Yes," Pyott admitted. "Yes, I know."

"Washington will carry the day, you know that," Aubrey

observed. "Gresham, as P.M., and the rest of the Cabinet will have to sanction whatever the President wishes to happen— however much they dislike the medicine."

"But they have not yet done so—"

"And we have run out of *time!*"

Momentarily, Giles Pyott's cheeks glowed with anger, then he turned on his heel. "Very well," he snapped, "very well."

Aubrey hurried after him as he mounted the ladder to the communications gallery. "Tell Waterford he must check this KGB activity," he called. Pyott stopped and turned.

"No!"

"Yes," Aubrey insisted. "We have to know whether or not Gant is alive—we have to know when, and if, they take him alive. Everything could depend upon it."

Pyott paused, his brow furrowed, his cheeks hot. Then he nodded. He, too, could not escape the conclusions Aubrey offered; could not escape his imprisonment within the situation. Aubrey—the covert world that he and Buckholz represented— was his jailer. He saw himself within a fortress, a castle. The politicians had erected the outer walls; they could be breached, or removed, or their existence could be denied as circumstances dictated. But Pyott knew himself to be imprisoned within the keep of the castle, and the walls of the keep had been made by Aubrey and Buckholz and the Mig-31 and its pilot. The walls were impenetrable, inescapable. He nodded.

"Very well," he announced angrily. "Very well."

He opened the door to the communications gallery. Aubrey scurried in behind him.

He was floundering through the snow now. They still had not released the dogs, but he could hear them barking close behind him. The snow was deep, almost solid, restraining him, pulling him back. He had abandoned the floor of the shallow valley, keeping to the slope, but even here the snow lay heaped and traplike near bushes and boulders. He slipped often. The effects of the hot food were gone. He was utterly weary.

When he had halted last, he had checked the map. More than three miles from the village, perhaps another sixteen— fifteen now, or a little more?—to the Norwegian border, to villages, to police, to another state where he might be safe. Safe—?

They wouldn't let him remain. They would take him back.

He stumbled, his wrist hurt as his weight collapsed on it, the .22 rifle ploughed into the snow. Furiously, he shook the barrel; snow fluttered away from it. The sky was black and clear, the stars like gleaming stones. Silver light from a thin paring of new moon lay lightly on the snow. He climbed groggily to his feet and looked behind him. Noise of dogs, and a glimpse of lights. The distant sound of one of the helicopters. He did not know where the choppers were, and it worried him. They buzzed at his imagination like flies, as audible in his head as if they were physically present, their belly lights streaming along the floor of the valley, searching for his footprints. One of them had to be ahead, its platoon already fanned out and sweeping slowly back towards him, in radio contact with the pursuit behind him.

Radio—

He had known, had hidden the fact from himself.

Radio.

It winded him like a blow, the admission of their technology, their ability to communicate. Even now, at that precise moment, he was pinpointed.

He looked up at the black sky with its faint sheen, its glittering stars. At any moment, the choppers would come. The pursuit was too close now not to be able to locate him. Somewhere along the valley floor, just—*there* . . .

A finger was tracing contours, the twisting course of the valley. A helicopter would bank, turn—

He ran. Ice glittered on a bush, and he brushed savagely against the obstacle. The rifle bumped against his thigh, against the heavy waterproof trousers. His chest hurt with the temperature of the air he was inhaling. The survival pack bumped and strained and dragged at his back. He glanced behind once more—

Lights.

Noise—*ahead*—

Men had been dropped out of earshot, ahead of him, and were working their way back down the valley from the north-west towards him. Pincer.

He stopped running, bent double. He listened. A thin breeze had carried the noises. Shuffling, the clinking of metal, the slither of cross-country skis. The barking of a single dog. Behind him, more dogs, more men, and wobbling flashlight beams. No rotor noise. Nothing. Surprise.

The two groups of Russians were no more than a few hundred yards apart. He began to struggle up the slope, out of the valley. Icy rock betrayed him, a hollow trapped his leg with soft, deep snow. His chest heaved, his back bent under the weight of the survival pack so that his face was inches from the glittering snow. He climbed, feet sinking, body elongating so that he threatened to become stretched out, flat on his stomach. His legs refused to push him faster or further. He used his hands, the .22 clogging with snow as he used it as a stick.

Crest. Dark sky above white snow like a close horizon.

He staggered, pushed up from all fours to try to stand upright. He gasped for breath, saw the legs, saw the Arctic camouflage, shook his head in weary disbelief, saw the next man perhaps fifty yards away, already turning in his direction, saw, saw—

He cried out in a wild yell of protest, and used the rifle like a club, striking at the white form on the crest of the slope. The Russian fell away with a grunt, rolling down the steeper slope on the other side. Gant staggered after the rolling body, as if to strike it again, then leapt tiredly over it and charged on down the steep slope.

Trees. A patch of black forest, then the flatness of what might be a frozen lake beyond. The ground leveling out. The trees offering cover, the barrel of his rifle clogged with snow—

He careered on, just keeping his balance. Whistles and the noise of dogs behind him, but no shooting. He ran on, floundering with huge strides towards the trees.

4 / **RECOVERY**

The Westland Lynx Mk 86 helicopter, its Royal Norwegian
Air Force markings concealed, dropped towards the arrowlike
shape of the lake. Alan Waterford, sitting in the copilot's seat,
watched intently as the ghostly ice moved up towards him,
and the surface snow became distressed from the downdraft
of the rotors. He ignored the noises from the main fuselage as
the four-man Royal Marine SBS team prepared to leave the
helicopter. Instead, he watched the ice.

"Hold it there," he ordered the pilot. The downdraft was
winnowing the surface snow, but there was no billowing
effect. Waterford did not want the surface obscured, the
snow boiling around the cockpit like steam, as it would if they

dropped any lower. Even so, a few crystals were melting on the perspex. Beyond the smear they made, the ice looked unbroken and innocent as it narrowed towards the neck of the lake where Eastoe's infrared pictures had revealed a patch of dark, exposed water.

The Lynx steadied at its altitude and began to drift slowly over the ice, the faintest of shadows towed behind it like a cloth. Waterford craned ahead and to one side, searching the surface. As with the photographs, he could see no evidence that an airframe had broken up over the lake. There appeared to be only the one patch of clear water and jostling, broken ice right at the end of the lake.

No undercarriage tracks, but he could not count on them. There could have been a light snow flurry, or the wind could have covered them as effectively as fresh snow. Had he landed the plane, or ejected before it ever reached the lake? And if he'd landed, how efficient in saving the airframe and the electronics and the rest of the Mig-31's secrets had the American been in his terror of drowning? Or had he left the cockpit before the plane began to break through the ice?

Behind him, the SBS men, all trained divers, were preparing to discover the answers to his questions. It was too late and too dark to assess fire damage to the trees on the shore. Gant had to be alive—the Russian activity confirmed that—but had he ejected or landed?

The Lynx moved towards the trees. The patch of dull black water was visible now; ominous. Waterford removed his headset and stood in a crouch. His bulk seemed to fill the cockpit like a malevolent shadow. The pilot, a Norwegian lieutenant, glanced up at him.

"I can't put down this side of the trees—I'm not risking the ice. Tell them they'll have to walk." He grinned.

"They're used to it," Waterford grunted and clambered back into the main cabin of the helicopter. Four men in Arctic camouflage looked up at him. Beneath the white, loose tunics and trousers, they were wearing their wet suits. Oxygen tanks, cutting equipment, lamps, rifles, lay near the closed main door. "You're going to have to walk it," Waterford announced to a concerted groan. He ignored it. He spoke to the unit's leader, a lieutenant. "You know what they want, Brooke—evidence that the airframe is intact—don't give it to the buggers unless it's absolutely true. *Any* damage— any at all—has to be spotted. And don't forget the pictures for Auntie Aubrey's album, to go alongside the pressed flowers . . ." He grinned, but it seemed a mirthless exercise of his lips. "Keep your heads down—you are not, repeat not, to be detected under any circumstances. And," he looked at his watch, "Gunnar tells me we have no more than an hour to look for our American friend—even if we don't run into trouble—so that's all the time you've got. And, sergeant?"

"Sir?"

"Make sure you conceal that commpack properly—we won't be the last of our side in and out of here, I'm sure of that, and they'll all want to talk to London as quickly as possible." Waterford indicated one of the packs near the sergeant's feet. "This'll give them satellite direct—don't leave it where a reindeer can piss on it and fuse the bloody thing."

"Certainly not, sir," the sergeant replied. "Commpack not to be left where reindeer may piss on it—sir! One question, sir?"

"Yes, sergeant?"

"Does the Major know the exact height to which a reindeer can piss, sir?"

The Lynx drifted slowly downwards. Waterford, smiling at the tension-releasing laughter in the cabin, glanced at the window in the main door. Snow surrounded them like steam. They were almost down. As he observed the fact, the Lynx touched, bounced as if rubber, settled. Immediately, the rotors began to wind down, their noise more throaty, ugly. The sergeant slid back the main cabin door.

"Out you get—quick as you can," the lieutenant ordered, nodding at Waterford. Packs and equipment were flung out of the door. Through his camouflage parka, the night temperature chilled Waterford. He felt the tip of his nose harden with the cold. When they had dropped to the ground, he moved to the cabin door.

"Good luck. One hour—and I'm counting." He waved, almost dismissively, and slammed the sliding door closed, locking it. Then he climbed back into the cockpit and regained his seat, rubbing his hands. He slipped on the inertia-reel belt, then his headset. "O.K., Gunnar—let's see if we can find this lost American chap, shall we?"

The Lynx jumped into the air almost at once, the rotors whining up, the blades becoming a dish that caught the moonlight. The four SBS men were already trudging briskly into the trees, laden with their equipment. The helicopter banked out over the lake, and headed northwest. The ice diminished behind them.

There was no night sight on the folding .22 rifle. There were six rounds, each to be fed separately into the breech. It was a weapon of survival—for Arctic hares for the solid tablet stove or any fire he might have been able to light—but not for defense. Never for offense. Gant had no idea how much stopping power the slim, toylike rifle possessed, and he hesitated to find out. The nearest of the Russians, white-tunicked, white-legginged, Kalashnikov AKM carried across his chest, was moving with great caution from fir-bole to low bush to fir-bole. The dogs had been kept back, still leashed; perhaps moving with the remainder of the unit to encircle the clump of trees in which they knew he was hiding.

Time had run out. His only advantage was that they wanted him alive. They would have definite, incontrovertible orders not to kill him. Maim him they might, but he would be alive when they reached Murmansk or Moscow or wherever.

The frozen lake was behind him, as clean and smooth as white paper, almost phosphorescent in the moonlight. His breath smoked around him like a scarf; he wondered that the approaching Russian had not yet caught sight of it, not heard the noise of his breathing. Forty yards, he guessed. A glimpse of another white shape, flattening itself behind a fir, farther off. The noise of the dogs.

And, omnipresent and above the trees, the rotors of two of the helicopters. He had glimpsed one of them, its outline clear for a moment before he had been blinded by the searching belly light. Slim, long-tailed MiL-4s. Frost glittered on the dark trunk of the fir at the fuzzy edge of his vision. He had now recovered his night vision after the searchlight, except for a small, bright spot at the center of the Russian's chest as he sighted along the seemingly inadequate barrel of the rifle. The man bulked large around the retinal image of the searchlight. Gant could not miss at that range.

Still he hesitated, sensing the moment at the eye of the storm; sensing that any move he now made would be his last. Capture was inevitable. So, why kill—?

Then he squeezed the trigger, knowing the true futility of the attack. A sharp little crack like a twig broken, and the

white-dressed Russian flung up his arms and fell slowly
backwards. Snow drifted down, disturbed by the downdraft,
onto Gant's head and shoulders. Beyond the body, which did
not move, did not begin to scrabble towards the nearest
cover, another white form whisked behind a dark trunk. Gant
turned towards the lake, regretting, loathing the gesture of
the kill. Through the trees, the shore appeared empty.

Orders shouted, the crackle of a radio somewhere, the
din of the dogs. His head turned back towards the body, then
once more to the lake. A light was creeping across the ice.
Above it, as if walking hesitantly on the beam, a MiL-4 came
into view. The ice glared. He heard the noise of dogs
released— released, unleashed, loose . . .

He began to run, even though some part of him knew
they would be trained not to harm him if he remained still.
He could not help himself. He had to run. The dogs were
loose.

Yowling behind him, a shot high over his head. Small,
low branches whipping at his face, depositing snow in his
eyes and mouth and nostrils. He held on to the rifle with
both hands, almost heaving the air aside as he ran out of the
trees, across the snow-covered, slippery stones of the shore,
out onto the surface snow that made the ice tactile, surefooted.
The MiL-4 turned its baleful black face of a cockpit in his
direction, and the beam of the searchlight licked across the
ice towards him.

No more trees, no more cover, his mind kept repeating,
attuned to the frantic beating in his ears, but he could not
regret the sky. The trees had hemmed him, formed a prison
before he was, indeed, captured. The MiL slipped over him
like a huge, moving blanket, whirling up the snow around
him, cleaning the ice and making it suddenly treacherous. He
staggered, then whirled round.

The leading Alsatian was out of the trees, hardly hesitating as it met the stones on the shore and then the smoother
ice. He raised the .22, and fired. The dog skidded, sliding on
towards him, mouth gaping. He looked up. A face appeared
at the open cabin door of the helicopter. It was grinning,
savagely. Gant fumblingly ejected the cartridge, thrust a new
round into the breech, raised the gun—two more dogs, now,
on the ice, but he could no longer care even about dogs—and
fired. The head ducked back inside the helicopter, but Gant
knew he had not hurt it.

He ran on. Skating, slipping, then hurrying through patches of undisturbed snow. Then the MiL slid towards him again, pinning him in the searchlight beam. Whistles, men on the shore . . .

He reloaded the .22, but the dog was on him, its leap driving him backwards, struggling to keep his balance. He was winded, but as he doubled over he struck the dog across the head with the rifle. The Alsatian twisted away, yelping. The other dog watched, suddenly more wary. Gant stood his ground, watching the men approach behind the dogs, caught for their benefit in the glare of the searchlight. The rotors above him hammered, drowning thought.

He knew he would not move now. It was finished. He was defeated. Or perhaps satisfied at having protested, struggled enough. He had made his gesture. Energy drained away, as if drawn out of him by the light. Both dogs now crouched on the ice, growling, only yards from him. The first troops were forty yards away.

Then the crackling of a loudspeaker from the MiL above him: "Major Gant—please put down your weapons. Major Gant—put down your weapons."

The dogs seemed more alert now. The men had hesitated. He held up the rifle slowly, then threw it aside. He drew the Makarov with his left hand, butt first, and dropped it. The white-clad troops hurried towards him. Beyond them, the second and third MiL-4s slid over the trees and out onto the lake. He hunched his shoulders, thrusting his hands into the pockets of the check jacket. He might have been waiting for a bus. One of the two approaching MiLs settled onto the ice and its rotors slowed.

Ten yards. Seven . . .

The dogs were quiet, tongues lolling, suspicious and forgiving.

Fourth MiL, rotors hammering, its fuselage slim and knifelike as it banked savagely. The searchlight blinked off him, loping away across the ice as the helicopter above moved as if startled. Gant looked up. Nose-on, closing and dropping swiftly. The Russian troops looked up, halted, uncertain. The dogs growled.

MiL-4 . . . ?

Sharp-nosed, not round-nosed as it whipped into full silhouette. Concealed markings, not unmarked like the others. Sharp-nosed, and a white-clad form at the open cabin door, gesturing. The MiL that had hung above him sidled towards the newcomer, much as a dog might have investigated a bitch. The newcomer rose rapidly, hopping over the MiL and closing on his still figure on the ice. The form waved. The helicopter danced closer, then away, enticing him.

The second and third MiLs wound up their rotors, both having landed. The airborne MiL-4 swung nose-on, closing. The form bellowed something. He did not know in what language, but it did not seem to be Russian.

Sharp-nosed . . .

Lynx—

The language was English. He moved his feet, lifted his reluctant legs and began to run. The dogs were up, shaking themselves, moving more quickly than himself. The Lynx helicopter danced slowly away, tempting him to reach it, hovering only feet above the ice. The winch had been swung out of the main cabin and its rescue wire trailed like a black snake across the ice.

He slipped, righted himself, plunged on, arms flailing. One of the dogs snapped at him, leaping at his side. He flung his arm at it, fist clenched. The dog rolled and skidded away. Twenty yards, fifteen—

He kicked out at the second dog—the first was recovering, moving again—missed, kicked again, almost losing his balance. The dog watched for its opportunity. Ten yards. Only ten—

Eight, seven, five . . . the wire was almost underfoot, the Lynx rising a little so that he could grasp it without bending, be heaved upwards immediately . . .

The noise of the dogs. Something ripped at his calf, making him stagger. A yard, no more, the face of someone yelling and cursing, firing over his head. The dogs yelping, whining suddenly . . .

He touched the wire—

Then the helicopter was flung away from him. The ice came up, he was winded, the searchlight came back, something pressed down on him, almost smothering him. He smelt onions, felt hot breathing on his cold face. His head cracked against the ice. He groaned. More dogs, renewed barking, as if they expressed his howl of despair.

He watched the Lynx lift away, the cabin door slam shut, the helicopter hop over the nearer of the two MiLs, skitter like a flung stone towards the trees . . .

The Russian soldier who had knocked him over in a

flying tackle got slowly, heavily to his feet. Despite his efforts, he seemed satisfied. Other faces crowded around him, dipped into the glare of the searchlight. The light began to hurt, dazzling him as if it was being filtered through a diamond. He closed his eyes and lay back. His calf hurt where the dog had torn at it.

He heard the distant noise of the fleeing Lynx and the rotors of a pursuing MiL. Then nothing except the rotors above him, the shudder of the downdraft, the cloud of snow around him, and the sense that he was dreaming . . .

Dreaming of the Lynx, dreaming that he was being lifted, carried . . . dreaming . . .

Waterford slammed the main cabin door of the Lynx with a curse, heaving at it to expel his rage. He locked it furiously, as if breaking into the environment outside rather than making something secure. Then he staggered as the pilot flung the Lynx into a violent alteration of course. He grabbed a handhold and looked out of the cabin window. The lake streamed beneath them. Craning, he could catch the lights of one of the MiLs, a sullen wash upon the ice. Then they were over trees, and Waterford clambered back into the cockpit, regained his seat and his headset, and strapped himself in. In the copilot's mirror, Waterford could see two of the MiLs dropping slowly behind them. The third would be loading Gant aboard and scrambling for home. The Lynx was approaching its top ground-level speed, perhaps forty miles an hour faster than the Russian helicopters.

"We're in Norway," Gunnar announced casually and without any slowing of the Lynx. "They will not follow, I think."

They flashed over car headlights, glaring as they twisted along a north-south road, then the scattered, muffled lights of a small village.

"More important things to do," Waterford muttered, his hands clenched on his thighs as if gripping something tightly. He could hear himself grinding his teeth. To have missed him by a yard—a *yard*—! "Oh, *fuck* it!" he raged.

"They've dropped back—shaking sticks at us, I expect, now that we have been seen off the property." Gunnar chuckled. "Are you all right, Major?"

"No."

"You don't like losing?"

"I *hate* losing."

"We were too lucky even to find them—it could not hold." Gunnar altered course. Two white dots registered on the radar. "Ah. They are heading east, very quickly now. Soon we will lose track of them, they are very low." The dots already appeared to lose sharpness, becoming pale smears. There were other smudges on the screen from the general ground clutter. The MiLs and the Lynx were all too low for effective radar tracking; which had exaggerated their luck in stumbling onto the Russians.

Only to lose him, Waterford thought. "How long?" he asked.

"A matter of minutes." Cloud was building above the canopy of the cockpit, the sliver of moon threatened. To the east, it might already be snowing on the Russian border. "In a few minutes, we can return to the lake."

"We're all fucked if that plane's in one piece!" Waterford growled.

"Well done, Colonel—well done!"

It was difficult not to smile at Andropov's enthusiasm—smile *with* it, Vladimirov corrected himself. Smile in concert. The War Command Center was like the scene of a promotion or medal-presentation party, though the guests were not yet drunk. But they had done it—!

"My congratulations, too, Colonel," Vladimirov added into the microphone. He and Andropov watched one another until they heard the Border Guard commander's reply.

"Thank you, Comrade General—thank you."

"What of the other helicopter?" Andropov asked Vladimirov. "It was Norwegian, I presume?"

"The Nimrod knew we were looking. It, too, was looking. *We* found him. Soon, he will tell us what happened to the Mig-31. What he has done with it."

Andropov leaned towards the transmitter once more. The operator seemed to flinch slightly from the proximity of the Chairman of the KGB. "Transfer him to Murmansk with all possible speed, Colonel—then he'll be flown to Moscow . . ." He turned away from the transmitter, and added to Vladimirov: "Midday tomorrow, at the latest. He'll be here by midday." Andropov removed his spectacles and wiped them. His narrow features sagged. "It has been a very long day," he said nonchalantly, "and now I feel tired." He suppressed a yawn.

"I, too." Vladimirov watched the Chairman replace his gold-rimmed spectacles. When he looked up once more, brushing the disturbed wings of hair above his ears, his confidence had returned. Pleasure had been succeeded by calculation. It was evident that the capture of Gant was of some kind of political significance to Andropov. Already, the incident was being prepared as a piece of propaganda, something to be used against the military, or employed to impress the rest of the Politburo. Their temporary, uncomfortable alliance was at an end.

"Of course, General." The remark was a sneer, a comment upon energy, on advancing age. Vladimirov straightened his form, standing three or four inches taller than Andropov. The Chairman turned away. His grey suit could not match the uniform and he realized it.

The Border Guard commander acknowledged his orders, almost unnoticed.

"I'll arrange for a transport aircraft to be standing by. The weather is worsening east of Murmansk, but there will be no delay. A detachment of GRU troops will provide an escort for the American—"

Andropov turned sharply. "Make certain they fulfill their duties, Comrade General," he snapped icily.

Vladimirov's cheeks burned. "Of course."

"Then I will say goodnight," Andropov offered without mollification, as a bodyguard placed the Chairman's overcoat over his shoulders and then handed him his fur hat. He tipped his gloves to his forehead in salute to Vladimirov, and then exited from the War Command Center.

Vladimirov turned to the map table. On impulse, almost as if reaching for a bottle or a sedative, he said: "Give me the area of the capture again."

Slowly, tantalizingly, the north of Finnish Lapland and the coast of Norway at the northern edge of the projection, appeared then hardened on the table. It was a relatively small area, it had to be . . . the man had not used his parachute, he must have *landed* the Mig—

Or survived a crash-landing.

North to south, no more than fifty or sixty miles, east to west, eighty miles—it could be narrowed down within that area by time, by Gant's condition, by his rate and mode of travel. He *must* have been *with* the aircraft when it grounded.

Where?

His hand stroked the surface of the table, glowing white and green and blue as it moved, catching the colors, fuzzy bright colors . . .

Vladimirov blinked and yawned. He was bone-weary; he needed sleep.

He could sleep, he told himself with an undiminished thrill of satisfaction, until the following midday. Gant knew, Gant would tell them . . .

He stifled another yawn, and blinked the hypnosis of the map and its colors out of his head.

"Stand down all personnel—transfer the transmission monitoring to the operations room here," he instructed quickly, anxious now to get out into the cold night air, to reinvigorate himself with the chill. "And—well done, all of you. Well done."

A chorused murmur of satisfaction and assent vanished behind him as he closed the door of the War Command Center. In the compartment aft of it lay his cap, uniform greatcoat, and his gloves. How long ago had he laid them down? When he had boarded this aircraft in Moscow, on his way to witness the weapons trials of the production prototype— a million years ago . . . yesterday . . . ?

He looked at his watch. Eleven. No, today still. Early that morning.

He rubbed his eyes and picked up his greatcoat.

Brooke reached out his hand and stroked the metal of the fuselage, just behind the headlike nose and cockpit. It was like stroking some huge, sleeping pet whose body retreated out of the fuzzy glare of his lamp into the dark water. He had swum down the length of the airframe, lifting slowly over the huge wing, gripping the edges of the massive tailpipes as he rounded the tail section, his lamp dancing wildly off the contours of the plane. He had propelled himself forward towards the second great spread wing. His flippers had touched against the metal as he lifted over it, before he returned to the nose section.

It had taken no more than minutes to find the intact airframe. His sergeant had been first down, after he had checked and then hidden the satellite commpack which would carry any transmissions from the site direct to a geostationary communications satellite, and on to London. Almost at once, Sergeant Dawson had been confronted by the blunt, ugly nose of the Mig-31. His lamp had disappeared beneath the new thin coating of ice, for which Brooke was grateful, since their search would now be undetectable from the air. He had made the preliminary inspection while Brooke and the two corporals had scouted the shore of the lake, the closest trees and the ice itself for the homing device whose carrier wave Eastoe had picked up. They had searched most carefully where the ice had congregated into rougher, jerry-built shapes, presumably from the break-up after the Mig had landed. They had found it jammed between two resoldered plates of ice, after Dawson had returned to the surface and was warming himself with coffee. Brooke had switched it off, and then listened to Dawson's preliminary damage report. The undercarriage door appeared to have been buckled, there was cannon damage in the port wing and in two places along the fuselage where fuel lines might have been ruptured, but the cockpit was closed—some water inside, but not much—and the aircraft appeared to have been fully shut down, presumably by Gant.

Brooke understood the significance of the report. The intact airframe was more dangerous, a hundred times more dangerous, than shards and pieces of wreckage on the floor of the lake. The Bilyarsk project continued to exist. He had dived himself the moment Dawson had finished, instructing one of the corporals—the best among them with an underwater camera—to prepare for a full photographic record.

The aircraft had awed him. Its size, of course, was huge in the partial, weak light of his lamp. More than that, its black paint, its almost total absence of markings, its preying-mantis head, its drooping wings, made it alien; most of all, its location beneath the frozen lake was sufficient to make it mesmeric, almost nightmarish as his lamp's beam danced over it.

The corporal grinned behind his facemask as Brooke jumped at the heavily gloved hand on his shoulder. Bubbles, air tanks, facemask, all fitted the scene and the airframe. He nodded, indicating the length of the fuselage, the undercarriage, the wings. Almost at once, the corporal, propelling the large underwater camera steadily in front of him, its flash

unit like a blank television screen, began swimming along the
airframe. The flash unit fired time after time. Each time a
part of the fuselage glared. Gunports, wing section, tail,
tailpipes, belly of the airframe, undercarriage, wing, cockpit
. . . the light flashed again and again as each part of the Mig
was recorded.

Brooke almost felt betrayal under the ice as he recalled
the explosive charges they carried in one of the packs. They
had no orders, but the airframe was intact . . . the easiest
way to solve the problem, from London's point of view,
would be to plant and detonate enough explosive to shatter
the airframe, melt the electronics, destroy the hydraulics—
kill the aircraft. *That* aircraft, that huge thing in the repeated
glare of the flash or in the beam he played almost lovingly
over it. He was surprised by his own sentiments; perhaps it
was the too-familiar expectation of wreckage whenever he
dived. Bodies, twisted metal, charred plates, signals of damage and destruction everywhere. But this—? It was complete,
almost untouched; salvageable.

Impossible. They'd be ordered to destroy it.

The corporal swam towards Brooke, his thumb erect.
Brooke slapped his shoulder and the corporal swam towards
the surface. His form bumped along the last feet of ice, and
then he was only a half-body in the beam of light, legs
flapping lazily, moving away to where the shore sloped
upwards. Brooke danced his lamp over the Mig once more,
and then rose to the surface. He was becoming very cold. He
left the aircraft in the darkness in which he had discovered it.

As he waded out of the lake, he saw Waterford, white-
clad, waiting for him, and already in conversation with the
corporal. Waterford patted the camera equipment much as
he touched everything; large, possessive, dangerous contacts.
Dawson handed the corporal towels and a mug of coffee.
Waterford waited for Brooke to remove his facemask. The
moment they confronted one another, even before Dawson
could take Brooke's air tanks, Waterford said:

"Well? Looks as if he taxied it to the shore and found the
ice too thin?" Brooke nodded.

"It seems like it. The stream would have continued to
drain the lake for a while before it froze over. It must flow
pretty quickly in summer—it's not a deep channel, anyway.
It left thin ice and a nice big air pocket. Oops!"

"The corporal tells me the airframe's factory-fresh. Is

that true?" It sounded like an accusation, a laying of blame upon the Royal Marine lieutenant.

Brooke nodded. "Almost. Even the undercart is intact—one of the doors is buckled, but—"

"Christ! That's all we need. So the silly sod landed the bloody thing in one piece, did he?" Again, Brooke nodded.

"He must have done," he said. "Even closed the canopy before he left—God, Major, you should see the thing—!"

"No, thanks!" Then he continued, as much to himself as to Brooke: "I almost had the poor sod . . ." His hand clenched into a grip in front of him, almost touching Brooke's chest. "He was as close to me as you are now. Sheer bloody luck we found him—but they'd found him, too. Some bloody Ivan tackled him just as he had hold of the wire . . . we could have had him here *now*, for Christ's sake—!" Then, more calmly and even more ominously, he added: "Having been that close to rescue, having looked in my face, into the cabin of the Lynx behind me, he'll go to pieces now—fast. From what I've heard of him, he's halfway off his head already. He's going to last about five minutes when they start to question him." He looked out over the lake. "By tomorrow, the Russians will be crawling over this place like ants. Getting ready to cart the thing home."

"You think so?"

Waterford's face was grim. "I've seen them, laddie," he snapped sourly. "In Belfast, in Cyprus, Borneo, the Oman—I've seen how *communicative* people can be when they're put to it." His square, stone-cut features were bleak as he spoke. "Gant, poor sod, won't be able to help himself . . . and I haven't helped him either, arriving like the Seventh Cavalry just *after* they've burned down the fort!" He threw up his hands, and added: "O.K., let's tell Aubrey the good news—Dawson, have you hidden that commpack successfully? Will it work for the next lot in?"

"Reindeers permitting, yes, sir," Dawson replied.

"He's going to love this, that podgy little clever-dick—Christ, is he going to love this!"

The rain blew out of the darkness like something alive and impishly malevolent. Aubrey had closed his umbrella because it threatened to turn inside out in every gust of searching wind, but he held his hat jammed onto his head.

Buckholz walked beside him, bareheaded, chilly and soaked, hands thrust in his pockets, head bent against the splashes and gouts of rain. They had been silent for some minutes. Buckholz, numbed by the signals they had received via the satellite link, as he knew Aubrey must be, had no wish to interrupt the silence. The splashing of the rain against the administration building windows as they passed, the faint noises from the Officers' Mess, their clicking or sloshing footsteps, the sudden yells of the wind, all expressed his mood and deadened it at the same time. He was able not to think, not to consider.

Aubrey dabbed at puddles with the ferrule of his umbrella, breaking up their rippling reflections of light. As always to Buckholz, his anger seemed no grander than petulance. Yet it was real and deep. The smaller, older man shivered at the intrusion of rain into his collar, and expelled an angry, exasperated breath. Buckholz thought he might be about to speak, but they continued their patrol in silence. Down in the Ops Room, Curtin was trying to contact Pyott in London.

They had come to a dead stop, Buckholz had to admit. They needed fresh orders, a fresh guarantee of support, from Washington and London and Brussels and Oslo, and they had to make fresh approaches to the Finns. But—to what end? For what?

Buckholz brushed away the thoughts, his face cleansed of worried frowns by the splash of rain that met them as they turned the corner of the building, into a gleam of light from a doorway. Buckholz thought it was Bradnum, standing there in his uniform raincoat, but the RAF officer, whoever he was, saw them and turned suddenly back into the building. They passed the main door. Noises from the Mess emerged as warmly as the heat of a fire. They passed on, feet crunching on gravel, no longer clicking or splashing on concrete.

Finally, as if in the grip of a tormenting, unbearable secret he must blurt out, Aubrey turned to Buckholz and said, almost in a gasp: "They have *everything*, Charles—in the palm of . . . oh, dammit, they have *everything*!" Buckholz was prompted, for an instant, to pat Aubrey's shoulder, but desisted. The Englishman would find it patronizing, too gauchely American.

"I know, Kenneth—it's one hell of a blow."

"Both prizes, Charles—both of them, lost to us. The airframe is intact and less than forty miles from the Russian border, and the pilot is by now probably in Murmansk, if not on his way to Moscow!" Aubrey leaned towards Buckholz, lowering his voice to an intense whisper as he said: "And they will make him talk, Charles. Believe me, they will. He is alone, you see—their first and sharpest weapon. Before, he was never alone, not for a moment. He had help. Now, he will know he is alone, and that resistance, courage, defiance, all have no meaning. Sooner or later he will tell them where to find the airframe of the Firefox."

"I know you're right, Kenneth . . ."

"And, like me, you can see no way out?"

Buckholz shook his head emphatically, as if to dispel any lingering, foolish hope in Aubrey, who merely nodded once in reply to the gesture.

"No, all I can see is we've painted ourselves into a corner, Kenneth."

"I won't accept that—!"

"You *have* to, Kenneth. I have to talk to Washington again, you to London. And we have to tell them that, in our considered estimation, we've lost both ends of the operation—Gant and the Firefox." Buckholz shrugged expressively. Water ran from his short hair in droplets that gleamed in the light above the main doors of the administration building. "What else can we say, for God's sake?"

"You want me to order Waterford to set charges and destroy the airframe? Before it's too late to do so?" Aubrey challenged.

"Man, what else in your right mind can you do? You can't let them take it back over the border!"

"If only they didn't have Gant—!" Aubrey raged. "We'd then have the advantage of our knowledge. We could spend weeks examining the airframe, the electronics and avionics, the anti-radar, the thought-guidance systems . . . everything. But they *do* have him, and they'll make him talk!" His umbrella stabbed at the puddles that had gathered in the tire marks of a heavy vehicle. Stab, stab, stab, destroying the gleaming mirrors, the gasoline-rainbowed water.

"The Finns wouldn't let you—"

"It would have to be covert, I agree—"

"Sneaking around Finnish Lapland for weeks—civilian and military scientists . . . *underwater*? Come on, Kenneth, that's a dream and you know it."

"What good are *spies* to us now?" Aubrey asked, his tone that of someone dissociating himself from his lifelong profession.

"Good use enough to blow the airframe to pieces."

"Is that your *only* advice, Charles? It's not very constructive."

"Sorry."

Rain slapped at their faces and raincoats. Buckholz shivered, but Aubrey seemed not to notice.

"I should never have decided on that clever, so *clever*, flight across Finland—it should have been Norway—"

"Where they might have been waiting? The flight should have lasted a lot less than an hour and a half, there wasn't a risk—when you drew up the scenario."

"Thank you, Charles—it doesn't help, I'm afraid." The words were murmured. Aubrey walked a little away from the American, his head bent forward, oblivious of the falling rain. Water ran from the brim of his hat. Buckholz recognized the signals of intense concentration. He waited, looking up into the rain. The lights of Lincoln glowed dully on the clouds to the south.

Minutes later, Aubrey turned back to him. His face was determined. Buckholz, knowing the Englishman, recognized Aubrey's refusal to accept defeat.

"Very well—Waterford may lay his charges—he may need an opinion from someone here—but he is not to detonate them. I shall alert Shelley to talk to Edgecliffe and Moscow Station—they're to look out for Gant's arrival. We must know the moment he gets there, where they take him, how long we might have . . ."

"Why—?"

Aubrey did not seem to hear the question. Instead, he pursued his explanation. "I must talk to Hanni Vitsula in Helsinki." He smiled, briefly and for the first time. "Hanni has no love for Russians since they killed his father, and less love for Finlandization as a way of life. He will see the problem from our point of view."

"The Director-General of Finnish Intelligence is a government official, Kenneth, even if he is a friend of yours. What will he do?"

"I don't know—at the moment, we *need* friends, and he's one. Perhaps—oh, I don't know . . . I simply trust to a Finn's long memory. He's from the southeast himself—the part that now lies in Russia, what used to be known as

Karelia. He's never been back since he was a child." Aubrey raised his hands, palms outward, and desisted from the explanation, then added: "I don't know what to do, Charles—I'm merely running around in this old, deserted house, opening doors with a bang and whistling to myself in the dark. Who knows what may come of it?"

"You're hopeful something will?" Buckholz asked in surprise.

"No. But I must *try*—!"

Dawn was leaking into the heavily clouded sky as Gant stepped stiffly out of the large MiL-8 transport helicopter. Light puffs of snow pattered against the fuselage, melting almost at once and drizzling down the olive-drab camouflage paint. Two GRU guards stood on the tarmac of the helicopter base, Kalashnikovs pointed at him, and there were another four behind him in the MiL's main cabin. His hands were handcuffed in front of him. His right arm ached. It had been locked to one of the handholds above his hard seat for the entire journey. His whole body, however, submerged that pain in a general ache. It was difficult to move. His feet seemed numb, the wound the dog had made in his calf pained him, and he staggered as he reached the bottom of the steps. A guard held him upright, not ungently but with care to keep his rifle out of range of Gant's hands.

Then he was surrounded again by his full escort. A truck drew up near the parked MiL. Gant, with almost no interest, watched more guards debouch from it, noticed a staff car and emerging senior officers beyond it—curiosity rather than business had brought them, he thought. Then he raised his head so that he looked beyond the helicopter base down towards the town of Murmansk and the grey Kolafjord which disappeared northwards into the heavy mist and snow towards the Barents Sea. There was the smell of fish on the snowy wind. The hills behind the base were hidden by cloud. The transport airplane which was to transfer him to Moscow would just get off before the weather closed in sufficiently to prevent further flying.

He shook his head, half-amused. He wondered why he bothered about meteorological conditions. He was in the Soviet Union, and he was alone and he was manacled. It made no difference whether his location was Murmansk or Moscow; they were identical, cells in the same fortress prison.

He was gestured into the back of the military truck, and helped over the lowered tailgate when his legs appeared to fail him. He struggled in and sat down opposite one of the GRU guards, whose rifle was leveled. Everything was constant, and constantly repeated; wrists manacled, rifles leveled, box-like metal containers—trucks or aircraft did not matter—and this routine would proceed endlessly . . . endlessly . . .

He tried to believe that the routine would never change because, at the end of the journey, at the change of routine, they would begin to ask their questions. He did not wish to consider the abyss of failure that would open up then, in the first hours or even minutes of his interrogation. Thus, the journey possessed him, was everything.

The truck moved off with a jerk the moment the rest of his guards had boarded it. Gant watched the MiL shrink in size as they left it behind. The metal and canvas of the truck pressed close around him. Someone coughed; metal scraped, boot studs perhaps. Leather creaked. The engine of the truck throbbed. Through the V-shaped gap in the canvas at the back of the truck, he could see belching chimneys and anchored ships and grey water—most of all, he registered the movement of the truck itself.

After some minutes, a brief stop. Red and white pole, a guard room. Then a glimpse of runway, a control tower. Most of all, the renewed movement of the truck. He was still travelling, the journey was everything . . .

There was no destination. Only movement . . .

5 / **RESTRAINTS**

"I have divers—who also happen to be expert soldiers—at Kirkenes, sixty or seventy miles from our lake and our intact airframe . . . pray, what else do I need?" Aubrey asked, waggling his fork in Curtin's direction.

The USN Intelligence officer brushed a hand through his hair and adopted a lugubrious expression, staring down at his plate of bacon and eggs. Eventually, unnerved by the heavy silence around the breakfast table, he murmured a reply, clearing his throat as he did so as if in apology for what he said.

"A hell of a lot else, sir—too much, if you don't object to me saying so. Much too much."

Aubrey snorted, then stabbed his fork at the center of his remaining egg. Yolk oozed onto the plate. Buckholz glanced at Pyott, who had arrived no more than an hour earlier and evidently had not slept. The Deputy Director of the Covert Action Staff of the CIA searched the English soldier's face for signs of complicity; a willingness to squash Aubrey's ever more unrestrained imagination. Pyott, however, appeared willing to remain silent while Aubrey rambled, prodded, enquired, snapped.

Buckholz sighed audibly. "There's nothing you can do, Kenneth—nothing at all. You're clutching at straws." He spread his hands in front of his chest, in sign of pacification. "It's not realistic, it's not even adult, to scratch at this particular sore the way you're doing. Let's settle for your guy Waterford triggering the charges he's planted . . . ?"

Aubrey glared at him, his nostrils pinched and white, his lips bloodless. "Adult? Childish?" he repeated scathingly. "Do you think, when we play our suburban, late-century version of the Great Game, we are *ever* being adult?"

"Kenneth—" Pyott warned quietly.

"It was not *adult*—it was not the behavior of a *gentleman*—to throw prisoners under interrogation from helicopters, *pour encourager les autres*, in Southeast Asia!"

"Kenneth—be quiet!" Pyott snapped. "It was not civilized to sacrifice people for metal, lives for avionics—as you did, as we all have done with this operation." Pyott's face was white, highlighting the dark smudges beneath his eyes. Aubrey appeared abashed, even ashamed.

"Forgive me, Charles—I apologize for that remark," he said.

"It's long ago and far away—another country, " Buckholz replied.

"Thank you." Aubrey turned to Pyott immediately. The soldier saw that four hours' sleep had done nothing to improve Aubrey's temper or patience. He was the pestering, gifted child of SIS, and his impatience had become habitual, even incessant. Like the highly intelligent children he somehow suggested, he was solitary, frustrated, intolerantly and urgently alive inside his own mind. He could handle people with suavity and aplomb when he chose, but for the most part he regarded the world as a stumbling block, no more, placed between himself and his goal. Aubrey was simply—*too* clever.

"Kenneth—you are silently pleading with me," Pyott said with heavy humor. "What is it?"

"I—" Aubrey waved his hands over the table like a hypnotist. "I've seen airframes transported on motorways—in this country. Their wings are folded, or they are absent. What I need is someone to take the wings off this poor butterfly . . ."

Pyott nodded to the Americans, requiring them to answer. Curtin, grinning suddenly and rubbing his hand through his hair once more, said: "You may have seen them—but you won't get trucks to move far enough and fast enough in Finnish Lapland at this time of the year. You don't even have roads they could use, always supposing they *could* move!"

Aubrey's face was taut with disappointed anger. "I see," he managed to utter.

"What you need is a chopper—a very big chopper," Curtin added. Aubrey's face brightened.

"Which one?" He immediately placed a small, gold-bound notebook beside his plate, and touched the tip of a pencil to his tongue. "Pray, what is the name of this marvelous beast?"

"You need the new Sikorsky Skyhook—it could lift fifty thousand pounds in a sling load with no trouble."

"And—this helicopter could transport the airframe?"

"It might take it as much as two hours to get the Firefox back into Norway from the lake. The problem is—the closest one is probably in Germany, as far south as Wiesbaden."

"But it could transport it, in a single lift, all the way out of Finland?"

"Yes."

"Christ, Gene—you're getting as crazy as he is!" Buckholz exclaimed. "Have you seen the weather forecasts for that area? You'd be real lucky to get the Skyhook *up* there, never mind operating!"

"I'm afraid that's true, Mr. Aubrey," Curtin reluctantly agreed.

"Could it lift it straight out of the lake?" Aubrey persisted.

Curtin nodded. "But, I suggest you have winches as a backup, to haul that airplane's ass out of the water onto dry land. The Skyhook would like that—and the weather wouldn't help a straight lift, either." He watched Aubrey scribbling furiously in his tiny notebook, and added, as if dictating: "From Waterford's report, it must have run backwards into deep water—you could winch it out, up the slope, along a portable roadway . . ."

"Just a moment!" Pyott snapped. "I'm going to put—a hypothetical case, shall we say?—to the RAF's Field Recovery Unit at Abingdon. I want an *expert* opinion—with apologies to Captain Curtin—on all this speculation." He stood up, dabbing his lips, then dropped his napkin on the table. "I shan't be long," he offered in a cheery voice.

When the door had closed behind him, Buckholz leaned over the table and whispered fiercely at Aubrey: "We know men and machines can do *anything* you want them to—but what about politicians, Kenneth? You haven't gotten a dime's worth of change out of the Finns since yesterday. Even your buddy in Helsinki isn't too crazy about more interference from us—"

"*Or* from the Russians . . ."

"Don't count on that," Buckholz said abruptly.

Ignoring him, Aubrey addressed Curtin. "What else do I need?"

"I agree with Director Buckholz, Mr. Aubrey—you need the politicians to say yes to you. But, if you're asking me, I'd think about maybe even dismantling the airplane and taking it away in pieces—in case you haven't gotten a Skyhook to the lake. You could hide the pieces and go back later . . . ?" Curtin shrugged. "So," he continued, "you need technicians, equipment, winches and pulleys, cutting tools, airframe experts, and a hell of a lot more besides, all gathered around your lake, and you need the utmost secrecy and you need *time*."

"How much time?"

"From beginning to end—a lot of days."

"And Gant isn't going to be able to give you that time, Kenneth," Buckholz supplied, staring at his fingertips as he spread them on either side of his cup of coffee. They drummed pointlessly, without discernible rhythm. "Gant hasn't got any time left, so neither do we." He looked up from the table, shaking his head. "This whole conversation's pointless."

"Don't say that—"

"I have to, Kenneth. All right, you're the guy, the main man, the one who dreamed up this crazy scheme—and almost made it work—but it hasn't worked. Blow the damned airframe into little pieces!"

Aubrey stood up. "And that is your considered, your *expert*, opinion, Charles?" he asked.

Buckholz nodded. "That's it."

"Then I beg to disagree." He looked at his plate with an old man's reluctance to leave food uneaten, then shook his head. "I must talk to London—to Helsinki *via* London, to be exact. You gentlemen will excuse me."

He closed the door of the small dining room in the Mess behind him. A secure line direct to Shelley at Queen Anne's Gate had been installed in the bedroom he had been allocated. He went heavily up the staircase, his mind whirling with the possibilities of his scheme. Pride stung him into desire. He wanted action, activity, organization, a *scenario*. He would not let the aircraft go; could not bring himself to destroy the airframe. Guilt, too, hounded him now; had awakened him in the short night when he had tried to sleep. Guilt for Fenton, who had been tricked to his brutal murder on the bank of the Moskva after doing good work trailblazing for Gant; guilt for Pavel Upenskoy, guilt for Baranovich and Semelovsky and Kreshin, all of whom had died at his orders, or had been considered no more than expendable in promoting the success of the operation. It was a heavy toll of good people; the best people.

To destroy the airframe now, scatter it over the bed of the frozen lake, would be more criminal than creating the circumstances of those deaths. Gant was lost. Strangely, he did not feel any acute guilt at the American's loss . . . but the others, yes.

He closed the door behind him and crossed to the telephone. He felt a physical sensation of weight between his shoulderblades, slowing him, wearing him down. He felt he would only rid himself of it if he recovered the Firefox; would only reduce and lighten it if he *tried* for such a recovery.

He dialed Shelley's number.

"Peter?"

"Yes, sir. Good morning."

"What news?"

"As far as we can tell, he hasn't arrived yet . . . sorry."

"Put me through immediately to Hanni Vitsula, Peter. I must talk to him. I'll wait until you call me back."

He replaced the receiver, and rubbed his hands on his thighs. Sitting on the edge of the bed, he recaptured the position his body had adopted when he first woke and made to rise. Hunched, small, lost. Guilt, yes—guilt and pride.

Two emotions to move mountains; or bury people beneath mountains.

Stop it, he told himself, sitting upright, hands thrust into his pockets. Prepare yourself for the next step, for this conversation.

The Finns—more precisely, the Finnish Cabinet Defense Committee under the chairmanship of the Prime Minister— had agreed to the overflight of the Firefox and to certain, very limited backup facilities and incursions of Finnish airspace. Aubrey had been tempted by a new mood in the country, under the new government, to use Finnish airspace rather than order Gant to fly the longer journey down the spine of Norway to rendezvous with the British Airways flight from Stockholm to London. Infrared invisibility would have been guaranteed by the aircraft's proximity to the civilian airliner for the last crucial stage of its flight across the North Sea. The Finns had agreed because "Finlandization" had become a term of abuse, an insult to a resurgent mood of independence in the country. But—

But, but, but . . .

Army deserters crossing from the Soviet Union into Finland had been publicized, and not handed back. Granted asylum. Key industrial projects in the Soviet Union designed and built by the Finns had been halted or suspended until more acceptable trade agreements and repayment terms had been agreed. All good signs . . .

But, but, but—

The telephone rang, startling Aubrey out of his reverie of justification and optimism. He snatched at the receiver.

"Yes?"

"Director Vitsula," Shelley said, and then he heard, more distantly, the voice of the Director-General of Finnish Intelligence.

"Good morning, Kenneth."

"Good morning, Hanni—"

"What is this business we have to discuss—your aide tells me it is urgent . . . is that so?"

"I'm afraid it is."

"What has changed since last night?"

"Nothing—except our attitude here to what we discovered."

"Yes."

"What is the feeling at present in your Cabinet Defense Committee?"

"Deadlock—I can put it no more hopefully than that."

"What about the Russians?"

"I think they are more angry with them than with your country and the Americans. They do not know about—your little escapade, only about the overflight by the Nimrod, which they permitted, in the event . . . but, there has been a leak in the newspapers here—"

"*What?*"

"Only concerning intrusions into our airspace by Soviet fighters—nothing more. But the Prime Minister had made the most serious protest to Moscow concerning the matter."

"Is there any hope there, Hanni?" Aubrey was speaking very loudly now because the Finn's voice seemed more distant.

"Hope for what?"

"A—" Aubrey hesitated, then said: "That matter we talked about last night . . . a fishing expedition."

"Kenneth—I have seen the Foreign Minister and the Prime Minister—nothing, I'm afraid."

"Do they understand?"

"Yes, Kenneth, they understand. They are not unsympathetic. But—troops, vehicles, helicopters—it would be easier to ignore the whole problem, or drop a bomb in the lake . . ."

Aubrey, enraged, snapped: "What is it they want?"

"Ah," Vitsula sighed. In front of his reply, as if coming from the next room, the line crackled and spat. "Reciprocity and access were two of the words being tentatively used, I believe," Vitsula said.

"Would they agree, in that case?" Aubrey snapped.

"I—don't know. It might . . . soften them."

"It's a high price."

"Higher than you think. Access to highest levels, access to the codes, access to the scenarios regarding Scandinavia . . ."

"You mean your people want a full Intelligence partnership with NATO while remaining neutral?" Aubrey asked, taken aback. He rubbed his forehead, wiping slowly and with force at the creases he found, as if they surprised him. "It's *your* price, of course."

"My suggestion, yes."

"In return?"

"We would keep our heads down—three wise monkeys."

"For how long?"

"I—don't know . . . how long must you have?"

"*I* don't know!"

"Then you must think it over—just one more thing, Kenneth—"

"Yes?"

"Can you assure me—give me your word—that our friends across the border know nothing, nothing at all, of the whereabouts of their property? I must have that assurance, Kenneth, before I do anything more. Are you able to give it?"

Aubrey envisaged Gant's face for an instant, cleared his throat, and said: "Yes. I can give you that assurance. They are in complete ignorance."

"Thank you. When do we talk again?"

"Later. I will talk to London and to Washington."

"Good."

"The price is very high."

"So are the risks."

The young KGB colonel, whose shoulder boards and uniform seemed remarkably new, had hurried aboard the Antonov An-26 short-haul transport aircraft with the eagerness of someone meeting a dear relative. Gant watched him clatter up the lowered beaver-tail ramp into the fuselage, his eyes seeking along the row of tip-up seats. Gant was seated on one of them, hands manacled in front of him, a guard on either side, the remaining GRU men positioned on the opposite side of the fuselage.

The young colonel stood in front of the American, hands on his hips, appraising him frankly but without malice. There might have been something akin to admiration in his gaze. Then, almost smiling, he turned to the officer in charge of the guard detachment.

"O.K., he's ours now," he said.

As if he had been overheard, KGB men in civilian clothes clambered up the ramp into the aircraft's belly. The cold of the day outside followed them, striking through Gant's check woolen jacket and the waterproof trousers. He shook his head, trying to fully wake himself. It had been surprisingly easy to sleep in the noisy main compartment, surrounded by guards. Now he was hungry. The journey was almost over—

bath, food at the end of it. He knew why his mind had narrowed and was working at this fiction.

"Major Gant—would you accompany us, please," the young colonel requested. The four civilian-clothed KGB men stood behind him.

Gant stood up, stamping the cramp out of his calves and thighs. The dog bite in his calf ached. The GRU men were already at their ease. Cigarette smoke was pungent in the cold air. The colonel reached out a steadying hand, but Gant motioned it angrily away. The officer nodded almost respectfully.

Gant moved towards the ramp and the tarmac outside, a KGB man close on either side. Their arms touched his as they moved, he could smell staleness and smoke on one of the suits, mustiness on an overcoat. The men's faces were pinched and whitened with the cold. Gant shivered as the sleet blew into his face.

The officer was suddenly beside him, one of his guards having dropped back a step.

"I'm Colonel Dmitri Priabin," he explained, the rank still a strange, pleasant taste on his tongue. "I found you," he added, gesturing the American towards a rank of black limousines drawn up on the tarmac. Gant's attention wandered over the military airfield. Familiar, except for the aircraft types and their markings.

"Yeah?" he murmured. "Found?"

Priabin's hand was on the door handle of the second and largest limousine, a Zil. He nodded. The grin was boyish, the eyes alert, clever, studious. "Almost in time," he explained. "You were on our computer files, of course. But—it was an accident, even then. A *minute* too late, no more than that!" He laughed.

"What happened to your boss?" Gant asked suddenly. Priabin's face frowned, then cleared.

"Colonel Kontarsky is—in disgrace, I'm afraid." His head had turned from side to side, as if checking that his new shoulder boards remained in place. "However, will you please get in the car."

"Where are we going?"

Priabin grinned reprovingly. "Come, come, Major—you know that as well as I. Please . . . ?" He opened the door and gestured for Gant to get in. The American clambered into the Zil. The other rear door opened and a KGB man—the one whose overcoat smelt of mothballs and disuse—slid in next to him. Priabin got into the front passenger seat. The KGB man who was scented with harsh tobacco followed Gant into the car. He was pressed between them. No guns had been drawn. Priabin turned to watch the American as the driver accelerated towards the perimeter fence of the airbase. Passes were shown at the guardroom, and then they were turning onto the main road, towards Moscow.

Why hadn't he used his overcoat? Gant wondered irrelevantly, the smell of mothballs and mustiness overpowering now.

"Where did you discover that overcoat, Oleg?" Priabin asked good-humoredly, wrinkling his nose. "It can't have been used for years." Gant grinned crookedly.

"My son took mine before I was up," Oleg grumbled. "You know what kids are like, sir. What's yours is theirs—what's theirs is their own." He tossed his head in mock disgust.

The midday traffic was light on the Volgograd road as they passed through farmland and forest; deceptive countryside, flat and passive like his home state. Only the black car in front and the two black cars behind forced his real context and status upon him. Industrial smoke belched beyond woodland ahead of them, from chimneys scrawled against the grey sky. The sleet slithered on the windscreen as the wipers flicked at it.

"I might make you walk the rest of the way," Priabin said to Oleg, smiling. "Get rid of that smell, at any rate." He returned his attention to Gant. "A pity about the aircraft," he murmured conversationally.

"Sure," Gant replied. "A real crying shame." He converted himself in his own mind to a laconic, simple, truculent figure; as if flexing the first muscles he would use in a contest yet to come. "It caught fire," Gant added.

"Mm. You ejected, then?"

"What else, man? I saw it go." He nodded vigorously. In his mind, from the vantage point of his ejector seat, he saw his Phantom explode in Vietnam. That had been the moment before the quick, breathtaking rush through the trees, the catching jolt as the chute caught and held him, the arrival of the party of armed gooks . . .

He continued nodding. Priabin rubbed his top lip with his forefinger. "Yes," he remarked. "You have certainly seen aircraft destroyed—blown up . . . ?" His hands made the expansive gesture of a mushrooming cloud. Gant contented himself with a final, decisive nod. "What a pity—all that money wasted," Priabin said soothingly. "I hope they believe you," he added quickly.

Gant's eyes narrowed, but his features remained passive. Outside the car, a suburban town in the Moscow *oblast* offered low factory units, chimneys, then wet-black streets and hurrying figures. Scarved or fur-hatted women, a preponderance of black, unfashionable winter overcoats, short fur-lined boots and galoshes. Old-fashioned, poor. Again, the familiar . . .

They halted at traffic lights. He felt the two bodies on either side come to greater alertness. He relaxed, slumping back against the seat. The Zil moved off as the lights changed. Billboards stared down, alcohol and cheese and chocolate rivaling the flags and the Party portraits for his attention. The town straggled away behind them in the sleet, and an airliner dropped out of the cloudbase towards the Bykovo airport on their right. There was little that was unfamiliar, except the city ahead crowding on its hills like a vast gathering of people waiting for important news. Four days before, when he had entered it from the northwest, from Cheremetievo, he hadn't noticed the hills. Now, the city might have been Italian; a holiday destination that had strayed to some wet, cold northern latitude.

He gave up trying to assimilate the city, change its nature. For him, it was now no larger than Dzerzhinsky Street and the Lubyanka prison behind the dignified facade of KGB headquarters. They passed beneath a railway bridge. Sparks flashed against the sullen sky from a passing train's overhead cage. He was holding on, but only just, only just—

Just keeping out the future. It was beginning to ooze through a hairline crack in the dam he had built with inadequate materials, but he was holding on . . .

Priabin scrutinized him carefully, keenly, as they drove along the wide Volgogradski Prospekt towards the inner ring road, the Garden Ring. He saw the onion domes of a church and a building near it that was large enough, alien enough to Gant, to have been a monastery. He was startled by the outline of a distant bridge over the Moskva as a gap between buildings revealed it to him. Beyond the monastery, against the sky and almost obscured by the sleet, he saw the

Krasnokholmski Bridge. He remembered its lights blurring with sudden tears as Vassily jerked his head back and held him while Pavel beat Fenton's face into an unrecognizable blood-covered dough.

He saw that his hands were shaking when he followed Priabin's keen gaze downwards, towards his lap. He clenched them, ground his teeth, and looked up.

"Yeah," he said sullenly. Priabin had evidently seen the bridge, for he said:

"Well-remembered scenes, mm, Major?" Then he shrugged, and added: "It was clever—ruthless, but clever. I'm afraid it doesn't make you the most popular visitor to Moscow."

Taganskaia Square. They crossed it quickly, using the central lane marked with its broad yellow lines which was free of all but official traffic at any time. Ahead of the cars, Gant saw ugly concrete blocks towering above yellow-stuccoed buildings and monuments and columned arches.

Priabin turned to follow his gaze. A huge hotel block drifted past the Zil's windows. People hurried beneath, dwarfed, hunched into overcoats. There were very few umbrellas. Apart from the buildings, that was the most alien thing he had seen. Most of the people wore hats, or scarves, but there were almost no umbrellas. It *was* an alien place.

Priabin turned back to Gant. Ahead, through the smeared passage of the wipers, the city seemed to hurry like a crowd towards the center. The streets narrowed, appeared to squeeze closer. The distance from Red Square to the KGB's headquarters was perhaps no more than two minutes' drive.

"Welcome to Moscow, Major Gant," Priabin said, grinning.

The dam broke. Gant was no longer able to fend off the future. It broke over him. His hands would not keep still on his lap, however hard he watched them, however much he willed them to stop.

"It's remarkably astute of the Finns, in my opinion," Aubrey observed to Buckholz as they stood at the plot table. Yellow, red, and green tape was stretched between pins. The futuristic model of the Firefox remained where he had placed it, squatting on the lake. It ought to be *under* the table, he observed to himself irreverently. "Everyone has their price, especially governments, and the Finns have been very clever at deciding upon theirs—but then, Hanni Vitsula is a clever man."

"Sure," Buckholz grumbled.

"They don't want Russians in Finland, collecting and taking back their most secret warplane—think of the bad publicity that would give this new Finnish government . . . and they certainly wouldn't want to destroy it themselves, and have to own up to the Russians—too much diplomatic flak for anyone's liking there. So, what do they do? Give us the job of cleaning their stables for them, and making us pay an exorbitant price for the privilege of so doing! One really has to admire them."

"Does one?" Buckholz asked reluctantly, sarcastically.

"*I* think so, Charles—oh, don't be such a spoilsport. In the end I don't suppose it will come down to us giving them very much more than we do already. You know that as well as I do. What is it that is really upsetting you? The fact that your President, at the eager prompting of the Chiefs of Staff, the entire Pentagon, the NSA and your own Director, have ordered us to rescue the airframe if we humanly can?"

Aubrey's complacent smile irritated the American, made him unreasonable; even disposed to violence. Washington had given him explicit orders, outlined a specific course of action; pressured London into agreement, into the supply of men and facilities and materials. Buckholz was angry with Aubrey for anticipating, in his insatiable desire for success, the way in which the President's Crisis Management Committee would resolve the matter. An all-night meeting, a morning of computer-discussed scenarios, and the White House had agreed with Aubrey. The attempt must be made, and the Finns made to allow it.

Charles Buckholz felt he now appeared stupid, narrow, defeatist. Aubrey had forced such a view of himself upon him, and he therefore disliked Aubrey intensely at that moment. He disliked Pyott, too, he thought, as the soldier, now attired in a dark suit rather than his uniform, entered the Ops Room, a sheaf of papers in one hand. To Buckholz's extreme irritation, he proceeded to wave them like a flag above his head as he came towards them.

"Well?" Aubrey asked eagerly. Pyott, on reaching them, seemed disconcerted by Buckholz's sullen expression and glinting eyes. "Oh, don't mind Charles," Aubrey remarked airily. "He's sulking because the President ignored his Jeremiad this morning!" Then he turned to Pyott again. "Is that Abingdon's shopping list?"

"Yes, it is."

"Good. And how were JIC and the Chiefs of Staff, not to mention Andrew Gresham, our revered leader?"

"Sullen," Pyott observed maliciously, looking at Buckholz with amusement. "At least, Gresham and the Cabinet Defense Committee are writhing at the pressure the President is putting on them—but wilting, of course. JIC is fence-sitting, and the Chiefs of Staff are promising the moon in the way of assistance!"

Aubrey grinned broadly, almost snatching the sheaf of papers from the taller Pyott. Pyott handed them to him, and brushed at his moustache; a preening gesture, Buckholz thought.

"Kids," he remarked. "You're like kids."

"Charles," Pyott soothed. "Let's not get into that again."

"It's not a game—not even your old imperial Great Game, Giles," the American said heavily, leaning on clenched knuckles on the plot table; a heavy, reluctant figure, someone to be taken seriously. "Kenneth's idea of Christmas, this is," he continued. "And maybe yours." He looked at each of them in turn, intently, then he added: "The President never mentioned Gant, though—uh? Not a Goddamned word!" Buckholz threw his hands up in the air, continuing with great vehemence: "What did he do, uh? Stand in front of the green-tinted window in the Oval Office, put his hand on his heart and tell the Chiefs of Staff and the gathered multitudes that Mitchell Gant was a true American and he'd never talk to the damned Russkies!" Pyott dropped his glance. His eyes seemed to cast about on the plot table for something he had mislaid. Aubrey, too, seemed abashed. "You haven't got a chance—not the ghost of a chance—because they've got him and they're going to make him talk. Today, or tomorrow, or maybe if you're lucky the poor dumb bastard will hold out until the day after tomorrow—but eventually, he's going to tell them go look in the lake, comrades. That's where it is. And if he holds out that long, you might just have gotten it out of the lake before they arrive—they won't even have to fish for it!"

Buckholz glared at them, then turned on his heel and walked noisily across the Ops Room towards the door. He slammed it behind him.

Aubrey stared at the plot table and the colored tapes

marking supply routes and aircraft types and journey times and dropping zones. The sheaf of papers he held tightly in his right hand quivered at the lower edge of eyesight. He could hear his own breathing, nasal but barely under control. Finland appeared so accessible on the plot table. Colored tape stretched out towards it from the U.K., from Norway. The black model of the Firefox sat stolidly on the pinprick of the lake. The quivering sheets in his hand were the foundation, the scenario.

And yet Buckholz was right.

The telephone startled him. He looked at Pyott almost wildly. The soldier crossed the room to the foldaway table on which the secure telephone rested.

"Yes?" he asked, then immediately held out the receiver to Aubrey. It seemed slippery as soon as he touched it. "Shelley."

"Yes, Peter?" he asked anxiously. "Yes . . . yes . . . I see—they're certain, yes, yes, I appreciate they are . . . very well. Yes, the surveillance must be of the best, they may not keep him there . . . yes, Peter. Thank you." He put down the telephone heavily. Pyott, in response to Aubrey's bewildered glance, furiously rubbed at his moustache with a crooked right forefinger. "He's arrived," Aubrey announced in a voice that might, in less serious circumstances, have sounded comically gloomy. "Almost an hour ago, he was driven into Moscow Center." He glanced up at the large clock on the Ops Room wall. It was as if he could hear it ticking in the empty silence of the underground room. "Damn it!" he cried, thumping the foldaway table with his fist. "Damn and blast it, it's already *begun!*"

They had taken him directly to Andropov's office. The cobbled courtyard behind the main building had seemed desolate and ice-cold, gleaming with melted sleet. He had glimpsed the old buildings of the Lubyanka as they hurried him from the car. The office of the KGB Chairman seemed like some kind of bribe. Warm, opulently furnished with embroidered sofas and Oriental carpets, paneled walls, tall windows looking down on Dzerzhinsky Square and Marx Prospekt. He was given a drink—bourbon, which he disliked but which they might have assumed was to his taste. It burned his chest and stomach, but the sensation, after the chilling cold of the cobbled courtyard, was comforting.

Andropov watched him from behind his large, intricately carved French desk, hands steepled, face not unkindly. Merely curious. A tall, uniformed man stood at his side, outlined against the artificial whiteness provided by the net curtains. His eyes gleamed even in half-shadow. Gant sat on a delicate antique chair covered with embroidered silk, cradling his drink, while Priabin stood behind him. There was no one else in the room, but the illusion of innocence that the smallness of the company at first provided, soon dissipated. Instead, the status and size of the office, the heavy silence, the furnishings, the intensity of the air force general's gaze, and the patent and insatiable curiosity on Andropov's face began to unnerve him.

Vladimirov, standing beside Andropov, was aware of a slow-growing cramp in his left calf. The sense of stiffness reminded him of how motionless he had remained since Gant entered the room; a stillness of body that belied the state of his emotions and thoughts. After a night's sleep and breakfast with his wife and the reading of a treasured letter from their only son regarding his promotion to deputy director of the power station in Sverdlovsk, he realized that he hated Gant. It was some kind of delayed stress reaction, he concluded. He had suspected it in the staff car as he was being driven to the Center from his apartment. Suspected it even as he recalled his son's childhood, his poor academic record at school, the fudging that had got him into a technical university, his dislike of the armed forces and his choice of a career in electricity. In Andropov's office, drinking coffee, engaging in the halting small-talk that was all the Chairman could command, he had begun to be more certain. When they had brought the American in—weary, disoriented, fearful—he had known with certainty that he hated him. No admiration, no ex-flyer's fellow-feeling, no *objectivity* at all . . .

Gant had almost ruined him, almost made him fail; almost outwitted him. He had destroyed the other prototype and lost the one he had stolen. He would be made to pay.

Eventually, Andropov cleared his throat with a small, polite sound, smoothed his silk tie, and said: "Major Gant—Major Mitchell Gant . . ." He smiled thinly. "We have—asked you to come here today to tell us what you have done with the prototype Mig-31 which you removed from the secret complex at Bilyarsk, early yesterday morning—what have you to say?" The tone was an attempt at silkiness, at a kind of indirect, ironic humor. Priabin sensed that Andropov was unused to the tone, had had little use for it in the past.

"It blew up—I told him," Gant replied sullenly, gesturing over his shoulder at Priabin. Andropov's gaze flickered to the young colonel's face, then back to Gant.

"I see. You, of course, ejected?" Gant nodded. "Where, precisely? Would you describe the incident for us? General Vladimirov is most interested to know what became of the aircraft—aren't you, General?"

"Yes," Vladimirov replied in a choked voice. The American's sullen, insulting voice, his pretence to stupidity, further angered him. Even now, he was preparing to play a game with them.

Gant sniffed. "Could I have another drink?" he asked, holding out his glass.

"Of course. Colonel—?"

Priabin brought the bottle, half-filled the crystal tumbler, returned the bottle to the dark, inlaid cabinet against one paneled wall. Then he resumed his stance behind Gant. Gant swallowed, cleared his throat, and said:

"The airplane was breaking up and on fire . . ." Vietnam, he reminded himself. Remember the cockpit, filling with smoke. "The cockpit was full of smoke . . ."

"What caused this damage?" Vladimirov suddenly snapped.

"Cannon fire—the second of the two Mig-25s was on my tail. I tried to shake him off, but my fuel was too low already . . . we flew into a closed valley, he came up first and I thought I'd gotten him . . . I had, then he got me . . . I hit the button and got out of there fast . . . I don't know if he did . . . ?" He looked up then, at Andropov. Vladimirov was a tall and threatening shadow at his side.

"You lost fuel—why?" Vladimirov asked.

"The second Firefox—must have ruptured my fuel lines. I was trying to glide her all the way to Bardufoss when your Mig-25s sighted me visually. I was in a corner. I didn't have the fuel to outrun them."

"I ordered them to shepherd you back."

"They almost did—I was lucky, I guess."

Vladimirov was silent for a moment, and then he burst out: "Now I am certain you are lying, Gant!"

"What do you mean, General?" Andropov asked, turning his head to look at Vladimirov.

Vladimirov rounded the desk and moved towards Gant's chair. Gant could see the one clenched fist for a moment before the other hand closed over it, calming it. Then Vladimirov said: "Not you. Never you, Gant. Your life is a mess, you live like a hermit, you couldn't keep a job if you were given one . . . But, you don't rid the world of yourself, you don't give in to the mounting evidence of failure. And why?" Vladimirov leaned forward, his face level with Gant's eyes. "Why? You are a badly wrapped parcel, Major, and you are held together only by an unsurpassed egotism. You really do believe you are the finest pilot in the world, perhaps ever. *You* would never be *lucky*! Not you—you could never admit it!"

As Vladimirov turned triumphantly to Andropov, his face reddened with emotion and delight, Gant said: "If I'm so fucking clever, General, then what the hell did I do to get rid of the airplane?" Vladimirov turned back to Gant. "Your guy blew my ass out of the sky."

"*Liar!*" Vladimirov shouted. The fist he had been cradling swung at Gant's head. One of the legs of the delicate French chair snapped like a twig as Gant tumbled onto the carpet. The bourbon spilled, seeping onto the polished floor. Gant's head turned. His dazed vision encountered Priabin's boots in fuzzy close-up. He waited to be kicked.

"Can we possibly do it in four days, Giles?" Aubrey asked. Curtin, whose timetable they were discussing, also looked at the tall soldier.

"With this shopping list of Curtin's—it might be possible. *If*, and only if, everything works like clockwork. It won't, of course, but this is theoretically feasible."

"Very well—what have we got so far?" Aubrey said, more in the nature of an announcement than an enquiry. He pushed away his plate—lunch had been served in the Ops Room, a white cloth laid over two pushed-together foldaway tables. Buckholz had not joined them. Aubrey studied the last of the claret in his glass, then swallowed it. "Giles?"

"Politically, we're O.K., with the crucial exception of the Finns. Their Cabinet still has to decide."

"Yes, yes—" Aubrey interrupted impatiently, waving his

hand, then standing up, thrusting his hands deeply into his pockets as soon as he had done so. His professorial manner angered Pyott. Aubrey paced alongside the plot table while Pyott continued.

"Washington and London have agreed that the rescue is to be attempted, and that it continues as a covert operation—deniable and disownable if and when necessary. Therefore, we report only to the Cabinet Secretary here, who represents Number Ten and the JIC, while Charles will report via his Director to the Chief of Staff at the White House so that the President may be kept in touch."

"Good, good. That gives us a free hand. Now, what about the substance of the meal?"

"One Hercules has been requisitioned from RAF Lyneham. We think Kirkenes makes the better HQ. Despite the greater range of facilities at Bardufoss, it's too far away . . ." Aubrey was bending over the plot table. Pyott glanced at Curtin, nodded, and they joined him, Curtin having sipped at his glass of water before rising. Aubrey gazed at the map as if he coveted it; a stylized portrait of a conqueror. Pyott waved his hand over the plot table like a conjuror. "Bardufoss—" he said. "Kirkenes—" He cleared his throat. "We have the transport, we have the troops to set up a defensive perimeter, SBS already in Kirkenes . . . we have a Royal Engineer detachment—winches, tripods, pulleys, cutting gear . . . RAF engineers, four of those and appropriate tools . . . Curtin has our giant Sikorsky Skyhook fueling now for its first hop from—where is it, Gene?"

Curtin grinned at the use of his Christian name; his welcome to the comfortable circle of conspiracy. "Germany, Giles." His smile did not diminish. Eventually, Pyott nodded, accepting the familiarity. "We have to finalize the refueling points—this baby can't travel more than two hundred miles on a full tank of gas . . . that means two, maybe three refuelings before she gets her ass out of Germany, since she's coming up from Wiesbaden. Then there's Denmark, Sweden—we don't anticipate problems with their neutrality—and she's going to come awful slowly up Sweden and across Lapland to the lake . . . And the weather reports are getting worse, Mr. Aubrey, they really are." Curtin looked dubious, uncertain; as if he had blasphemed. Aubrey glared at him.

"And there," Giles Pyott said heavily, looking hard at Aubrey, "is where the best laid plans, et cetera, will stumble and fall. You have no backup, Kenneth. No fallback. No second line." He continued to stare at Aubrey.

Eventually, Aubrey shrugged. His face was chastened, and angry. Once more, the image of the frustrated, gifted child came to Pyott. Aubrey really was almost impossible—

"Giles, there can be no fallback or backup or whatever you wish to call it. The best we could hope for, if the Skyhook does not arrive, is to remove some of the more vital systems from the airframe, then destroy it. Which is why this plan *must* work!"

"Too much hinges on the weather and a single large helicopter, Kenneth. If the ice were thick enough to bear the weight of a Hercules . . ." He brushed at his moustache, a flicking motion. "But it won't. Waterford's people are certain of that. Even if it landed, and the ice held, it wouldn't bear the weight of the Hercules with the dismantled Firefox inside its cargo compartment."

Aubrey glanced from Pyott to Curtin, then back to Pyott. "Have you too been rehearsing this?" he asked with evident sarcasm. "I, too, have digested Waterford's reports. I *know* there is no alternative to the Sikorsky. It must arrive. It is *our* job to prepare for its arrival!"

Pyott shrugged, then relented and said to Curtin: "And how have you been getting on?"

"We've had experts study the pictures of the lake, we've spoken to one of your university professors—"

"Gilchrist at King's," Pyott explained casually. "Geologist—actually knows the area."

"What does he say?"

"He pointed out, having seen the pictures, that we might have to do some tree-felling if we want to drag anything out of that lake. Brooke's detailed report on depth of water, slope of the shore, indicated the same thing."

"So—tree-felling. Easy to pick up visually by any overflight."

"I agree. It will have to be made to look—natural . . ."

"How many drops?" Aubrey asked.

"All our people—thirty to forty, including SBS—could go in the first drop, onto the lake. Any non-parachutists will have to be taken in by Lynx helicopter. Equipment can go in a second drop. A lot of what we need is at Bardufoss already our good fortune."

"When?" Aubrey burst out.

"If you get permission from the Finns—if all the pressure being exerted finally makes them bend—tonight."

"Then I must talk to Hanni Vitsula—!" Aubrey exclaimed, hurrying from a lingering glance at the plot table towards the telephone. As soon as he moved, Pyott and Curtin began murmuring rapidly as they leaned over the table. Aubrey dialed the Queen Anne's Gate number, then requested Shelley's extension, having satisfactorily and impatiently identified himself.

"Peter—get me Helsinki at once . . . what? No, nothing. I see—yes, Peter, I realize the importance of the matter, and yes, it does worry me—however, will you please get Director Vitsula on the telephone!" Aubrey realized that Pyott and Curtin were watching him. He could see the model of the Firefox on the table between them, as if they had moved apart solely to reveal it. For a moment, his eyesight became unfocused, the model seemed almost to dissolve as he thought of Gant. The telephone connection clicked and stuttered.

"Kenneth?" he heard Vitsula say at a great distance.

"Yes, Hanni—can you hear me?" It was a ridiculous remark, clashing absurdly with the colored tapes, with a loaded Hercules transport aircraft and a giant Sikorsky helicopter flying several hundreds of miles north.

"Perfectly, Kenneth—you caught me as I was about to call you."

"You have news?" Pyott and Curtin had stopped murmuring. Both of them were staring in his direction. "Good news, I hope."

"All communications are to be between the two of us."

"I understand—our people have the same idea."

"Good. Then I can tell you that you have—you would call it, I think, a qualified yes."

"Qualified? How?"

"There is a strict time limit."

"We feel we need a minimum of four days—"

"Then I am sorry, but you do not have it. Forty-eight hours is the offer I am authorized to make. No negotiations."

"Forty-eight hours? Impossible—!"

"Nevertheless, that is the offer. After that, Finnish units will move into the area, seal it off, and inform the Soviet Union of the precise location of their aircraft. I think my government sees some political advantages in this course of action . . ."

"It's still impossible, Hanni," Aubrey almost pleaded.

"It is a fact, however. Perhaps you will consider it more carefully . . . ?"

"Forty-eight hours—from when?"

"The clock is already running. Noon today—GMT, of course. It is already less than forty-eight, Kenneth."

They had not hit him again. He had not been kicked. He had lain there for almost a minute, staring at the drying white rime of dampness around the toes of Priabin's boots until the young colonel had helped him to his feet. Vladimirov had stared through the net curtains, out of the tall windows down towards the square for a long time. Then Andropov had ordered a map to be brought in. A secretary spread it on the surface of the large, ornate desk, and then retired. Gant, reseated on a more substantial chair, waited. The broken, delicate French chair had been removed from the room.

Andropov rose and spoke briefly to Vladimirov at the window—the general sucked his bruised knuckles while the Chairman talked—and then sat down once more. Slowly, Vladimirov turned from the window. Light fell on his profile for an instant, and Gant recognized that the man was in no way calmed or mollified. He wondered whether he was the most dangerous, or merely the most obvious, enemy in the room.

"Major Gant," Andropov began, crooking his finger at the American, "there would appear to be some discrepancies in your account—would you show us, please, on this map?"

Gant got up slowly and moved to the desk. The map was a large-scale projection of northern Finland and Norway, and the Kola Peninsula area of the Soviet Union. It was weighted down where it had been unrolled by a gold inkstand and a large paperweight that might have been jade.

"General Vladimirov," Andropov commanded quietly. "You wish to ask the Major some questions?"

"Yes," Vladimirov replied tensely. He remained on the opposite side of the desk from Gant. His long forefinger tapped over the map like a blind man's stick, probing and uncertain. Gant saw only the lake for a moment, then refocused. "Where was the Mig-25 destroyed?"

Gant hesitated, counting the seconds as he had begun to do in the long silence after Priabin had helped him to his feet. Each second of silence was valuable; he had no idea why. It simply postponed . . .

"There, as far as I can remember," he said at last.

Vladimirov's finger tapped the map. "Quite so. Correct. This is the closed valley you described—there is wreckage at this point, here . . ." Gant nodded. Vladimirov did not continue. His finger merely continued to tap at the indicated point on the map. Gant looked up into his face. His eyes gleamed. The general was barely in control of his emotions, but Gant saw clearly the lucid, suspicious intelligence of the man. He might be the most obvious enemy in the room— perhaps he was also the most intelligent? Certainly, he was the most expert . . .

"So?" Gant said in a surly tone. The general's lips twitched. "Wreckage? I told you that."

"Strangely, though, our reconnaissance photographs— which have been examined by experts—indicate no signs of wreckage from the Mig-31. How would you account for that, Major?"

Think, think—

"Uh—it's got to be around there somewhere . . ." In control of his features, he straightened and looked at Vladimirov. "I hit the button, the airplane was on fire, I parted company from the seat, I saw the airplane explode—how far away it was by that time I don't know."

"And you landed—?"

"Less than a mile from the Mig-25's wreckage, I guess . . ."

"So you consider that a radius of—oh, what, ten miles? A radius of ten miles around that point would contain the wreckage of the Mig-31?"

"Can't be more than that. It was a couple of seconds, maybe ten—speed was down, and I saw the explosion . . ." He nodded, inwardly envisaging that moment of suspension as the burning Phantom raced away from him and he turned over and over before parting company with the ejector seat— then the Phantom had exploded, a bright orange ball of flame . . . Yes, that was it. Hold onto that. With luck, the reconnaissance photographs were of too narrow a strip. Time, time—

"I see," Vladimirov murmured, fingering his top lip, making little hollow plopping sounds as he tapped it against his teeth. Then he bent to Andropov's intercom, and snapped: "Bring in the exhibit, please."

One of Andropov's bodyguards from the outer office

dragged something that looked like a rucksack into the room, then left as Andropov's wave dismissed them. Gant stared at Andropov, who was smiling. Then he looked into Vladimirov's face. The general's mouth was working, as if he were chewing at something indigestible and cold. Finally, Gant looked back towards the pack. Priabin bent to pick it up. His smile was almost radiant. He brought it to the desk and dropped it at Gant's feet.

"Your parachute, I imagine?" Andropov remarked.

"No—!"

"There are not too many of these lying casually unused in the snow of Finnish Lapland. In fact, I should be surprised if there were *any* others . . . A pity. I believed your story— except that I knew about this, of course."

Gant leaned on the desk. "That's not my chute, man! The airplane blew up just after I ejected. I buried my chute near the landing point. Where did you find this?"

"Exactly where you had buried it. Not far, in fact, from the village where you borrowed those clothes—which smell of Lapp, I must observe. Dung, grease and sweat . . ."

"*It's not my chute!*" Gant shouted.

"It is, Gant," Vladimirov snapped. "You landed that aircraft somewhere—where was it? Where *is* it?"

"No—"

Andropov pressed the buzzer on his intercom. Immediately, two of his personal bodyguards, torsoes large and muscled beneath their suits, stepped into the room. Gant watched them, tensing himself, counting the last futile seconds. Now he knew why he had been counting. It was a record of the time before *this* began, before the pain.

His fists clenched. Priabin's hand was at his holster. The two large men moved swiftly, lightly towards him, almost as if they floated over the carpet. They were close—he tensed—

Stomach, jaw, back, head, legs, side . . .

As he fell, they punched then kicked. Perhaps a dozen blows were struck before he lay stretched on the floor, each a separate, new, agonizing pain. It was an assault. Frighteningly fast, terrifyingly damaging. He felt paralyzed, unable to move, hardly able to breathe and groan.

Then he was dragged to his feet. His breath disappeared again. He was doubled over in their grasp. Their holds on his forearms and elbows were separate, distinct, new pains. Head hanging, he looked up at Andropov's smiling face. A white handkerchief was held over his mouth and nose, as if they intended suffocating him. But it was loose. It was simply to prevent blood falling on the carpet, the desk.

"He does know, Vladimirov?" he heard the Chairman of the KGB ask quietly.

Vladimirov seemed disappointed that the beating had stopped. "Oh, yes, he knows," he replied. "He knows precisely. He's the only one who does."

"Very well—this must be done quickly—" Gant felt his stomach heave, his body struggle inside the chain mail of the spreading, burning pain. Andropov pressed his intercom, and snapped: "Tell the Unit to prepare for an important arrival." Then he looked at Gant. There was distaste, probably at the blood staining the white handkerchief. He nodded dismissively. "Take him to the Unit. Tell them to prepare him for interrogation—within the hour!"

Gant was swung around, dragged towards the door. As he passed the young colonel, Priabin was smiling a sad, wise, confident smile. You'll tell, the smile and the eyes announced. Bad luck, but you'll tell . . .

"Kenneth, it's impossible!" Forty-eight hours is a strict, complete, *total* impossibility. Please take my word for it." Pyott shook his head sadly.

"But, if we leave tonight . . . ?" Aubrey persisted.

Again, Pyott shook his head. "I'm afraid no. *We* could be in position by tomorrow. But, the Sikorsky would not be there and half our supplies would not be there. That would leave us less than twenty-four hours to lift the airframe and get it over the border!"

"Giles, don't be stubborn—"

"You are the one who is being stubborn, Kenneth, for Heaven's sake—! I lose all patience with you. The discussion is *closed*. It cannot be done in the time available. We must decline the Finnish offer."

"It's there—intact. The prize is still there—"

"Unfortunately," Pyott replied with freezing irony, "we have been scratched from the race."

"Damn you, Giles—" Aubrey breathed, looking around at Curtin and then Buckholz for support. The argument had been in progress for almost an hour. They had skirted the plot table, paced beside it, leaned upon it, as if it were the dock, the judge's seat, the gallery of a court. And ended where they had begun, the Americans siding with Pyott and Aubrey more and more exasperated.

"I'm sorry you feel like that, Kenneth, but—damn your insufferable self-esteem, your pride. *That's* what is at the root of the matter—*your* success or failure . . ." Aubrey's face was white with rage, with admission. Pyott dropped his gaze and murmured an apology.

Buckholz looked at his watch. Curtin coughed, shuffled his feet, glancing at the plot table where symbols and counters, even torn slips of paper with folded bases to make them stand like cardboard soldiers, indicated their state of readiness. Outside, on the tarmac, the Hercules transport stood awaiting them. It was being loaded with supplies flown in from specialist RAF and army units. Aubrey had been up to see it once; he was gloating when he descended again to the soured atmosphere of the Ops Room.

Buckholz and Curtin waited. Pyott glanced at the plot table. Nothing more than a box of child's toys, stirring memories but of no use to the adult.

Aubrey hurried to the telephone the moment it began to ring. He snatched up the receiver.

"Yes?" he demanded breathlessly. "Peter—what is it? What—you're certain of it . . . followed the car, saw it drive in . . . no, there can't be any doubt—yes, Peter, thank you." He put down the receiver with great and pointless deliberation. There was, he knew, nothing to consider or think about— nothing to delay his agreement with Pyott that the operation was impossible . . . more impossible now than stealing the aircraft had ever been. He studied each of them in turn.

"Well?" Pyott demanded.

"Well? Well?" Aubrey snapped. "Gant has been transferred to the KGB Unit out on the Mira Prospekt—" He waited for their reaction. He could see that they sensed his depression, but the name meant little or nothing to them. "It is a unit operated for the KGB by the Serbsky Institute. They are going to interrogate Gant under drugs, gentlemen—I'm afraid we do not have forty-eight hours, after all . . . we probably do not have twenty-four, perhaps not even twelve . . ." He sighed, then added: "Gant will not be able to help himself. He will tell them *everything!*"

PART TWO
THE AGENT

   This is most strange,
That she whom even now was your best object,
. . . . should in this trice of time
Commit a thing so monstrous to dismantle
So many folds of favor. Sure her offense
Must be of such unnatural degree
That monsters it; or your fore-vouched affection
Fall into taint.

   —*King Lear*, I:1

6 / **ECHOES IN A TUNNEL**

The dream required the presence of his father. His father had to be made to walk along the Mira Prospekt and be seen from the vantage point of a passing black car. If he could make his father walk in a northerly direction, if he could slow down the moving car to a curbside crawl, if, if, if . . .

It was important to remember the Mira Prospekt. Important, too, to remember the room in the moments before the needle, the pause, the unconsciousness. White, clinical, smelling faintly of antiseptic, rubber, ether, furnished with an operating table and hard chairs. Most important to remember the faces . . .

Vlad—i—mir—ov—

The Soviet general looked like his father now, but Gant remembered who he was. White coats—doctors . . . Guards, a nurse, others he did not know. He tried to see his father's face, but was forced to allow the shirtsleeved, shambling figure to wear Vladimirov's features. However, he made him move and glance from side to side like his father. The imaginary car slowed, sliding along the curb, and Gant peered at the passing faces as they kept pace with his father's intoxicated, shiftless, shameful progress. Nurse, doctor with the needle, other doctor, guard, man in suit—who was he?—Andropov, Priabin—no, no—!

Pavel, Baranovich, Semelovsky, Kreshin, Fenton—his face like red-dyed dough—other faces . . . Gant concentrated. He could see, ahead of them and farther along the Mira Prospekt, against the snow-laden clouds, the huge cosmonaut's monument of a rocket stop its narrowing trail of golden fire. His father was an insect-figure moving towards it, then the car turned off the road, moving at a snail's pace behind the shambling, despicable gait he knew so well. His father was heading through tall iron gates towards the front entrance of a large house hidden from the busy road by tall, thick, dark hedges.

It looked like the house of a dream, but it was real. He recollected the steps, the door opening—nurse's uniform, guards' uniforms—and two flights of marble staircase. His father had disappeared into one of the ground floor rooms, he thought. It did not matter. Each time he retraced his journey, his father reappeared to hold the memories together.

It was important to remember the journey. To remember the black limousine, the pressure of the two bodyguards' frames on either side of him; to remember the Mira Prospekt and to remember the house, the steps, the door, the marble staircase, the columns and doorways and ornamental urns and pots, the old furniture, the white room and its smells, the doctors, guards, Vladimirov. Vital to remember the hard chair, the straps about his wrists and ankles, the needle . . . held up, spurt of colorless fluid, hovering, moving closer, skin pinched up, needle inserted . . .

In his dream, he was sweating profusely with the effort of memory—but he had done it! He had remembered it all while the dream still contained him . . .

Remembered everything, everything that informed him that he was under interrogation, that he was drugged and prepared—probably sodium pentothal followed by Benzedrine, or some other two drugs in harness. He was only dreaming now while they waited for the first drug to take effect, he was certain of it . . . then the stimulant would jolt him into wakefulness, dreamy and slow or hyperactive he did not know, but when it happened the questions would begin—

And he had remembered everything! He knew where he was, he knew why he was there. He knew they would ask him questions about—about . . . ?

Gant panicked in his dream, felt himself chilled and burned by his fear. He could not remember *why* he was there!

Don't, he told himself, don't . . . *I have to* . . . don't, secret, don't . . .

He had remembered everything—he had remembered enough.

Pinprick—?

His skin crawled. Pinprick? He was instantly wary . . . something else—quickly, something else, quickly . . . just before the needle, as he looked down at the needle, as his skin was pinched into a little hillock and the needle went in, something else . . . ?

Watch, watch *watch*—

They hadn't taken off his watch, he had been staring at it as his eyes snapped shut and he was suddenly in darkness. He had told himself to remember the time, to look when he awoke again. Time—

It was getting light. Murmur of voices that was more than the dream-traffic on the Mira Prospekt. People constructing sentences, discussing, arguing . . . waiting for him to awaken.

Light—his head was lifted, eyelid plucked at, a blurred form moved away, and a fuzzy light was revealed which did not seem to hurt his eyes.

Pinprick again. A few moments, and he was able to see more clearly. Doctors, nurses, uniforms. White room. It's starting, he told himself with great difficulty. He seemed to be trapped in a heavy, translucent oil, his thoughts moving with extreme difficulty. It wasn't like the dream—he had swum easily through the dream, raced with it. Now, his body—he was aware of it quite clearly—was laden, his eyes focused slowly and he could almost feel them moving in his head as he transferred his gaze from face to face. He saw a doctor nod, slowed down like a failing movie reel.

He remembered the watch. Focused with exaggerated slowness. Read the time. It did not seem meaningful. Thirty minutes had passed. It did not seem to matter. Father on the street outside, a long gallery on the second floor lined by tall ornamental urns . . . It did not matter. None of it mattered. He was trapped in his body which was trapped in the translucent oil. He watched the faces around his chair, as dull and unmoving as a fish on the watery side of an aquarium's tank. He stared out at the human faces, unthinking.

Vladimirov watched Gant carefully. The doctor assured him that the man was prepared. He could be interrogated immediately. He was now capable of suggestion. Vladimirov savored the helplessness of the American strapped in the chair, which was itself bolted to the floor of the clinical room. More than the bruising on the face, and the swollen lip he had himself inflicted even before the bodyguards had operated upon the American, he enjoyed the man's present helplessness. It satisfied his craving for superiority, his desire for the restoration of his self-esteem. This—*thing* in the chair, drugged and animal-like, could never have succeeded against him. Now, indeed, the thing in the chair was about to tell them everything it knew—

Where he had hidden the Mig-31. After that—his life preserved only for the length of time required to locate the aircraft—he would be disposed of together with the other rubbish that accumulated in such a place; in a Forensic Psychiatry Unit of the KGB.

He turned to the plainclothed KGB officer who had been assigned by Andropov. He and his two fellow-officers were experts in interrogation by the use of drugs. Most of their work was performed at this Unit on the Mira Prospekt. The man probably had a research degree in psychiatric medicine or clinical psychology.

Vladimirov suppressed the contempt he felt for the tall, angular, harmless-seeming man next to him. The man is only doing what you wish of him. He smiled and turned to the tape deck that rested on a metal-legged table behind them. Wires trailed across the floor to speakers arranged on either side of Gant.

"These haven't been edited. I have only the flimsiest

acquaintance with them, Comrade General—" the interrogator complained.

"But you approve their use?" Vladimirov asked firmly. "Comrade Colonel Doctor," he added to emphasize the politeness and formality of their circumstances.

The interrogator nodded. "To begin with, yes," he replied. "But the man outside may be of more use. This form of induced regression often has no more than a limited application. We must use it to warm him up, perhaps, make him familiar with the area we want to investigate—but sooner or later, he must be more fully regressed, as himself, not someone else." The interrogator smiled. "He must be debriefed, and believe he is being debriefed." When Vladimirov did not return his pale-lipped smile, he rubbed a long-fingered hand through sparse sandy hair, and added: "We will retrieve what you have lost in your head, Comrade General. Don't worry about it." It was a stiff, formal insult; an assertion of authority, too. Vladimirov nodded thoughtfully by way of reply. The interrogator glanced at Gant, then nodded to one of his senior assistants, who switched on the tape deck. He watched the leader tape move between the reels, then said to Vladimirov: "He speaks Russian sufficiently well to understand this?"

Vladimirov glanced at Gant, as if to assure himself that the American was not eavesdropping, then nodded. "He does."

"Very well, then. Let us see what occurs."

Gant heard the static, the mechanized voices, the clicks and bleeps of communication; recognizing them, knowing them as well as he knew his own past. UHF communication between a pilot and his ground control. The sound seemed all around him, enveloping him as if he were wearing a headset, as if *he* were the pilot. He listened, his eyeballs moving slowly, rustily; unfocused. He absorbed the conversation, his awareness pricked and heated and engaged by the brief exchanges. His hands hung heavily at the ends of his wrists, and his body seemed a great way below him. His attention seemed like a little peak rising above dense jungle foliage which nothing could penetrate. He listened. The words enveloped him. He was back in the cockpit of the Firefox.

"I've got him—! . . . vapor trail, climbing through sixty thousand . . . must get into the tail cone to avoid his infrared . . ." Whose infrared—? "I'll have to slot in quickly behind him . . . climbing past me now . . . contrail still visible .

seventy thousand now, climbing up past me . . . come on, come on—please confirm orders . . ."

"Kill," Gant heard.

"Two missiles launched . . . he's seen them, the American's seen them, come on—he's got the nose up, he's into a climb, rolling to the right . . . missed . . . Bilyarsk control, I'm reporting both missiles failed to make contact . . ."

Gant listened. It was *him*, and yet he remembered what was being described . . . *his* violent evasive action . . . it was strange, inexplicable. It was in Russian, it was a Mig-31, yet not him. There was a pressure, almost too strong to resist, which suggested *he* was the pilot, the speaker . . . yet somehow he knew it was the test pilot he had killed, flying the second prototype Firefox. It enfolded him after that moment of lucidity. He was back in the cockpit.

"Missed him again . . . ! Wait, he's going into a spin, he's got himself caught in a spin . . . he's losing altitude, going down fast, falling like a leaf . . . I'm diving, right on his tail . . ." Gant heard his own breathing accelerate, become more violent, as if the white room—dimly seen—was hot and airless. His blood pumped wildly, he could hear his heart racing. He sweated. "I'm right on his tail—he can't pull out of the spin—he's going to fall straight into the sea, he can't do anything about it—!" Gant groaned, hearing the noise at a great distance. "Thirty thousand feet now, he's falling like a stone—he's dumped the undercarriage . . . wait, the nose-down's getting steeper, twenty thousand feet now . . . he's leveling out, he's got her back under control . . . I'm right on his tail . . ." Gant was groaning now, stirring his hands and legs against the straps, moving his head slowly, heavily back and forth like a wounded animal. He might have been protesting, repeating *No, no, no* over and over, but he could not be sure of that. He knew the end of the story, the climax. He knew what was going to happen to him as he followed the American down and leveled out behind him, the cold Arctic Ocean below them—he *knew*!

"Careful, careful . . . I'm on his tail . . . careful . . . he's doing nothing, he's given up . . . nothing—he's beaten and he knows it . . . I've *got*—" Gant was minutely, vividly alive to the change of tone, the terror that replaced excitement. He *knew* what would happen . . . he could *see* the other Firefox ahead of him, knew what the American was going to do, knew he hadn't given up . . . "Oh, *God*—!"

Gant, too, screamed out the words, then his head lolled forward as if he had lost consciousness. The tape ran on, hissing with static. Tretsov was dead. Vladimirov was watching Gant with a look almost of awe on his face. He shuddered at the identification of the American with the dead Tretsov. The manner in which the American had played Tretsov's role, acted as if he, too, were suddenly going to kill, then die—uncanny. Unnerving. Gant was nobody now, or anybody they cared to suggest. Perhaps he could believe himself anyone at all, anywhere they said . . . ?

"Mm," the interrogator said beside him. "Perhaps not quite the effect you wished for . . . but, from his file, I suggest the effect is not without merit."

"How?"

"He has his own nightmares—his delayed stress syndrome I think he will be sufficiently easy to convince that it was his own nightmare he experienced . . ." He smiled. "When I heard your tape, I projected we might make just such an impression on him . . ." One of his assistants nodded obsequiously as the interrogator glanced at him. "Illness," he continued, "shock. We can work on this now. Very well— bring him round again, to the same level of awareness, no lower . . . and bring in our mimic." He looked at Vladimirov. "I hope the voice is good enough. We have tapes of the Englishman, of course—innocuous material, mostly gathered at long range in outdoor situations . . . the imitation seems to me sufficient." He smiled again, studying the unconscious Gant and the white-coated doctor bending over him, pointing the needle down towards Gant's bared arm. "He'll probably accept the man whatever he sounds like . . ."

The light, the resolving faces and the familiar voice all came to Gant in the same moment. White room . . . He was sitting up—why had he expected to be lying down—? Yes, nurse's uniform, he was in hospital . . . nightmare? He listened to the voice; familiar—changed, somehow foreign-tinted, but familiar. He listened to Kenneth Aubrey as he spoke slowly and soothingly. His eyes concentrated on the only two figures he could see, a nurse and a doctor. They stood directly in front of him . . . Aubrey must be behind him as he murmured gently, confidentially in his ear. Nurse, doctor— where was he? What had happened to him? His body felt dull, heavy, but without pain. What had happened?

The voice explained.

"You're recuperating very quickly, very fully, Mitchell," Aubrey said soothingly. "We're all very pleased with you . . . but time presses us. You're the only one who can help us . . . time is pressing, you must try to remember . . ."

Remember?

There were things to remember, yes . . .

What?

Street, shambling figure, black car—

Who? Where?

Aubrey continued, frightening him, making him cling to the familiar voice. Crash, he thought. Crash? Dead. "You seem to have been suffering from some sort of localized amnesia, Mitchell. Even from delusions . . . You've been very ill, my boy. Very ill. But, you're getting better now. If only you could *remember*—if only you could tell us where the aircraft *is*!"

Street, shambling figure, f—ather . . . black car, gates, corridors, white room . . . *remember*—

"Do you remember, Mitchell?" Aubrey asked soothingly.

Gant felt his head nod, as distant a signal as another's head or hand might have made. "Yes," he heard himself reply, but the voice was thick with phlegm, strangely flat. "Yes . . ."

A murmur of voices, then, before Aubrey said: "You remember exactly what happened after you destroyed the second Mig-31—the second Firefox?" Aubrey's voice was silky, soothing, gentle. Gant nodded again. He remembered. There had been things to remember. These things—?

Street—blank—car—figure ahead—huge sculpture of a rocket's exhaust—street—blank—figure, catch up with the figure see his face—blank—house—steps—corridor—blank—watch—blank—watch—blank—

It was a series of pictures, but the cartridge of slides had been improperly loaded. There were gaps, frequent large gaps. Blank—car—blank . . . *remember* . . .

"What do you remember, Mitchell?" Aubrey asked once more. "After you destroyed the second Firefox, what happened then? We know that you destroyed the two Mig-25Fs— you remembered that much. Do you still remember?" Gant nodded. "Good. The first one you took out in the clouds, and the second one almost got you . . . but you survived and the aircraft survived . . . what did you do next? What did you do, Mitchell? Time is of the essence. We haven't much time if we're to prevent it falling into their hands . . . what did you do with it, Mitchell?" The voice insisted. Yet it soothed, too. It was almost hypnotic. There seemed to be a window behind the doctor and the nurse, through which Gant could see . . . what was it? London. Big Ben? Yes, Big Ben. There seemed to be a bright patch of color at the corner of his vision, perhaps flowers in a vase? He could see Big Ben—he was almost home—he was safe . . .

And Aubrey's voice went on, seductively soft, hypnotic, comforting.

"Where, Mitchell, where? Where did you land the aircraft? You can remember, Mitchell . . . try—please try to remember . . ."

"Ye—ess . . ." he breathed slowly, painfully.

"Good, Mitchell, good. You *can* remember!"

"Yes," he enunciated more clearly. He *was* feeling better. Whatever had happened to him, he was on the mend. His memory had come back. Aubrey would be delighted, they might yet rescue the airframe from the bottom of the lake—

Lake—

No!

"No!" his voice cried an instant after his mind. "No—!"

He was drowning and burning in the lake. His drug-confused memory had jolted awake against his utter terror of drowning. Wrapped in icy water, then in the same instant wrapped in burning fire—

His nightmare engulfed him.

"No—!"

Vladimirov stared at the interrogator, at the mimic bending near Gant, whose earpiece picked up every question suggested by the interrogator and the general, then he stared at the nurse, the doctor bending towards Gant, at Gant himself—

"What's happening?" he asked, then, more loudly: "What the hell's happening to him?"

Vladimirov found himself staring at the slide projected on one of the white walls, the one opposite Gant. A London scene, looking across the Thames towards the Palace of Westminster and Big Ben. Now that Gant was screaming, over and over, that single denying word, the illusion seemed pathetic, totally unreal. Like the flowers someone had placed against the wall. Who would be fooled by such things, even under drugs? Gant was evading him again, evading him—!

He shook off the angry, restraining hand of the senior interrogator and crossed the room. Gant's eyes were staring blankly, his mouth was open like that of a drowning man, but instead of precious air bubbles it was the one word *No!* which emerged, over and over again. Vladimirov looked up, confused.

"What is it?" he shouted. "What is it?"

The interrogator reached Vladimirov's side. The doctor was checking Gant's pulse, his pupil dilation, his respiration. When he had finished, he shrugged, murmuring an apology at the interrogator.

"Put him out."

"No—!" Vladimirov protested. He bent over Gant. "He *knows!* He was about to tell us . . ." The mimic had moved away, removed his earpiece; anxious not to be blamed. "*Do* something!"

"Put him out," the interrogator repeated. "Shut him up! We'll make another attempt later—" He turned to Vladimirov. "It is simply a matter of time. We have stumbled upon something that is interfering with the illusion. There's always a risk of tripping over something in a dark tunnel . . ."

The doctor injected Gant. After a moment, he stopped repeating his one word of protest. His head slumped forward, his body slackened.

"How long?" Vladimirov asked, biting his lower lip. "How long?"

"A few hours—this evening. We'll start from a different point. With more careful preparation. Think of it as mining for gold—only the last inches of rock lie between us and the richest seam in the world!" He smiled. "Next time, he'll tell us."

Dmitri Priabin shivered in his uniform greatcoat as he watched Anna's son playing soccer on the snow-covered grass of the Gorky Park of Culture and Rest. The bench on which he was seated was rimed with frost which sparkled in the orange sodium lights. Beneath the lights which lined the paths through the park, Maxim and his friends would play until it was fully dark, and then on into the night, if they were allowed. He felt indulgent, despite the cold, though he knew that when Anna arrived she would scold all of them, him most of all for allowing them to get cold and damp and tired. He smiled at the thought, and at the high, childish voices, the imitations of star players' protests and antics. He contented himself with occasional glances towards the gigantic stone porch and architrave that marked the main entrance to the park. Beyond it, traffic roared homewards on the Sadovaya Ring and along the Lenin Prospekt. Workers hurried through the park, one or two of them stopping for a moment to watch the boys' soccer game; stamping their cold feet, rubbing gloved hands before rushing on into the gathering dusk.

Maxim had new soccer shoes—Dynamo First-Class—which Priabin had purchased for the boy's birthday the previous week. The ball also belonged to Maxim. He watched as Anna's son dribbled past two friend-opponents and slid it inside the tall metal rod which marked one goalpost. Maxim pranced, hands in the air, after he had scored. Another boy protested at offside while the very diminutive goalkeeper picked himself out of the snow after his desperate, unavailing dive for the ball. Priabin clapped his gloved hands, laughing, then looked at his watch. Time to go—at least to begin to round them up.

He glanced towards the architrave and the Communist Party symbols carved upon it. Then, from beneath the curving weight of the stone porch, he saw Anna Borisovna Akhmerovna emerge, and he found his breath catching, as it almost always did when he unexpectedly caught sight of her; when it was no more than a few moments before she would be at his side. Hurriedly, with a great show of concern, he stood up and walked through the snow, waving his arms, collecting the teams. All the time, he was aware of her approach, half-amused, half eager, almost to the point of desperation. He still could not properly catch his breath. The boys crowded reluctantly, protestingly around his tall figure. He continued to wave his arms in shepherding gestures, turning eventually to where he knew she had stopped. Red-faced and puffing, he knew he could easily have appeared to be one of the schoolboys. He was taller and heavier, but closer to their age-group than he was to the woman who stood on the frosty path, arms folded, head slightly on one side, appraising the group of which he formed the centerpiece.

"I didn't realize the time . . . you're late, anyway," he protested. Maxim waved shyly, a gesture he could not prevent but which was muted out of deference to his friends and the rough masculinity of their recent activity.

"Who won?" she called.

"I—don't know," he laughed.

"Maxim's team—lucky swines!" one boy explained.

"No luck in it!" Maxim retorted.

Priabin walked towards Anna, feeling his cheeks glow. She was wearing a fur coat and hat and long black leather boots. Her fair hair escaped untidily from the hat. Her face was pale from the cold. Priabin could not bear not to touch her, but contented himself with a peck on her cold cheek and a murmured endearment. Her gloved hand touched the side of his face, briefly; his skin seemed to burn more heatedly afterwards.

"Come on—all of you," she ordered. "Collect your things. Change out of those wet shoes before you go anywhere! No, no, coats on first or you'll all catch pneumonia!"

The boys fought for places on the bench. Cold fingers fumbled and tugged at wet, icy bootlaces. Bodies that had wisps of steam about them in the freezing air struggled into overcoats and anoraks and thick jackets. The sons of civil servants, schoolteachers, one of them even the son of a Soviet film star. Boys from the same expensive block of apartments as Maxim. From the place where he lived with Anna—

"Come on," he said. "Hot dogs and hamburgers all round— but only if you're quick!" He turned to Anna. "One good thing the Olympics did, from their point of view. We now have Muscovite hot-dog stands . . ." He sniffed the air loudly. "I can smell the onions from here!" he exclaimed. The boys hurried into their shoes and boots and colored wellingtons. Knitted caps and scarves, and they were finally ready. Priabin handed Maxim a crumpled heap of ruble notes, and nodded towards the stone porch and the Lenin Prospekt beyond. "Your treat," he said. "And none of you stray away from the stand before we get there!"

Noisily, the party of soccer players and would-be diners ran off. Soccer shoes, trailed carelessly, clattered on the frosty path as they ran. The ball bobbed between them before it was retrieved.

"He's not going to take any chances with that ball!" Priabin laughed.

"Like his mother," Anna replied, slipping her arm into that of Priabin. "He can recognize a good thing when he sees it!"

"Bless you," Priabin said awkwardly, blushing. He patted

her hand. She leaned her face against the shoulder of his greatcoat, then said mischievously:

"Those new shoulder-boards are very hard."

He burst into laughter. The noise of the traffic was louder as they walked towards the archway. Away to their left, across the darkening park, the double line of lights along the banks of the river were fuzzy. An icy mist hung above the Moskva. Priabin shivered. He had remembered their argument the previous evening.

As if she read his thoughts, Anna murmured: "I'm sorry about last night—"

"It doesn't matter."

"I'm still glad about that damned aircraft—I'm still glad it's been stolen, it's *gone*—!" she added vehemently, as if making an effort to fully recapture her emotions of the previous night; rekindling their argument.

"I know," he soothed.

"When I think—!" she burst out afresh, but he patted her hand, then grabbed her closer to him.

"I *know* it," he murmured. "I know it."

He detested the vehemence of her blind, unreasoning hatred of the Mig-31 project. It was an intellectual hatred, the worst kind. He had loathed the previous evening and the argument that had seemed to leap out of the empty wine bottle like a djinn. He had been totally unprepared for it. He had informed her of the death of Baranovich at Bilyarsk almost casually, his head light with wine and the meal she had cooked to celebrate his promotion. He had been high on drink, and on his colonelcy. Blind. He hadn't seen the argument coming, hadn't watched her closely enough. Baranovich had been the trigger. As he held her now, he could hear her yelling at him across the dining table.

"*Baranovich is dead?*" she had asked. "*You pass me the information like a bundle of old clothes? Your project—your damnable bloody project has killed Baranovich? His mind was—priceless! And that filthy project killed him!*"

There was much more of it. Priabin crushed Anna's body to him to prevent the workings of memory, feeling her slightness beneath the heavy fur coat. She struggled away from him.

"What is it?" she asked, studying him intently.

He shook his head. "Nothing—nothing now . . ." He could hardly bear to quarrel with her. It seemed like an absence from her each time he did. He was not a jealous man. Not jealous, but possessive. He had to possess her, and things had to be right, always right, between them. No darkness, no cloudy days.

Yet Baranovich's death was a cloud, a darkness, even though he tried to ignore it.

"Come on, then. The boys will be getting cold—in spite of their hot dogs!" She reached for his hand, like an elder sister, and pulled him towards the arch and the traffic beyond. He matched his step to hers. The flushed lightness of his mood had disappeared, and he blamed Baranovich, the dead Jew. Anna had met him no more than three or four times. He was not a friend, not even a real acquaintance. Instead, he had become some kind of hero to her; even a symbol.

He shook his head, but the train of thought persisted. It was almost six years earlier, from Anna's account, that her role with the Secretariat of the Ministry of Health had brought her into contact with a Jewish scientist. He had developed a prototype wheelchair for the totally disabled, which used thought guidance via microelectronics for its motive power and ability to maneuver. Anna had taken up the project with an enthusiasm amounting to missionary zeal. After eighteen months, the project had been scrapped.

Correction, he admitted to himself. He could hear the group of boys around the hot-dog stand now, above the rumble of the traffic. The smell of the onions was heavy, almost nauseating. Correction. The Ministry of Defense had acquired the project for its anticipated military applications; acquired Baranovich, too. The design for the wheelchair which was never built found its way eventually into the Mig-31 as a thought-guided weapons system.

Anna had never forgiven them for that, for creating a means of more efficient destruction out of the prototype for a wheelchair.

Them—?

Everyone. The military, the civil service, the Politburo— even himself. She had never forgiven anyone.

"Come on, come on," he said with forced enthusiasm as the boys gathered around him, full mouths grinning, feet shuffling, the lights of passing cars playing over the group. The hot-dog seller stamped and rubbed his hands. Onion breath smoked from the stand. "Where's your car?" he asked Anna. She gestured down the Lenin Prospekt. "See you at the apartment, then," he said. "Take as many as you can . . . the rest of us will get the metro."

She nodded, and smiled encouragingly. He knew his face was dark with memory. He nodded. "O.K.—all those for the metro, follow me!" He marched off pompously, making Anna laugh. The boys, except for Maxim and the film star's son, followed in his wake, giggling.

Priabin waved to her without turning round. He envisaged her clearly. Thirty-eight, small-faced, assured, fashionable, ambitious. A senior assistant secretary to the Secretary to the Ministry of Health; a prominent and successful civil servant. Her income was greater than his.

As they clattered down the steps into the Park Kultury metro station, he thought that last night he had begun to understand her. He started fishing for the fare money in his trouser pockets, hitching up the skirts of his greatcoat to do so, his gloves clamped between his teeth. Yes, he had at last begun to understand.

It was that damned project. It had always been that damned Bilyarsk project. She had wanted revenge for what they had done, for never developing and mass-producing that bloody wheelchair.

So, she had begun to work for the Americans . . .

He gripped a handful of change and small denomination notes and heaved them out of his pocket.

She had begun to work for the Americans . . .

"We have one chance—just one," Aubrey said with heavy emphasis. "If we can get in before this approaching front brings winter's last fling with it—" He tapped the projected satellite photograph with a pointer "—then perhaps we can beat the Russians *and* the Finns to the Firefox." Pyott, who was operating the slide projector, flicked backwards and forwards through the satellite pictures as soon as Aubrey paused. They fluttered grey and white on the old man's face as he stood in front of the screen, pointer still raised. Finally, Pyott switched off the projector. Buckholz put on the Ops Room lights. "Well?" Aubrey asked. "Well, Giles?"

Pyott shook his head and fiddled with his moustache. "This front is producing heavy snow at the moment, and it's bringing a lot more behind it—heavy snow, high winds, even the possibility of electrical storms. As you so neatly put it,

Kenneth, it's winter's last fling over northern Europe and Scandinavia—I don't know. I really don't know."

"It won't take us forty-eight hours to arrive on the site, Giles—"

"I realize that, Kenneth. But, the Skyhook's already making very slow time . we shall be very, very lucky if it gets there at all."

"The winches we have are capable of moving something as heavy as the Firefox. She'll have to be winched out of the lake."

"And then what do you do with her?"

"The Skyhook *will* arrive."

"And if it doesn't?"

"Then we must salvage what we can and destroy the rest!" Aubrey turned his back on Pyott and crossed to the plot table. Curtin, seated on a folding chair, watched him in silence. Buckholz appeared genuinely distressed and firmly in a dilemma. Aubrey glared at the black model of the Mig-31, at the map of Finland and northern Norway, at the colored tapes and symbols.

He turned on his three companions. "Come on," he said more pleasantly, "decide. The Finns don't want the aircraft on their territory. If we removed it before the Russians found out, they'd be delighted with us! Their strong language is bluff—*mostly* bluff. We have placed them in an awkward spot. In twenty-four hours, perhaps less, no aircraft will be able to fly in that area, there will be no aerial reconnaissance to interrupt us. There will be no detachment of Finnish troops flown in, either. We would be on our own. *We*—at least our forward detachments—are little more than sixty miles from the lake. We're *nearer* than anyone else! One full Hercules transport could drop all our requirements and our people *at* the spot!"

Aubrey paused. He felt like an orator who had come from the wings towards the podium and discovered an extremely thin, utterly disgruntled audience. Buckholz, instead of looking in his direction, seemed to be looking to Pyott for an answer. Curtin was doing no more than acting out his subordinate rank. Pyott was brushing his moustache as vigorously as if attempting to remove a stain from his features.

"I—" Buckholz began, still not looking at Aubrey. "My government wants this thing cleared up—I don't mind telling you, gentlemen, Washington is becoming just a little impatient . . ." Aubrey watched Buckholz's face. The Deputy Director of the CIA had said nothing of his last lengthy telephone conversation with Langley. This, apparently, was the burden of it. "I've argued the weather, the logistics, the lack of a fallback operation, the political dangers and pitfalls . . the White House still wants action . . ." Now, he turned directly to Aubrey, and added: "I have my orders, Kenneth. I don't like them, but I have to try to carry them out. I don't have any answers, but I sure *want* some!" It was evident that Buckholz had been browbeaten by Washington. He had been ordered to mount some kind of recovery operation, however much he rejected any such idea. Buckholz shrugged. "It has to be done—something has to be done."

"What about Mitchell Gant, Mr. Aubrey?" Curtin asked sharply.

Aubrey glared at him. Then he transferred his gaze to Pyott. "There is the *absolute* time-limit, Giles," he said. "Gant will be unable to hold out for very long against drugs—my God, they could persuade him he was being debriefed by Charles and he'd be likely to believe it! So—the Russians, who will also be watching the weather, will move soon. Or—they will wait until the weather clears. It's going to be coming from their direction—they'll have it sooner than we will—it might just give us enough time, it might just persuade them to wait—" He cleared his throat of its intended, husky sincerity. "I think it is worth the chance. Don't you?"

Pyott looked up then. His face was clouded by doubts, by a hundred considerations. His features were maplike. He stared at his knuckles as they whitened on the edge of the plot table.

"I agree—that the weather is swinging around the low and moving west across Russia—" he said slowly and at last. "I agree, too, that they will be hampered, even grounded, before we are. I accept that they may, just *may*, wait until it clears before they take their first look . . . *But*—"

Aubrey harried his opponent. "We can withdraw, melt back into the landscape, if we find the Russians there . . . if we find them arriving *while* we're there, we can do the same . . ." Again, he cleared his throat. "I don't need to remind you that possession of the intact airframe by the Soviet Union—despite the deaths of Baranovich and the others at Bilyarsk—will mean that the Firefox project continues. We shall be where we were last year, before we ever thought of this—this *escapade!*" Aubrey paused for effect. Pyott's face expressed vivid uncertainty. JIC and the Cabinet Office had left the decision, the final decision, to Aubrey and Pyott. "Our people are waiting to embark. Waterford and his SBS people are gathered at Kirkenes . . ." Aubrey soothed. "We are only *hours* away—"

"And the Russians may be only minutes away!" Pyott snapped.

"Nothing is happening at the moment," Aubrey countered.

"As you say," Pyott replied with heavy irony. "At the *moment*, nothing is happening."

"Giles!" Aubrey exclaimed. "Giles, for God's sake, *commit!* This aircraft is still the threat it was yesterday and last year. It is invisible to radar, its electronic systems are a generation ahead of ours, it flies twice as fast as our fastest fighter! It is a *threat!* Commit, Giles—one way or the other, *commit.*"

In the heavy ensuing silence, Buckholz cleared his throat. Curtin's chair scraped on the floor as he shifted his weight. Pyott stared at his knuckles. Aubrey's left hand made futile, uncertain sweeps over the plot table.

Then Pyott looked up. "Very well—*very well.* Talk to Hanni Vitsula in Helsinki. Tell him we're on our way!"

"Giles!" Aubrey exclaimed with the excitement of a child. "Giles—well done!"

"Kenneth!" Giles Pyott replied in an offended tone. "It is not a matter for congratulation. Damn your scheme and damn that airplane!" He stretched his arms wide. "I hope to God we never find out whether or not it holds the balance of terror—and I hope to God we don't find out it's a *dud!*"

"You know as well as I do—"

"Don't lecture me! I know what that anti-radar system would do if it were used on a Cruise missile or an ICBM or a MIRV—I *know* where thought-guided weaponry could take the Russians in five years or less . . . I've *heard* your arguments, I've heard the Pentagon on the subject—I don't need to be reminded!"

"Don't be such a sore loser, Giles," Buckholz grumbled.

Pyott turned to the American. "I sometimes think the profession of arms is as morally delectable as the oldest profession itself," he announced freezingly.

"Don't despise we night-soil men, Giles," Aubrey soothed. "Better this way—"

Pyott banged the plot table with his fist. "Let's get on

with it, shall we? Charles—you'll be on-site, but Waterford has *military* command—you understand?" Buckholz nodded. "I must stay here—"

"And *I* shall set up HQ in Kirkenes!" Aubrey announced brightly. "Shall we go?"

He seemed to be lying down. He concluded, very slowly, that he must be in bed. The ceiling was chalk-white. It reminded him of other familiar ceilings. People were whispering out of his sight, like mice in a corner of the room . . . it had to be a room, there was a white ceiling and the beginnings of white walls. His head felt very heavy. He could not be bothered to move it to check. There was the ether smell—it was a hospital room. A bedside light shone in his peripheral vision, and cast a glow on the ceiling. It must be night.

Whispering—?

Whispering in English, he thought Why did that matter? What else would they talk in . . . ?

He had once known the answer to that question, had known the alternative, strange, indecipherable language they might have spoken . . . but not in a hospital room.

In a bamboo cage—

They poked him with long sticks like goads. Then the little girl had burned, dissolved in napalm fire . . .

He shuddered and groaned. He remembered. Remembered, too, why he was in hospital. His body remembered resentment, even hatred, and he tried to move. His arms were restrained. Or too tired and heavy to lift.

A face appeared above him, floating below the ceiling. A starched cap on dark hair. A nurse. She examined his eyes—a man did, too—and there was more murmuring . . .

He tried to listen. It seemed to concern him. American—? His mind formed the word very slowly, as if he were in class, learning to spell a new and difficult word. American . . .

A strong face floated above him. It wobbled—no, someone was shaking his head. He heard the American voice again as soon as the head whisked out of sight.

"Poor bastard . . . what the hell did he go through, Aubrey?" He heard the words quite distinctly now, though the effort of eavesdropping made him sweat. "My God, those injuries—!"

Injuries? Heavy unmoving arms, the answer came back.

Legs he could not feel . . . yes, they prickled with sweat, but he could not move them. He did not try to move his head. Perhaps it did not move. He was stretched out—

He listened, terrified. "The doctors are doing their best for him," the English voice replied. "We have the best surgeons for him . . ."

"And?"

"Who can say? He may walk again—"

Gant gagged on self-pity. It enveloped him, filled his mouth as though he were drowning.

"And he never told them anything . . . not a damn word. Even when they started to break him to pieces, he never told them a damn thing!"

"He's a very brave man," Aubrey replied. Aubrey—yes, it was Aubrey . . . the self-pity welled in his eyes, bubbled in his throat as soon as he opened his mouth. He was drowning in it; only the unwilled and even unwanted pride kept him afloat, like a life jacket.

His eyes were wet. The ceiling was pale and unclear, the glow of the lamp fuzzy, like a light shining down through deep, clear water. The voices appeared to have stopped, as if they wished him to hear no more. Aubrey and an American . . .

He had been asleep. Or they had given him something. Chillingly, he remembered himself screaming. It was the nightmare. The little girl erupting in flame, her form dissolving. Yes, that was it. Yet he remembered water, too, as his mind tried to understand what he had overheard. He remembered water, and drowning—? It was hard to think of it, difficult to concentrate, but he made the effort because he could not bear to allow any other thoughts to return. Deep water, dark . . . fire down there, too—? Water, drowning, his left hand trapped, but his right hand moving . . .

A shape retreating into the dark water, like a huge fish. Black. Airframe . . .

He shouted, then. Just once.

"No—!"

Two faces hovered over him. He did not recognize them. The nurse mopped his forehead, soothed him with clucking noises. He was injured, yes . . .

No—

Yes . . .

Someone was speaking now. To him.

Explaining—

He listened avidly and in terror. "You ejected, Mitchell." It was the American voice. "You ejected from the Mig-31 when it was on fire . . . at least, that's what we conclude from your—your burns . . ." He gasped and swallowed. Burns—? "It exploded in midair. You say you saw that, even in the pain you must have been in . . . It exploded—"

He moved his head very slowly, wondering whether they would realize it was a negative sign. He did not trust himself to speak. His throat and mouth were full of water which he could not swallow. His father would hit him if he spat in the house . . .

No one seemed to have noticed. The American voice continued.

"On the ball to the last . . ." He must have been addressing Aubrey again. Gant strained to hear, holding his breath. "They must have found him unconscious and airlifted him direct to Moscow." Gant tried to remember. He could not remember the ejection from the aircraft or the explosion. Then he could. But that was—was Vietnam, where the cage and the little girl had been . . . he shook his head very slowly. Someone quickly held his face, checked his eyes, and vanished. The voice continued. "And in that condition, they beat up on him until he couldn't take any more. Christ, those people over there—!"

Gant drifted. His father was walking towards a huge golden spire that narrowed towards the top, like the exhaust of a rocket leaving its launch platform. Gant could not explain the fleeting image. He let himself drift. It was better than listening. It was better than the creeping sensations of pain that possessed him in legs and trunk and head and arms—

Pinprick.

He stopped drifting almost at once and the American voice seemed louder. He did not dare to turn his head. His father disappeared behind a tall dark hedge; vanished.

"We'd better ask him—"

"We must be certain." That was Aubrey. "Yes, we must make certain."

"The problem is—the *real* problem," the American said, "is to make him believe he's safe now. He can stop being brave and silent."

"I agree."

A face overhead. The strong, sandy-haired man. Smiling.

The collar tabs of a uniform, medal ribbons. Shoulder boards. USAF. An Air Force General. Blue dress uniform. Comforting. He opened his mouth. A bubbling noise came out. He clenched it shut again. The general smiled at him. The American general smiled.

"Mitch—Major Gant . . . Mitch—listen to me, boy. You're safe now. We're going to make you well again. I promise you that. We just need to know one thing—you're certain the aircraft exploded? You are certain? They can't get their hands on it again—can they?" Gant realized the bed near his shoulder was being patted, slowly and gently; reassuringly. "We need to be sure of that."

"We're not tiring him too much, are we, doctor—in his condition?" That was Aubrey, speaking somewhere out of sight.

"Quiet, Aubrey," the general said, then looked back at Gant. "Now, Mitch, how much can you remember? Are you *certain* the Firefox exploded?"

Gant swallowed. He listened. Aubrey was talking, still talking, to the doctor. Concern—? A tongue clicking like a grasshopper, a low somber tone.

Then he heard it.

"He's dying, I'm afraid . . . I'm sorry, but there's nothing I can do about it—"

"Shut up!" the general snapped.

"Hurry!" Aubrey replied. "We must be sure!"

Gant was shaking his head more quickly, with a huge and desperate effort of will and muscle. "No," he said.

The general looked very sad. "I'm afraid so, Mitch. It—Christ, it wasn't what they did so much as the burns. When you ejected, boy, it was already too late—but help us now. Tell us the airplane exploded. That's what we need to know. Tell us. Please."

"No—it didn't . . . didn't . . ." Gant sobbed. "I'm not burned. It's not—I couldn't be . . . didn't . . ."

"Didn't what, Mitch? What didn't happen?"

"I—didn't eject—" If he told them, explained to them, they would realize their mistake. They wouldn't say he was dying from burns, not then. They'd realize they'd made a mistake, an awful mistake, if he could prove he landed the airplane . . .

"What? Mitch, what are you saying?"

"I landed—landed . . ."

"Oh my God—! Aubrey, did you hear that? He landed the airplane!"

"No—!"

"Yes—!" Gant cried out. "Yes!"

The general leaned over him. Gant could smell a violet-scented breath-sweetener. The face was concerned. The eyes pleaded. He suddenly looked like the general who had decorated Gant on the flight deck of the aircraft carrier in the South China Sea—looked just like him or his twin brother. The resemblance comforted Gant, made him want to speak. He smiled. Just as on that previous occasion, he smiled at the general. He had wished he had been able to send the official photographs to his mother—but she was dead . . .

He realized he was in a trough. Like the sea-swell beneath the carrier's hull, he was in a trough. The general's face was a moment of calm.

He wouldn't have sent the photograph to his father, not in a lifetime, not in a million years . . .

Father—

Street, monument, dark hedge, front door, corridors, marble staircase, urns, white room, white room white room white—

The finding of his thread appalled him. He tried to shrink from the general whose face bore down on him, enlarging like the opening jaws of a fish—

Fish. Black fish—airframe. Water—drowning. Firefox—lake, sleeve trapped, cut free, airframe intact . . .

He knew he was out of the trough now. He even knew, for the briefest moment, that he was drugged. He knew where he was, he knew he was being deceived, he knew he must say nothing. Then that moment went. He wanted to talk. Had to talk.

"Dying . . . dying . . . dying—dying, dying, dying . . ." Seemed to be all the general was saying, though his lips did not move except to make his smile broader. The words seemed to come out of the air and fill the room. He disbelieved them for a moment then did not know why he disbelieved . . .

Then—

"He's not dying!" Aubrey's voice. "For God's sake, he didn't crash—he didn't eject—the aircraft's still out there somewhere." Aubrey did not come into view. The general's face looked away. His head shook sadly. An earpiece and a wire came out of the general's ear. Gant realized he was deaf.

His father had worn an uglier, more obvious one. The general was deaf.

"He's dying, Kenneth . . ." He turned back to Gant. "Tell us the airplane was destroyed."

Deaf—would he hear? Gant reached up—huge effort, sweat bathing his body, but he grabbed the general's uniform and pulled him nearer so that he could hear. He placed his lips near the general's ear, near the earpiece . . .

"Not burned . . . not burned . . ." Something seemed to hurry him, quicken inside him like an increase in adrenalin. He began to babble incoherently, desperately trying to make himself understood. "Not burned . . . drowning . . . drowning—on fire, but water, water . . . not burned . . . landed, not burned . . . water . . ."

The general's earpiece fell from his ear. Gant lay back in abject apology. His body twitched with adrenalin, or something. He felt *too* alive, a collection of jangling nerve endings. He scrabbled for the earpiece. The general shouted at him, jerked away, but Gant held the earpiece. A long wire snake unreeled in his hand, seemingly alive. There was nothing at the other end of the wire, no box in the general's breast pocket, like his father had. The wire trailed away out of sight.

Someone shouted, almost a snarl. He did not understand the language. Truth bubbled in his throat as self-pity had done. He gritted his teeth, held the words back, making them into a growl . . .

He did not know why he was stopping himself from speaking. The adrenalin demanded it. His body twitched and jumped with it. If he could tell, say everything, then he could relax. He must tell—must tell . . .

He sat up, jerkily, quickly, mechanically. Sat up in bed. Not bad for a dying man . . .

Not dying—tell—explain—in the lake . . .

"Not—explain!" he said through his teeth, looking around him. "Listen!" he cried.

He saw two figures in one corner of the room. And flowers. And other faces. Nurse, doctor, general, man in suit—

Two generals. Blue and brown—

They stared at each other, the two generals.

"Listen to me!" Gant screamed. He had to tell them now—he had to. He would burst, explode, if he didn't get the words out . . . he had to tell them. "Listen!"

He moved, tried to put his legs out of the bed but they

would not move and he felt himself tumble forward. The floor rushed up at him, blue and white tiles. He dived at it, striking it with all the force of the energy surging through him.

Vladimirov rushed forward, shaking off the interrogator's restraining arm garbed in the USAF uniform, and knelt by the unconscious American. Blood seeped from Gant's forehead where it had struck the tiles. Vladimirov, in his frustrated rage, smeared it over Gant's face and neck like some horrific tribal badge of manhood. Then he turned to look at the interrogator in his American uniform.

"You had him!" he raged. "You had him in the palm of your hand—!"

The doctor lifted Gant's body back onto the bed. Then the nurse wiped the smeared blood from his face and dabbed antiseptic on the spreading, livid bruise. Vladimirov stood up and moved away from the bed. Gant was breathing stertorously, his chest heaving up and down as the last effects of the stimulant surged through his body. Uselessly—

"It is a matter of time," the interrogator said, checking the earpiece the doctor had removed from Gant's hands. He had used it to listen to the comments of his aide, seated in another room in front of a bank of monitors where hidden cameras focused on eye movements, muscular reaction, a hundred other tiny factors. He shook his head ruefully. "A pity—but next time for certain—"

Vladimirov grabbed him by the upper arms. "I *want* that information—I want it tonight!"

"He has to be allowed to rest now. We have to clear his system before we try again."

"I want that information!"

"You'll have it—before morning," the interrogator snapped, shaking off Vladimirov's fierce grip. "Before morning!"

The Hercules transport, bathed in hard white light, sat like a stranded whale at the end of the runway. Beyond it, the lights of Lincoln created a dull, furnacelike glow on the underside of the low clouds. As he stood with Pyott near the RAF Land Rover which would ferry him to the transport aircraft, Aubrey was impatient. The breeze lifted Pyott's grey hair and disheveled it. It gave a wild, almost prophetic emphasis to the gloomy expression on his features.

Buckholz and Curtin were already on board. The Hercules

waited only for Aubrey. The small, routine Ops Room was behind him. He had left it, and the larger underground room beneath it, with a sense of freedom, of advantages gained, of willfully having got his own way. Now, Pyott held him—like the Ancient Mariner, Aubrey thought irreverently, and then said:

"Well, Giles, I wasn't on my way to a wedding, but you've nevertheless detained me. What is it you want to say?" His smile was an attempt to jostle Pyott into a more acquiescent mood. The soldier smoothed down his wind-blown hair and returned the smile.

"I want your assurance, Kenneth— " he began.

"Oh, don't be so solemn!" Aubrey chided.

"Kenneth—damn it, you're impossible! I want your assurance, your *solemn word* that, if the Skyhook does not arrive before the deadline expires—you will destroy the air-frame completely."

"Oh, Giles—"

"Don't 'Oh, Giles' me, Kenneth. The airframe must not be left intact for anyone else to retrieve. You must salvage the most important systems and then destroy the rest. Now, do I have your word on it?" He paused, then added: "It's too serious for anything less than your word. I know it isn't in your orders—you've persuaded everyone that your precious Skyhook *will* arrive—but, you must make certain the Firefox is not recovered by the Soviet Union. That is imperative."

Aubrey patted Pyott's arm, just at the elbow. "I promise, Giles, that the Firefox will not fall into the wrong hands. Don't worry—you'll give yourself ulcers."

"*You* will give me ulcers, Kenneth."

Aubrey looked across the tarmac. His gamble was beginning. He knew that Pyott was right, that his entire fortune was staked on breaks in the weather and a single helicopter already in difficulties and behind schedule. And, for himself, he was on the point of laying down his cards.

Gant, he thought suddenly, and shivered. He pulled the collar of his overcoat around his neck and ears, but felt no warmer.

"Good luck," Pyott said, holding out his hand.

"What? Oh, yes— " Aubrey returned the handshake. There was no trace of excitement left in his body; nothing now but cold and fear and nerves.

7 / **FELONY IN PROGRESS**

His head hurt. It was heavy and seemed grossly enlarged, a huge melonlike thing. He could not lift it from the pillows. Faint lights washed across the ceiling, but he could not hear the noise of passing traffic. When he breathed in, there was the smell of ether. Hospital. The word filled him with a vague dread. His body seemed jumpily alert, filled with an undefined tension.

Hospital. Ether smell. He found the thread once more. Street, hedges, steps, door, hall, marble staircase, gallery with ornamental urns, white room, white room—

He stifled a groan. This was not the same room, not the same bed. He had been moved. After . . . after his interrogation under drugs . . .

155

Gant understood. He raised his heavy arm. The watch was still there. In the darkness, the hands glowed. A little before ten. He let his arm drop, tired of supporting its weight. He was aware of other bodies; aware of muttered or snorting breaths. People were sleeping in the room. He pushed with his hands against the mattress, easing his heavy body half-upright against the headboard. Slowly, sweating with the effort and stifling his heavy breathing, he turned his head from side to side. A night light over one of the beds helped him to see the contours and outlines of the small ward in which he had been placed. It was a brief glance. He slid down in the bed again when he saw the male nurse sitting near the double doors. The man was dimly lit by a small tensor lamp, and silhouetted against the light entering through small, opaque panes in the doors. He appeared to be reading a book. When he lay flat again he wondered if he had warned the nurse he was conscious, and listened for the scrape of his chair. Eventually satisfied, he closed his eyes and pictured the room.

There were six beds, three of them occupied by sleeping—drugged?—figures. One's head was heavily bandaged, the second was identifiably male, the third, on the far side of the room and away from the weak light, was in deep shadow. The windows of the ward were barred. In a wash of headlights from outside, he had seen the vertical lines of the bars and the wire-reinforced glass beyond them. The male nurse near the only exit from the ward was muscular, probably armed.

Gant listened, but the nurse did not move. So intently was he listening that he heard a page of the book being turned. Then he relaxed, and immediately the small victory of knowing and mapping his surroundings dissipated. He was trapped in the room; parked there until he was again required for interrogation. He knew he had been interrogated twice; he knew they were only waiting until his body recovered sufficiently to be drugged once more; he knew that they could convince him of anything while he was drugged; he knew that at the next interrogation he would tell them what they wanted to know.

He remembered the USAF general in his uniform, he remembered Aubrey's voice. He remembered the scrambled and confused mess his thoughts and awareness had become. He understood the furious, undeniable desire to tell the truth that had come over him, and which they would induce in him again . . .

Burns?

He touched himself carefully. He was wearing a sweatshirt and shorts. His legs did not hurt when he touched them, nor did his arms or face. There was a lump on his temple, but he remembered the tiles rushing up at him. They had saved him from telling.

But he had believed he was dying—

That was the real measure of their power over him, of his inability to continue resisting.

The sweat was cold on his body. His hands lay beside his thighs, reminding him he no longer possessed even trousers. Nothing but a sweatshirt—no shirt, no jacket, no shoes. He was helpless. Like the figures in the other beds, who were probably criminals or even dissidents, he had ceased to exist. Isolation swamped him.

He struggled to escape it by following the thread back into his interrogation. His removal to this silent ward might mean he had told them everything, that they had finished with him while they checked the truth of his story—had he told them?

Slowly, cautiously, he sifted through the wreckage—father, aircraft carrier, burns, Aubrey, the lake, drowning, burning, ejecting . . . the tiles, the tiles . . .

He had been sitting up, screaming for them to listen to him. What had he said? He squeezed his eyes shut, concentrating. What had he said?

He could not stifle the audible sigh of relief when he was certain. Nothing. He had not told them. They did not know.

He listened as the nurse's chair scraped on the linoleum. He heard the footsteps approach. The light over his bed flicked on. Gant controlled his eyelids, his lips. The seconds passed. He tried to breathe normally. The light went out, the footsteps retreated, the chair scraped once more. The nurse grunted as he sat down. Gant heard the book being picked up, reopened, pages being shuffled.

He was sweating freely once more. It had taken a vast effort of control and made him realize how weak he was. The nurse would have been capable of plucking him upright with one hand and dragging him from the bed without effort. He could never overpower him.

And there was no weapon. His itchy, sweating hands,

tense yet without strength, did not constitute a weapon. And there was nothing else. He could never take the nurse's gun away from him, even if he wore one.

He heard the chiming of a clock somewhere, a small, silvery, unreal sound. Ten. He must have been asleep for hours. In all probability they would be coming soon. They were pressed for time. There was an almost frantic sense of urgency about their pursuit of what he knew. There was no reason for it—no one else knew of his whereabouts or the location of the airplane, but they could not seem to stop until it was over.

So they would come, and he would be helpless. Weaponless and helpless.

Mitchell Gant lay in the dark waiting for the doctors and interrogators. The bandaged head of one of the other patients loomed in his thoughts. A mummy, almost. Something, like himself, long dead and forgotten.

He felt himself once more on the point of losing the struggle against his sense of isolation . . .

Aubrey felt the nose of the Hercules C-130K dip towards the carpet of gleaming cloud he could see through the round porthole in the fuselage. It still lay far below them, stippled and endless. The moon was brilliant, the stars as hard as diamonds. It was difficult to believe that from that black, light-punctured clearness would come weather conditions even worse than they had anticipated when the aircraft took off from Scampton.

He removed the headset, his conversation with Waterford at Kirkenes at an end. As he stared through the porthole, the clouds seemed to drift slowly up to meet them. They were still flying north along the Norwegian coast, inside the Arctic Circle. The pilot was taking the Hercules down as low as he could, to deceive the long-range Russian radars, before turning to an easterly heading which would take them towards Kirkenes. To all intents and purposes, the Hercules would have dropped out of radar contact west of Bardufoss and be assumed to be a routine transport flight to the Norwegian NATO base.

Aubrey fretted, even though he attempted to allay his mood by losing himself in the mesmeric effect of the clouds. It might have been a white desert landscape with wind-

shaped rocks rising from its surface. The self-hypnosis held
momentarily, then dissipated. Aubrey transferred his gaze to
the whale-ribbed, bare, hard-lit interior of the transport aircraft.

It was almost done, they were almost there. He was for
the moment in suspension, unable to do more. It was always
the most frustrating, dragging part of an intelligence operation—the flight, the drive, the train journey, whatever it was
. . . just before the border was crossed, the building entered,
the target sighted. Useless tension, pointless adrenalin. He
did not *control* the thing at that moment—

Five huge pallets of equipment were secured in the aft
section of the cargo compartment. The team of fifteen men
lounged or stretched or checked equipment. Charles Buckholz
once more familiarized himself with the cargo manifest, in
conversation with the WRAF Air Loadmaster. Curtin was
standing at a folding table on which lay a large-scale map. He
was talking to the Hercules's copilot. Everything had been
decided, the briefings had been completed. This was repeti-
tion to occupy time, nothing more.

The Hercules would land at Kirkenes, and Aubrey,
Buckholz and the other members of the team without parachute training would disembark. Waterford and his SBS unit,
twenty-five men in total, would then embark, and the Hercules
would take them and their equipment to the area of the lake.
The dropping zone for the parachutists had already been
selected; the surface of the lake. Waterford had confirmed its
suitability. Once the men had dropped, the Hercules would
make a low-level run and the five pallets of equipment would
simply be dropped, without parachutes, from the rear cargo
doors. At first, Aubrey had considered the method primitive,
unsophisticated, potentially dangerous to the valuable equipment—especially the winches. RAF reassurances had failed
to convince him, even though he accepted them. It still
seemed an *amateurish* manner of accomplishing the drop.

Above the Norwegian border with Finland, Eastoe's
AWACS Nimrod was back on-station. It would operate in an
airborne, early-warning capacity, a long-range spyplane, ob-
serving the Russian border for any and every sign of movement.
Also, it would provide a backup communications link with
Washington, London, Helsinki, and the lake to supplement
the direct satellite link established when Waterford's initial
search party had left the commpack at the lake.

He turned away from the scene. Buckholz and the non-parachutists would be flown in by RNAF Lynx helicopters, arriving no more than an hour behind Waterford's party. Aubrey looked at his watch. Ten-thirty. By four-thirty, the whole party would be in place at the lake, where the Firefox lay in twenty-six feet of icy water.

Twenty-six feet. It was hardly submerged. A man standing on the fuselage would have his head above water. Eighty feet in length—the tailfins in perhaps thirty-four feet of dark water—with a wingspan of fifty feet, it had to be winched no more than one hundred and fifty feet before it was ashore. Or, preferably, plucked out of the water like a hooked fish by the Skyhook which had refueled on the German-Danish border thirty minutes earlier. The figures were temptingly simple, the task easy to achieve. Yet he could not believe in it, in its success.

Gant—

The nose of the Hercules was dipping into the clouds when the operator of the communications console that had been installed for Aubrey's use, turned to him.

"There's a coded signal coming in, sir—from Helsinki." He attended to his headset, nodding as the high-speed, frequency-agile message ended. "There's no need to reply, sir. They've signed off."

"Very well—run it."

The operator flicked switches, dabbed at a miniature keyboard set into the console, and hidden tapes whirred. It was Hanni Vitsula's voice.

"Charles!" Aubrey called.

Buckholz arrived as the replayed voice chuckled, then said: "Don't rely on the weather, Kenneth. Forty-eight hours from midnight tonight is our final, repeat final offer. Our forecasts suggest it might be easier to reach the site than you're supposing . . . don't expect us not to arrive. Good luck. Message ends. Out."

Buckholz shook his head ruefully.

"He guesses we're relying on getting ourselves socked in by the weather. Think he'll decide to move in before the deadline?"

Aubrey waved his hand dismissively. "No. But, otherwise he means what he says." He slapped his hands on his thighs. "Well, that's it. Your President has gained us the dubious bonus of a few more hours." Through the porthole,

Aubrey could see the grey cloud pressing and drizzling against the perspex. "But that's all the time we have."

"Let's just you and me hope the weather turns real sour, uh?"

"Then we will have lost the game, Charles. The Skyhook will never arrive in the weather you're hoping for!"

Dmitri Priabin turned slowly and gently onto his back and sat up. In the soft lamplight, he stared intently at the hollow of Anna's naked back, as if he were studying the contours of a strange and new country. Eventually, he clasped his hands behind his head, leaned back, and stared at the ceiling. He pursed his lips, pulled dismissive, laconic faces, prevented a sigh, but knew that the time of recrimination had once more arrived. He slipped from the bed and hoped she would not wake.

He sat cross-legged on a padded chair. He could taste the onions from the hot dog one of the boys had pressed upon him, unable himself to finish it. He belched silently behind his clenched hand. Yes, onions—it recurred more strongly than the wine, than dinner, than the vodka. It was more persistent than the taste of the perfume from her neck and breasts on his tongue and lips.

Onions—recrimination. Both brought back the park and the metro station and the other reminders of her treachery that had assailed him at the ticket counter so that the clerk's face had changed from puzzlement to nerves before he had recollected himself sufficiently to buy the tickets.

Now, recrimination, guilt, fear all returned like some emotional malaria as she slept. It was an illness which never left him, only remained dormant.

He leant forward, resting his chin on his fist, studying her.

He lived on the verge of a precipice. He had done so ever since the momentary looks of guilt and fear he had noticed when he had answered unexpected telephone calls, looks which had vanished again as soon as he put down the receiver and shrugged. And, he reminded himself, he always put it down with the sense that he had been speaking to an American who spoke good but very formal Russian.

He had lived on the cliff edge ever since he began to follow her himself. Ever since he witnessed her make covert contact with a man who might have been her Case Officer. Ever since he had tailed that Case Officer to a known CIA safe house . . .

He had been on the edge for six, almost seven months—

She stirred, alarming him, as if surprised in some deep disloyalty of his own. She turned onto her back but did not wake. Her flattened breasts were revealed as her unconscious hand pushed the bedclothes down. It was a strangely erotic exposure; crudely inviting. He studied her unlined, sleeping face; unlined except where the brow was creased even while she slept. He felt tears prick his eyes, and because he could never bring himself to even begin to tell her that he knew, that he wanted to help . . .

Recrimination, palpable as the taste of onions—

As soon as he had moved into her apartment, he had looked for bugs. He had spent the whole of that moving day checking the telephone, pictures, walls, floorboards, cupboards, wardrobes, bed. His relief at finding no traces of surveillance or bugging had overwhelmed him. As soon as he had straightened from pushing back the last corner of fitted carpet, he had had to rush to the bathroom and vomit into the avocado-colored toilet.

For weeks after that he had been unable to rest until he had checked the files, checked her office, followed her to discover whether anyone else was following her. He had become like a jealous lover, or like the private investigator such a lover might have employed.

Like a spy—

Gradually, he came to believe that it was only he who knew. There was no evidence, no one was gathering information, no one even suspected.

What she supplied was not state secrets, it was little more than high-grade gossip. Details of the Soviet Union's social services, housing programs, illnesses, alcoholism—the temperature of Soviet society—which would be useful to them in building their total picture of the Soviet state. Promotions inside the Secretariat and the Politburo and the ministries, glimpses of the workings or stumblings of the Soviet economy, matters of that kind—

Almost not like spying at all. Little more than indiscreet gossip, careless talk which was overheard by strangers.

Priabin could make himself believe that. She was not an important agent, hardly an agent at all. Revenge, disgust with the system that preferred weapons to a wheelchair, had made her do it, were her motives. He could understand that. How much the suicide of her husband, in unexplained circumstances years before she met Baranovich and his damned wheelchair, had to do with it, he had no idea. He preferred the motive of revenge. It gave her a certain honest dignity.

Recrimination. He was certain she did not suspect he knew. He blamed, even hated himself for not telling her, for not weaning her away from the addiction, for not saving her. But he dare not risk losing her . . .

His possessiveness was strengthened, made blind by his knowledge of her secret. He dare not let her be caught. He could not bear the thought of losing her. Should anything ever threaten their relationship—

He choked silently. He could not even complete the thought. Could not begin to imagine what he would do, what would happen, if he lost her, if she ever left.

He stood up and crossed the room swiftly to kneel by the bed. Very gently, he kissed each flattened breast, each erect nipple. Then he continued to kneel, as if partaking in a further religious ceremony. He could not let her go, but he could not let her be discovered. He must speak to her—

He could never admit his knowledge—

Angrily, he stood up. She stirred and moaned lightly, half-turning away from him. The glow of the lamp fell on the fine down along her arm. He watched, then walked swiftly into the bathroom. He did not switch on the light because he had no wish to see himself in the long, beveled mirror. Instead, he fumbled in the poor light that came from the open doorway, found a glass and filled it with tepid water.

Recrimination. *He must do something—!*

But, he would lose her—

His mouth was dry and the taste of onions was making him feel nauseated.

Whispering near the door, as it squeaked shut once more. Gant came awake immediately, shocked that he had dozed, making a vast effort to stop his left arm rising from the bed to display his watch. He breathed in, slowly and deeply, and listened.

Dressing change . . . who? He was sufficiently propped up by the pillows to see the two figures at the table without lifting his head. Starched cap, long hair tied back. The male nurse had put down his book. Gant saw him nod, then the woman began moving across his line of sight towards—his bed?—no, the bandaged patient, the mummy. Gant relaxed, and immediately the sense of isolation returned. He did not know how he had slept, or for how long. How had he been capable of sleep?

He could see the nurse's back as she bent over the second bed from his own. She had flicked on the overhead light. The mummified head murmured. It might have been a stifled groan. Gant watched gauze bandage being unrolled, stretched upwards by a slim arm in the muted light. Something glinted, and the arm fell. The mummy murmured again in a frightened tone, as if someone intended him harm. Something glinted, and clicked lightly.

More clicking, like the sound of distant hedge clippers . . .

Gant felt his body tensing itself without his will. His hands curled and uncurled, his arms lifted slightly, testing their own weight. His body felt compact, less weary. Bruised, though. The drugs had worn off, leaving the pain of his brief, violent beating.

The nurse was murmuring, the mummy seemed to protest. Then her arm stretched again in the light. Then the clicking noise, and something slim and metal gleamed. And, at the moment of realization, as his thoughts caught up with his body, he heard footsteps coming down the corridor towards the ward, and he moved.

One chance, only one . . .

He flicked the bedclothes away, rolled, wondered for an instant what strength he had, and then rolled across the nearest bed, his right hand reaching for her arm, his body closing with hers, knocking the breath out of her. Gleam of the scissors, her frightened mouth and eyes turning to him, the eyes of the mummy and the half-exposed, purple cheek and swollen mouth. Then he dragged the nurse sideways so that they did not topple on the patient, and whirled round—

"Don't—!" he yelled in Russian, feeling his legs buckle but holding the snatched scissors at the girl's throat, the blade imitating a slight downward stabbing motion. "Don't *think* about it!"

The male nurse was on his feet, his hand reaching into his short white coat to where a breast pocket or a shoulder holster would be. Then he was bumped forward as the doors opened behind him. *The doctor—*

Gant recognized the man and fought off the weakness that followed his realization of how late he had left it. He moved forward with the nurse in front of him, even as the doctor was asking what was happening and breaking off in mid-sentence as he understood.

"Over here!" Gant yelled, pushing the reluctant nurse forward. The doctor snapped on the main strip lights, which flickered and then glared on the scene. There were two plainclothed guards with him. A stretcher waited behind them; he could see it through a gap where one of the guards still held the door half open. "Move!" His voice sounded panicky. His legs felt weak, even shuffling at that snail's pace. The scissors gleamed. He pressed the point of them down, touching the girl's throat. It would not take a minute more, perhaps only seconds, before they moved out of shock and drew their guns and killed the girl and took him for interrogation as if nothing had occurred.

The male nurse moved slowly, reluctantly. Three yards separated them now, then only two, but Gant hesitated because the maneuver seemed too complicated. He lacked the necessary coordination. The man's eyes were quick and alert, the girl had gone soft and unresisting in his arms. Both of them were beginning to think he was already beaten. In the man's face Gant could already detect his anticipation of what might happen to the girl when he made his move, and his lack of concern.

One of the guards was moving his hand very slowly to the breast of his jacket. The doctor, sensing the approaching moment of violence, had made a single step to one side, away from the doors. Two yards, a yard and a half—

Now—!

His left hand gripped the girl's arm, his arm across her breasts. He spun her away from him, flinging her to the left. Then he kicked at the male nurse with his bare right foot, almost losing his balance, striking at the groin. He had already dropped the scissors to the floor. He grabbed the nurse, hoisted him upright, fumbled in the man's coat, withdrew the Makarov. Awkwardly, he juggled the pistol until it pointed towards the group at the doors.

"Back off!" he snapped. "Out! Move!" He waggled the gun in their direction.

The doctor was flat against the wall. He slid along it and slipped through the doors behind the two guards. Gant turned the nurse, who was groaning softly, still clutching his genitals, and prodded him through the doors—

Alarm, hand reaching for it—

Gant moved, bringing the pistol's barrel down on the extended wrist of one of the guards as he reached towards the wall at the side of the door. The man groaned as something cracked. The violence thrilled Gant, made him feel stronger. As the guard slumped against the wall, Gant kicked his legs away and the man sat in a moaning, untidy heap. Gant waggled the gun at the remaining guard and the doctor.

What to do—?

Guide them—but what about the alarms—? Guide—alarms . . .

"Move!" he said. "Go on—move! Get out of here!" There did not seem to be any other alarms down the corridor. "Take him—get out." He indicated the guard sitting against the wall, eyes malevolent, one hand clutching the other like a precious, damaged possession. The second guard bent, helped the injured man to his feet, and then the two of them began to hurry down the corridor, the doctor following them, casting occasional glances over his shoulder.

Gant held the nurse against the wall, arm across the man's throat. The girl had not emerged from the ward, but he knew she would sound the alarm the moment the corridor was clear—he knew, too, that the guards were hurrying to the nearest alarm . . . the male nurse understood. His eyes anticipated what he might be able to inflict on Gant before the doctors and interrogators ordered him to desist.

Which way—?

He gripped the nurse's shoulder, pressing his forearm against the man's windpipe. Which way—? His feet were cold on the linoleum. He was aware of his bare legs.

The alarm sounded above their heads. Someone had triggered every alarm in the building; overlapping, continuous ringing.

"Which way up?" he barked. "Up to the top of the house? Which way?"

He released his grip on the man. The alarm just above their heads was deafening. The nurse hesitated—then shrugged. It was no more than a postponement of his intentions towards the American. He pointed along the corridor, his body adopting a submissive stance. Gant motioned him forward with the pistol. At first, Gant's legs moved reluctantly, and then he was running, his bare feet slapping on the linoleum, the gun clutched in both hands.

At the end of the corridor, the nurse turned left. The ether smell and the cream walls they had left behind suddenly clashed with ornamental urns and carpets and upright chairs against paneled walls. A short gallery overlooking the main hall—the clatter of boots on the tiles below—and then they were climbing a steep wooden staircase that twisted back on itself, then climbed again. Gant glimpsed another corridor, wide and paneled. Heavy, unrestored oil paintings retreated along the walls. Snowbound hunting scenes, a rich, faded carpet, a frowning, heavy Czarist face, then more stairs. Bare walls, old plain wallpaper swollen with damp. Colder. His feet resented the uncarpeted, dirty floor of the next corridor.

The nurse halted. The gun prodded his back. He half turned. Gant struck his shoulder with the pistol. The man groaned.

"Where?"

The alarms were all distant now. He heard no sounds of pursuit. He caught the musty, warm smell of animal cages. The nurse went ahead of him down the corridor. He opened a door. Ether smell, overhead lamps, an operating table. A surgery or another interrogation room. They passed into a pharmacy, then into a room from which the animal-straw scent emerged strongly. Monkeys chattered as the lights were switched on—Gant realized the man was leaving a trail of turned-on lights for others to follow, but ignored the danger.

Rats in cages, an operating table, loudspeakers, instruments. Monkeys. In one cage, a cat mewed pitifully. An electrode emerged from its shaved, plastered head. Gant shuddered with the cold of the sight. The room itself was warm, the smell overpowering. Straw and urine and food. A bird chirped somewhere.

"Undress!" Gant ordered. The nurse watched him, weighed him. Gant felt himself swaying on his feet, his breath coming heavily, raggedly. "Undress—clothes on the floor!" Still the man hesitated. "Do it! I don't give shit whether you live or die, I just want your clothes!"

The man's resolve snapped and he undressed swiftly. At

a movement of the pistol, he kicked the little heap of clothes towards Gant. Gant watched him. The cat mewed again. Gant glanced at it, its protruding electrode touching the wire of the cage. Its food was uneaten. The nurse moved. Gant struck out with the barrel of the Makarov, hardly moving his eyes from the cat's gaze. The nurse held his head and stumbled against a cage of white mice, spilling them onto the floor. They scattered and clambered over his underclothed body, making for the room's corners. The nurse lay still, blood seeping from his temple down the side of his face. Hurriedly, Gant climbed into the jeans, then the shirt. He leaned against a table as he put on the shoes that were at least a size too large Then he buttoned the white coat. He brushed dust from the uniform. Still the nurse did not move. A mouse emerged from behind him, sniffed the air and the body, then skittered away beneath one of the tables.

Gant turned swiftly and left the room, switching off the lights. As he closed the door, he heard the monkey chatter die, heard the scamper of mice paws. He switched off the pharmacy lights, then the lights of the interrogation room. As he closed the door behind him, at the moment when he wanted only to pause and recover his breath, someone turned into the corridor. Booted feet. He looked round wildly.

A uniformed KGB man strode towards him. The Kalashnikov in his hands hesitated to draw a bead on a white hospital coat.

"Anything up here?" he asked.

Gant shook his head. "Only the mice," he managed to say.

The guard laughed. "The bloody American's loose," he said. "You know?" Gant nodded. The guard was already reaching into his breast pocket. The packet of cigarettes emerged before Gant could react. "Smoke?" Gant shook his head. He was sufficiently aware to keep his bruised temple out of the guard's direct line of sight. The man struck a match, the cigarette's acrid smoke was pungent in the bare corridor. The man smoked secretively, as if at every moment he expected the appearance of one of his officers. Seconds extended to a half-minute, three-quarters . . .

"I'd better get back down," Gant explained.

"Plenty down there rushing around—say you heard a noise up here . . . thorough search." He grinned, his stony face opening as if a rock had cracked apart. "They like that, officers—" He spat, without malice, more out of habit.

"I'd better go—" Gant said. The guard shrugged.

"I'll take a couple of minutes more," he said.

Gant hesitated. If he left the man here—? The cigarette had not burned halfway to its cardboard tube. Two, three minutes—? The nurse . . .

"You all right?" the guard asked. Gant turned directly to him. Immediately, he realized the guard was staring at his bruised temple and swollen lip. Something slow but certain began to form behind the man's eyes.

"Yes, sure," Gant said, then struck at the man's face. The guard half-stepped, half-fell backwards against the wall. There had seemed no strength in the blow. Gant moved inside the rifle and struck again, and again, his fists beginning to flail at the man because he felt he would be unable to overpower him.

The guard slid down the wall to end in a slumped crouch, rifle between his knees. Gant ran, clattered down the first flight of stairs, glimpsed the ranks of oil paintings again, took the second flight as quickly as he could in the slopping shoes, and reached the gallery overlooking the main hall. He almost collided with a man in uniform. Lieutenant. KGB.

"What is it?" the officer asked. Someone else in uniform emerged from another room. The alarms were loud. Gant shook his head.

"I thought I saw him—" he began.

"Where? Up there?"

"No, coming down this way . . . it was just a glimpse. I could have been wrong . . ."

"Very well."

There were four people on the gallery now, two in uniform, one in a white coat, one in a suit. Gant did not recognize any of the faces, but knew he could not be certain. He did not know how many people had seen him since his arrival.

"Are you the one he escaped from?" the officer asked.

Gant nodded, shamefaced. "Yes."

"I thought so," the lieutenant sneered, nodding at the livid bruise. "Serves you right. God help you if they don't catch up with him—your mother won't know you!" He turned, motioning to the guard in uniform. "Up these stairs—*he* might have missed him!" Laughing, the officer followed the guard up the stairs.

Gant looked over the gallery, down into the main hall. Two men in white coats were moving up the sweep of the marble staircase to the first floor. Someone who might have been the American general during his interrogation followed behind them. He moved slowly and angrily.

Gant walked swiftly along the gallery, opened a door at the end of it, and found himself at the head of a flight of narrow stairs. He clattered down them, one hand bracing himself against the bare plaster of the wall because he was increasingly afraid to make demands upon his body. It seemed like the fuel leak in the Firefox, the gauges in the red, waiting for the first, hesitant sound of the engines dying. He felt he might suddenly seize up, be unable to move.

The stairs twisted to the right, then descended again. Ground level—? A narrow corridor, quarry-tiled. He opened the door at the end of it. A room that might once have been a vast kitchen was now dotted with armchairs, a television set, radio, a still-smoking cigarette which had fallen onto the carpet from the ashtray where it had been left. He stepped on it, grinding it into the carpet—

They wouldn't rescue the monkeys and the cat if the place took fire . . .

He left the room by a door at the far end of it, knocking over a half-full glass of beer as he brushed past a small table, then he crossed a narrow passage. Through frosted glass, moonlight shone; almost impossibly, it was an outside door. A shudder ran through his body. Coats, uniform greatcoats, scarves and hats hung from pegs inside the door. He shuffled through them, found a navy pea coat, snatched at a bright scarf, and tried the outside door.

It opened. He slipped through, closed it softly behind him. The alarms were still loud. Outside alarms—

He judged himself to be at the rear of the house. Blocks of somber flats marched away from him. Lights from the house spilled onto the gravel that surrounded the building. Here, the dark hedges were replaced by a high stone wall, against which a car was parked. Gant ran to it.

The wind was cold once he moved out of the lee of the house. He shrugged on the coat and wrapped the scarf around his face. He thrust the pistol into his right-hand pocket. He tried each door of the car. All of them were locked.

The door opened behind him. He turned slowly, attempting to deflect suspicion. Two men—no, a third armed man behind them, in uniform. More lights flickered on in the ground floor rooms, throwing their glow at him.

Vladimirov stepped forward, the guard moving swiftly to his side, his rifle raised to his shoulder and aimed directly at Gant. Vladimirov's face was chilled by the wind and half in shadow, but Gant saw his smile of undiluted pleasure. Hopelessly, he tugged at the door handle behind him. Locked.

Two men at one corner of the building, rounding it, slowing, then moving forward. A solitary figure at the other end of the building. The wall behind him, Vladimirov in front—

Vladimirov moved forward, closing on Gant. The guard kept his rifle at his shoulder. His aim did not waver. Two white-coated doctors, emerging from the doorway, shivered with the raw cold. Two plainclothed KGB men followed them.

He turned, then, and mounted the bonnet of the car, feeling the weakness of his legs as he clambered onto the car's roof. The thin metal flexed beneath his weight. A bullet smacked flatly into the wall, inches from his face.

Vladimirov screamed at the guard. "His *legs*! His legs—don't *kill* him!"

He turned to the wall, elated as if by alcohol or drugs. He jumped, scrabbled, his fingers clutching then being skinned by the rough stone as he slid back to the roof of the car.

"Stop him!"

Footsteps running on the gravel. He did not bother to look, knowing there was time for only one more effort. He stood up, swayed—heard footsteps skidding only feet away and heavy shoes striking the metal of the car's bonnet—and jumped.

Clung, heaved, felt the weakness again, heaved once more, his face sliding inch by inch up the stone, then the wind hitting into his face as it cleared the wall. Something touched, then grabbed at his left leg. He lashed out. Two bullets smacked against the stone near his left hand, then he heaved himself astride the wall. Looking down, he blanched at the drop. Two more bullets, the heat of one of the rounds searing his leg below the knee. He swung both legs over the wall, and dropped towards the pavement. A car passed, headlights on. A quiet side street—

He crumpled as he hit the pavement, sitting down hard. He questioned his ankles, waiting for the pain of a sprain or twist. Then he stood up. Looked up. A face appeared. He drew the Makarov and fired at it. The bullet chipped dust from the capping stone. The head disappeared. He glanced up and down the street. Ill-lit canyons opened between blocks of flats. The street lamps were dim and few. He ran across the street, sensing the moment he reached deep shadow.

Sensing, too, the opening of gates, the switching on of engines, the beginnings of pursuit. His leg ached but he thought the flesh only scorched. He had escaped. He did not consider the alien city, not yet—only the concealing night as he ran.

"The Hercules flies south along the airway—my people drop by parachute, the Hercules drops off the Russian radars as if landing at Ivalo, then doubles back below the radar net and makes a low-level pass—booting these five pallets out of the cargo door as it goes . . ." Waterford broke off, and turned from Aubrey to the pilot. "One smoke flare enough of a marker for you?" he asked. The pilot nodded. Waterford returned his gaze to Aubrey. "Buckholz and the non-parachutists will come in on the two Lynx helicopters we've got here." Without even the trace of a smile, he added: "Simple."

Aubrey was nodding abstractedly. When Waterford had finished speaking, he looked up. "Very well." He glanced at his watch. "You'll be ready for takeoff in . . . ?"

"One hour maximum," the pilot answered.

"Good." Aubrey's gaze traversed the interior of the transport aircraft. The SBS men under Waterford's command were now coming aboard, bringing their weapons, packs, skis, and diving equipment with them. In conjunction with the WRAF Air Loadmaster, Brooke and another marine officer were checking the manifest of the equipment the aircraft had brought from Scampton. Aubrey wondered whether or not he should address the marines.

"Sir—" It was the radio operator.

"What is it?"

"London requests immediate signals contact, sir—it's Mr. Shelley. Utmost priority."

"I'll come at once." He crossed the cargo compartment

of the Hercules with an agitated swiftness, then seated himself in front of the console. He waited until the operator nodded, and then he began speaking. "Peter—Aubrey here. What is the problem?"

He waited impatiently. He had sanctioned the use of high-speed transmission rather than one-time encoding because of the greater ease and speed of communication, voice-to-voice. Yet still the conversations seemed endless, punctuated by silences which fearful guesswork attempted to fill. A light indicated that Shelley's voice was now being recorded at high speed within the console. The operator dabbed at keys, and he heard Shelley's voice; breathless, as if not quite slowed to normal speed on the tape.

"Sir—it's Gant. He's escaped from the Unit on the Mira Prospekt . . . " Shelley seemed to pause, as if for a reply, then appeared to remind himself that he was not at the other end of a telephone line. "We had someone watching the Unit, and they witnessed the alarms, the whole fuss . . . he must have got over the wall at the back, but our man couldn't find hide nor hair of him. But there was complete and utter panic among the KGB. A huge search is underway already . . . "

Shelley faltered rather than stopped. Immediately, Aubrey said: "Peter—wait until I get Charles Buckholz here, please. You're certain there's an extensive search for him?" He turned and raised his voice. "Waterford—get Buckholz—at once, please."

Waterford disappeared immediately through one of the paratroop doors in the side of the fuselage. Buckholz was supervising the loading of the two Lynx helicopters, parked near the Hercules on the ramp of Kirkenes airfield. Aubrey's fingers drummed on the side of the console. It sounded as hollow as an empty drum.

Shelley's voice came back soon after the red light flicked on once more.

"In answer to your question, sir, the British and American embassies are bottled up—no explanation, no official contact, but the cars are outside in force. They're waiting for the lines to go dead any minute now. Our low-grade people still on the streets are ringing in with reports of high-level KGB activity—*saturation* cover, was the term David Edgecliffe used. Shall I hang on now, sir?"

Aubrey turned on the swivel chair. Buckholz, his face half-hidden by the fur trimming of a white parka hood, clambered through the paratroop door, Waterford behind him. He hurried to Aubrey's side.

"He's got out—!" Aubrey blurted. "Damn it, but he's got out of that unit—they're looking for him all over Moscow!" Buckholz grinned and slapped Aubrey's shoulder heavily. But, even before he could speak, Aubrey clicked his fingers—a dull sound in his heavy gloves—and said excitedly: "Saturation cover, the Moscow Head of Station reports—you realize what that means, Charles? Do you *realize*? My *God* . . ."

"What?"

"They don't know—they didn't *break* him—!" He gripped the sleeve of Buckholz's parka, tugging at the material. "If they *knew*, they wouldn't have every available man on the streets of Moscow looking for him—they *need* him!"

"That's just a guess . . . they don't want us to get him back—"

"Squadron Leader—!" Aubrey called to the pilot of the Hercules. "Contact Eastoe—I want an up-to-the-minute report on border activity." The pilot nodded and began moving forward towards the flight deck. "I don't believe he's told them, Charles—I don't believe they *know*!"

"It's only a matter of time, Kenneth—he can't survive on the streets for long. Can we get someone to him?"

Aubrey turned to the console. The operator nodded. "Peter—what are the chances of finding him?"

He waited, listening to Buckholz's heavy breathing, his eyes willing the red light to wink off.

Then Shelley was speaking once more. "Edgecliffe's signal was very clear, sir—and I checked at once. Every known contact, every member of the embassy staff outside the building, is already under surveillance. Edgecliffe reminded me." Shelley's voice hesitated, and then added in a more mumbled tone: "We—used up the best people two days ago—especially Pavel. He's still very angry about losing Pavel—"

"To the devil with Edgecliffe's anger!" The operator flicked at the keyboard to try to overtake Aubrey's unexpected, rushed reply. "Is there no one? Do they have any idea where he might be?" As his questions were transmitted, he turned to Buckholz. "You realize that the time limit is expanding, Charles? Gant has given us a stay of execution." The pilot appeared from the flight deck, shutting the door behind him. "Any activity?" Aubrey asked.

"No change in the situation."

"See, Charles—they don't know!"

"Where does that leave us? They could pick him up any time. Maybe we ought to pray he gets run over by a bus!"

Shelley's voice anticipated Aubrey's reply.

"No information, sir. Moscow Station personnel simply can't move—it's the same for the Americans. We have a few low-grade watchers who Edgecliffe has been using, but no one he could use to give help, even if he knew where to look. He's got out, but that seems to be as far as anyone can go, sir. We can't do anything for him."

Aubrey stood up, punching his right hand into the palm of his left; a dull concussion. He looked almost wildly around the crowded, murmurously noisy interior of the Hercules. Breath smoked. Runway and perimeter lights gleamed beyond the lowered cargo ramp. It was as if Aubrey expected to find a volunteer from among the marines and RAF personnel around him. His eyes rested on Buckholz.

"We must do something, Charles—something to try to keep him out of their hands! Now we have this slim chance—now we might be given all the time we need . . . he mustn't go back into the Unit!"

"I agree—so? What the hell do you expect me to do about it?"

"Think, Charles—*think*!"

"What? Kenneth, what in hell do you *want* me to think?"

Aubrey strutted a few intense, excited steps from Buckholz, then returned to the console. "Peter—do we have anybody . . . anybody we can use?"

He waited in silence, his brow creased, his face intent, until Shelley replied.

"Not a native Russian who's capable of finding him, making contact, shielding him, and none of our officials could get near him. We might be able to locate him, with a great deal of luck, but there's no one we could trust to take care of him—in whichever way you wish—" Shelley added in a softer, almost apologetic voice. Aubrey wrinkled his nose in disgust.

"I'm not having him killed!" Aubrey snapped, turning on Buckholz so that he understood his decision.

"Even if you find him, you mean?" Buckholz observed with heavy irony. "Let's face facts, Kenneth. You're hamstrung—our two services are hamstrung in Moscow. We don't know

where he is, where he might go . . . and we couldn't reach
him to help him if we did!"

Aubrey stretched out his hands imploringly, but his face
was flushed with anger. "Then give me someone who *can*
help him! Charles, the CIA must have someone—a Russian
with the resource, the nerves and the intelligence to help
Gant? Give me one of your Category-A Sources, Charles!"

"I can't authorize that, Kenneth."

"To save Gant—to save all this, perhaps . . . ?" His arms
encompassed the entire contents of the cargo compartment;
men, equipment, purpose. "Give me one of your Sources.
Someone with freedom of movement. Someone who can
travel!"

Buckholz was silent for some time. Aubrey allowed him
to pace the cargo compartment, his face thoughtful. His
mittened hands rubbed at his cheeks or alternately held his
chin. Aubrey instructed Shelley to remain in full contact, and
to wait, then he spent the endless minutes of Buckholz's
silence furiously reviewing his own extensive knowledge of
the CIA's Moscow operations.

They were avid for information, and lavish in their cor-
ruption and persuasion of agents. They had dozens of Russians in key positions who supplied them with high-grade
information. They were designated Category-A Sources. Any
one of them might be young enough, resourceful enough to
locate and assist Gant . . . Get him out of Moscow . . . ?

But, would Charles agree? Would he endanger one of
the CIA's key Sources for the sake of *possibly* finding, *possibly*
assisting Gant?

Eventually, Buckholz stood in front of him once more.
He nodded, slightly and only once.

"Source *Burgoyne*," he said enigmatically. "I'll have to
confirm with Langley . . . Source *Burgoyne* seems the most—
expendable." He flinched as he saw the look on Aubrey's
face, then snapped: "Like Fenton and Pavel and even
Baranovich—you were pretty *wasteful* there, Kenneth."

"Damn you, Charles," Aubrey breathed, but his face was
white with admission and a surprising self-disgust. "*Burgoyne*
is less important than your other Sources, I suppose?" he
asked acidly. "How many Category-A Sources are there at
present, Charles?"

"Maybe thirty—scattered through the ministries, the

Secretariat, the Supreme Soviet, top industrial concerns, the Narodny Bank—"

"And *Burgoyne* is one of the least significant, I take it?"

"You got it. I—we've tried to persuade her to request—"

"*Her?*"

"Right. A woman. We've tried to get her to move into more sensitive areas for years now—she won't. She's useful, but she's not *crucial*, as you put it. You want her or not?"

Aubrey pondered for a moment, then brightened: "Yes, I'll take her. A female companion would avert suspicion, and she must have intelligence or resource or you wouldn't have tried to get her into more useful work. She can travel with some ease . . . Yes, I'll take her. Does the code name *Burgoyne* suffice to wake the sleeper?"

"It does. Let me talk to Shelley. I'll supply the telephone number. It's then up to you what you do with her. She's a limited asset and no longer our concern—she'll be all yours!" Buckholz grinned crookedly.

Aubrey moved away from the console. Fenton, Pavel, and now Source *Burgoyne* . . .

"What's her name?" he asked without turning around.

"Anna—Anna Akhmerovna. She's a widow. Touching forty. She has almost complete freedom of movement. Just one thing, though. She lives with a KGB officer, if I remember correctly."

Aubrey turned on his heel.

"*What—?*"

"She's the one you're going to get, Kenneth. Langley would never agree to any of the others."

Aubrey turned away. His mind raced, skipping over crevasses and chasms that opened beneath his optimism, threatening to swallow it. If Gant could be saved—? Edgecliffe could work up a suitable escape route, provide good papers, the woman was good cover . . .

Buckholz completed his instructions to Shelley, then addressed Aubrey. "You still want London, Kenneth?"

"I do!" He faced Buckholz once more. "I'll save him if I can," he murmured. "And her—I'll save her, too!" It was mere bravado and he knew it, as did the American, who merely shrugged.

"I don't think you can win this one, Kenneth. You'll just be losing the Company a useful agent. You'll get *Burgoyne* killed along with Gant."

"No I won't, Charles!"

Buckholz snatched off his mittens angrily, and held up the fingers of his left hand, splayed. He counted them off with his right forefinger, folding them into his palm at each of the names he recited.

"Fenton—Pavel—Baranovich—Semelovsky—Kreshin—Glazunov—the old man at the warehouse, I forget his name . . ."

"Damn you, be quiet!" Again, Aubrey's face was white and his mouth trembled. Appalled, he witnessed the appearance of guilt in his mind. It made his heart race, his stomach turn. Guilt— Shakily, he said: "Then I will atone, Charles— I'll save Gant *and* your Source *Burgoyne*! Now, let me talk to Shelley—!"

"Yes, Comrade Deputy Chairman—yes, of course. I'll come at once!" Priabin put down the bedside receiver and turned to Anna, his face flushed with an almost boyish pride and self-importance. Anna watched him, watched his innocent pleasure spreading in a broad grin.

"What is it?" she asked sleepily, glancing at the traveling clock on her bedside cabinet, propped open in its leather case. Two o'clock. Then she yawned, as if the reminder of the lateness of the hour and her interrupted sleep had wearied her.

"Orders," he said almost blithely, getting out of bed and opening the sliding door of the fitted wardrobe.

"You're going out?"

"I am. Panic stations—" he answered, hoisting his uniform trousers then pulling his shirt from its hanger. He buttoned it hastily, looking down at each button as he did so. He talked as he dressed. "Your friend the American pilot is on the loose—seems they mislaid him—" He looked up and grinned. His tie was draped over a chair. He snatched it up and began to knot it.

"What happened?" She was leaning on one elbow, her small breasts invitingly exposed, nipples erect in the coolness of the bedroom. She shivered, then, and rubbed her goose-pimpled arms. Then she stretched. Priabin hunted for his jacket in the wardrobe.

"Some monstrous screw-up, I expect. Deputy Chairmen don't give explanations over the telephone to newly-promoted colonels." He thrust his arms into the jacket, and buttoned it. "Where's my cap?"

"When will you be back?"

He shrugged. "Can't say, love. I'm appointed one of the coordinators of the search. They've got saturation cover on the streets as a matter of routine, now they want people like me to sort it out . . ." He stopped smiling. "And people to blame, no doubt, if he gets away. Still, we colonels must bear our appointed loads—" The smile was back. He moved to the bed, bent and kissed her. She folded her arms behind his neck, holding him in the kiss.

"Take care," she murmured.

"I'll watch my back." He grinned. "I suppose you're a little bit on his side, aren't you—with your attitude to the project?"

She shook her head vehemently. "Not if he endangers you," she said.

He winked and crossed to the door. "See you," he said, and opened the door. "I love you." He closed the door behind him. Anna heard the front door of the apartment close quietly a few moments later. Doubtless, he had paused only to collect his holster and greatcoat from the rack in the hall.

She shivered, rubbing her arms again. She swung her legs out of bed, crossed to the door and took down her dressing gown. Warm and sensible, but silk-lined. She buttoned it quickly.

As she crossed the hall, she listened at Maxim's door. Satisfied he had not awoken, she went into the kitchen. Her anxiety at Priabin's departure was usual, even though disproportionate. To her, every departure was only the prelude to a meeting where he would be ordered to arrest her.

She turned on one of the small fluorescent lights beneath the kitchen cabinets. It gave the room a hard but confined glow which she could tolerate. It preserved a quality of secretive darkness the room had possessed when she entered it. She switched on the percolator, having checked that enough coffee remained in it.

What was it—? What had disturbed her so much? It wasn't simply her recurring nightmare of discovery and arrest . . . no. It was something—the arrival of fate as palpably as a knock on the door. Yes, that was it. A sense of fate, renewed by the American's escape. It had been with her ever since Dmitri was transferred to security on the Bilyarsk project.

Baranovich's wheelchair had begun her double life—Dmitri had moved closer to that double life when he was transferred. Now, leading the hunt for the American, he seemed in some vague and shadowy way to threaten her. There *was* something fateful about the whole affair.

Of course, Dmitri knew. She had known that for months. She had learned to live with that terror; it had been a mad dog in the back garden, gradually tamed and thus ignored. He would not give her away and therefore lose her—not yet, at least, and perhaps not ever.

To go *back*, she thought bitterly, pouring the heated coffee into a thick brown mug. Just to go *back* . . .

The futile recrimination wailed like a lost child in her head. Baranovich, and before that, her husband. Suicide because he had lost his academic post—*samizdat* copies of banned writings in his locked drawer at the university—

She had had to live with the knowledge that he had killed himself to protect her. She had known nothing until the KGB told her, after she had found him dead in the bath, afloat in red water—*Samizdats*, meetings, planned protests, anti-Soviet activities. A dangerous criminal, her loving, gentle, innocent husband? It was impossible to believe; impossible, later, not to realize that he had had the courage to face them, to undergo imprisonment. He had killed himself to protect her, to free her from the stigma of being the wife of a prisoner, a *zek* in the Gulag—

Gradually, very, very gradually, she had returned to life and to her career from that dark tunnel where he had left her. And then Baranovich, corrupted forcibly from his idealistic work—his wheelchair—to build a warplane more destructive than anything ever known . . .

That had been the breaking point. Not her husband's suicide but the destruction of Baranovich's project. She had made her first contact with an American diplomat-agent at the next embassy cocktail party she attended.

And then Dmitri, and Dmitri working to protect that damned, infernal aircraft project, and Dmitri discovering her double life—

And now hunting the American. It *was* fate. She could not disbelieve it. It was a time of ill omen—

If only they would let her go, if only she could go back, her mind wailed like a lost child—if only . . .

The coffee scalded her mouth as she sipped it, then

spilled onto her dressing gown as the telephone startled her.
She put down the mug, staring at her quivering hands. Then
she snatched at the receiver hanging on the kitchen wall, as if
to protect her sleeping son from its intrusion.

"Yes?" she asked breathlessly.

"*Burgoyne*, is that you?" a voice asked in English.

"What—?" she breathed. "I—I'm afraid I don't understand . . ." She spoke very deliberately in Russian.

"But I do," the voice said. It sounded English—but if it
was, then why not an American accent—? She felt panic
mount in her, filling her throat.

"Who is this, please?" she asked as calmly as she could.

"Listen carefully, *Burgoyne*—my name is Edgecliffe, British Embassy. This line is secure at my end, and I know yours
is not tapped—I also know that Colonel Priabin left the apartment ten minutes ago. You're alone, except for your son . . ."
The details were as palpably nauseating as hands pawing
her, caressing her body beneath the dressing gown.

"What do you *want*?" Now, at last, she spoke in English.

"Your help. Please listen carefully. You may confirm my
identity and instructions with your Case Officer, if you wish.
When I have finished. You've been loaned to us, *Burgoyne*,
by your present employers, to do a special job."

"What—?"

"Colonel Priabin, no doubt, has been summoned to the
Center to take charge of some part of the search for the
escaped American pilot—we want your help to find him
before your lover does . . ." There was a chuckle at the other
end of the line. "We're a little limited as far as resources are
concerned—we need your help."

"Go to hell!" Suddenly, she was frighteningly angry,
hardly able to speak, so full was her throat, so tense her
whole body. "Go to hell, whoever you are!"

"Listen to me, *Burgoyne*!" the Englishman snapped. "I
don't have time to play games. You'll do as you're told.
Otherwise, well, you know what might happen to you—enough
of that, however. It will be up to you to get our American
friend out of Moscow, once we've located him. I'll have
papers for the two of you, travel permits, everything—and a
full scenario in a matter of hours. All you have to do is be
ready to move when I tell you."

He fell silent, and into that quiet Anna dropped the

small pebble of her voice. "And what if—if Colonel Priabin catches him?"

"Then we won't require your services. You can carry on with your life as before."

"But what do I tell *him*—what about my *son*—?"

"I'm sure you can discover a sick relative somewhere if you try hard enough. You have many friends, I'm told. Send your son to stay with one of them. Or with your father, perhaps?"

"Just like that—?"

"Everything is just like that, I'm afraid. You don't have a choice. None at all. You must comply with our wishes—I'm sure you realize that. I won't even bother to assure you that if the KGB recaptures the American they will get back their aircraft—the one you loathe so much. Even though that is true, it isn't necessary to persuade you, *Burgoyne*, because you *must* do as we say and you are intelligent enough to realize it."

"But—how? *How?*" Anna asked.

"The details have yet to be decided. Simply prepare yourself for a journey, perhaps by train. Be ready to move as soon as it becomes necessary."

"I *can't*—" she wailed.

"You must. And, who knows? With your connection with Colonel Priabin, our American might be safer with you than anyone else we might have been loaned—mm? Goodbye for the present, *Burgoyne*. I'll be in touch—soon."

The line clicked, then purred. Anna sat for some minutes, staring into the receiver, as if the man who owned the voice might emerge from it, oozing smokily out like an appearing djinn. One hot, angry, frightened tear fell on her upturned wrist. Then she lifted her head to the pine-paneled ceiling of the kitchen, and howled like an animal in pain.

It was the absence of pedestrians that worried him most. In the small hours, he might have expected the streets to have emptied, but there had been no crowds and little traffic from the time he had vanished into the dark canyons between the endless blocks of apartments. It had taken him more than two hours to work his way back into the center of Moscow via side-streets and alleys and lanes and waste ground. And all the time he did so, he knew he was moving slowly but certainly into the mouth of the trawling net the KGB and the police had cast for him.

Sirens, prowling cars, foot patrols, even helicopters. From the Mira Prospekt he had moved east, then north, then west, using the deeper darkness of open spaces, sports complexes, recreation parks, climbing their frosty railings, resting in the deep shadow of trees; fighting his rising panic and sense of isolation as though they were two attackers in the darkness. He passed through Dzerzhinsky Park which contained the Ostankino television tower; the park surrounding the army museum; the zoo park. He kept away from the streets as much as he could; avoided streetlights.

The shops of the Kalinin Prospekt were lit like fish tanks. Above the windows, ranks of unlit offices marched towards Tchaikovsky Street and the American Embassy. Gant knew, though he suppressed the knowledge, that it would be guarded— barred to him. But he needed a destination, an objective. It was the only one he could enlarge in his mind and store with the comforts of safety, help, food, sleep. During his two hours of walking and skulking and scuttling across lit spaces and shrinking into doorways and behind trees, the embassy had become furnished and warmed in his imagination. There was no need to imagine anything after its doors opened. When the door closed behind him, he would be safe. It would be over.

He stared down the Kalinin Prospekt as if studying a minefield. Two foot patrols, two parked police cars, another cruising slowly towards him from the direction of the Kalinin Bridge. It would be a gauntlet he would not pass. He turned right, into the sparsely lit Malaya Molchanovka Street. Ranks of tall offices and department stores retreated towards Tchaikovsky Street and the bridge on his left. The street was empty, except for the quick darting shape of a cat crossing the road. Gant hurried, hands thrust into the pockets of the short coat, the cap he had found in one of those pockets pulled down over his eyes. He had abandoned the white coat. His heels were raw from the rubbing of the too-big shoes, and the pain in his calf where the dog had bitten him had resurfaced now that the effect of the drugs and sedatives had disappeared. He stamped out the memory of the frozen lake and the Lynx helicopter only yards from him, waiting to save him.

He heard music coming from a still lit window as he

passed a low apartment block opposite the rear of a cinema. A child cried somewhere, startled from sleep. A car turned the corner from the Kalinin Prospekt behind him, and he forced himself not to run but to turn into the entrance of another apartment block. The outer door was not locked. He pushed his way inside. The foyer smelt of cabbage and greasy cooking. He flattened against the wall and waited.

The car drifted slowly along the street. For a moment, a spotlight played on the entrance, washing over the walls of the foyer. Then it was gone. Quivering, he returned to the street. The police car had turned off. He hurried on, head down, breath smoking around him, feet hurting, leg stiffening.

He reached the corner of Tchaikovsky Street. It was wide and at first glance almost empty. It formed part of the Sadovaya Ring of boulevards around the inner city. It was lined on each broad pavement by trees. A red-and-white-striped tent, unexpectedly, occupied one curb. Flashing yellow lights, a roped-off section, the noise of a compressor. Road works of some kind. He crossed the Kalinin Prospekt, seeing the same foot patrols and parked cars, and began to move cautiously down the boulevard, keeping to the shadows of the trees. The street-lighting was good here; betraying. His eyes sought each shadow, trying to dissolve it.

A parked car; he paused. The embassy was number nineteen, less than a hundred yards away, an ugly, postwar building. He could clearly see its facade, safe behind railings and the emblem of the eagle, illuminated by the yellowish street lighting. Just the single car . . .

He repressed the leap of optimism. He must not believe in the single car and its two occupants he could see as shadows through the rear window. He had to *look*—!

Road works. Six men, two leaning on shovels, one leaning on a pneumatic drill, three others using pickaxes in slow, rhythmical movements. He waited, turning his attention to the windows of the buildings, especially the second and third floors. There were smaller, brightly painted houses jammed incongruously between the Stalinist-style apartment blocks, frowned upon by the concrete towers. Gant studied the windows. A car passed, but did not stop, did not even slow down. He looked at his watch, a nervous, hardly aware reaction. Most of the curtains were drawn, most of the lights were off. One or two of the windows were open, even in the cold weather. He watched until his eyes were confused with dots and with dancing, unfocused images of windows, but he saw nothing to make him suspicious.

Excitement began to mount through his chilled body. There would be a marine behind the gates. Once he opened his mouth . . . he needed only one word, his name . . . the startled marine would open the gates and he would be safe . . .

Against belief, it seemed the guard was minimal. Perhaps they expected him to try the British Embassy—?

He forced himself to study the windows again. Nothing. After ten minutes, nothing. Parked cars too far down the boulevard, only the one near the gates. And the road works—

He looked at the six workmen. The drill was working now, so were the two men with shovels. The other three, the men wielding the pickaxes, had stopped to rest under the spindly legs of the spotlights they had erected. The noise of the drill violated the silence of the street. Each of the three resting men faced in a different direction as he leaned on his pick-handle. Each head moved rhythmically, slowly, traversing an area of Tchaikovsky Street.

The red-and-white-striped tent was twenty yards from the embassy gates. The six men were not workmen. The roadworks were a fake.

Gant swallowed bile and backed away from the shelter of the tree. He had passed a telephone box. In shadow, he hurried back towards it, entering and slamming its door behind him. Immediately, his tension and fear clouded the glass. He fumbled for coins—there were coins in the pockets of the jeans—and dialed the number of the embassy. It sprang out of his memory without effort, a signal of his necessity. He withdrew his finger from the dial and waited. The telephone clicked, then the noise became a loud, continuous tone. He joggled the rest and dialed once more. The same loud, unceasing noise sounded in his ears.

The lines to the embassy had been cut off at the switchboard. There was no way to reach them.

He clenched his fist and banged it gently but intensely against the small mirror above the coin box. He swallowed, and shook his head. Illusions of safety dissipated. Then, furiously, he dialed another number, and waited, holding his breath.

The ringing tone—

They'd left the lines to the British Embassy—he would be able to talk to them, he *would*—

"Come on, come on . . ."

The operator on the embassy switchboard—a night-duty man—answered. Asked his name, his business . . . there seemed a note of expectant caution. Gant felt relief fill him, the words hurried into incoherence even before he began speaking—

Then he heard the clicks, three of them.

He stood there, mouth open, not daring to speak. The man on the switchboard insisted, his voice more demanding and, at the same time, more suspicious. Gant heard the man breathing as he waited for a reply. He understood the clicks, and wondered whether the switchboard operator had heard them—must have heard them . . .

The line was tapped. They'd left it open, hoping he would call. A tracer was probably at work now, seeking him.

"Caller?" Gant did not reply. He stared at the mouthpiece. Distantly, he heard the operator say: "I'm sorry, caller . . ." Then the connection was broken. The operator had circumvented the tracer both of them knew had been put on the call. Gant continued to stare at the receiver, then slammed it onto the rest, heaving open the door of the box almost blindly.

He looked down the wide boulevard. Red-and-white-striped tent, six men, one parked car. He would never make it. He knew he did not dare to make the attempt.

He felt the wetness in his eyes and rubbed angrily at them. He jammed his hands in his pockets, hunching his body until its shivering stilled. Then he turned his back on the American Embassy.

Gant did not see the shadowy figure slip from beneath one of the trees on the opposite side of Tchaikovsky Street and hurry after him.

8 / THE STRANGERS

The noise of her anguish had woken Maxim. The eleven-year-old had come into the kitchen, startled and half-awake, rubbing his eyes, his mouth already working with anticipated fears for his mother. Instantly, as quickly as sniffing back her tears and dragging the sleeve of her dressing gown across her eyes, she had transformed herself once more into the figure he expected and needed. Even his immediate enquiries had been half-hearted. Being allowed to sit with her, drinking fruit juice, had been in itself a comfort, a reassertion of normality. He had gone back to bed satisfied.

Once she was alone in the kitchen, Anna buried her terror in activity. She called her Case Officer at the embassy, and he confirmed her sentence. The image of punishment had occurred to her with bitter humor. When the line suddenly went dead, the humor vanished and she felt chilled and isolated. She had put down the telephone, forcing herself not to consider the implications, not to consider her own danger. Instead, she began to build her fabric of deception. It would have to be an old aunt in Kazan—she didn't even have a telephone, though she lived in comfort, so Dmitri couldn't check on her story, nor could the ministry or her superiors . . .

She ticked off the benefits on her fingers.

Then, Maxim—

Her father, naturally; the boy's grandfather. The father who had assiduously promoted her career and had protected her from censure and suspicion after her husband's suicide. Her father, who had once risen to the position of first secretary of the party organization of the Moscow Oblast region, and had thus been a member of the Party Central Committee. His retirement to a *dacha* outside Moscow had been honorable, luxurious. He still had the weight, the contacts and friendships to protect Maxim if something went wrong.

She swallowed. Maxim would enjoy a few days in the woods outside the city. The old man had taken up wildlife photography as a hobby. He had even bought Maxim a small Japanese camera for his birthday.

Maxim would enjoy—

She was sobbing. The camera had become inextricably linked in her mind with the Dynamo First-Class soccer shoes that had been Dmitri's present. The two presents, their images so clear in her mind, pained her.

She sniffed loudly after a time, and shook her head as if to clear it of memory and association. Blonde hair flicked over her brow. She tugged it away from her forehead.

If it worked—if, if, if, *if*—she might be away for only a couple of days, perhaps three at the most. If she helped the American successfully, did what they wanted her to do, then she would be back with presents and an explanation that her aunt was a little better and she could stay away no longer . . .

If—

If not, she would have preserved her son from the shipwreck. Her father had protected her; now he could do the same for her son, his grandson. His task would be simple. Narrow and bigoted though his political and social ideas were—a surviving splinter of the Stalinist period who cut and bruised at every encounter with her newer, more liberal ideas—he had always been a kindly, though authoritative father; and an indulgent, fond grandparent. Maxim liked him, they would get on.

"No . . ." she whispered slowly, intensely. It was as if she were already giving her son away. Not if she could help it—not if she could win.

Dmitri's knowledge, her eventual safety from the KGB, her continued function as a Category-A Source for the CIA—

She would face those problems afterwards.

The telephone rang. She glared at it as if it had been a hated voice, then snatched the receiver from the wall.

"Yes—?" It might be Dmitri, but the second of silence before she heard Edgecliffe's voice, told her it was not.

"*Burgoyne?* Listen carefully. The American is still loose in the city. He hasn't been arrested or spotted by the police. We had someone in contact with him, but he shook them off—we presume he thought the man was KGB. We think he's tried our embassy and the American embassy. He realizes by now that he can't find a bolt-hole in either place . . ."

"And?" Anna snapped, determined that Edgecliffe should hear nothing but competence, resource—however much that played the Englishman's game.

"The papers are ready—we'll have them delivered before morning. We shall require you to take the American to Leningrad, by train. You and he must manage the station as best you can."

"Leningrad?"

"You'll be met. I'll tell you how and where when we have it finalized. He'll be taken into Finland—what you do will be up to you. Your exit can be arranged—"

"No—!"

"I should consider it carefully, if I were you," Edgecliffe warned. "We're offering you a way out."

"A passport to nowhere," she sneered.

"As you wish. Think about it. We will want you to board the Leningrad train this afternoon . . . there'll be clothes for the American, delivered with his papers. Some sort of disguise. Your job will be to get him to Leningrad."

"Your job is to find him first."

Edgecliffe chuckled, an almost pleasant sound. "I realize that. Be ready to leave your apartment the moment I call on you to do so. Once we locate him, he's in your hands. You'll make contact—it's too risky for us to try."

"And if you don't find him today?"

"Then it may be too late—he's running out of time. However, you'll stand by until you hear otherwise. Have you made your arrangements?"

"Don't worry—they'll be made."

"Then expect the papers and another call." He hesitated, then added: "Good luck."

Anna replaced the receiver without replying. She watched as the shadow of the cord stilled against the tiled wall. It formed a tightly coiled noose below the telephone.

She hoped, fervently hoped to the point of prayer, that Dmitri would catch the American. He had the short remainder of the night, the morning, noon, the afternoon.

Please, please . . .

Priabin stood in front of the large-scale map, rubbing his chin with his left hand. Moscow's main line stations were represented by colored pins. His right arm was folded across his chest as he pondered his responsibility; the seven principal stations for long-distance routes, and one of the four airports around the city, Cheremetievo in his case. His whole department had been seconded, and he occupied Kontarsky's old office in Moscow Center, coordinating the surveillance. Dmitri Priabin was grateful for the static nature of his participation. At least his men were not walking the streets, combing the parks and open spaces, searching the apartment blocks, the empty houses, the building sites and the shops. Nor were they manning roadblocks in the freezing night.

And yet—and this was the splinter in his satisfaction since he had left Anna—it might be his people who let Gant slip. If he got out of the city, it might well be by train. And Gant could bring him down just as effectively as he had ruined Kontarsky.

Surely they had to find Gant soon? It was impossible for the man to roam the city undetected. He was alone, without friends or contacts. The SIS and CIA were bottled up in their apartments, embassies, compounds, safe houses. There was no one to help him, hide him, provide him with papers, protect him. The man was utterly, entirely alone.

His forefinger touched each of the colored pins in turn,

as if for luck. His hand described a circle around the inner city—Leningrad Station, Riga Station, Savolovsky Station, Belorussia, Kiev, Pavolets, Kurskaia.

And the principal airport to Leningrad and Scandinavia at Cheremetievo, northeast of the city—

He looked at his watch. Time to make another tour of the stations and drive out to the airport—yes, he would do that. It was suddenly urgent, necessary to remind his men of the stakes, the risks.

The intercom sounded on his desk.

"Yes?" he asked, depressing the switch.

"General Vladimirov wishes to see you, Comrade Colonel," the secretary informed him. The girl had a heavy cold, and her mood had not been lightened by having to work this extra duty.

"Where?"

"He's here, Comrade Colonel."

"Very well—send the general in at once!"

Priabin took up a position in front of Kontarsky's—*his*— desk, almost posed, exuding confidence. He had sensed something overbearing about the general when he had been aboard the First Secretary's Tupolev. Priabin wanted to make a good impression; he did not wish to appear an interloper in that office—some sort of caretaker. His secretary opened the door, nose buried in her handkerchief, much to Vladimirov's evident distaste, and ushered the general in. She slammed the door immediately.

Priabin held out his hand. Vladimirov took it briefly. Priabin studied the older man's eyes. Bloodshot, but intense with purpose. He evidently had not slept for even a small part of the night. Priabin understood that Vladimirov's pride had been insulted and diminished by what the American had done. Only hours before he had been confined and on the point of revealing the truth, yet now he was at large again. To Vladimirov, his bad luck must have seemed like a continuing taunt.

"General—I'm honored. What can I do to help you? Please sit down—" Priabin indicated a chair near the desk. Vladimirov shook his head.

"Tell me your arrangements, your dispositions—all of them," he ordered sharply, without preamble of any kind. "Quickly, Colonel—I haven't time to waste!"

The Deputy Chairman had briefed Priabin sufficiently

for the authority exuded by Vladimirov not to come as a surprise. However, he was abashed by the peremptory, almost violent expression of it. Vladimirov had been placed in command of the hunt for the American—an unusual step, since he was not KGB or even GRU—but that position was a KGB safeguard. Only Vladimirov would fall if the American eluded them—no one in the KGB would suffer. Priabin almost felt sorry for the older man, even as he bridled at his tone.

Swiftly, he explained the disposition of forces, using the map on its easel. Vladimirov stood near him. There was a faint smell of whisky and pastilles on his breath. He nodded violently, his rage and impatience barely concealed. When Priabin had finished his outline, Vladimirov studied him with the same piercing glance he had bestowed on the map and its pins.

"So," he remarked at last, "you will simply wait until he makes himself known to one of your men and then arrest him?" The sarcasm was evident and stinging. Vladimirov raised an eyebrow in further emphasis. Priabin felt his face redden and grow hot.

"These—are normal, tried-and-tested security procedures, Comrade General," he said with heavy slowness.

"It was normal security that allowed the American to escape from the hospital."

"I—"

"I have toured three departments in this building of yours so far," Vladimirov pursued, "and in each of them I have heard variations on the same refrain. *Routine—normal—usual* . . . even from Deputy Chairmen and Directors of Departments and their principal Deputy Directors and Assistant Deputy Directors—" His arms were in the air, expressing exasperated hopelessness. "People who should know better, *much* better, tell me the same things you do! Do you think it is enough, Colonel? Do you think you are doing all you can to apprehend the most important escapee in the whole of the Soviet Union?" Priabin glanced towards the door, whether for signs of help or out of embarrassment he could not be certain. The general raged on. "This organization of yours has too much experience with *prisoners* and not enough with escapers." His lips parted in a thin, mirthless, arrogant smile. "You're not up to the job, perhaps?" His left eyebrow lifted ironically once more. The expression did nothing to alleviate the heavy anger of the eyes. He turned back to the map. "Well?" he asked. "You've nothing to say? Nothing at all? Not an idea in your head, mm?"

Priabin cleared his throat and composed his reddened features. He was already considering how best, how painlessly, he could maneuver the general out of his office.

"I—am sorry you're not satisfied, Comrade General. You are, of course, unfamiliar with our methods . . ."

Vladimirov turned on him. The white light from the table lamp fell on his cheek, giving it the dead, flat appearance of skin that had undergone plastic surgery. A lock of grey hair fell across the older man's creased forehead. He flicked it back into place.

"Unfamiliar? Aren't jailers very conventional—the same the world over?" he hissed. "Dolts, buffoons with clubs and guns? Well? Have you an idea in your head, or not?"

Priabin stared at the map. A circle of pins, the weave of a net. Other maps in other rooms displayed other pins. A huge trawlnet being dragged across the city. He must surely be netted soon. The Sadovaya Ring, Red Square, the river, the broad avenues and boulevards, the narrow streets, the buildings and monuments—Gant was *alone* out there. He'd walked that city only once in his life before, and that for little more than an hour, on his way to rendezvous with the now dead agent Pavel Upenskoy.

Priabin clenched his fist; began beating it into the palm of his left hand. Red Square from the Moskva Hotel, past GUM, down to the river—the murder had taken place there, then they'd fled via the metro to the warehouse on Kirov Street . . . then he'd been driven out of Moscow in a truck the next morning. He didn't even *know* the city, not at all—!

His forefinger traced the route that Gant, in his disguise as Orton, must have taken from the Moskva Hotel to his rendezvous near the bridge. Having reached the Pavolets metro station, he traced the route once more.

"Well, what is it, man?" Vladimirov asked impatiently. "Are you awake or half-asleep?"

Priabin turned on the general, grinning. "I think I'm awake, Comrade General!" he said with something akin to elation in his voice. It was at least enough of an idea to get rid of this uncomfortable old man.

"What is it?" Vladimirov's excitement was hungry and dangerous.

"Gant knows very little of Moscow. He must reason someone would be looking for him, he's valuable. If they know he's out, and they probably do, then they'd have people looking for him—low-grade people, unofficials, anyone they could get out of bed on a cold night—! He might, just *might*, retrace his steps. It's the only piece of knowledge they all share—the route he took to his meeting with Pavel Upenskoy and the others."

Vladimirov looked doubtful. Then he nodded, once.

"They might make an assumption—*he* might make it . . ." He stared at Priabin. "Well, where do you begin? Quickly, man—where?"

Priabin flicked the intercom switch. "Bring me the files on Upenskoy's cell—yes, all of them. Every name!" He glanced up. How many were there—Upenskoy, the old man, Boris Glazunov who died under interrogation, Vassily who'd disappeared without trace, one or two others, suspects only . . . it didn't seem much, but it was something. A beginning.

"He'll wait for daylight, if he tries it . . . for the crowds," Priabin explained, once more facing the map. At that moment, he almost believed in his own idea, so convincing was his act for the imperious air force general. "Yes, he needs the daylight and the cover of the crowds." He turned as his secretary entered. She deposited the files, sneezed, and left. Vladimirov wiped the cover of one of the files. The name borne by the file was that of Boris Glazunov. Vladimirov opened it eagerly, in desperate, almost pathetic ignorance. It seemed a foolish idea to Priabin, but it appeared to more than satisfy the general. He shook his head gently.

Vladimirov looked up. "Well, help me, man! There are names, addresses, relatives in here, in each of them. Put them all under surveillance. And get me the departments responsible for street surveillance in the areas you pointed out to me—quickly! Don't just stand there, Colonel—earn your salary for once!"

The Hercules had completed its southward run, utilizing the airway and a civilian call sign and flight number. The pilot had requested landing instructions from Ivalo airport and dropped below the Russian radar net. Then, using visual and electronic navigation, and its radar in the mapping mode, it had flown northwards once more, heading for the dropping zone. The SBS unit had departed from the two paratroop doors during the first run over the lake at 3,500 feet.

First light was no more than a greyness in the sky, patched with darker cloud. Snow flurried across the windscreen, causing the copilot to intermittently operate the wipers.

Every light on the Hercules had been extinguished.

"All clear ramp doors and depressurizing," the pilot heard the loadmaster announce over his headset. "Ramp opening, ramp down and locked."

"Roger. Ninety seconds to Initial Point."

"After I.P., heading two-one-five, skipper," the navigator informed him.

"Roger—two-fifteen."

"I.P. mark—now."

"Roger . . . turning to two-one-five . . . two-one-five steady." Ahead of the aircraft, the dawn attempted to lighten the sky beyond the flurrying snow. The wipers cleared the screen. Stunted and dwarf trees confused the pilot's sense of distance. "Speed coming back to one-sixty knots." The undulating, snow-blurred outlines of the land seemed to rush just beneath the belly of the aircraft. "Wheels down," the pilot announced. "Flaps down." It was a precaution, in case the aircraft came into contact with the ground. "Lamp on, Diane—"

"O.K.—ready this end," the loadmaster replied.

"Lake in sight," the copilot said.

Ahead of them, beyond the last, straggling trees, the apparently smooth surface of the frozen lake stretched away, narrowing as it did so. Trees crowded down to the shore, like a fence around the ice.

"Got it. Keep the wipers on." Snow rushed at and alongside them. "I've got the smoke marker—"

"Altitude fifteen feet . . . twelve . . . ten . . ."

"Standby—five, four, three, two, one . . . Go!"

The nose of the Hercules tilted up slightly as the five pallets followed each other, sliding off their metal tracks and disappearing through the open ramp. The aircraft seemed to bob up, floating on a slight swell.

"Drop good—all away, clean and tight. Ground party already beginning to recover . . . ready to close up this end."

"Roger, Diane, standby for ramp closing."

The Hercules passed southwards over the narrow neck of the lake. A stronger flurry of snow rushed at them, obscuring the pilot's glimpse of tiny, moving figures on the ice. Then the lake was behind them.

"Initial heading—two-two-four."

"Roger—turning on to two-two-four . . . ramp closed."

The Hercules skimmed the stunted trees to the south of the lake. Whenever the flurries of snow revealed the horizon, the lightening sky appeared full of dark, heavier cloud.

Delaying his decision for as long as possible, Gant watched the apartment block of stained, weatherbeaten grey concrete that overlooked the Riga Station on the Mira Prospekt. In the windy, snowy light of dawn, he watched the first overcoated, booted, scarved inhabitants leaving for work. Cheap curtains had been drawn back at a hundred windows; faces had glanced at the day without enthusiasm. The traffic had begun to flow along the wide street. Trains left the station noisily and arrived in increasing numbers from the northern and north-eastern suburbs.

He had returned to the Mira Prospekt almost by the route he had taken to the U.S. Embassy, taking to the streets only when they began to fill with the first flow of workers heading into the inner city. He had made better time once there were hundreds of other pedestrians. He had even risked a short trolley-bus ride, but the sense of the closeness of other bodies, the growing claustrophobia of the self-imposed trap, had forced him to walk the remaining distance.

He was there simply because he remembered the address of Boris Glazunov, whom he had impersonated during the truck journey from Moscow to Bilyarsk with Pavel. Boris Glazunov was married—he remembered the details of the papers Pavel had given him. Boris Glazunov had been arrested, but perhaps they would know someone—a name, an address, a codeword, something . . .

He had passed the warehouse near Kirov Street where he had spent the night after Fenton had been killed. It was locked and empty. The old man, too, must have been arrested. He had hurried away from there, alert and fearful. Glazunov's was the only other address he knew belonging to anyone even remotely connected with the operation to steal the Firefox. He had at least to try.

He was cold, but no longer hungry. He had drunk a bowl of thick soup, eaten bread and a thick-crusted, greydoughed meat pie from a stall selling hot food to early workers. It was parked near a building site on the Sadovaya Ring. The food gave him indigestion but temporarily rid him of his growing sense of unreality. He could not decide the center of the unreality. It frightened him. He had learned to be wary, alert, clever—but to what purpose? What could he do? How many days and nights could he spend on the streets, without papers and with a diminishing supply of rubles and kopecks, eating from steaming food-stalls and riding claustrophobic trams and trolley-buses? He could see no end to it—and that was his real fear.

He waited for twenty minutes, until he was certain that the apartment block was not under surveillance, that no one and no cars were halted suspiciously for long periods, that no police or KGB had arrived. The traffic thickened—Party limousines sped past old saloon cars and heavy trucks, using the yellow-painted center lane. The trains came and went monotonously. People left the apartment block, and its companions lining the Mira Prospekt, in greater and greater numbers.

Eventually, he was stamping his feet in the too-big shoes as much with impatience as cold, and then he crossed the thoroughfare at the nearest pedestrian lights and climbed the steps to the foyer of the apartment block.

"Yes—quickly. You must come at once. The Gargarin apartment block on the Mira Prospekt, near the Kulakov intersection. Please hurry—you must bring your car . . . the American has just entered the apartment block—no, I do not know whether they are waiting for him. It is the apartment of someone who—was arrested, but I do not know what happened to his family . . . but I have just seen a KGB car pull up in front of the block. Yes, someone must have spotted him, someone I did not see. What? They're sitting in the car still . . . I must go in and warn him—yes, you must hurry. Park in Kulakov Lane. What is your car? Yes, and the number— quickly, please. No, no, they are still sitting in the car—I think that must mean there are people already inside . . . I must hurry. Please reach Kulakov Lane as quickly as you can!"

*　　*　　*

The wide, grubby foyer of the apartment block possessed a sticky, stained linoleum floor. It was badly in need of a fresh coat of cream paint. One of the six elevators did not work. Gant, unnoticed amid the hurrying tenants leaving the building, attempted to envisage Glazunov's papers as they had been handed to him by Pavel. He could see the grainy identification picture which was later replaced by one of himself, he could see the name, see the overlying official stamps, the address . . .

The number, the number—

A hurrying woman bumped into him, seemed to search his face with a scowl on her own features, then hurried away. The tiny incident drained him of energy . . . concentrate—

Apartment—four, four, five—? Five-four, yes, five-four . . . nine, nine—! Apartment 549. He stood in front of a set of elevator doors. Only odd-numbered floors were served by the elevators on that side of the foyer. For a moment, the foyer appeared entirely empty, except for the concierge— who might or might not have been more than that—who was reading *Pravda* behind his counter. From the open door behind him, leading to his own quarters, came the smell of percolated coffee. There was also the noise of a radio. Gant half-turned his head as he heard footsteps. High-heeled shoes— boots—and a long, warm coat. Fur hat. The pert daughter of the house, dressed beyond her station. The concierge was also the KGB official and informer. Gant's head snapped back to face the doors of the elevator. The foyer was silent, empty. No elevators arrived. The seconds passed. Gant forced himself to remain still.

Then an elevator door opened on the opposite side of the hall. Footsteps, hurry—

He glanced around towards the concierge. He was still reading his paper, uninterested in anyone who passed; apparently uninterested in Gant. Someone called him, and he turned his head, then went in, shutting the door behind him. The elevator door in front of Gant opened. He waited until the elevator was empty, entered, and pressed the fifth-floor button. It seemed a tiny but important victory that the concierge had taken no interest in him. He probably thought it was someone coming back for something he'd forgotten, if he thought at all.

People tried to press into the elevator on the fifth floor before he could get out. He squeezed through them, not ungrateful for the press of their bodies, their scents and smells. He did not resent or fear them for that brief moment. Then the door closed and he was alone in the corridor. Linoleum, chipped and stained, on the floor, a succession of brown-painted doors, dirty green paintwork on the walls. It was an infinitely depressing place. He checked his direction, then followed the trail of mounting numbers on the doors. Some of them were missing. Radios played pop music loudly behind many of the doors, as if to drown out something else.

Five-four-nine. He raised his fist, and hesitated. He listened. Radio playing, but not loudly. No other human noises. He looked back down the corridor. No one. Swallowing, breathing deeply, he knocked loudly on Boris Glazunov's door.

At the third knock, as if at a general signal or alarm, a number of things happened. The elevator doors sighed open, and Gant turned his head. A young man emerged, saw him—

The door opened. Gant turned. A tall man faced him, a grin already spreading over his face as he evidently recognized the caller. Someone spoke from inside the flat, a man with an authoritative tone. The young man near the elevator shouted. His voice seemed full of warning.

Gant's hand remembered the Makarov in the coat pocket, and clenched around its butt. The tall man's grin spread. His hand moved from behind his back, slowly and confidently. He was intent upon the widening fear in Gant's eyes. The young man was running towards him down the corridor shouting, his shoes clattering on the linoleum.

Gant half-turned. He half-drew his hand from his pocket. Then the young man, ten yards away, skidded to a stop and yelled his name. A plea rather than a challenge. The tall man had stepped forward through the doorway, his hand now holding a pistol, bringing it up to level on Gant's stomach. Gant squeezed the trigger of the Makarov, firing through the material of the coat pocket. The noise was deafening, ringing down the corridor, pursued by the explosion of the tall man's gun, which discharged into the ceiling. Plaster dust fell on Gant's hair and shoulders.

"Quickly! Gant—quickly!" the young man shouted, grabbing his sleeve. Gant thought the face familiar, distorted by urgency as it was. A second KGB man was emerging from the room at the end of the apartment's hall. Gant fired twice, wildly. The man ducked out of sight. Gant heard a window slide protestingly up, felt chilly air on his face. "Come!"

Gant crossed to the window and the iron fire escape. The young man climbed out and began to descend. There was frozen snow and ice on the rail and the steps. The young man danced carefully down them as quickly as he could. Gant watched the door of apartment five-four-nine as he climbed over the window sill and felt for the first step. Then he was outside, shaking with cold and reaction.

Familiar—the face behind the two or three days' stubble of dark beard—familiar . . .

He clattered down the first flight, then the second, slipping once, pursuing Vassily—

Vassily—!

He had helped Pavel throw Fenton's body into the river. He had disappeared after the metro journey, near the warehouse. Vassily. Gant looked back up the twisting fire escape. A face had appeared at the window, a walkie-talkie clamped to its cheek. He saw a pistol, too, and then looked down once more, aware of the treacherous nature of the ice-covered steps.

Relief, the excitement of danger being met and overcome, filled Gant. Vassily bobbed ahead of him, half a flight further down. He chased him.

First floor—ground floor. Rear of the building. Lock-up garages, trash cans, a soccer goal painted on a brick wall. He bumped into Vassily, almost breathless.

"Vassily—!"

Vassily grinned. "Come. Quickly . . ."

They ran across the courtyard. Then Vassily jumped at a garage door, clinging to the low roof, kicking his legs, easing himself up and onto the felted roof. Gant followed. He could hear whistles and shouts now, but no noise of vehicles other than the muted roar of traffic on the Mira Prospekt. Vassily crouched as he ran across the roof, then he jumped out of sight. Again, Gant followed.

He dropped into a snowy patch of garden. A dog barked. Vassily was already climbing a fence when Gant caught up with him. Gant heaved himself over the fence and dropped into an icy alleyway. Vassily ran to the corner of what appeared to be a narrow, quiet street. When Gant reached him, he said:

"I hope she is here . . ."

There were a few parked cars. Vassily seemed to be searching for one in particular, reciting license plates half under his breath. Gant's chest hurt with the effort of drawing in the icy air.

"Is—?" he began spluttering.

"Yes—there!"

They ran across the street. *She?* Who? Vassily bent to peer at the driver of the car, then nodded. He pushed Gant into the back seat and climbed in after him.

"Get down, both of you!" the driver snapped as she eased the car away from the pavement, then turned left. Gant's face was against Vassily's arm. He could taste the worn leather of his jacket.

"They were—waiting," Gant said as the car turned right, traveling at no more than thirty miles an hour once it had done so.

Vassily's face, close to his own, frowned. He nodded his head vigorously. "Yes. I was not sure. I was watching you. The moment you entered the building, a car pulled up in front. It was KGB, but they did not get out. I knew then that they were waiting for you." A police car passed them, siren flashing, heading in the direction of the Mira Prospekt. "I was almost too late!"

"How long have you been following me?"

"Most of the night."

"Why didn't you make contact?"

"He was ordered not to!" the driver snapped. "He always obeys orders—we all do!" Gant felt the force of the driver's resentment.

"Are we being followed, Comrade?" Vassily asked very formally, surprising Gant. His face was serious, perhaps in awe of the driver.

"No."

Gant felt the car turn sharply left. After a silence, he raised his head, and was shocked to see the cosmonaut's monument, the rocket atop its narrowing trail of golden fire, drifting past the car windows. He clenched his hands together to stop them shaking. They were near the Unit, heading for it—!

"What is it?"

"Where are we going?" he snapped in a high, fearful voice. They were leaving the monument behind them now.

"We have a place . . ." Vassily assured him.

"A change of clothes for you," the driver said. "A change of appearance. Papers. Everything is to be provided for you." The resentment was deep, angry. The woman disliked, even hated him. Who in hell was she?

"O.K.—what then?"

"I must get you out of Moscow."

"And Vassily?"

"Vassily is not trusted—not as much as is necessary." Vassily shrugged at her words. He grinned, almost pathetically. "They do not consider he is capable of the task."

"And you are?"

The car had stopped at traffic lights. Gant could see them through the windscreen. The car was almost new, the fawn-colored fabric of the seats very clean. It was a large saloon. Gant was suspicious. Then the blonde woman turned her head, so that she was in profile as she answered him.

"I have certain qualifications," she announced. "The greatest of which is my capacity to be blackmailed into helping you. I am told Vassily is someone who keeps changing addresses, who deals in black-market goods as well as espionage work. He is useful, but not *their* person! I am."

She turned her head as the lights changed. The car drew away, accelerating. They passed the Ostankino television tower, like a steel needle against the heavy sky. Gant stared at Vassily, disconcerted, troubled by the woman's resentment. Almost afraid of help now that it had come.

Waterford lifted his head as the noise of the chainsaw ceased. At the far end of the clearing that had been made and was still being enlarged, a tree fell drunkenly forwards with a noise like the concussion of a rifle. Immediately, branches were lopped from it and stacked for later use in general camouflage. At the perimeter of the clearing which reached from the shore of the frozen lake back into the trees in a rough semicircle, bundles of white netting lay ready for use. Already, much of the camouflage netting had been strung between the trees, forming what might have been the roof of a huge, open-sided tent.

Two RAF mechanics were laying and checking nylon ropes which stretched from the trees that held the winches down to the shore. They had selected the stoutest trees, capable of taking the strain imposed by the three chain-lever winches which would be used to haul the Firefox out of the lake. The winches were anchored to the trees and additional steel anchor pins had been hammered into the frozen ground—not reaching a sufficient depth in the soil to completely satisfy Waterford or the Senior Engineering Officer from Abingdon. Even the Royal Engineer mechanics who would operate the winches were unconvinced there was a sufficient safety margin. They would only know, however, when they tried.

Waterford returned his attention to the group of marines around him. Six of the SBS unit were seconded as divers, which left the eighteen in front of him in full arctic combat kit. The group was framed by upright or slightly leaning pairs of long cross-country skis and vertical ski poles. Each man bore a laden pack on his back. Nine of them also carried radio equipment. They were assigned to work in pairs rather than their more usual threes and fours, and their duties were reconnaissance rather than defense. His early warning system, he thought—which was all they could be with their small numbers.

Their rifles were slung in white canvas sleeves across their chests, below their snow goggles. The usual mixed bag favored by an elite force such as SBS—some standard LlAls, a few 7.62 sniper rifles, one or two of the new, short-stock 5.56 Enfields, and a couple of the very latest 4.7mm Heckler & Koch caseless rifles. Even in their disguising sleeves, they possessed the appearance of plastic planks narrowing at one end. Waterford himself had one, for evaluation on behalf of the army. He thought it ugly, futuristic, and effective, firing its bullets from a solid block of propellant rather than a cartridge case. It had the stopping power and accuracy to penetrate a steel helmet at more than five hundred meters. He appreciated the weapon.

Looking at the rifles, he reminded himself he must stress yet again the reconnaissance nature of their duties. He moved two paces to the unfolded map on its collapsible table. The eighteen SBS marines crowded around him. Their breaths climbed above them like smoke from a chimney. Flurries of snow struck Waterford's face and settled on the map. Angrily, he brushed them away.

"Right, you gung-ho buggers—now you've got yourselves together, I just want to remind you what you're supposed to be doing. I'll keep it simple so you won't have to take notes . . ." He tapped at the map with a gloved forefinger.

"You're on recce *not* engagement duties. You have your headings and you know the maximum distance you should go. It's a scouting perimeter, nothing more solid than that. Beyond the trees—beyond three or four kilometers, that is—the country is rolling, with mixed thickets and lots of open areas. Find the best observation posts, and sit tight. Report in only at specified times and keep it brief. We're not playing requests for Grandma and Aunt Glad and the rest of the family this time. Unless, of course, you wake up to find yourself being buggered by a huge, hairy Russian soldier—in which case, don't wait for your allocated time slot—just yell *Rape!* and get out of there." They laughed. "As far as we know, there's nothing out there. We don't expect trouble, we don't *want* trouble, but we want to know if it's coming. So, make sure your dinky new radios work, and keep hold of the nice new binoculars M.O.D. issued you, and—good luck. Any questions?"

"Reinforcements, sir?" a lieutenant asked. "I mean, if it comes to it . . . ?" He gestured round him.

"I know. You'd like to know there's a Herky Bird full of your mates ready to drop in—well, they'll be at Bardufoss if they're needed. But, just remember this is a nice quiet pub—we don't want a bloody awful punch-up in the lounge bar, if we can possibly help it! O.K.?" More laughter, then Waterford said: "Anyway, you're the lucky ones—think of this lot having to break all the ice and dig away at the bank until it's a nice shallow incline, then lay runway repair mats. O.K., let's confirm your O.P. sites, shall we? Cross and Blackwell?"

"Blackburn, sir," one of the marines corrected him amid anticipated and preconditioned laughter at a familiar joke.

"Cross and *Blackburn*—your heading?" Waterford replied, his face expressionless as he stared at the radiating lines on his map that led from the lake to the observation sites he had decided on for the nine pairs of marines. Not so much the thin as the transparent red line, he remarked to himself.

Buckholz turned to look at Waterford, and then returned his attention to Brooke. Evidently, Waterford knew how to handle his men. The laughter that had distracted the CIA's Deputy Director was high-pitched, nervous. The SBS men were, like most elite forces, somewhat too thoroughbred in behavior when not in action. Buckholz had found that to be true of U.S. Special Forces men in Vietnam. But, they were there to function, not for show . . .

Brooke stood with his air canisters at his feet, a white parka over his wet suit. Two other divers had joined them, one bringing coffee. Buckholz sipped at it now. The snow pattered against the back of his parka and the wind buffeted him.

"This is vital," he reiterated, sensing Brooke's resentment of his inexpert interference. He criticized it in himself. He did not mean to imitate his own grandmother, but he simply could not help it. Brooke had already been down twice through the jagged hole they had broken in the ice. His damage report had been expert, thorough. His inspection of the undercarriage, especially, had been positive in conclusion. Then he and two others had removed the charges they had laid when they had first found the Firefox. Now, Buckholz had ordered them to make another check on the undercarriage. "You have to be certain—really, really certain, that those three legs are going to be able to take the strain of the winching. She's got to come out of there by the strength in her legs . . ."

"Yes, sir," Brooke said stiffly.

Buckholz grinned. "O.K., I know I'm fussing—but humor me, uh?"

Brooke returned his grin. "O.K., sir—I'll double-check."

"Good boy."

"Mr. Buckholz?"

Buckholz turned in the direction of the call. The chainsaw was at work again. Snow flurried into his face. The sky was dark grey, the snow almost constant now, and the wind had increased from around five to more than ten knots. Sure, it was all helping to mask the signs of the air drop and their prints out on the lake, but it was reducing visibility at times to less than thirty yards. From the shore, it was difficult to see across the clearing to the Royal Engineer corporal using the chainsaw. He mistrusted the weather. A small example of its crippling effect had been the three hours of searching required to locate the contents of one burst pack out on the ice. Yes, more than anything it was the weather that made him fuss and triple-check. It held the key. Worst of all, the weather was delaying the Skyhook so much that they couldn't now assume it would arrive when they had winched out the Firefox. Buckholz worried that the flying crane would never arrive, and they would have to destroy the Firefox where it stood.

Damn the weather.

"What is it?" he called into the gusting wind.

"Mr. Aubrey, sir," the radio operator called. He was bent over the control console of the commpack as he crouched behind a canvas windbreak reinforced by lopped tree branches. A dish aerial rose to the height of the lowest overhanging branches of the tree canopy on the shoreline.

"O.K., tell him I'm coming." He turned back to Brooke, hesitated, then said: "O.K., you bums—do your thing." Brooke smiled as the American walked away.

"Mr. Aubrey said it was urgent, sir."

"Sure," Buckholz replied, attempting a grin. "With him, everything is. O.K.—put me through." He shivered. At least in the Lynx helicopter, one of two that had brought in the non-parachutists and which were now tied down and camouflaged on the far side of the lake, it had been crowded but warm. He looked at the coffee mug in his mittened hand. He hadn't been warm since . . . too old, that was the trouble. Thin blood. Buckholz devoutly wished Aubrey his own present discomfort.

The operator keyed in the voice scrambling code and paused for the light which would signify the console was ready to transmit. Then he sent his call sign and received an acknowledgment a few seconds later. He nodded to Buckholz, who held the microphone close to his lips, as if about to whisper.

He was assailed by a sense of foreboding, which made him pause before he said: "O.K., 'Mother,' go ahead. What's on your mind? Over." The conversational, almost jocular tone was deliberate, as if it could fend off what he sensed was approaching bad news. He heard Aubrey's voice through the one earpiece of the headset that he pressed against the side of his head.

"Bad news, I'm afraid, 'Fisherman.' The Skyhook has had to put down at a military airfield in southern Sweden for repairs. I'm assured that the repairs are minor, something to do with the rotors being out of balance. Caused by the bad weather they've been forced to fly through. However, even more important, they can't yet give an accurate estimate of the length of the delay. I'm sorry. Over."

"Hell! Give it to me straight, 'Mother.' Don't bullshit me. I'm a big boy and I can take it. Over."

"At least tomorrow afternoon—that's the earliest they could be with you. Over."

"But they *will* come? Over."

"They must! When do you think you'll be able to begin winching out? Over."

"Some time around midnight tonight. Before first light, the Firefox will be on land. And no Skyhook! Over."

"It will come, 'Fisherman'—it will come. Over."

"If it doesn't arrive by eight, I'm planting the charges and we start ripping out the thought-guidance and anti-radar systems! Over."

"It will arrive, 'Fisherman'—just be patient. Over."

"Get the damn weather changed, will you? Over."

"I'll do what I can, 'Fisherman.' Meanwhile, prayer might be advisable. Over."

"I'll pray, 'Mother'—I'll pray. Out."

Buckholz looked around him. The SBS two-man reconnaissance units were vanishing behind the weather and the trees, on their way out of the camp. He could hardly see the last of them. Brooke had already descended with one of the other divers. In the silence after the chainsaw had ceased, a stunted tree fell with a crack like the beginning of a landslide.

Buckholz looked up. The snow was heavier, the wind colder, stronger.

"Yeah, I'll pray," he said. "I just hope He can hear me above this wind!"

He had been like a thief, an intruder, in her apartment. She had had to be careful, almost obsessive, about the things he picked up, touched, used. She was coming back—she had determined on that—and Dmitri would be coming back there, too. There must be no traces of any other man—this American least of all. After each cup of coffee, after the one small whisky, after the lunch she had prepared, she washed cups and glasses and plates and dried them and put them away. The actions prevented discovery and occupied her; distracting her from the growing claustrophobia of her apartment now that it contained the American. His presence was so, so *palpable*, so inescapable.

He spoke little after he had accepted her story. She had no idea what his feelings were towards her, towards his own future. He was tired—for two hours he had dozed in the armchair in which he had first sat down—and his experiences in the Unit on the Mira Prospekt, about which he remained silent, had worn at him. He seemed almost unliving, so passive and withdrawn was he. It was as if he had come to effect her arrest himself, wrench this life away from her.

The suit that Vassily had brought, with his papers, was a good, sober one of foreign cloth and cut. Three-piece. Pads fattened his lean face and half-glasses added age. Once he had shaved and showered and donned his disguise, he appeared almost like one of her senior colleagues in the Secretariat . . . which was what his papers declared he was, a civil servant traveling to Leningrad on ministry business. The bluff was bold, designed to attract attention but deflect scrutiny. The American seemed easy with the disguise, his body adopting a stiffly correct uprightness, seeming to add inches to his height. The dark overcoat would finish the portrait of a bureaucrat.

They left the apartment at four. In the elevator, when someone she knew from the floor below her own got in, she murmured to him in businesslike, formal tones, having greeted the neighbor. It was evident from what she said that she was accompanying a colleague; her overnight bag and his small leather suitcase suggested the length of their stay. Gant's brief replies were in practiced Russian. He seemed at ease, but she could not be certain. The part he was playing protected him like a carapace.

The taxi, a checkered band along the doors and side panels, was waiting outside the apartment block. The traffic on Kutuzovsky Prospekt was heavy, but sedate. The cars were larger and moved more slowly. The Party limousines seemed almost to line up in the central lane. The driver put their bags in the trunk and they slid into the back seat. Gant unfolded a newspaper and pretended to read as soon as the door was closed behind him; obscuring his features from the driving mirror.

"Leningrad Station," Anna said.

She thought of Maxim. The dog, and her father, had welcomed him. The dog seemed suspicious of her, as if picking up her mood, and this suspicion seemed to communicate itself to her father. But he did not ask, except after her health and after her KGB lover. A couple of days, she assured him . . .

For her office, she had a heavy cold. For Dmitri, it was a

sudden trip to Leningrad—no, by train, the afternoon flight was full and she enjoyed train journeys . . . what business? Oh, some complicated case of fraud at one of the hospitals, the disappearance of clothing, money . . . no, not a police matter yet, until she had seen the records . . . yes, love to you, love, love . . .

She had almost betrayed something then, over the telephone. Choking back tears, choking back the desire to prolong the call, she had rung off before he became concerned at the strangeness underlying her reassurances.

She had left Gant in the apartment while she delivered Maxim to her father's *dacha*. No one, he said when she returned, had called at the door, no one had rung. When she entered the apartment, it had seemed like a stranger's home.

They crossed the river by the Kalinin Bridge and picked up the Sadovaya Ring. Blocks of apartments lined their route. Gant fastidiously concentrated on his newspaper while she stared absently through the window, hand cupping her chin. She determined not to notice the city either to right or left of her, because she would not allow herself even to consider she might be taking some final journey through Moscow. There was the bulk of the Peking Hotel with its pink facade incongruous against the snow-filled sky. If she concentrated on the apartment blocks to the left, even though she saw Gant in profile all the time, their grey, weather-stained concrete and countless, anonymous windows deadened her sense of Moscow. It could be any modern city, anywhere in the world.

They left the Ring at Kirov Street, passing between the twin, guardianlike towers of the Leningrad Hotel and the Ministry of Public Works. Komsomolskaya Square, with its three main-line railway stations, closed around them. The taxi pulled up beneath the portico of the Leningrad Station. She got out first, and Gant paid the fare, and a slender tip which caused the taxi driver to mutter under his breath but which he might have expected from a bureaucrat such as the man who had ridden in his taxi, his nose in his newspaper.

Snow speckled the shoulders of Gant's overcoat. He jammed his fur hat on his head, adjusted his half-glasses, and studied Anna. She saw his keen, appraising glance and felt challenged, even insulted, by it. This man, who had done nothing, said little. Then, surprisingly, he smiled briefly.

"O.K.," he said, handing her her overnight bag. "They'll be checking papers. I'll get in line first, you go to the ladies' room or something so that you're further back in line. I'll collect the tickets."

She nodded, feeling suddenly undermined and nervous. He had, by taking control of the situation, deflated her little air pocket of confidence and self-reliance. He gripped her arm as he saw her hands shaking.

"Take it easy," he said, not unkindly, bending his head close to hers. "You've done O.K. up to now—just take it easy."

She nodded, more vigorously. "I—I'm all right." She changed her grip on her bag, and added: "Very well. But, be careful . . ."

They walked under the portico into the smallest of the square's three stations. Marble pedestals, at shoulder height, displayed countless, ever-vigilant busts of Lenin placing the station concourse under eternal surveillance. The roof of the station arched above them, glass and steel, the ribs of a huge animal. The station was busy with the first commuters. Gant read the Departures board. Anna slipped away from him towards the toilets. Then, walking with an easy confidence, turning his head with the appearance of casual interest, he made for the ticket reservations counter. He picked out uniforms, overcoats, guns, bulky figures questioning arriving passengers. He felt himself moving through a network of invisible alarm beams. Yet it was not as before, it was not like the metro when he had trailed at Pavel's side, trying to keep up, trying to adapt and adjust. He had spent most of the day preparing for this. He had temporarily forgotten Gant.

He arrived at the window and, with the appropriate impatient authority, bent and spoke into the grille set above the swiveling wooden begging bowl that issued the tickets and snatched the payment for them. He asked for his reserved tickets—yes, his secretary had reserved them that morning. He sounded as if he already anticipated some confusion, some mistake on the part of the ticket clerk, a small balding, grey-faced man in a jacket with a worn collar, and frayed shirt cuffs. He fumbled with his book of reserved tickets, fumbled out the appropriate ones. There were two styles of first-class on Soviet trains, and Anna had reserved seats at the front of the train, where the best carriages were always placed, the ones with two-seater compartments, heating, air-conditioning, radio—and restaurant service. The most expensive seats; the Party seats.

Gant paid for the tickets with large-denomination notes. They, too, were an element of disguise. Almost new notes. Declarations of privilege.

He turned away from the window, pocketing his change and picking up his suitcase. A leather-coated man watched him, and he tensed. It was really beginning now—

He pretended not to notice the man and headed across the wide concourse towards the platforms. A second man appeared on the point of stopping him, but assessed his clothing and bearing and let him continue. He hardly looked at his face, hardly noticed the features above the well-cut formal suit and behind the glinting half-glasses. Conventionally, they did not expect him to arrive at the station; if he did, they would expect him to sneak, to lounge, to slip through— not to stroll. He reached the ticket barrier. The long Leningrad express stretched away to where the dark-grey sky and the snow canceled the perspective. He joined the line. Tickets and papers, of course. The KGB man who informed him was more deferential than he was to the man ahead of him or the woman behind. Gant pursed his lips in affected irritation.

Two people ahead of him. Suddenly, he wanted to know where she was in the line. The man's papers being inspected with great thoroughness, with absolute leisure. Would his stand up? Where was she?

Stop it.

Where—? Would they—? Did they have pictures—?

Yes, behind them, pinned to the side of the ticket barrier, next to a notice about the penalties for not purchasing the correct ticket for any journey—a silhouette of a figure being grabbed and held by a taller figure, the sense of a struggle, of an arrest—

Stop it.

He dabbed his forehead with his sleeve, pretending to remove his fur hat to disguise the gesture.

The picture taken of him at the motorway barrier, when his papers said he was Glazunov . . . next to that, something they must have obtained from the Center's Records Directorate computer—himself in USAF uniform, taken perhaps eight or nine years before. He had been much younger then, he told himself, much—

Beneath the pictures, he was described as an enemy agent, spy and saboteur. He was sought with the utmost urgency. People were instructed to be vigilant.

The hairpiece they had given him was an expensive one, one that had been purchased in the West, in all probability. It was, Vassily had said, grinning, better even than Tito's had been. Yet, deliberately, it looked false. His hair was too short from having to wear the helmet with its thought-guidance sensors to be anything but noticeable. A wig which looked like a wig was deemed a bolder call to attention. Were he suspicious, he would not wear an evident hairpiece. His motive would be considered to be vanity.

He replaced his fur hat. The youthful hair showed beneath it, a slightly different shade from his own.

He handed over the tickets, and gave the KGB man his papers, drawing them from his breast pocket. The ticket collector asked the reason for the second ticket, and Gant turned his head loftily, indicating Anna when he saw her three places behind him. He waved her forward without consulting the KGB man. A man in the line scowled, resenting authority and privilege. Gant introduced her offhandedly to the KGB man, and she passed over her papers.

To Anna, he paid no attention. To Gant, he was respectful, studying him from beneath narrowed eyelids. He scrutinized the papers for a long time, but did not glance behind him at the photographs. The hairpiece seemed to amuse him but he was nervous of revealing his smile and his contempt. Eventually, he handed back the two sets of papers, and nodded.

"A good journey, Comrade," he said with insolent mock-servility. Gant pretended to study the name displayed beneath the man's picture on the ID card clipped to his breast pocket—but only for a moment. The man winced visibly.

They passed through the barrier onto the platform. Gant felt his legs weaken, his hands shake. But he did not falter in his stride.

"Are you all right?" Anna asked.

"Yes," he replied without looking at her.

Side by side, in silence, they walked down the long, wide platform, past the newspaper shop, the candy shop, the gift shop, the coffee shop. Gant imperiously waved away a porter.

Bullshit, he thought. It's keeping you going, just bullshit. And he wondered who had suggested the disguise and the false identity and how well they knew him. It helped. To playact arrogance helped. Bullshit—

They reached the designated carriage. Gant looked at his

watch. Fifteen minutes before the train left. They found their compartment, claimed their seats. He was grateful for the relative safety of the twin-berth compartment. No one would be able to intrude.

"A magazine or newspaper, Comrade Ossipov?" Anna asked him as he lifted their cases onto the rack. "Some candy?"

"No . . . ah, perhaps a magazine. *Soviet Science World?*" he replied, smiling at the pantomime. "Yes."

"Very well, Comrade Ossipov," Anna said, and left the compartment.

He watched her climb down onto the platform and make for the newsstand. She looked small and vulnerable as she passed two uniformed KGB men with guns on their shoulders. She had been angry, he remembered—blazingly angry—when she had seen his false papers. Secretariat, like herself. They were forcing her to use her own papers rather than the set they provided, which described her as his wife. She had been insulted and challenged. She'd chosen to travel as his professional colleague. There was some declaration in it, he thought, some assertion of herself, of her personal life.

She disappeared into the shop. Gant began to relax. The hairpiece felt as hot and constricting as the fur hat he had removed. He brushed flecks, and creases, from his suit. He unfolded the newspaper. He began to allow time to pass more slowly, feeling his whole body relax, inch back from the pitch of tension he had experienced at the ticket barrier. It had worked, had worked, he repeated to himself over and over like a calming spell. The woman was excellent cover. In the time available, in the extreme situation in which they had found themselves, Aubrey's people in Moscow had done well, very well.

He glanced out of the window, directly after looking at his watch. Four minutes to departure time—she was talking to a man in uniform, a young colonel in the KGB. Fifteen yards from the window. She *knew* him—

Four minutes—she was smiling—three minutes fifty—she was *smiling!*

Gant felt his body constrict into a straitjacket, his fists rest heavily on his knees, his eyes begin to dart about the carriage . . .

Who *was* she—? What was she *doing?*

Anna leaned up to him, and kissed Dmitri Priabin, aware of Gant's staring face fifteen yards away.

"What a surprise!" she exclaimed.

Holding her arms, as if to restrain her, he grinned. "Duty, my love—duty. I'm here in my official capacity, inspecting the security arrangements. I didn't know whether or not you'd arrived."

She looked pointedly at her watch. "Only a couple of minutes," she murmured.

"*Soviet Science World?*" he asked, looking at the top of one of the magazines under her arm. "Looking for more wheelchair projects? No, I'm sorry," he added when he saw her face darken. "That was cheap." He bent to kiss her, and she responded. She had half-turned and she could see Gant clearly as she pressed against Dmitri's chest. He looked betrayed, frightened. She could not tell him—

She pushed away. "I'd better get on the train, I suppose."

"When will you be back?"

"A couple of days."

"You didn't leave a hotel number."

"I'll ring you—tonight."

"What is all this business?" he asked, taking her arm—an image of arrest?—and walking her towards the door of the carriage. She leaned against him, trying to display the innocence of the meeting to Gant. She smiled broadly. She could not tell if Gant relaxed. He continued to watch them very obviously. Had Dmitri seen him—?

And she realized, with a horrible, sickening force, that the hunter and the hunted were eight yards from each other. She was certain that even she would have recognized Gant beneath that disguise, beneath the ridiculous hairpiece, even from those grainy pictures of him near the ticket barrier . . .

"Oh, some petty fiddling, they think. It's got to be verified before the police are called in."

"No drugs?" he asked in all seriousness.

"No—clothing, sterile supplies, all kinds of silly things— sometimes I think people will steal anything in this country! It may even be a fraud on the part of the suppliers because they're behind with their production schedules—I'm not sure yet. But it has to be investigated." She whirled him round suddenly, and smiled up into his face. "Never mind about that—just say you'll miss me!" A part of her awareness was stunned at the ease with which she lied.

"I will—like hell." He kissed her. She pressed her mouth against his, held his head between her hands, clung to his neck as the kiss continued. It *was* a farewell, to something.

A whistle blew. She pulled away from Priabin. "I must go—"

"Come on, then—on you get!" He was blithe, confident she would be away for no more than two days, enjoying this tiny interlude in the search for Gant. He handed her onto the train, and slammed the door. She leaned out of the window and kissed him again.

The train moved. He stepped back. She waved, blew him a further kiss, which he returned. He grinned like a schoolboy. She waved furiously, already ten yards away.

Hers must be the nearest compartment of the first-class carriage, the others were full, two faces at each window. Who was she traveling with—? He waved. The train gathered speed, twenty yards away now—

He began running, still waving. He took the first two steps because he wanted to keep her in sight as long as possible—and then the third and fourth steps and all the others because of the face at the window. Strangely, he did not falter in his waving.

He was ten yards away, and puffing for breath, when he recognized the face at the window; confirmed the suspicion that had dashed over him like cold water. And saw, too, the horrified, appalled look on Anna's face when he transferred his gaze to her.

And knew, then—

Gant.

Traveling with Anna. Anna, helping him . . .

Gant.

9 / **EN ROUTE**

Kirkenes civilian airfield possessed the very temporary appearance of a forward position likely to be abandoned at any moment, crouching uneasily just inside the Norwegian border with the Soviet Union. Its low wooden buildings did not seem entirely explained by its latitude or the Norwegian style of architecture. Instead, they suggested impermanence; the reluctance to invest in Kirkenes—just in case. Aubrey had been allocated a low, barracklike hut behind the control tower, part of the Fire Section, into which was crammed the communications equipment, the maps, charts, telephones, and men he would need to employ. The windows looked out over the iron-grey water of the Korsfjord, and beyond it the peaks on Skogerøya, the Varangerfjord and the Barents Sea. The water was a fitful sight through the slanting snow showers. The main room of the hut smelt strongly of the numerous paraffin stoves that supplemented the main woodburning stove. The noise of a twenty-eight-volt generator outside the hut intruded. Power cables snaked over windowsills. The edges of the windowpanes were foggy. It was a depressing place; an image of exile, or defeat.

Aubrey stared out of the windows at the sleet, attempting to imagine the weather conditions that the Skyhook lifting helicopter had encountered on its slow journey from Germany, and the even worse conditions that would prevail if it ever took off again from the airbase in southern Sweden. He had been in communication with the helicopter's U.S. Army pilot, and with the senior engineering officer at the airbase. Repairs to the rotors were proving a slower, more complex, more serious task than had at first been anticipated. Parts were required which the Swedes did not have; parts which, at present, could not be flown in.

The Skyhook was crucial. *No fallback*, Giles Pyott had said. Everything depending on better weather and a single helicopter . . . If the Firefox was to be removed from the site, they could not dispense with the helicopter. Aubrey knew that he, too, had fallen for the spurious, glamorous excitement of the helicopter lift, just as the politicians had done. There was no way in which an aircraft capable of carrying the dismantled pieces of the airframe, an extra forty-five thousand pounds weight, could land and take off at the lake. They could not have got trucks through—too much snow and no roads.

Now, he knew that the bad weather might last a week. It would worsen for the remainder of that day, and though the following day might begin a little better, it would rapidly close in once more. There might be short breaks, windows in the weather, but they were unpredictable. By the time it finally cleared, the Finns would have cordoned off the entire area and informed the Russians where they could find their precious Mig-31—!

Aubrey choked silently on his enraged frustration. He was helpless; bound and gagged. He could do nothing, *nothing*! Unless the Skyhook arrived before the expiration of the deadline, at midnight the following night, then it would all have been wasted, all have been for nothing.

And he would have failed, and he would have to attempt to live with the increasing sense of guilt he felt concerning the people who had died. Aubrey shook his head. He did not want to have to do that. It was an unfamiliar feeling, and it pained him. He had no defenses against it.

All he could see ahead of him were the explosive charges clamped to the airframe, the mutilated cockpit instrument panel and systems consoles—then the bang. Snow, earth, metal—then nothing!

Damn, damn, damn, damn—

Guilt thrust itself once more into his consciousness, a weed growing through concrete. Pavel, Semelovsky, Fenton, Baranovich—especially Baranovich. He had killed them all, only to fail to catch the ball they had thrown.

Damn the weather and the helicopter . . .

And damn Kenneth Aubrey!

"Mr. Aubrey?" It was the voice of his radio operator. The communications equipment from the Hercules had been transferred to the hut.

Aubrey turned his head to respond, thankful for the interruption. One of the Norwegian army guards passed the window, face held to one side against the blowing sleet and snow. "What is it?" Aubrey asked.

Curtin was at the top of a pair of stepladders, leaning against a huge map of the Finnmark, the Kirkenes area, and Finnish Lapland. He was intently applying red-flagged pins to the map, designating Soviet activity along the border. There were no red flags inside Finland. There had been little movement along the border, and no aerial reconnaissance since the weather had worsened, according to reports from Eastoe in the Nimrod.

"Mr. Shelley from London, sir," the radio operator replied. Aubrey joined him at the console, lowering his overcoated body onto a flimsy-looking swivel chair. He had retained his coat as a vague protest at inactivity, as if to suggest he might be called away at any moment or be engaged in some furious travel. Aubrey had to feel that his own sojourn at Kirkenes was utterly transitory.

"Hello, Peter—what can I do for you?" he said offhandedly.

After a few moments, when the Receive light had winked out and the tape had rerun, he heard Shelley say: "Just to report that they're on the train, both of them. One of our scouts saw them go through the barrier, inspection and everything." Shelley sounded pleased. The rescue of Gant was working like clockwork, and it irritated Aubrey. Shelley would have an easy and notable success with it—

He crushed his anger in the silence. Shelley was waiting for a comment.

"Well done, Peter—is everything else in place?"

"Harris will pick them up at the station outside Leningrad—Kolpino—when they leave the train. He'll have the travel warrants and the visas for them to cross into Finland. Director-General Vitsula has agreed that a team will meet them at the border, just to take the weight off their shoulders when they've got that far. It's looking good on the operations board—fingers crossed, sir."

Aubrey waited beyond the time when the Transmit light indicated that he could speak once more. Shelley's success made him envious. It had been *his* idea to try to rescue Gant and the woman the CIA was prepared to throw away—and now under Shelley's control it looked as though it might work.

And yet, it was the damned aircraft that he really wanted! The Firefox—that was the real prize—the big one, as Charles Buckholz might have described it. The big one . . .

"Well done, Peter," he repeated eventually. "Keep me informed. Harris should do a good job—he's worked for us before. Out."

He stood up and returned to the window, wrapping his overcoat testily and showily about him. Curtin watched him from the top of his stepladders, tossed his head and grinned, and went back to his map and his pins. A gap in the sleet again showed Aubrey the lower slopes of the lumpy, barren peaks of Skogerøya and the grey, featureless Varangerfjord beyond them. An awful place—

A mirror of failure.

At least Gant would be saved—

And Aubrey admitted that at that moment Gant seemed a poor prize without the aircraft he had stolen.

Dmitri Priabin continued to stare as the last carriage and the guard's van moved around the curve of the line just beyond the end of the platform. Then the train was masked by an oncoming express. Anna and Gant had disappeared.

His thoughts were in a turmoil. He felt paralyzed and weakened to such a degree that it was difficult to remain standing; impossible to move—to turn and walk or run to the nearest telephone, the nearest fellow-officer—

That flight of his imagination horrified him. *He had actually thought of telling someone—of reporting it to his superiors—!*

His hands were shaking. Nerves in his forearms made them seem chilly, even beneath his greatcoat. He rubbed his arms to stop them quivering. As he did so, he realized his body was bent. He was leaning forward as if he were about to vomit. He straightened up very slowly, his eyelids still pressed tightly together—warding off what he had witnessed or retaining the dampness behind them. The pain of it, the waves of shock, went on like a series of coronaries, each one worse than the one before. He could not escape the image—*her face, Gant's disguised but recognizable face*, together.

He heard himself breathing very quickly. He sniffed loudly, and wiped surreptitiously at his eyes. He was facing down the length of the platform. And Oleg was coming towards him from the barrier, still wearing the overcoat that smelled of mothballs.

"Damn," he muttered between gritted teeth.

Suddenly, Oleg was an enemy. A KGB man. A spycatcher. He must know nothing.

"You all right, Colonel?" the older man asked in a not unkindly tone. "You look a bit pale."

Dmitri tried to smile. It was more like the expression of a wince at sharp pain. "Yes, all right, just indigestion."

"Oh—Comrade Akhmerovna got off all right, then, did she?" Oleg persisted, smiling; almost winking as he continued: "Did you catch a glimpse of the bloke she was with, sir?" The grin was broad, jokey, knowing. Priabin stifled a groan. "Traveling on business, like you said, but with this bloke wearing a hairpiece." He continued to grin at Priabin, expecting a jocular reply. "You might have trouble there, sir," he added. Priabin again provided a slim, pale smile.

"One of her colleagues in the Secretariat, I gather," he said stiffly, and moved away. He had to find somewhere to think, to decide. It was racing beyond him, he was losing control, falling apart—Oleg was making him want to scream— he felt he would explode if he didn't get away from him.

He strode towards the barrier, hearing Oleg's sarcastic:

"Sorry I mentioned it, Colonel sir," behind him. *Don't upset the man!* He paused and turned. "It was a very obvious wig," he said with studied lightness. Then he smiled. Oleg returned the expression, nodding and chuckling.

"Wasn't it, though—what a shocker! They always make me laugh, wigs. Don't know why—haven't got much myself—but, wigs—!" He burst into laughter. Priabin joined in for a moment.

"That indigestion all right, sir?" Oleg asked solicitously.

"Bit better, thanks."

"You got anything?" he asked, fishing in his pocket and bringing out a wrapper of indigestion tablets. "These are good—get them in the *beryozhka* shop. American, they are. Better than those peppermint things they make in Minsk. Try one." He held out the wrapper. There was fluff from his pocket on it. Priabin did not dare risk reaching out his hand. He could envisage fumbling with the wrapper, tearing it, spilling the tablets, arousing Oleg's suspicions.

"Don't do anything for me. It's vodka I need!" he announced as heartily as he could.

"Come on, then, sir—"

Priabin shook his head. "I've taken enough time off—better get on with my tour of inspection." He shrugged. "See you, Oleg."

He touched his cap with his gloves and walked off.

"A real pity, sir—" he heard Oleg offer.

"What?" he snapped, turning on his heel.

Oleg was holding out the wrapper of indigestion tablets. "These," he said. "They smell of mothballs—taste of 'em, too. Don't blame you refusing."

Priabin smiled. "Goodbye, Oleg." He strode towards the ticket barrier, passed through it with a nod to the KGB man who must have inspected Gant's papers, glimpsed the poster displaying the pictures of the American pilot, and passed into the station's main concourse. A wig . . . attracting attention to a distraction. See the wig, see the silly vanity, the lifestyle and personality it suggests—miss the pilot beneath.

The air outside the Leningrad station was cold. It was as if he had walked into a sheet of glass. He breathed deeply, many times. His head would not clear. It was like a night sky against which rockets and other fireworks burst. Crazy, useless schemes, exploding, leaving their fading images on an inward eye. He had no idea what to do

Except he knew he could not report her. He could not tell his superiors, could not tell Vladimirov, that the woman he lived with, the woman he loved, was aiding Gant in his escape from Moscow. They would arrest her, interrogate her, make her talk—then dispose of her. Into a pine box or into one of the Gulags, it was the same thing in the end. Reporting her would be her death sentence.

"Gant—!" he murmured fiercely, clenching his fists, then pulling on his gloves in a violently expressive manner. "Gant—"

Anna was running a terrible risk. She was in the utmost danger.

He clattered down the station steps towards his limousine. Where?

What to do?

They were going to Leningrad—in all probability, they'd leave the train before it reached the city. Someone would be waiting for them, an Englishman or an American . . .

And then it struck him, jolting him like a blow across the face. *She was leaving—leaving with the American—she was getting out—*

He climbed into the back of the black car and slammed the door behind him.

"The apartment!" he snapped.

The driver turned out into the square. Railway stations all around the square. Images of departure, of fleeing.

He did not know what to do. He knew only that he must not lose her. He had to bring her back. He had to stop her leaving. He could not bear to lose her. She *couldn't* run out on him—! He had kept her secret, he had protected her—she *couldn't* leave him now—!

The train gathered speed, passing the television tower, its top hidden by low, grey clouds. Sleet melted on the window, becoming elongating tadpoles of water. The closest suburban stations all exhibited the same functional, deserted appearance as they headed northwest out of Moscow. The compartment was warm. A loudspeaker softly provided Tchaikovsky. Gant did not know how to begin the conversation he knew he must have with the distraught woman who sat opposite him. She was staring at her hands, which seemed to fight each other in her lap. Her lover, she had replied to his first question. The man she lived with. He had been unable to find another question to ask. Instead, he had stared out of the window as if surprised that the train was still moving, still being allowed to continue its journey.

Finally, as the suburbs flattened into parkland, grey and white beneath the driving snow and low clouds, and then rose again into the old town of Khimki-Kovrino, Gant turned away from the window.

"What will he do?" he asked, staring at his own hands, as if imitating the woman's supplicatory posture. She looked up, startled back to her present surroundings. Her features appeared bruised with emotion.

"What—?" she replied in Russian. He wondered whether her use of her native language—he had spoken in English—was some way of keeping him at a distance. Or simply security?

"I said, what will he do, the man you live with?" he repeated in Russian.

She shook her head. "I don't know—!"

"He knew it was me," Gant explained unnecessarily. "And he guessed we were together." He cleared his throat. "What would he make of it?"

"He knows about me!" she exclaimed, beating her fists in a quick little tattoo on her thighs. "He already *knows*—!"

"Jesus H. Christ . . ." Gant breathed, leaning back in his seat. The small compartment was hot, even though he had removed his formal overcoat and unbuttoned his jacket. He fiddled with the half-glasses on his nose, but did not remove them. "He knows about you . . ." he repeated in English.

"He's known about me for a long time. He's done nothing about it. He—" She looked up, and essayed a smile. "He's very much in love—" She might have been talking of a favorite son and another woman. "It pains him—sometimes he can't sleep—but he protects me . . ."

"Christ—" Gant rubbed his forehead, inspecting his fingers for dampness. Very little. He was surprised. He checked his body. Hot, yes, but no sense of rising panic. The movement of the train, northwest towards Leningrad and the border, lulled his body. The first stop was Kalinin, a hundred miles from Moscow. Perhaps they were safe until then.

He could not panic, he decided. The woman had coped, coped with much more, over a much longer time. While she remained almost calm, so would he.

"Listen," he said, leaning forward, reaching out his fingertips. She withdrew her hand, holding it against her breasts. He sat back. "Listen—think about it. What will he do? What will he think?"

"I—God, I don't know . . ."

"Will he—will he blame the CIA? Will he blame me?"

"What do you mean?"

The daylight outside was failing. It was as dark as late evening already. The tadpoles of melted sleet wriggled across the window. A collective farm lay unused beneath a layer of snow. A tractor huddled near a hedge.

"Does he love you enough to blame everyone else except you for what he saw?" Gant explained with some exasperation. "Is he that blind? Will he blame the CIA, the British, me—?"

"Instead of me?" Gant nodded. "Perhaps—"

"Will he report us to his superiors? Will they stop the train?"

"I—don't think so . . ." Anna's brow creased into deep lines. Gant guessed her age to be around thirty-eight or -nine. Older than the young colonel he had seen on the platform. He leaned back and closed his eyes. What had he seen? Seen her trying to reassure him . . . yes. He'd understood that there was no danger, even through his shock. What else—? The man? Smiling, laughing, holding her—

His *face* when she climbed aboard the train, in the moment before he saw Gant—?

Love. Something from paintings, almost religious—what was it? Adoration—? Adoration . . .

And he began to believe that they were safe . . . safe, unless—

"Could he follow us?" Gant asked sharply.

"What?"

"Could he arrange to follow us—*himself*?"

"Why?"

"To kill me."

"Why?"

"He might—just might work it out. If he believes in you, he'll blame me most of all, lady. And he could keep your dark secret and put the clock back to yesterday, if he killed me. I wouldn't even be able to tell tales on you." The Makarov was in the suitcase. Later, he would think about transferring it to his inside pocket.

"Do you think he would do that?"

Gant shrugged. "He might—you know him, not me.

You've screwed up what was a nice neat assignment. He could either hate you, or me. There's no one else to attract his interest." Gant leaned back, closing his eyes. His lack of panic surprised him.

Maybe it was the woman's presence? She was a talisman who had, perhaps, become a hostage. He felt safe with her. Adoration . . . yes. Priabin was besotted with the woman, and he could use that to his advantage. Priabin might come after them, but he wouldn't betray her, give her up.

He'd blame the good old U.S. of A. and one of its citizens in particular. Yes, he'd want to kill Gant.

Gant could not believe his luck. The car journey after Vassily had helped him, the apartment for most of the day, the disguise and the easy access to the platform and the train—they were all dreamlike, unreal. It had been going too well.

But this—this was real luck.

He found himself thinking aloud: "This is real luck . . ."

Immediately, the woman's face narrowed. She despised him. He could not help that. *Real luck*. He might have had thousands of KGB looking for him, but now, thanks to her, he had only one who was looking in the right place. And, as they say, his lips were sealed.

It was working out. He could make it, with those odds. The papers and the disguise had stood up, would stand up. Harris would be meeting them at a quiet suburban station with a car and new documents. And, if he kept Anna by his side or in front of him like a shield, he had nothing to worry about . . . nothing at all.

"Stop it!" she said intently. He opened his eyes. "Stop it!"

"What—?"

"You're smiling—you're *enjoying* it!" She was very close to tears. Her teeth nibbled at her full lower lip. Her pale, drawn features seemed inappropriate to the expensive hairstyle, the costly, fashionable clothes.

"All right," he said. "I'm sorry. It was good not to be the one who's really alone for a change. I *am* sorry."

She nodded. "I—" she began.

"Could you go back?"

"I don't know—I thought so, before, before—"

"Take it easy. Maybe the Company will lay off, if this all works out?" He watched her shaking her head. The blonde hair flicked from side to side. On the platform, she had seemed so much in control, so much the stronger partner. But she was weakened by her own love. She wasn't so much afraid of getting caught as of losing her lover. Well, maybe the Company would release her if she pulled this off . . . ? Miracles did sometimes happen.

He looked at his watch. Five hours to Kolpino. They had tickets for the restaurant car. She'd have to make up before she appeared in public—

Gant retreated from concern. It complicated matters. She was, effectively, his hostage, and that was the easiest and most satisfactory way to think of her.

Dmitri Priabin had dismissed his driver when the car dropped him at Anna's apartment. He had hurried from the elevator and fumblingly unlocked the door as if half-expecting to find her there. The apartment was, of course, empty.

He tore the expected letter open, glanced at the excuse of business in Leningrad, his eyes highlighting the love that constituted the remainder of the letter. Then he crushed it, threw it across the room, and retrieved it only moments later, thrusting it into his pocket. Without conscious decision, he had packed a suitcase with a civilian outfit—a disguise, he thought—and then he had left the apartment once more, slamming the door hollowly behind him. Maxim was with her father—whatever happened, the boy was safe. And it was important that he was safe. Whatever happened to Anna, whatever was discovered—whatever part he played himself— her father could protect his grandson even if he could not save his daughter.

In one way, then, it would be clean.

He hailed a taxi. Conscious thought seemed to have caught up with bodily activity, and he ordered the driver to take him to Cheremetievo airport.

Flights to Leningrad—

He had to inspect the airport security anyway, it lay under his authority. They would expect to see him.

And what would he do? What was he planning that required the suitcase on the seat beside him? He did not really know. Thought had not yet overtaken reaction, to discover what lay in the future. It, like his body, was content simply to be active. He was hurrying to the airport—he appeared to be pursuing . . .

Who and what was he pursuing?

His hand touched the holster at his hip, providing the answer. The American—Gant. He wanted to kill Gant. He *would* kill Gant—! In his death lay safety. Anna would be safe, *he* would be safe.

The driver had a bald, shining head. His ears were red and prominent. The sleet flew at the windscreen, rushing towards the wipers, then sliding jellylike to either side. It was hypnotic.

Priabin shook his head, waking himself. If there was a flight to Leningrad, he could overtake them. They would leave the train before the terminus, though—

If he obtained a list of stations where the express stopped, he could perhaps decide which was the farthest station from Leningrad where they might get off or be met by someone. If he traveled back along the line to that station and waited for the train, then—if they didn't get off, he could board it. Board it and confront them—

Like a cuckolded husband, he could not help thinking, hating the image. He could kill Gant—shot resisting arrest. He could live with Vladimirov's rage, and Anna could disappear into the Leningrad night. He'd spotted Gant, followed him . . .

He should have boarded the train then, *in Moscow—!*

No, no . . .

He'd had no plan, then. He'd have blundered in like the cuckold, not the rescuer.

And, when he'd killed Gant, what would the Americans do to Anna? Would they guess who and why and assume she'd been a party to it?

And turn her over to his own organization?

He sweated, even though the heating of the taxi was primitive. He banged his fist slowly, mesmerically against the leather of his suitcase. Have to hide that at the airport, get on the aircraft at the last moment, mustn't be seen by his own men . . .

Any of his personal subordinates posted there? He didn't think so, but was not sure. Have to be careful—

It's awful, he thought. The mess is awful, awful—

He sat back in the corner of his seat, out of view of the driver's mirror, because he knew his face was pale and cold and utterly confused. He could not see the end of it. He could not believe that he could save Anna. He rubbed one gloved hand over his face, as if trying to remodel his expression with heavy stroking movements.

Each time he thought about his situation, the main priority appeared to be to save Anna. Get her away from the American, get her back safely to Moscow, reinstall her in her apartment. Life could go on, then—from that point.

But, each time he considered the priority and agreed with it, he thought of Gant and the desire to kill him rose like nausea in his chest and throat and it became difficult to consider Anna's safety or his own. Gant's death increasingly thrust itself upon him as a course of action that was inevitable.

"Then, while we do not have the pilot, we must return to our search for the aircraft," Chairman Andropov announced. At his side, Vladimirov did not demur, even though he understood that this was little more than another deflection of blame in his direction. A similar move to his surprise appointment as security coordinator of the hunt for the American.

Strangely, he did not resent his assigned role as scapegoat. Rather, it increased his sense that he was the only man—the only one of all of them—capable of recovering the Mig-31. Even when the First Secretary nodded his agreement with Andropov and looked immediately towards him, Vladimirov felt no resentment and little anxiety. He was prepared, even equable, as he awaited an outburst from the Soviet leader.

It came almost at once, beginning on a low, histrionically calm note.

"Gant must be found," he announced from behind his desk. The Kremlin office had once been used by Stalin. It was not the great anteroom where all visitors were cowed and fearful long before they ever reached the huge desk behind which Stalin had sat, but nevertheless it was a large, high-ceilinged room with a tall marble fireplace and massive, dark furniture. It daunted visitors, and it expressed the Soviet leader's ideas of his own personality and authority. Khrushchev had used a much smaller room. This First Secretary had moved to another floor of the Arsenal building, and the windows of his office and the luxurious apartment beyond it stared across a triangle of grass and trees towards the Senate and the rooms once occupied by V.I Lenin

"Yes, First Secretary," Vladimirov replied.

"And so must the aircraft—Gant is only the key to the aircraft. You agree, General Vladimirov?"

"Of course, First Secretary. Of course—" He bit down upon the rising irony in his tone. He rubbed his hands on the carved arms of the huge chair in which he sat before the mahogany desk with its lion's feet.

"Then where *is* the aircraft? Where is it *now*?" The First Secretary got up, pushing back his chair noisily on the parquet flooring. He strode to the window, hands clasped behind his back. He looked out at the failing light, the white trees and grass, the windows of Lenin's office. "*Where is the aircraft*?" he repeated without turning.

Vladimirov did not need to glance at Andropov to realize the satisfaction that would show on his features. To think *that* man, the *secret policeman*, might become the successor to the grey-haired buffoon at the window. Vladimirov, unable to suppress his contempt, was pleased that neither of them could see his face. But, just to think of it . . . ! Andropov was already a member, perhaps the most powerful member, of the inner cabal of the Politburo. He was rumored to be about to resign as Chairman of the KGB, to become head of the General Secretariat of the Party, thereby broadening his power base. Andropov might one day sit behind that very desk .

Andropov would have the Lenin offices opened up again, Vladimirov thought bitterly. They would become offices once more rather than a museum—*his* offices.

"I—have people working on that. We have selected a number of landing sites, First Secretary; places where the American could have landed the Mig-31 " The words were automatic.

"These I should like to see," the First Secretary said, turning slowly and overdramatically to face into the room once more. "And—the American told you nothing under the most intense interrogation?"

Vladimirov gambled. There *was* something there, in those tapes—he was certain of it

"I'd like you to listen to it—and Chairman Andropov of course—to the tapes his people made. I'm sure we're missing something there."

He heard the First Secretary sigh with satisfaction. All the man wanted, ever wanted, was his authority recognized

He wanted the scent of subordination strong in every room he entered. It was easy . . .

Careful, Vladimirov warned himself. He stood up slowly as the First Secretary passed him. The two bureaucrats in grey suits preceded him to the door. Their coattails were creased with sitting. He had managed a few hours' sleep late the previous night, a shower and a change of uniform. He followed the two men through the outer offices where the Soviet leader waved secretaries back to their desks. Two bodyguards fell in behind Vladimirov—a prisoner's escort, he thought for an instant, then smiled inwardly.

They used the elevator to the ground floor. It was only a single floor's descent, but the elevator was modern, air-conditioned and emitted quiet piped music. Guards saluted with uptilted rifles as they passed across the marble floor towards the main doors. The two bodyguards hurried a little way ahead, then issued umbrellas from a rack beside the doors. Vladimirov took an umbrella, but disdained the galoshes the two guards were now fitting over the shoes of the First Secretary and the Chairman. The image of the guards kneeling before the two men was too striking not to be savored.

They cautiously stepped out into the darkening evening, descending the swept, damp marble steps of the Arsenal like very old men. Birch trees and snow-covered lawns were dyed pale orange by the lights. Vladimirov walked alongside his companions. The Kremlin was a place he did not often visit, and he tilted back his umbrella to gain a clearer view of the palaces and cathedrals within the walls, thereby displaying what the other two might sniggeringly have called his provincialism, his gaucheness.

The place was a monument to absolutism. Even the cathedrals repelled rather than invited. There was little sense of quiet expressed by their facades, nothing of sanctuary. The red towers, topped by their neon Party stars, ringed the buildings; penned them. They were heading towards the largest of the new buildings, the Palace of Congresses, which, together with the Senate, contained most of the government offices within the Kremlin complex. To Vladimirov, it looked like a glass and concrete weed growing up modernistically amid the planted, massive, tropical flowers of the older buildings.

The wind splashed sleet against his shaven cheeks, chilling his skin. Yet he continued to stare, to appraise, until they reached the main doorway of the Palace of Congresses. They passed the guards on duty and entered the main foyer of the glass building. Heavy chandeliers hung from the ceiling. Vladimirov followed the First Secretary and Andropov across the tiled floor—a huge modern mosaic depicting the inevitable triumph of Socialism—towards the reinforced steel doors of a special elevator. They descended six floors before the elevator sighed to a stop. Guards faced them as they entered a corridor of whitewashed concrete. Steel doors, like the watertight doors of a submarine, confronted them. The bodyguards inserted plastic identity tags into the locks, and the doors opened.

Vladimirov inhaled deeply as he once more prepared to enter what bright, cynical young army officers who had served there called the *Führerbunker*. Beyond what was little more than an airlock, where more identity tags were inserted into computerized locks, examined, and returned, a second steel door opened onto a vast underground room. They stepped into a command center which mirrored not only that in the Tupolev but also those deep beneath the Moscow Garrison's HQ and his own air force headquarters southeast of the city. He followed the others across the room, then mounted a metal ladder onto a gantry which overlooked the command center. A long glassed-in gallery formed the control room of the underground complex.

All this, Vladimirov thought, the means of obliterating most of the earth, is being used for no more than a skirmish, a small fuss on the border. The insight increased his sense of well-being. Officers saluted, operators sat more erect and alert as they entered. Vladimirov immediately directed the Soviet leader's attention to the fiber-optic map against one wall; a smaller version of the huge perspex screen erected on the main floor of the underground center. It was edge-lit, computer-fed, like the map-table aboard the Tupolev, and at that moment it displayed Finnish Lapland. There were patches of light on the screen, dotted like growths of luminous fungus across Lapland.

"We've selected these sites, First Secretary—" Vladimirov began, using a light-pen to pick out each of the small glowing points. "These are the only places where the terrain would allow an aircraft to land." He was confident now. He'd already spent two or three hours in this control room. Its occupants were military personnel—with a sprinkling of KGB and GRU and GLAVPUR people, of course, but soldiers in the main, soldiers first—and he was at home amid the paraphernalia of electronic warfare and computer strategy. He picked out, too, a line of small red dots. "This is the American's route, from the point at which the Chairman's Border Guards picked up his trail." The light-pen's arrow bounced along the row of dots, as if picking out a melody. "He traveled in the same general direction, and we deduce that he was making directly from the point where he left the aircraft to the Norwegian border at its closest point. Paint in the suggested route, in both directions, please."

The red dots became a white line, extending roughly northwest to southeast. It crossed lakes, valleys, minor roads, forest tracks, frozen rivers. In the northwest, it terminated at the border, while to the southeast it halted at the shores of Lake Inari.

"Time is crucial here," Vladimirov continued in the tone of a kindly, expert lecturer of greatly superior intelligence. "We know when the second Mig-25 was destroyed, we know when we first found traces of Gant. We know how fast he was able to travel, and we can begin to deduce distances. This white line is far too extended, of course—therefore, we consider that the Mig-31 must be somewhere in this area . . ." The arrow of the light-pen described a circle. When the arrow bobbed away, off the map, the computer had traced a circle, as if the pen had drawn on the perspex. It was perhaps twenty miles in diameter.

"Very good," the First Secretary announced with evident sarcasm. "Very good—the Mig-31 is in Finnish Lapland!" He turned to Vladimirov. "We *know* that, General—we already know that!" It was obvious that the Soviet leader had simply been waiting for this opportunity to harangue and threaten. Now he had an audience, and it was one that pleased him—the military; the despised and feared military. He would humiliate one of their heroes in front of them, show them their idol's feet of clay. Vladimirov steeled himself to control his features and remain silent. "Find it! *You* find that aircraft, *today*. And you, Andropov," he added in a less hectoring voice, "find the pilot." He turned as if to leave, his bodyguards already opening the door of the control room and making room for him to pass. Then he returned his gaze to

Vladimirov. "It must be found," he said. "I do not need to remind you of the consequences if it is not found—today."

He left the control room. Abashed, Andropov immediately wiped his spectacles with his silk handkerchief. There was a sheen of perspiration on his brow. His nostrils were narrow with rage. Vladimirov, feeling the resentment of his body begin to dissipate, realized two things concerning the Chairman of the KGB. He was playing for perhaps higher stakes than Vladimirov himself—and he was uncertain of his allies in the Politburo if he could still be bullied by the present First Secretary. Therefore, Andropov would now become an ally; untrusted and dangerous, but an ally. The Soviet leader had included him in the catalogue of blame should Gant and the Mig-31 not be found.

As if to confirm his thoughts, Andropov moved towards the perspex map, closer to Vladimirov. He smiled, an expression that turned to its habitual ironic shape almost as soon as it formed on his lips.

"If you wish for a more—sympathetic?—audience, I offer myself, General Vladimirov," he said quietly.

Vladimirov nodded. "Accepted, Comrade Chairman."

"Good—now, I understand the logic of your deductions thus far—but, how could he have landed the aircraft? In that terrain—it is snowbound, surely?"

"Yes, it is. However, we think his best chance would have been a forest track or minor road."

"Would *he* have thought of it?"

"I think so. I think he would have felt himself—shall we say—challenged, to do it? He is possessed of a massive certainty of his own worth and talents. He would have tried, I think. He must have tried, because of the parachute. And he was uninjured, which I think means the airframe is virtually undamaged—certainly recoverable, certainly a threat if recovered by the Americans or the British. So, all we have to do, Comrade Chairman, is to find it."

"A forest track or a minor road—still covered with snow—"

"Out of fuel, with little risk of fire, he might have risked landing on snow. Too deep, and I agree he would turn tail-over-nose and break up. But, with the winds and the weather over the past weeks, we think that at least some of these tracks could have had sufficiently little depth of snow to help rather than destroy the Mig."

"And there are two of these tracks within your circle also

crossed by the white line predicting his route," Andropov observed. He bent closer to the map, then clicked his fingers. "You're ignoring these lakes," he said. "Might he not have used a frozen lake?"

Vladimirov shook his head. "We discounted them. Our aerial reconnaissance immediately after the loss of the second Foxbat showed nothing. On a lake, he could not have hidden the Mig."

Andropov shrugged. "I see," he said. "Very well. What is the scale of this map?"

"We are talking about a matter of fifty or sixty kilometers from our border, at its closest point, to this road, another fifteen to this one here." The arrow of the light-pen danced like a moth on the surface of the map.

"You have ordered a new aerial reconnaissance?"

Vladimirov shook his head. "All we could do in this weather is high-altitude infrared, and that airframe is as cold as the landscape around it by now. We won't have photographs. Any search would have to be on the ground. We should have to cross the border—a small party . . ."

"But then, your deductions would have to be correct. They would have to be accurate—extremely accurate for a small party."

"Working back along this white line, into the circle—sufficiently spread out, they could cover a wide area—"

"As long as the weather gets no worse and visibility drops no further—and just so long as the aircraft is not buried under the snow by now!"

Vladimirov shook his head. He enjoyed the Chairman's scepticism. It enlivened the debate and cemented their alliance. "I think it's under the trees somewhere—he taxied it off a road under the trees."

"And left it like a parked car?"

"Just like a parked car."

Andropov looked doubtful. "Is there any other way?" he asked.

"Your experts have been examining the tapes of Gant's interrogations ever since he escaped, in the hope of finding something, some concrete piece of evidence to indicate what he did with the aircraft." Vladimirov's features hardened as he remembered. His hand squeezed the material of Andropov's jacket sleeve. The Chairman seemed not to resent the grip on his arm. "He was about to tell us—on the point of telling, when he knocked himself out. He was within an inch—!" He held up his fingers, almost closed together. "An inch, no more—"

"But, he didn't—"

Vladimirov shook his head. "Your people are good, but they seem unable—"

"I'll have the tapes brought here, together with their report," Andropov promised. "Meanwhile—I suggest a reconnaissance party consisting of Border Guards?" Vladimirov nodded. "I take it their helicopters can fly in the weather they're experiencing up there?"

"Just."

"Then they must be ready to move at once. Where do you suggest they begin?"

The arrow of the light-pen wobbled up the perspex map, alighting above the white line of Gant's suspected journey.

"Here's where they found evidence that he had made camp, slept. All the other traces—parachute found here, village here, capture—are further to the northwest. I suggest we have your party dropped here, and that they work backwards along this line, perhaps making for the closest forest track, here . . ." The arrow buzzed almost dementedly above the line.

Andropov studied the map, then simply said: "Very well— I'll issue orders for a reconnaissance party to prepare for an immediate border crossing—please have the coordinates and any other advice ready for them."

Gant pushed down the window of the compartment. Snow flurried against his face. The drab provincial station on the edge of the town of Chudovo was almost deserted. A handful of passengers gingerly left the train, as if stepping into an alien environment. Boots and galoshes slipped on the snow-covered platform. Lights gleamed through the snow. The train hummed. One or two uniformed guards, railway police, individuals in leather coats or heavy mackintoshes checked papers. There was one more stop and perhaps forty minutes before Kolpino, where they must leave the train to meet Harris. To explain their through tickets to Leningrad, Anna would assume a sudden indisposition, a need for fresh air, a slight fever that might be infectious. The local hospital might be required . . .

It seemed slack and fortuitous to Gant, but he sensed that it would work. A small country station in a suburban town, the staff tired and bored, their unexpected visitors important Party officials. Panache and bluff would convey them from the station to Harris's car with little trouble. A suggestion of food poisoning, though the restaurant meal had been good, might further the bluff.

It didn't matter, he thought. Priabin had not boarded the train here at Chudovo—and if he was waiting for them in Leningrad, as Anna thought he might, then he was powerless. Gant had as good a hostage as he could have wished for. That thought satisfied him, though it gave him no pleasure. He heard the guard's whistle, saw the swinging lamp the man held winking at the far end of the train, and withdrew his head from the icy air and closed the window. When he turned to Anna, he saw that she had pulled her coat over her shoulders and was shivering.

"Practicing—right?" he said. She looked at him vehemently. "Sorry—" He nodded his head towards the window. "No sign of trouble," he added, sitting down opposite her. The train journey had lulled him; every passing mile had reinforced his sense of having broken through the net tightening around him. Not so for Anna, apparently. The journey might have been one into exile. She was still terrified of what Priabin might do.

She fumbled in her bag, drew out a gold lighter and cigarette case, and lit a filtered American cigarette. The brand of cigarette was as unconscious as the habit of smoking; a badge, long worn, of success. She blew the smoke towards the ceiling. Her hand was shaking.

She shook her head, softly and rhythmically, at some inward image or idea. She appeared as if alone in the compartment. It was evident she blamed him, entirely, for her situation; just as her lover would be doing by now. The thought chilled Gant.

Was there a way out for them? Could they manage, between them, his own capture or death and their safety? He suspected that both she and Priabin would be concentrating their entire energies on finding such a solution.

Killing him would be the easiest way.

The train gathered speed, the last of the station lights flashed past. The darkness of the night pressed at the windows. Snow was caught by the lights of their compartment, beyond the reflection of his features. He stared at himself, his cheeks fattened by the pads, his face changed by the addition of the half-glasses. They might kill him, if they ever got together and considered it—

The door of the compartment slid back. Anna was sitting bolt upright. Gant's eyes flicked up towards the reflection of the newcomer. Civilian clothes, he thought with a sense of relief.

Then he saw the drawn pistol and the distraught and grim features of the man holding it. Only then did Gant turn his head.

"Dmitri—!" Anna cried.

Gant felt numb with shock, as if his fears had conjured the man into the compartment. Priabin *had* boarded the train at Chudovo. Priabin with a pistol. The KGB officer who was Anna's lover had reached the end of his particular journey, and he had found his answer. A simple and obvious answer.

Kill Gant.

"Out," Aubrey said, limply handing the microphone to the radio operator. He turned away from the console, and almost bumped into Curtin, who had been standing at his shoulder throughout the conversation with the senior engineering officer at the Swedish airbase. Curtin shrugged, but Aubrey appeared not to notice the gesture. "Damn," he breathed through clenched teeth. The single word seemed invested with a great weight of anger and frustration, even something as dark as defeat.

"It's one hell of a piece of bad luck—" Curtin began, but Aubrey turned on him, glaring.

"Bad luck! *Bad luck?* It is a monumental fall coming after pride, Curtin—that's what it is! It is entirely and utterly my own fault." Curtin made to interrupt, but Aubrey gestured him to silence. "It is *my* fault! I was warned—Giles Pyott warned me, as you did yourself, as Buckholz did. I chose to take no heed. I chose not to listen." He clenched his hands together at his lips. He paced the hut, intent upon recrimination. Eventually, he turned to Curtin and said: "We know that Gant is on the train. In a matter of hours he will be across the border into Finland—it has proceeded with the smooth regularity of clockwork. Harris is at Kolpino to meet them. We know that the aircraft will emerge from the lake within the next few hours—*and we can't do anything to remove it!* We will have salvaged it simply for the *Russians* to collect!"

"You couldn't fight the weather."

"I should never have *ignored* the weather! That was my sin. Pride, Eugene, *pride*—!"

"Bad luck."

"No—!" He began pacing the room again, murmuring to himself like a child learning by rote. "Thirty-six hours, even then they're not certain—almost twelve hours after the deadline expires—and the weather may not allow them to continue. Pyott told me not to rely on the Skyhook, but I ignored that . . . now I have been shown my error!" He did not pause in his pacing. The radio operator huddled over his equipment, ignoring Aubrey's voice. Curtin perched himself on the edge of a folding table, carefully balancing his weight. Aubrey continued with his catalogue of self-blame. He forcibly reminded Curtin of an animal newly caged in a zoo, pacing the boundaries of its prison, seeking a way of escape. "I didn't listen, I didn't damn well *listen*—! I knew best—Nanny knows best. Nothing left now but to rip out the systems we most want and blow the airframe to pieces—and I still want that aircraft." Curtin strained to catch what followed. "I owe it to them . . . but I can't—there's no way—!"

Then he turned to Curtin, arms akimbo as if begging for some relief of mind.

"What—?" Curtin said, spreading his own arms, unable to understand what Aubrey required and reluctant to intrude.

Aubrey's lips worked silently. Then he burst out: "If only the damned plane would *fly!*"

Curtin grinned in embarrassment. "Yeah," he said. "If only."

Aubrey closed his eyes. "If the Firefox could fly . . ." Then he looked up and announced to Curtin: "They would leave me in peace, then, wouldn't they?"

"I don't understand?"

Aubrey disowned his words, his hand sawing through the fuggy, paraffin-smelling air. Then he wiped his lips, as if what he had said amounted to little more than a geriatric dribble of sounds.

"I'm sorry," he said with exaggerated, ingratiating apology. "I forgot myself for a moment." He moved closer to Curtin, placing himself near the heat from the wood-burning stove, rubbing his hands as if cold. He looked directly at Curtin instead of the floorboards of the hut, and said: "Forgive me for asking—but the aircraft could not fly, of course?"

Curtin shook his head. "No . . ." he said. The word was intended to be definite, to end the speculation he could see beginning to cloud Aubrey's pale eyes, but it faded into a neutral, hesitant denial. Aubrey seized upon it.

"You don't seem sure—"

"I am sure."

"Then why not *be* definite!" Aubrey snapped, his face sagging into disappointed folds once more.

"I am, but—"

"But what?"

"I—it's been immersed in water for more than forty-eight hours . . . you've got a smidgeon more than twenty-four hours . . ." Curtin shook his head, almost smiling. "It *is* impossible," he announced. "I'm sure of it."

Aubrey persisted: "As a matter of interest, why did you hesitate?"

"Because—well, because I've heard of Navy planes getting a ducking and making a comeback—" He held up his hands to stop a torrent of questions from Aubrey. "It took weeks, Mr. Aubrey—*weeks!* Well, maybe one week anyway. I just remembered it had happened, is all. It doesn't help you. *Us.*"

"You mean the aircraft is immediately damaged by immersion in water?"

"Sure, the damage starts at once."

"But the damage is not irreparable?" Aubrey's voice hectored, bullied. Curtin felt interrogated, and resented the small, arrogant Englishman who was too clever for his own good and too self-satisfied ever to admit defeat.

"That depends on how it went in, whether it was all shut down, sealed . . . Hell—!"

"What is the matter?"

"I don't know the answers, for Christ's sake! You're crazy, Mr. Aubrey, sir, crazy." He climbed off the table and stretched luxuriously, as if about to retire. The gesture was intended to infuriate Aubrey and it succeeded.

"Damn you, Curtin—stay where you are and answer my questions!" He pressed close to the American, undeterred by his greater height and bulk. Curtin thought, quite irreverently, that Aubrey was squaring up to him, ready to fight.

"O.K., O.K.—if it passes the time," he murmured, regaining his perch on the table.

"Just answer me this—could the Firefox fly?"

Curtin shrugged, hesitated, and then said: "I don't know—and that's the truth."

"Then, who would know?"

"Why don't you ask the Senior Engineering Officer—what's his name, Moresby? The guy from Abingdon. He's standing right next to the airplane, he knows the state it's in—ask him!"

The radio operator was sitting erect in his seat. "Get me Squadron Leader Moresby, at once." Then he looked at Curtin and held up his hand, displaying his fingers in sequence as he spoke. "We have the pilot, almost safe . . . we have the runway—the lake . . . we have twenty-four hours . . . the aircraft needs to fly fifty or a hundred miles, no more, to be safe from recapture. Is that asking too much?"

"Much too much—but you don't want an answer, I guess," Curtin murmured.

"Squadron Leader Moresby, sir—"

"I'm coming, I'm coming—" Aubrey's eyes gleamed, almost fanatically. "I *won't* let it go!" he said. "Not yet, anyway. I *won't!*"

10 / NESSIE

"Don't kill him, Dmitri—! Dmitri, *think*—!"

Gant's hand had stopped reaching for his breast pocket. He remembered that he had not transferred the Makarov from his suitcase. Priabin's pistol was pointed directly at him, even though the man was staring into Anna's face. His head had flicked towards her the moment she shouted. Gant remained motionless, an observer of the scene. There was no way in which he could move quickly enough across the compartment, before Priabin had time to shoot him. He forced himself to remain still

"Anna—?" Priabin exclaimed in the tone of a child that does not understand a parental order. He was being prevented from doing something he very much wanted to accomplish.

"Don't kill him, Dmitri," Anna repeated, her hand moving slowly towards his gun. He kept it trained on Gant and out of range of her grasp. "How can I escape from this if you kill him?"

Priabin appeared deeply confused. "You? But, you come with me. You'll be safe, then—"

"Do you think they'll allow that? Don't you think they'll know I *allowed* him to be killed? It's a trap, Dmitri—I have to do what they want!"

He held out his left hand, and she caught it with the fierce, clamping grip of a vise. She clung to him, he to her. Then he shook her hand, gently.

"It won't be like that," he said soothingly. Gant saw that he was sweating, and not simply because of the heating in the compartment. He was almost feverish with purpose. And now he was witnessing his schemes begin to dissolve. "It won't *be* like that!" he reiterated more firmly, attempting to persuade himself.

"It will," she said, "I know it will—you don't know them."

"Believe her," Gant added, and they both looked at him with utter hatred. He quailed. Priabin was still a man in shock and panic, revolving harebrained schemes to save his mistress. The situation eluded Gant. He did not understand how to use it to his advantage. He was certain that the wrong word would act like a spark on the Russian.

"Shut up!" Priabin snapped unnecessarily.

Gant squeezed into the corner of his seat, his eyes flicking upwards for an instant to his suitcase. There was no chance.

As if room had been made for him, Priabin sat down at the other end of the seat, the gun still aimed at Gant. Gant felt the cold of the window against which his back was pressed seeping through his jacket, between his shoulderblades.

Priabin spoke to Anna without looking at her. He still held her hand. Anna's fingers were white and bloodless, twisted in his.

"Listen to me, Anna," he began. "If he tells us where the aircraft is—you know, don't you?" Gant nodded carefully, his face expressionless. "If he tells us, we can pass that information on. We—we could get out of it like that. All they want is to know where the plane is, nothing else—that's their only interest in him. I can say . . . can say that I followed a hunch, or he was reported to me as seen boarding the train, *alone*—we struggled, the gun went off, but he'd told me everything . . . !" He stared at her. "It would work!"

"And they'd be sure as hell to turn you over, Anna," Gant said quietly. He realized he could not remain silent. Ever since he had noticed the bloodless fingers gripping those of Priabin, he had understood that she was not a contestant, rather the prize for which he was fighting with Priabin. If she became persuaded of her lover's case, then she would allow Gant to die. She hated him as much as Priabin did. At his words, Priabin's gun jabbed forward in little threatening movements. The man's eyes were grey, and now as unyielding as slate. His face wore a sheen of perspiration, and his cheeks were flushed. He looked feverish. "Believe me," Gant added, forcing himself to continue, "I know them. They've wasted people on this operation already— he knows that. Even Baranovich." The name was like a stinging blow across her face. "They'll use anybody. He's right—the man's right. They're only taking care of me because I know too much. I mustn't fall into the wrong hands." He attempted to smile at Priabin. "That's why they used you. But, you have to see it through, Anna. I'm sorry, but you have to. If you get me away—then they'll maybe let you off the hook. I'll try to make them do that."

"Don't believe him!" Priabin shouted.

"Dmitri, keep your voice down!" Anna snapped fearfully at him. Her eyes had glanced into the corridor.

"Pull down the blinds," Gant said.

Priabin released Anna's hand. He tugged at the blind above his head, sliding it down behind him. Anna rubbed her white hand. Gant turned, watched Priabin for a moment in the window, looked out at the snow flying past the train, and heard Anna draw down her blind. He turned back to Priabin. He would not jump from the train, not yet. He might just win the game—

"O.K.," Gant said in English, as before. Priabin's English was better than Anna's. "That's better. I will try to help—but I can't help if I'm dead . . . can I?" He turned to Priabin. "Look, comrade, I know you want to kill me, and I know why. But *I'm* no volunteer, either, just like her. *I* didn't pull her name out of a hat, so let's get blame out of the way, uh?"

"I'm not going to let you go," Priabin replied immediately. He had wiped the sweat from his forehead. He was calmer now; he held rather than gripped Anna's hand. Yet Gant saw that he was now perhaps more dangerous.

"If you turn me in, I'll tell them where the airplane is—sure, I almost did a dozen times, I guess. But, I'd tell them about Anna, too . . . even if I didn't want to." He hurried on as the pistol in Priabin's hand waggled threateningly. "It would come out, under drugs. Man, you know that! I couldn't keep quiet even if I wanted to."

"So, I kill you."

"And the CIA tips off your bosses, and Anna goes into the bag and maybe you do, too. What in hell are you doing here, anyway? Where's your backup? Who else knows?" He had begun to grip Anna's hand tightly once more. Gant saw her wince, but he did not know if her pain came from the grip or from his words. "Face it, man, you've messed up!"

"No—!"

"Your hide's on the barn door along with hers!"

He wanted to look at his watch. He bent his head slowly, as if weighing his next words. Fifteen minutes before the train stopped at Kolpino, where Harris would be waiting with a rented car. He had fifteen minutes to persuade, or kill, Priabin. And he knew he had no chance of killing him.

"They don't expect her to go over with you to prove how loyal she's been, do they?" Priabin asked in contempt.

Gant shook his head. "They gave her the option," he said. "She turned them down."

Priabin looked at Anna. Her face was pale, frightened. Gant sensed her need to touch the KGB officer, reassure both of them by gentle, continuing physical contact. Priabin scrutinized her face.

"You weren't going?" he asked hoarsely. She shook her head.

"No."

He appeared utterly relieved. The situation, Gant realized, was more complex than he had thought. Part of Priabin behaved like a jealous lover pursuing his mistress and the other man in a love triangle he had invented. Probably, he did not realize it himself. But it formed another spark that might ignite him. Gant did not know the truth—did Anna intend to stay?

"Thank God," he breathed. It was touching, and dangerous. "I thought—I thought . ." Then he seemed to recollect Gant's presence, and broke off, returning his gaze to the American. There was a sharp, quick cleverness in his face now. He was weighing the alternatives.

"That's it, sonny," Gant said. "Think about it. It's all one big trap—a maze. You have to find a way out, just like the rest of us." He smiled carefully. "There's just the three of us. What are we going to do about it?"

"What are the arrangements for this man?" Priabin asked.

"We were to leave the train at Kolpino—" Priabin looked at his watch, and Gant quickly did the same. Twelve minutes. "—the next station. Someone will be waiting there for us, with a car."

"Then you're not needed!" Priabin exclaimed. "Don't you see, Anna, you're not needed!" You don't have to provide cover for him by traveling all the way to the border—you don't!"

Gant controlled his features as she looked at him pleadingly. Priabin had leapt upon the flaw, the escape route for Anna. Now, she would ally herself with him.

"They'd still hand you over," he said.

"No! What are you—one of their Category-A Sources, Anna?" She looked at him, and nodded.

And he had protected her, just as he was trying to do now.

"Yes, that's what my Case Officer says."

"Then you're important to them, don't believe you're not. If the American fails to get away, you wouldn't be blamed. If you hand him over to whoever is to meet him, then your part is finished. If he is killed trying to get out of the country, then you cannot be blamed . . ." He hurried on breathlessly, his hand shaking hers in time to the rhythm of his thoughts. Gant felt his stomach become watery. His eyes flicked to the rack and the closed, too-far-away suitcase. There was nothing he could do now, but wait.

Ten minutes to Kolpino—but Priabin already knew about the waiting man and the waiting car. He would understand that Gant would be given exit papers for Finland, that he would be hurried out of the Soviet Union to safety. There was nothing Gant could do as Priabin continued talking, his face young and excited, as if he were engaged in nothing more dramatic than watching a football match or opening Christmas presents.

"Stay on the train—leave the American to whoever is meeting him. Understand? Just continue to Leningrad, and then fly straight back to Moscow. You can be there by morning, in work on time, everything . . ."

"And you?" she asked. "What will you do?"

Priabin looked down at his pistol. A heavy Stechkin. "It doesn't matter," he murmured. "I'll be back in Moscow tomorrow."

"He's going to kill me, after waiting until you've averted your pretty eyes," Gant said. "He thinks it's the easy way out."

"No—!"

"Isn't it?" Priabin grinned, but the expression was more akin to a sneer. He knew, now, that he possessed all the high cards in the game. Gant had lost his hostage, his secrecy—soon, his life.

"No. You'll have killed me. They won't like that."

"The Americans?"

"No. Your bosses. Vladimirov, the First Secretary, your chairman . . . the *really* big boys won't like it!"

"I can live with demotion, with a rotten posting—just like Kontarsky will have to," Priabin said sullenly.

"She'll still be working for the Americans—"

And Priabin's face unclouded, beamed at Gant. "I've thought of that!" he said, laying down his last and best card. He turned to Anna. Gant quailed. "I've just thought of it—she can become an agent of mine! An agent of—a KGB officer who's just died, or retired, but I knew about her—he would have set you up, Anna, as a double agent, and you were passed on to me. I went to bed with you as well as made use of you. They'd believe that easily—!" Anna was horrified.

"I would have to go on, and on, and on—forever?" she asked.

"Safe!" he replied.

"But—I'd never be allowed to leave it, to get out?"

"Then why did you do it in the first place?" he snapped in a hard voice. "*Why?*"

Gant glanced at his watch. Six minutes. When the train slowed? Outside the station—? Would he be able to get to

Harris' car before Priabin did? He would be unarmed. But—jump?

"You ask me—? Why are you a policeman?"

"It's my job."

"I want to get out of it, Dmitri—I don't want to pretend to have been working for the Americans while really working for you!" Her voice was high, her eyes bright with tears. She had released his hand. Both her small hands were clenched into protective fists, in front of her breasts. She was shaking her head. She looked much older, almost plain, as she pleaded with Priabin. "I don't care what clever excuses you think up, I don't want to be trapped *forever*—!" She unclenched her right fist and dragged a lock of hair away from her eyes. Then she clenched her hand once more in front of her. She was staring at her lap, not at Priabin. "I don't—I *can't* go on with it, Dmitri . . ." Then she looked up. "If only I could go back—you don't know how much I'd give just to go back!"

Priabin appeared to be about to speak, but then he slumped back against the window blind, his eyes staring at Gant.

Gant said quietly: "Come with me to the border, Anna— get me out, and I promise they'll let you go. If you let him kill me, they'll turn you over to his people. His plan won't work because the Company won't let it work. My way, you have a chance—his way, you have none."

"You'll be his hostage, Anna."

"Sure she will. But, there's a way out at the end of it. All you'd do for her is to put her in the bag for the rest of her life—do you want that? *Really* want it?"

Priabin blinked slowly, heavily. His features expressed confusion, indecision. "I can't let you go," he said. Gant thought that he was speaking to Anna, but the remark was addressed to himself. "I can't do that."

Must be no more than three or four minutes, Gant told himself. Stay with this.

"You could go home, resign from the ministry, take a job where you're no use to them. They'll get angry, but they won't be able to stop you. And they won't turn you over just for the hell of it." His voice was soft, the syllables like careful footsteps through a minefield. She looked up at him, attentive, almost beginning to hope. Gant squashed a sense that he might be lying to her, that the Company might indeed turn against her and betray her to the KGB.

"I'll help," he said. "Get me to Finland—keep this guy off my back until we reach the border, and I promise you'll walk away free. Come to Helsinki with me—" he added urgently. Two minutes, was the train already beginning to slow—? "Talk to the Company—talk to Charlie Buckholz or to Aubrey . . ." The names confused her, but he pressed on: "Aubrey would be on your side. It wouldn't take long, don't come unless you want to. Just get me to the border alive. That way you have a chance—his way, there isn't a hope in hell you can get away free!"

The train was slowing—

Priabin stared at Gant, then at Anna. When his gaze returned to the American, there was a deep, unsatisfied hatred in his eyes. The pistol was still aimed at the center of Gant's chest, and the man was still intent upon using it. It depended on Anna. Now they were silent and watching him once more, he would have no chance of jumping from the door of the slowing train.

The lights of a small town through the snow. White fields. The green splash of a signal light at the trackside.

"Well?" he asked.

Anna looked up. She reached for Priabin's hand, and clutched it. Still looking at Gant, she said: "I must do it, Dmitri. I must do as he suggests—"

"No!"

"My darling, I *must*! You've wanted only to help me—we kept it from each other, but all you wanted to do was help me. Now, *please* help me. Help me, my darling. Let him go, and let me go with him. Don't follow us, don't stop us . . . I'll come back, I swear. You know I will. But let him get away, and we can both be free. They *will* do it, won't they?" she asked Gant.

He nodded. "The people I know—they'll let you go. I swear they will."

Station lights, rushing at first, then slowing to walking pace as they passed the window.

"Quickly, Anna," he said, looking at Priabin. The gun was cradled on his lap. His face was miserable, angry and defeated and fearful for her safety.

"Dmitri—"

He nodded, just as the train sighed to a complete stop. "Yes," he said, then added to Gant: "It had better work, American. It had better work!"

"It will. I swear—"

"Then get your coats and luggage. I'll escort you—"

"No," Gant said.

"Yes. Your excuse for leaving the train here is flimsy, suspicious. With me, you will be asked no questions."

"And afterwards?"

"I'll wait for the next train. I'll wait for you in Leningrad, Anna—"

She rushed into his arms while Gant gathered the coats and luggage. He felt the ache of their passion, the intensity of their relationship. He had walked through the minefield, but until now he had never realized quite how dangerous it had been. And, deep inside himself, he felt something he could only describe as envy.

He owed her. He would, at least, try on her behalf—

"Come on," he said, turning to them, interrupting their kiss, almost embarrassed by it. "Hurry—"

Brooke shone his lamp on the nosewheel strut of the Firefox for what might have been the tenth or twelfth time. He could not help his reaction, avoid the jumpy tension in his body. It reminded him vividly of that period of childhood when he had avoided walking on the cracks in paving stones, always followed the borders of rugs and carpets, always checked and checked again that the light was properly switched off—at first it had needed four checks, then six, then eight . . . He had thought he was mad, until he discovered that half his classmates engaged in the same obsessive routines. Checking the ropes around the three undercarriage legs was now the same kind of thing. He felt almost obsessional. They had to be right. The raising of the aircraft was about to begin, everything depended on these three nylon ropes, on his checking them . . .

He bobbed beside the nosewheel strut. The rope passed several times around it, wound over heavy padding to avoid damage to the undercarriage leg. For that reason, too, the rope was high on the leg. He tugged, quite unnecessarily, at the nylon rope once more, ran the beam of his lamp along it as it stretched away towards the shore.

Yes, he thought, nodding his head—yes.

He turned his back on the aircraft, his lamp's beam running over the MO-MAT that reached down from the shore to the nosewheel. The portable roadway was of fiberglass-reinforced plastic, and lay over the mud and rubble of the lake bed, the incline of the shore itself, and the trampled snow of the cleared site beyond that. The Firefox would be winched along its nonskid surface, moving easily and smoothly, in theory, up onto dry land. The light bounced and wobbled over the wafflelike appearance of the MO-MAT, then Brooke's head bobbed out of the water and he began walking easily up the lessened incline of the shore. As he removed his facemask, he saw Waterford and Buckholz, dressed in white parkas, silhouetted against the lights suspended from the perimeter trees. They were standing together on the MO-MAT, waiting for him.

Snow flew across the glow of the lights as Buckholz waved his hand in Brooke's direction. The SBS lieutenant returned the wave. It was all right—they could begin.

"Yes," he said, nodding. He turned to look at the frozen lake, just as the American and Waterford were doing. "Anything in the latest report from the Nimrod?" he asked. An SBS corporal took his air tanks and facemask, and Brooke climbed into the parka. He did not feel cold.

"Sod all," Waterford replied. "Nothing."

"They still don't have Gant—he's on his way to Leningrad," Buckholz said. "He didn't tell them."

Through the curtains of snow that seemed dragged across the scene at irregular intervals, Brooke located a lump of timber floating in the patch of clear water. It was wrapped in Dayglo tape, and was attached by a thin line to the nose of the Firefox. Beyond it, more difficult to make out but spectrally visible, a huge crucifix of planks and logs, similarly wrapped with luminous tape, represented the position of the aircraft under the ice. He and his divers had measured that outline. Now, all that remained was for the ice marked by the cross to be broken where it had thinly reformed after the plane had sunk. Then the winching operation could begin.

Brooke sensed the excitement in the American beside him. It matched his own. Waterford looked grim, but the expression was habitual. Brooke could not deduce any meaning from it.

Buckholz pressed an R/T handset to the side of his face, watching Brooke as he did so. "O.K.—diving party. Let's start clearing that ice."

Brooke's SBS divers moved down to the shore. Two of

them entered the clear water, walking like penguins down the MO-MAT, then drifting out towards the edge of the ice. They reached the crucifix's tip, and immediately began sawing at the new, thin ice, working outwards from each other around the cross. Two more SBS men moved onto the ice itself, armed with steel spikes and hammers. White light reached out towards them as one of the powerful lamps was adjusted.

Even through the deadened, snow-filled air, he could hear the hammering of steel spikes into the ice. To these, lines would be attached so that sawn-off sections of ice could be towed to the shore. His divers were furiously at work cutting away chunks as the steel spikes were hammered in. He glanced at his watch. Twelve-fifteen. On schedule.

Two plates of ice were dragged by lines across the widening patch of clear water to the shore, then manhandled onto the thicker ice. Twelve-thirty. Lengths of timber floated in clear water now. The cross was losing shape. The sawing and hammering continued.

They had left the ice intact for as long as possible for reasons of security. A Dayglo crucifix, too, would signal their presence, even in bad visibility, to any low-flying aircraft or helicopter. Two hours earlier, they had had cause to consider the delay a wise one. Helicopters had been reported by Eastoe, heading northwest into Finland. Agreed, they were well to the south of them at first and later northeast as they cruised the area of the lake where Gant had been captured, for almost an hour. Then they had retraced the route he had taken to that lake. Buckholz's party had waited in darkness and silence for their approach. It never came. The weather had worsened and the helicopters, picked up with difficulty by Eastoe's most sophisticated radar, had changed course and headed southeast to recross the border. Immediately, the lights had been switched on and the crucifix laid out on the ice to represent the fuselage and wings of the Firefox. Since then, Eastoe had reported no activity along the border. Presumably the Russians had decided against further helicopter reconnaissance in the weather conditions that now prevailed. It indicated that they did not know where to look, were ignorant of the location of the aircraft.

More plates of ice were dragged out of the water, which now receded to the edge of visibility. Then the scene was further obscured by a curtain of snow. The corporal had thrust a mug of coffee into Brooke's hand which he had accepted almost without noticing. He sipped at it now Twelve-thirty.

He turned his head. Royal Engineers were checking the nylon lines with the same kind of obsessiveness he had shown in relation to the undercarriage of the Firefox. Some abrasive surfaces were padded with logs of felled timber. The three trees which held the chain-lever winches were not equidistant, nor were they in a straight line. Therefore, the winching operation would be complex, and slow, in order to avoid snagging and rubbing against the undercarriage doors and to ensure that the airframe ascended the ramp of the MO-MAT in as straight a line as possible. The officer in charge of the party would be required to monitor the speed and progress of each winch and line—constantly.

Out on the ice, his divers had handed over the task of driving in the remaining steel pins to RAF engineers. They dropped into the dark water, to make a thorough final check for underwater obstacles—they had spent hours clearing rocks and rubble that afternoon—and to take up their monitoring positions. They would be watching the undercarriage for signs of strain or weakness, the ropes for the same—and both for the first movements.

Twelve-forty. Brooke's coffee was cold in the mug, and he threw it away with a flick of his wrist. It dyed the trampled snow at the edge of the MO-MAT's carpet. Two of the shore party were brushing at the wafflelike surface, keeping it as free of snow as possible.

Brooke watched Moresby, the squadron-leader from the Field Recovery Unit at Abingdon and their Senior Engineering Officer, ambling towards them. He nodded to Buckholz and Waterford, taking up the stance of a spectator immediately, hands thrust into his pockets, parka hood pulled around his face, shoulders hunched.

"As soon as we reach the level," he announced as if he had been engaged in a conversation for some time and was now answering one of a series of questions. "I'd expect her stopped—oh, here," he added, waving his arms to indicate the area just behind them where the slope of the shore all but disappeared. "I've had a word with the engineers and they're fairly certain we can hold her on the winches. In fact, I'd like to have a look inside the cockpit as soon as she clears the water."

Buckholz, unabashed, nodded. "O.K., Squadron Leader. Any self-destruct mechanism is entirely your baby. We'll order the winches to stop just as soon as she's clear of the water."

"Splendid. The anti-radar capability and the thought-guidance systems must be protected by some kind of self-destruct. Since the bang-seat wasn't used, they may not be armed. But they could, just could, be armed by immersion in water—some of these devices are. So—I think I'd better find out before the aircraft dries off." He smiled perfunctorily, saluted quickly, and ambled off once more.

"It won't be much of a bang," Waterford commented. "They won't have rigged the whole airframe to blow up, much too dangerous. Might kill the squadron-leader, of course, and give Aubrey a heart attack when he hears he's lost all the best stuff on board . . ."

"Thank you, Major," Buckholz retorted.

Out on the ice, the last plates were being manhandled onto the firmer ice. The channel of clear water stretched away into the darkness beyond the lights. Bits of luminous wood floated randomly. The cross had gone. The shore party had begun to return, and his divers were walking out of the water up the slope of the temporary roadway. They were grinning as they removed their facemasks. Brooke nodded, and one of the divers turned and slipped back into the water to take up a monitoring station. Brooke watched the beam of his lamp flicker palely, like the track of some glowing fish, as it moved away towards one of the wings of the submerged Firefox.

"Tell me, Major," Buckholz began, "did Aubrey call this operation *Nessie* because he thought he wouldn't get the airframe out of the water?" He was smiling as he asked the question.

Waterford tossed his head. "Aubrey's idea of a joke, Mr. Buckholz—just his idea of a joke." He smiled briefly, then added: "Time for me to check with the Apaches out there Excuse me."

Waterford's huge, solid calm had acted like a barrier, but now that he had moved away Brooke could sense the electric-ity of the scene, the tension felt by each man. The ice was clear, the lines checked, the divers on-station. Moresby was standing with the party of Royal Engineers at the rear of the scene, upstage. They were checking drills, and walkie-talkies

Then he scoured the ground around each of the trees selected to take one of the winches, checking anchorages and
knots. Eventually, he waved a hand towards Buckholz and
moved back towards Brooke and the American.

Brooke could smell soup on the snowy air. And coffee. It
would be served when—if—their first attempt proved successful and they got the airframe to move. Then, safe in the
knowledge that it was possible to move the plane, they would
be given a ten-minute break for food and drink. The winching
would take much of the night.

Buckholz's head swiveled inside the fur-edged hood of
his white parka as he checked with each section of the operation by walkie-talkie and hand signals. Then he turned to
Brooke. His grin was nervous, his face pale with cold and
excitement. Brooke grinned and gestured him to begin.

"O.K., everyone—let's catch *Nessie*, shall we?" he
announced, and immediately Buckholz turned his back on
the lake and looked towards the three teams manning the
winches. As the two men on each winch levered back and
forth easily and rhythmically, the nylon ropes tautened. The
teams slowed almost immediately at a command from the
Royal Engineer officer. The central pair stopped winching
altogether at his hand signal only moments later; quickly
followed by the pair to the left. The R.E. captain allowed the
right-hand winch to continue as he moved forward to check
the relative tension of each rope. A few seconds later, he
made a chopping motion with his hand, and the third winch
stopped.

Moresby, joining him, spoke briefly, then nodded.

Buckholz heard the captain call: "Numbers One, Two,
Three—haul away," and the ropes stretched, creaking slightly
in the silence. Buckholz noticed the silence only then, at the
first renewed sound of winching. He was aware, too, of the
stillness of everyone there, except the six men at the bases of
the trees which anchored the winches. Buckholz could sense
their effort now; both men on each winch were straining. "All
stop!" the captain called out. The lines had lifted from the
surface of the MO-MAT. To Buckholz, they appeared over-
stretched, ready to break. Then he felt the silence again and
realized he had thrust his hands into his pockets because they
were trembling.

One of the SBS divers slipped into the cleared dark
water and swam to the lines in turn, tying an orange marker

to each one at the point where it emerged from the water. Moresby, like some parody of a keen-eyed, grasping factory owner, had walked down to the shore and was studying the diver, as if about to sack or reprimand him. Hands behind his back, head craned forward, back slightly bent.

"Haul away, One, Two and Three!" he called out as the diver turned and swam towards him. The levers of the winches pumped evenly. More quickly, rhythmically, Buckholz felt, as if—

He watched the flags on the lines, almost mocking Moresby's intent, craning stance. Buckholz understood only what he was looking at, hardly considered what it would mean if—

He grinned, and exhaled, seeming to hear a communal sigh in the windy, snow-flown clearing. Moresby straightened up, hands still clasped behind his back, chest and stomach a little thrust out as if continuing to portray the factory owner whose school history book image would not desert Buckholz's thoughts.

The orange marker flags, all three of them, had moved off the surface of the water. The Firefox had moved. A facemasked head bobbed above the surface, gave a thumbs-up signal, and disappeared. The Firefox had rolled forward, perhaps no more than a few inches, but the undercarriage had withstood the initial strain of moving.

"One, Two and Three—haul away!" Moresby called over his shoulder, and the captain hand-signaled his three teams to begin in unison. The even rhythm of the levers was barely audible above the wind. Buckholz felt his heart racing, and grinned to himself.

His walkie-talkie bleeped.

"Yes?"

"Mr. Aubrey, sir—sorry, sir, it's Squadron Leader Moresby he wants . . . sorry, Mr. Buckholz."

"O.K., son."

Curiosity made him follow Moresby towards the windbreak which half-concealed the commpack and its operator. The RAF officer detoured to nod his congratulations to the three teams on the winches. The men were bent and heated now, creating the impression of labor as much as speed, effort more than achievement. They would be relieved within ten minutes by fresh teams. Moresby had already picked up the microphone. The look on his face puzzled Buckholz. Something like outrage. Again, he could not help but picture the British factory owner, this time faced with the prospect of a strike. He smiled, but the expression vanished a moment later.

"You want to ask me about *what*?" Moresby asked, his face expressing disbelief now that he had spoken. "Are you serious? Correction—you cannot *be* serious! Over." He looked up and saw Buckholz, and immediately waved him into the tiny enclave of the windbreak. The radio operator's glance was vivid with humor and the prospect of a quarrel.

"What is it?" Buckholz asked, and was waved to silence by Moresby, who was once more listening to Aubrey in Kirkenes.

Immediately Aubrey finished speaking, Moresby replied, his face flushed despite the cold. Within the hood of his grey-white parka, he appeared almost apoplectic. "I can't even begin to answer your questions, Mr. Aubrey. I have not worked with you on previous occasions, and I don't understand your sense of humor. What you propose is preposterous! Over."

"What the hell's going on?" Buckholz growled.

"He wants me—" Moresby began, then swallowed before he added: "—to tell him whether the aircraft could be prepared to fly again . . . to fly from here, to be exact! Absolutely out of the question—"

"You realize what this means?" Buckholz snapped. "He doesn't ask idle questions. It means the Sikorsky isn't coming, old boy, old buddy—he's just found out and he's clutching at straws. Give me the mike, Squadron Leader." Buckholz pressed one earpiece against the side of his head, and said: "Kenneth, this is Charles. Are you certain the Skyhook won't make it? Over."

Immediately, Aubrey replied: "I'm sorry, Charles, but—yes, I'm afraid so. There is no possibility of it arriving before the deadline—until it is well past, in fact. Over."

"So, where did you get this crazy idea from, Kenneth? The squadron-leader here doesn't think much of it."

"Absolute rubbish!" Moresby foamed.

"I realize that," Aubrey snapped. "Very tiresome. Over."

"I think you're as crazy as he does, in case you're interested. Over."

"Charles, there is simply no time to waste. I need a shopping list Curtin can transmit to Bardufoss—if they haven't got what is required, then we may be in trouble—please put Moresby back on. You listen if you want to . . ." There was the faintest tinge of a dry laughter in Aubrey's tone. It surprised and even angered Buckholz. It made the depth of his reaction to the first movement of the aircraft seem somehow exaggerated and adolescent.

"Listen," he snapped. "We have no one to fly the damn thing!" Then he added waspishly, as if formality was a further element of the ridiculous: "Over!"

"Gant and Source Burgoyne should be crossing the border into Finland within an hour or two. Gant will fly the aircraft." Aubrey sounded self-congratulatory. Buckholz understood why Giles Pyott, out of Aubrey's hearing, referred to him as a gifted, restless, hyperactive child. He *was* brilliant—a brilliant pain in the ass for much of the time.

"You mean you got an airplane that's still at the bottom of a lake and a pilot who's still inside Russia, and that's the groundplan for your idea? You're crazy if you think that will work!"

Moresby snatched at the headset. The radio operator plugged in a second headset and offered it to Buckholz with a grin. "Top ratings for this phone-in show, sir," he murmured. Buckholz snorted. It *was* the *laughter* he could not comprehend. From Aubrey in particular . . .

Laughter in the dark. Game-playing. And yet people like Aubrey, even Pyott, made him feel heavy-footed and stolid, somehow colonial and gauche. All of it angered him.

Before Moresby could speak, he snapped: "Get off the air, Kenneth. You're an asshole for ever suggesting such a crazy scheme! If the Skyhook can't make it, we'll dismantle what we can. You get a Chinook from Bardufoss to take us out before the deadline expires. Over."

"Sorry, Charles—I said you could *listen*. Is Moresby still there?"

"I'm here!"

"Good. Now, Squadron Leader, perhaps you'll be so good as to try to answer my question. Could the aircraft be prepared for a flight of, say—fifteen to twenty minutes' duration, at subsonic speed, of course? A distance of a couple of hundred miles? Please think very carefully."

Both Moresby and Buckholz had, by some unspoken common assent, turned their back on the commpack and its operator, and shuffled to the extent of their headset leads; as if to remove themselves from the communicable lunacy of Kenneth Aubrey. Both of them watched the fresh teams at the winches slip quickly into the easy, regular rhythm of the levering. The ropes, at the edge of clear vision out on the dark water, shook off silver drops of light. The marker flags were perhaps a few feet nearer the shore. A diver's head popped above the water. He removed his facemask and mouthpiece, and they heard him shout:

"Port wheels are almost on top of a rock. Stop winching and give me a crowbar!"

"One, Two, and Three—stop winching!"

Brooke, the skirts of his parka gathered up around his body, waded out into the water, which moved sluggishly around his legs, and handed the crowbar to his diver. Their conversation was brief. The diver disappeared.

Moresby seemed to recollect Aubrey. "I've already told you that it's impossible, Mr. Aubrey. Please forgive my outburst—didn't mean to sound raped."

"You were, buddy—or you will be," Buckholz growled beside him.

"But it is impossible. I'm concentrating on what kind of self-destruct may or may not be attached to the thought-guidance systems, the on-board computer and the anti-radar. If we don't locate the self-destruct, assuming there is one, you won't have anything left that's worth the time and effort already spent. Over."

"I realize that, Moresby. But, please, simply tell me—Captain Curtin is listening, pen poised—what would be needed if the Firefox were to fly again—from that lake?"

The diver's head popped above the surface again. Brooke had waited for him, and took the crowbar. Both of them gave the thumbs-up, and the engineer captain immediately ordered the three teams to recommence winching. Moresby sighed, then with an angry reluctance returned his attention to Aubrey. Buckholz willed him to utterly refute the Englishman as he felt the impact of the news concerning the Skyhook helicopter spread through him. They couldn't get the Firefox out. As simple as that. They were winching it out of the lake only to be unable to do any more than steal a few of its systems and instruments and samples of its airframe materials . . . and photographs. Countless photographs.

Buckholz understood Aubrey's refusal to surrender to the inevitable. But he could not share the man's new, impossible scheme. Which, he reminded himself, Aubrey was conjuring out of thin air just because he had left himself without any fallback plan—!

"Hot air blowers," Moresby snapped as if the information was being extracted by physical pain. "Undercover job, drying the airframe. That takes care of the airframe. Now you have a *dry* lump of metal. Do you wish me to go on? Over."

"Please continue, Squadron Leader. All this is most interesting. Over."

Moresby sighed at the sarcasm in Aubrey's voice. Buckholz watched the three orange flags dancing like great butterflies above the dark, soupy water as the ropes strained.

"Engines next, then. Drying out—then you have problems with igniters, lubrication, barometric controls, engine ancillaries, and fuel, of course. Number three—hydraulics and pneumatics. They could be O.K., after such a short immersion, but everything, repeat *everything*, would have to be thoroughly checked otherwise you could end up without undercarriage, air brakes, flaps. Four—the electrics. It would depend on what level of operation would be acceptable. Again, everything would have to be thoroughly checked, and any damage would have to be made good—you do have a private pipeline into the Mikoyan production line so that we have easy access to Russian spares, I suppose?" Moresby snorted; a noise not much like laughter but which Buckholz assumed was the air force officer's means of expressing amusement. "Five—instruments . . . the air-driven ones may be O.K., since the water may not have got into the instrument heads—but, the electrically driven gyro ones—I wouldn't even like to speculate on that. Over."

Buckholz sensed that Moresby had flung a great douche of cold water in Aubrey's direction and expected his ploy to work. He imagined Curtin scribbling furiously, shaking his head almost without pause. When he heard Aubrey's voice, however, he realized that he was undaunted.

"What about armaments? Over."

"For Heaven's sake, Aubrey!" Moresby exclaimed. "You'd have to talk to my armorer, but my guess is that you're up the creek on that tack."

"I see. But, thus far, apart from things mechanical and electronic, I would need experts in airframes, engines, hydraulics, control systems, electrics, avionics, instruments and weapons . . . in other words, a full ground crew who would be experienced in servicing military aircraft. That doesn't seem too tall an order . . . Over?"

"Don't forget the runway, fuel, oxygen, a set of jacks, tools that fit—I simply cannot see any way in which it is feasible. Impossible in less than twenty-four hours, which is what we have. Impossible in three days or more, even at Abingdon—never mind Lapland!"

"Get off the guy's back, Aubrey !" Buckholz snapped. "You haven't got a chance with this. You couldn't even get the stuff he needs here, never mind the men. Forget it. Arrange for that Chinook to pick us up at dusk tomorrow Jesus—!"

"What's the matter? Over."

"She—she's on her way up, Aubrey—she's on her way up!"

He had noticed the silence. Now, cheering filled it. The winches paused, the orange marker flags danced. Pearls of water dropped from the taut nylon lines. Cheering.

The nose of the Firefox had slipped above water, black and snoutlike, ugly and still threatening. Above it, like eyes, the perspex of the cockpit canopy stared at them. It was a sea creature, Aubrey's *Nessie*, watching them, waiting for them to be foolish enough to enter the water.

"Is she—?" he heard Aubrey ask in a quiet voice.

"Beautiful," Buckholz said. "Dangerous and beautiful. My God, when Gant first saw *that*—!"

"Now tell me not to try. Over," Aubrey replied sardonically.

"It's still impossible," Moresby interrupted. The winches began again. Inch by inch, the snout and cockpit slipped higher out of the water, sometimes lost in the flurries of snow, sometimes clearer and more deadly in appearance.

"The weather, Kenneth?"

"At dawn, something of a lull is anticipated . . . enough for a Hercules to make a low-level drop. One drop, of *everything* you need. Then the weather will close in again."

"So no one gets out of here?"

"The Met reports anticipate another such lull, late in the afternoon. The fronts will allow two windows in the weather. at dawn and around dusk. Over."

"That means less than twelve hours, Aubrey—"

"I realize that, Squadron Leader. However, you could have everything you need dropped on the lake at first light. If it doesn't work, I promise you will have my reluctant permission to utterly destroy the aircraft. Over."

Involuntarily, Buckholz's head flicked round so that he was looking at the Firefox. The leading edges of its huge wings were beginning to emerge. Now, it looked like something captured, caught in a net and dragged from its own element into the snowy air; a great manta ray rather than an aircraft. It mounted the slope, moving slowly, very slowly out of the water. Menace. Yes, Buckholz thought, it already exuded menace, even though there was no possibility it could ever fly again.

"I see," Moresby replied.

"It doesn't have a runway and we don't have any way of putting it back on the ice," Buckholz said quickly, aghast at the clear sound of disappointment in his voice. Over.

"Tractor tug and a great deal more MO-MAT," Moresby snapped. "Over."

"Gentlemen," Aubrey said calmly, all trace of satisfaction carefully excluded from his voice. "How long before the aircraft is ashore? Over."

"Two hours at least. Over."

"Then we have two hours, Squadron Leader, Charles. I suggest we begin talking in true earnest, don't you? Over."

Before he replied, Buckholz glanced at the Firefox. And felt Aubrey's stupidity in having no fallback, and his illogical, desperate brilliance in daring to assume the airplane could fly out of Lapland. And, he admitted, he too wanted her to fly again. She had to fly—

He glanced at Moresby, who shrugged. Then the air force officer nodded, even smiled. A tight little movement of his lips beneath his clipped moustache. "Very well," he breathed in the tone of an indulgent parent. "Very well."

"O.K., Kenneth. Give us a few minutes to round up some people whose opinions we need—then we'll throw it on the porch and see if the cat laps it up!" Buckholz felt a strange, almost boyish exhilaration. In front of him, the wings continued to emerge from the water. The black snout seemed to seek him, the cockpit to stare at him.

Menace.

"Just make sure you don't lose Superpilot at the last fence, uh, Kenneth?"

*　　*　　*

Vladimirov yawned. It was an exhalation of his tension rather than an expression of weariness. He quickly stifled it. The room was small and cramped, the tape recorder on the folding table almost its only furniture apart from a number of chairs stacked against one wall. The bare room accommodated himself, Andropov, and the senior interrogator from the KGB Unit on the Mira Prospekt. All three of them leaned their elbows on the table in the attitude of weary gamblers. A sheaf of pages—hurriedly typed and corrected and now overlaid with the interrogator's scribble—lay near the recorder. Vladimirov had a pad and ballpoint pen in front of him. He was no longer concerned to disguise the fact that he doodled occasionally. There were few words on his pad, and little meaning. Andropov's pad was clean, unmarked.

Vladimirov had lost his eagerness to hear Gant's sufferings under drugs, his hallucinations and illusions, his terror at dying and his attempts to persuade them that he was not. He had listened to the two interrogations several times in that cramped and almost fetid room, and he loathed something in himself that had actually anticipated the experience. When they had first arrived he had *wanted* to hear them. Now, he did not.

The tape continued in silence. Gant had hit his head on the floor, silencing himself. Nothing—

Vladimirov had learned nothing from rehearing Gant screaming for them to listen to him. Even with the volume turned down, it was horrid. He had helped to torture Gant. It was his shame that was being replayed in front of the Chairman of the KGB. Slowly, he looked up, and shrugged.

"Nothing," he murmured.

"Mm. Your opinion?" Andropov snapped at the interrogator, who flinched before he replied deferentially.

"Comrade Chairman," he began. Andropov appeared to be impatient, but could not quite bring himself to wave the deference aside. Instead, he merely pursed his mouth and nodded the man along. "I—am not familiar with the kind of information the general is seeking."

"Was the American about to reveal something or not?"

"You mean—?"

"From his condition, from the frenzy in his voice and manner at the end of the tape, was he trying to tell you something?" Andropov had begun to doodle on his pad as he talked. Strong, bold curves which vanished beneath heavy geometric shapes.

"Yes, Comrade Chairman."

"Then, what was it?"

"I—that I cannot say." The senior interrogator shrugged, brushed his hand through his hair, stared at his notes, shuffled them, looked up once more. He spread his hands. "I—he believed in me as an American general, and he believed that the man he could not see was Aubrey, the British—"

"I know who Aubrey is," Andropov interrupted icily.

"Yes, of course. He—he was attempting to assure us that he was not dying—"

"Because he knew he hadn't burned in the explosion you pretended had occurred on the Mig-31—yes, yes. We *all* understand that much. Now, what was he going to tell you? Vladimirov, surely there are some clues in what he said, what he couldn't help letting out?" Andropov's pale eyes gleamed behind his gold-rimmed spectacles. Vladimirov felt pressed. The Chairman's perspective was a larger one than his own. He wanted an answer so that he could avoid the First Secretary's censure, because if it was used against him, he might remain no more than a minor figure in the Politburo. However, his desire for an answer was no more urgent than Vladimirov's own. He wanted the Mig-31 more than ever. His insurance would be the recovery of the aircraft.

"Perhaps, but I can't see it. He does not talk—*anywhere*—about landing the aircraft."

"And yet he *must* have landed it?"

"Of course he did!" Vladimirov snapped testily. "Do you think he jumped out without using his parachute?" Almost immediately, the general signaled a silent apology. "Yes, he landed it," he said more softly. Then he looked at the interrogator. "Very well. Rewind the tape to the point—oh, where he first claims he wasn't burned . . . find that."

The interrogator looked at his rough transcript and then rewound the tape. He followed the numbers flicking back on the counter, checking it with the column of numerals at the edge of each page. Then he stabbed his finger down on the Stop button. He looked at Andropov, who nodded. The tape began to play.

The mimic playing the part of Aubrey cried out immediately: "He's not dying!" Vladimirov leaned forward, head cocked, intent upon the charade, trying to hear something through the illusion, through the familiarity of the dialogue; through his recurring shame. The interrogator in his guise as the American general murmured that Gant was, indeed, dying. Vladimirov remembered, and could clearly envisage Gant's hand crawling as if with a life of its own up the uniform worn by the interrogator. He had pulled out the earpiece through which the interrogator was receiving reports from those monitoring the television cameras focused on the bed. Gant tried to pull the interrogator towards him . . .

"Not burned, not burned . . ." he heard the American repeating. He seemed pressed to tell something, to explain, to correct their mistake. Vladimirov could not prevent the pluck of tension and excitement he felt in his tight chest. *Not burned, not burned* . . . What had been happening in his drugged, confused, disorientated head at that moment? What had he wanted to say so desperately?

Andropov's fingers tapped silently on the edge of the table, as if accompanying the words with appropriate music. The interrogator was merely performing a charade of concentration. He did not know what to look for. He had not been a pilot.

"Not burned . . . drowning . . . drowning—on fire, but water, water . . ." Gant continued on the tape, his voice mounting, losing control, trying to convince them that their diagnosis was wrong, that he was not dying of burns. "Not burned . . . landed—"

"Stop it!" Vladimirov shouted. The interrogator jumped, then pressed the button. "Very well—you heard that? He said that he *landed*—"

"And where does that get us?" Andropov asked with withering sarcasm. "You already knew that, didn't you?" He smiled thinly. "Now, *where* did he land? Which one of your roads or tracks?"

Vladimirov shrugged. "Begin again," he said.

". . . not burned—water . . ." Gant said immediately, then there was nothing but the noises of rustling clothes, hesitant footsteps. Vladimirov remembered, then. Gant had slumped back on the bed at that point. A little later, he was to sit up once more, and scream out *Listen!* and *Explain!*

But he had never explained, though they had listened. In his frenzy, his legs had become entangled in the bed-clothes and he had toppled out of the bed, striking his head and knocking himself unconscious. End of the affair—

Footsteps on the tape—or was it Andropov's drumming fingers? Breathing, murmurs that were indistinct, someone cursing, fumbling with something. Everyone waiting for the moment that had never arrived.

Not burned . . . Gant was not burned. He knew that. Vladimirov looked down at his pad. Almost unnoticed, he had torn off the sheet of doodles and had virtually carved words onto the sheet beneath.

He counted. Gant refuted his having been burned five times. He mentioned fire, though—just once. Vladimirov realized he had scribbled each of the words separately, each time they were spoken. Taking Gant's fevered dictation. He had written *water*, too. Gant had said that, apparently, three times. And, *drowning*—twice . . .

Burning, drowning, water, fire, landed . . .

Vladimirov realized how much depended upon the tapes, the solution, the moment. He *had* to find the answer—!

Water three times, drowning twice, landed once . . . His ballpoint pen almost surreptitiously linked the three circled words by trailing lines. *Drowning* and *water* were like balloons floating yet anchored above the word *landed* . . .

He remembered Andropov asking about the aircraft being landed on a frozen lake—

And then he knew.

Landed—water—drowning.

He had broken the code. He knew what Gant had done. He had landed the Mig-31 on a frozen lake, and the ice had given way and he had almost drowned. And there was no trace of the aircraft because the water had frozen over it.

He had discounted the lakes in the designated area because there was no shelter for that black aircraft standing on white snow and ice. But, *under* the ice—!

His hand was shaking. He looked up, to find Andropov watching him intently. Vladimirov hardly heard Gant shouting for attention in the moment before he tumbled to the floor. Andropov gestured for the tape to be switched off, and Vladimirov announced in a quiet, hoarse voice:

"The Mig-31 is at present under the ice of a frozen lake, Comrade Chairman. I am certain of it."

"Explain." Vladimirov did so. Andropov stared at him, his face expressionless. Then, in the ensuing silence, which seemed endless, his features became intently reflective. Andropov was evidently weighing the consequences of his acceptance of the general's theory. Eventually, the Chairman spoke. "I think we should consult the map. Perhaps you would lead on, General Vladimirov." Then he turned to the senior interrogator. "That will be all, Comrade Deputy Director. Thank you." It was evident that the senior interrogator derived little comfort from the flat, noncommittal tones.

Vladimirov reached the door. Andropov followed him into the huge underground room. Heads turned to them, then returned to appointed tasks, as they crossed the floor together and climbed the ladder onto the gallery. Expectant faces looked up as they entered the control room of the command center. Yet no one joined them at the fiber-optic map. Finnish Lapland remained as they had left it, except for a dotted red line that had inched southeast during their absence.

"Well?" Andropov asked, surrendering the consequences to Vladimirov.

The general traced the dotted red line with his finger. The reconnaissance party had made good time, moving on a very narrow front, retracing Gant's journey . . . from a lake, he reminded himself. Where? His finger continued southeastward, moving swiftly over the roads and tracks he had at first nominated. How could he have been so *stupid*—?

Two lakes, almost in a direct line with the route of the reconnaissance party; certainly within the tolerances which allowed for slight changes of direction by the American. One of the lakes was rounded, the other longer and narrower. He recalled the scale. Either might have done . . .

And there was a third lake to the north of that pair, and a fourth to the east. Four lakes. The red dotted line was closest to the pair of lakes. His finger tapped the surface of the map.

"There," he said. "First priority—a reconnaissance of those two lakes." He stared at Andropov until the chairman silently nodded his head. Then he said, more loudly: "Major, please check these coordinates, then transmit them to our reconnaissance party. At once!"

A young major in the GRU hurried forward to join them at the map.

11 / CROSSING THE BORDER

Harris stopped the hired car, switched off the engine, and turned in his seat. For a moment, he appeared to study Gant and Anna with a cool objectivity, then he said: "I'll just call in and check with my people in Leningrad. The border is ten miles up the road . . ." He pointed through the windscreen that was already smeared with snow now that the wipers had been switched off. "I don't want us to get caught out by any alarm or increased security. The Finns are waiting for us. They'll have signaled Leningrad in case of trouble. We passed a telephone box on the edge of the village." He smiled. "Best not to park near it—if anyone sees me now, they'll assume I'm a local. Just sit tight. I won't be long."

Harris opened the door. Snow gusted in. He climbed out and slammed the door behind him. Gant turned his head and watched him trudge away, back towards the few scattered lights of the tiny hamlet through which they had passed a minute earlier. Harris had driven off the main road, into a pull-off masked by tall bushes heavy with snow.

Harris disappeared from view. Gant turned to Anna.

"Check your papers again," he instructed. He pulled his own documents from his breast pocket, unbuttoning his overcoat to do so. As he opened the travel documents and visas, he wondered once more about Anna. She had accepted the papers Harris had supplied, and the cover story. She had examined the documents periodically during their three-hour car journey from Kolpino, via the outskirts of Leningrad and the industrial city of Vyborg. Yet he sensed that she still in no way associated herself with them. They were like a novel she had picked out for the journey and in which she had little interest.

Harris, a British businessman with a Helsinki base and frequent opportunity for business travel inside the Soviet Union, was to pose as a Finn when they reached the border. He possessed a Finnish passport and his visas had been stamped to indicate that he had traveled from Helsinki to Leningrad a few days before. Gant and Anna were to remain as Russians, and as members of the Secretariat. They were accompanying Harris from Leningrad to inspect his facilities on behalf of the Leningrad Party. Harris was in the metallurgical business, and factories and businesses in the area covered by the Leningrad *Oblast* required his products.

The covers were impressive, even unnerving to a border guard. The only suspicious circumstance was the time of arrival at the border and the manner of travel. Yet, Gant knew it would work. He no longer noticed the hairpiece and the half-glasses, and in the same fashion he no longer considered the flaws in Harris's plan.

The journey had helped, of course. The constant moving away and, after Moscow, the openness of the dark, snowbound countryside. Frozen lakes gleaming in scraps of moonlight between heavy snow showers. Moscow had hemmed him. It had been a huge trawlnet cast just for him. Here, he saw no evidence of the hunt and he accepted the innocent-seeming time at its face value. He even dozed in the back of the warm car, head nodding on his chest, waking periodically to glimpse the countryside or the lights of a village or see the snow rushing out of the night towards the windscreen.

But, Anna—?

It was as if some motive force within her had seized up. She seemed incapable of action or decision. He did not even know, this close to the edge of the Soviet Union, whether she really intended to cross with them. He could imagine her opening the door of the car, even as the red-and-white pole began to swing up, and start walking back down the road into Russia. Also, he did not know whether Priabin was to be trusted.

At Kolpino, he had looked like a man striving to cling to the wreckage of his life; trying not to display emotions he might normally have considered womanish. He had waved them through the inspection at the station, chatting to them, strutting a little with his superior rank, dropping hints of mystery and important Party business. He had watched them into Harris's hired car, had stood in the falling light of a lamp outside the station, a solitary and enigmatic figure, as they had driven off. Gant, glancing round, had the impression of a small figure with arm aloft. And then his sense of intruding upon some private act had made him turn away. Anna had remained with her head turned to the rear window long after a bend in the road had removed him from sight.

He did not think Priabin would follow them, or betray them at the border, because of Anna's safety. But, he was not quite certain. As they had all three left the train, Gant and he had come face to face for a moment. Priabin had still possessed the grim, almost fanatical look that had been on his features when he first entered their compartment—when he had intended shooting Gant.

Priabin still wanted to kill him.

"You are coming over?" Gant asked hoarsely, slipping his papers back into his breast pocket. He fiddled with the glasses on his nose, as if working himself back into a portrayal just before going onstage.

Anna looked up at him. She looked older, even in the semidarkness. He heard her shallow, quick breathing. He thought she was very minutely shaking her head, but it did not seem to be any kind of denial. He touched her hand as it lay on her lap. The hand jumped like a startled pet, but did not withdraw.

"It's going to be all right—I promise," he said. He had

made Harris support his idea, render assurances. Anna could be got back into the Soviet Union without difficulty—via the same route and within a couple of days. Harris knew Aubrey— yes. Did Aubrey have the necessary clout with the CIA—? Yes, Harris thought so. Yes, he didn't see any reason why she should not be let off the hook for getting Gant back to the West . . .

"A couple of days," he murmured, prompted by his memories of Harris's calm reassurances. "That's all it'll take, I promise you." He smiled crookedly, sorry that she could not see clearly the reassuring expression. "I'm big for them now—at the moment. I *can* get them to do what I want—get you out of it."

Her head was shaking now. "I can't believe it is going to work." She looked up at him, having taken his hand. "I do not blame you, Mitchell Gant—believe that, at least. You were just . . . the wrong man at the wrong time." She might have been talking of a ruinous love affair, one which had cost her her marriage. That heartfelt tone gave Gant an insight. For her, the relationship with Priabin had been somehow altered, perhaps even destroyed. She could not envisage a satisfactory future unless she restored her relationship with him.

Gant envied and pitied her. And realized the mutuality of their passion. Priabin's hatred narrowed to himself alone now, was as palpable as if the man had just put his head into the car. The three hours since they had left him would have done nothing to dissipate that hatred. It would have grown, perhaps run out of control like a forest fire.

And Gant knew that Priabin would not give up, would not be content to wait in a Leningrad hotel for her return.

"Listen to me," he said urgently. "You love him, he loves you. What is there to be afraid of? Only people like your Case Officer—nothing more dangerous than that. And the Company will be called off—! You won't have to worry . . . and it won't matter how long it takes to get cosy with Dmitri again. You'll have the time to do it. For Christ's sake, Anna, just cross this border with me and I promise you everything will work out!"

He gripped her hand fiercely. It lay dormant in his fist. He dropped it onto her lap, sighed, and slumped back in his seat.

After a long silence, he heard her say softly, almost

apologetically: "Very well. I have made up my mind. You are right. I will come with you."

He looked at her carefully. He could see the pale skin, and her cheeks seemed dry. Her eyes were in shadow. The touch of her hand did not seem pretended or assumed, and he believed her.

"O.K.," he said. "You've made the right choice. I know you have."

"Will he understand?"

"He knew all along—"

"But that was *different*—!" It was almost a wail.

"You mean—you weren't helping me, uh?" Gant snapped. "I wasn't the key to his career?"

"He wouldn't think like that."

"Maybe, maybe not. Whichever way you look at it, he owes me. He's a man with a lot of grief to unload, and I gave him all of it. I just hope he sits tight in Leningrad and boozes himself into self-pity. It could be safer for all of us."

"You mean—?"

"I don't mean anything. Let's just hope, uh?" He was angry that he had voiced his own fears precisely at the moment she had become reconciled to accompanying him. He glanced at his watch, holding its dial close to his face.

Harris had been gone for more than fifteen minutes.

He gripped the door handle.

"I'm going to look for Harris—stay here," he ordered.

"You think—?" she asked fearfully, as if Priabin threatened her, too. Priabin, yes, he thought. Both of us are afraid of the same man—

"I don't think anything. He could've slipped and broken a leg. I'll be back."

He pressed his fur hat onto his head and squinted into the blowing snow. Anna watched him as he trudged as quickly as he could out of the pull-off and onto the main road. The high bushes hid him.

Anna turned back, and stared at the thick coating of snow that obscured the windscreen. There were lighter, paperlike coverings on the side windows. The car was claustrophobic, small and cell-like. Her fears enlarged within it.

She had coped, so easily and successfully she had always *coped*—! But not with this.

She rubbed her hands down her face, as if scouring her

skin. She was trapped; utterly trapped. Only the American, whom she ought to have hated because he had acted as the catalyst of her ruin, offered her any hope of escape. If they would let her go—*if only they would let her go!*

Gant had said it didn't matter how much time it took to rebuild her relationship with Dmitri. He had promised her the time in which to do it. She could only believe him, because there was no other solution. No other way out.

The door of the car opened. She turned her head and stared into Dmitri's face. Her mouth opened, as if to protest at the appearance of a ghost, and then he had climbed into the rear of the car and was holding her in her arms. She gasped and clung to him. His overcoat was chilly and wet with melting snow. His cheek was cold against her temple, but it soothed her. She held onto him, even when he made as if to push her away, because the world was no larger than the material of his coat, the cold of his cheek, the noise of his labored breathing in her ear. Then he forced her to sit upright, holding her arms tightly enough to hurt. She studied his face in the darkness of the car. As his eyes adjusted to the gloom, he seemed to be searching her face for some emotion he feared to find.

"Dmitri—where . . . ?"

"No time, Anna," he said breathlessly, placing his gloved forefinger on her mouth. "Listen to me. Come back with me now. Please come back with me now—!" It was an order, but more than that, a plea. As if he saw into a black future, and wished to pull her back from it as from the edge of a cliff.

"What is it?"

"What do you mean? I want you to come with me. Quickly, before Gant returns. Let him cross the border by himself. We can be in Leningrad before morning, in Moscow by noon. Look, Anna, we can explain everything. I—I can explain in some way or other why I had to leave Moscow, why I traveled to Leningrad. No one need know you ever left the city. Come quickly now, before he returns . . ." He was eager to be gone, like a thief leaving a house he had ransacked. She did not understand his urgency. She did not understand why he was there, how he had followed them. There was something in his tone that lay beneath love, and she could not help her mistrust of it.

"Why? Dmitri, what's the matter—tell me . . . ?"

Her hands gripped his arms. They appeared to be jockeying for a position whereby one could use a wrestling throw upon the other. She shook her head slightly.

"There's nothing the matter. Now, come with me, Anna—quickly, before he returns—"

She knew, then. The anxiety was clear in his voice. Knew part of it, at least. "Where's Harris, Dmitri? Where is the driver? What will the American find?"

She shook his arms.

"It doesn't matter," he said softly.

"Tell me!"

"He's *dead!*"

"You *killed* him?"

"There was a struggle," he answered lamely.

"No there wasn't—!" she almost screamed, outraged more by his lie than by the death of Harris. "You killed him. Don't *lie* to me!"

"Come on—"

"No! Not until you tell me what will happen."

"Anna—!"

"No. What will happen?"

"Gant will be arrested at the border—perhaps even shot. Yes, best if he were shot . . ."

"You mean you've told them to expect him—expect *us?*" she asked, appalled, her hand covering her mouth, then both hands clamped upon her ears.

"No. Not yet. I came for you first."

"Dmitri—for God's sake, what are you *doing*—!"

"Saving you—saving us. Harris knew about you, Gant knows about you. He won't give himself up at the border when they try to arrest him—they'll have to kill him. You'll be safe, then."

"No—!"

"What matters most—him or us? Anna, if Gant dies no one will know you helped him. He won't be able to tell them—"

"And the CIA?" she asked bitterly. "They will know."

"No they won't! You can tell them he made you turn back, that he went on by himself while you returned to Leningrad . . . he and Harris were killed. It's easy—"

"*Easy?* Killing two people is easy?"

"Anna—forget all this. Just get out of the car, come with me and let him go on by himself. I'll—I won't call the border post, I'll let him go. I promise he'll be safe—"

"I don't believe you—you *want* him to die." She studied his face; even though he moved his head back and away from her, she could distinguish the gleam in his eyes. He did want Gant killed. Like a jealous lover, he wanted his rival dead.

The windows of the car were fogged. The snow was slushlike, beginning to slip down to the sills because of the warmth inside the car; their anger. She did not know what to do. Dmitri could not protect her from the CIA. She could not let Dmitri kill Gant. Because he was Dmitri, because she could not live with him if she acquiesced . . . she would learn to live with Harris's death, change it from murder into something else. But not Gant. She would have known beforehand, and would never escape it. "I can't let you . . ." she murmured eventually.

"What? You want to *protect* him?" Dmitri raged. "You want to go on being a *spy*, an agent? For the *Americans?*"

"Not for the Americans, not for him—for us. I can't *agree* to his murder, I can't let you murder him! Don't you see? I can't live with that—!"

"I can," he announced with cold solemnity. "I want to."

"Dmitri—"

He shook his head. "You're coming with me, Anna," he said, grabbing her arm. This time the pressure of his grip made her cry out. He pulled at her arm, opening the door with his other hand. "You're coming with me! You'll forget about this, you'll forget about everything . . ."

"No—!"

He grunted and twisted her arm, making her scream. "Come on, Anna," he snarled, threatening her. "Come on."

He twisted her arm further, almost seeming to Anna to be on the point of breaking it. Fire spread from her wrist to her elbow to her shoulder. She cried out again, looking wildly at him, unable to understand his rage, his desire to hurt her. "No—!"

"Come on—!" He pulled her upper body clear of the car. She lay almost horizontally on the seat. He bent and slapped her face. "Come on, come on—!" He wrenched at her arm. She screamed.

Then she felt the pressure, the agony, lessen. The skirt of his overcoat brushed her head, she saw feet slipping and struggling in the trampled snow by the wheel of the car, then something banged heavily against the front passenger door. She heard Gant's voice.

"What the hell is the matter with you?" Gant was breathing heavily, almost grunting out the words. She could hear Dmitri's rough breathing, too. She rolled back into a sitting position. Dmitri's back had wiped away the snow from the passenger window. The freezing air made her shiver violently. She held her injured arm gently, cradling it like a child in her other arm. "That's better," she heard Gant say. "Just take it easy." Then: "You all right, Anna?"

"Yes, yes," she managed to say thickly. Then she groaned as she moved.

"O.K.?"

"Yes." She got heavily out of the car, still cradling her arm. Dmitri looked at her, horrified. Gant's arm had been across his throat, his pistol at Dmitri's forehead. Now, the American stepped back, motioning her away from Dmitri. She obeyed.

"What the hell was happening when I came up?" Gant asked. Then he added: "You know he killed Harris?" She nodded. Addressing Dmitri, he said: "You stupid bastard. What the hell's the matter with you? You could get us all caught!"

"You I *want* caught!" Dmitri snapped back.

"O.K., comrade, I'm the biggest villain you ever met! That I can understand—but *her*? You're putting her in danger. You think you can just take her back, without guarantees from the Company? You're dumb—*too* dumb." Something else, something more dangerous, occurred to Gant at that moment, and he said: "Are they expecting us? *Are they?*" The pistol jabbed forward, at Dmitri Priabin's stomach. Anna gasped, then cried out:

"No! He hasn't told them yet—I swear he hasn't!"

"I believe you. *You*," he added, addressing Priabin, "what was the plan, uh? Kill Harris so we get into trouble at the border . . . or just me? Anna was going to walk? You'd have left me stranded, and you'd have made sure I got killed." Gant's features twisted in anger and contempt. "Get in the car," he snapped. "Back seat, with the window rolled right down—get in!" Priabin climbed reluctantly into the car and wound down the window. He glared out after the door was closed on him. He avoided looking at Anna. He rubbed his hands together between his knees, as if warming or washing them. Gant pocketed Priabin's heavy Stechkin automatic, keeping his own pistol leveled. "Anna—come here," he said. "Not too close."

She moved closer to Gant. Priabin's eyes blazed as she seemed to touch the American.

"I'm all right," she announced, now rubbing her injured arm. "I'm all right, Dmitri—"

"I'm sorry," he said, shamefaced.

"O.K., that's fine, real fine. Now, what do we do with him? If we leave him here, he'll call the Border Guard just as soon as he can. If we take him, he'll turn me in the first chance he gets—and that will mean he screws things up for you, too, Anna."

"No," Priabin protested sullenly.

"Wake up to the fact that I'm the only real chance she has of walking free of this whole mess!" Gant snapped angrily. "You let us cross the border and she'll be able to come back to you. Your way—she hasn't a prayer."

Priabin's face gleamed with hatred. He could not accept Anna as a gift of the American. He was not calculating, not operating, in any kind of professional capacity. He wanted to kill Gant, but it was because of Anna. He blamed the American for everything. The killing of Gant would be some kind of cleansing ritual; either that, or it would prove his manhood or keep his mistress or ensure their safety. Whatever the reason, the death of Gant was inextricably tangled with any solution he envisaged. Perhaps he wanted Gant dead as much as he wanted Anna safe.

"Dmitri, let us go," Anna pleaded, almost leaning into the car. "*Please* let us go. It has to be this way—I have to be free of them—!"

Gant was shocked at the depth of bitterness in her words. However, he addressed Priabin in a tone of laconic threat. "Well, Dmitri, speak up. You heard the lady. Will you let us go?" Priabin did not reply, did not even look at Gant. Gant said to Anna: "Will he let us go? Can you really believe he won't try to kill me?"

She glanced round at him, as if invited to participate in a betrayal. Then she shook her head. "No," she sobbed.

"Then he's a damn fool!" Gant snapped and strode swiftly to the window of the car. Priabin flinched. Anna made as if to cry out. Gant struck Priabin across the temple with the barrel of the Makarov. The Russian slumped away from the window, across the seat.

"No—!" Anna cried, gripping the sill, stumbling against Gant.

"He's alive! It just gives us time."

"Dmitri—"

"Get into the car and listen to his heartbeat if you don't believe me!"

"No, no, I believe you . . ." She mumbled. "Thank you, thank you."

"Don't waste time. Let me get him out of the car—he won't freeze in this coat." Grunting with effort as he spoke, Gant hauled Priabin out of the car and dragged him across the snow to the shelter of a heavy, snow-laden bush. Anna walked beside him, her eyes never leaving Priabin's face. When Gant lowered the unconscious Russian, she knelt by him. Gant watched her stroke the young man's face, gently touch the swelling on his temple. He walked away. The whole attitude of her body, the look on her face, was too much like prayer. "Are you coming?" he asked in an almost fearful tone.

He turned to look at her. She was still kneeling beside the unconscious Priabin. She touched his face slowly, gently. Then she stood up.

"He will be all right?"

"Just a headache."

"There is no other way, is there?"

"No. No sure way except coming with me."

"Will he believe that?" she asked, glancing down at Priabin again.

"I can't answer that."

"I don't believe he will . . ." She shrugged, and walked away from Priabin towards Gant. "But, I have no choice—do I?"

"No, you don't," he replied softly.

They reached the car and Gant opened the passenger door for her. She climbed in slowly and reluctantly, her face turning immediately to Priabin's body. He slammed the door and walked round to the driver's side. He brushed snow from his hairpiece, from the shoulders and knees of his clothing, then sat heavily in the driver's seat.

Harris had left the keys in the ignition. Gant had checked his pockets when he found the body, thrown into a snow-filled ditch near the telephone box.

"Christ," he breathed, remembering his shock on finding Harris's body and instantly realizing who had killed him. "Why the hell did he do it? How could he be so *blind?*" He shook his head, his hands fiercely gripping the steering wheel.

"I don't know—love?" Anna said.

"Crazy—"

"Yes, love." She was nodding to herself, confirming her analysis.

Gant looked at her. "Have you got the nerve to cross the border without Harris? If he's expected along with us, then we'll have to bluff it out—he fell ill in Leningrad, something like that . . . we're angry at being delayed and having to cross the damn border in the middle of the night for talks early tomorrow. Can you do that?"

She nodded. "Yes, I can do that."

"O.K. We have ten miles rehearsal time. We might just make it before that crazy bastard wakes up."

"Do you understand why he did it?"

"It doesn't matter—"

"It does! He's a murderer. I have to find a reason for that."

"O.K. . . ."

"Harris and you—you were taking me away from him. He didn't believe I would come back . . ." She choked back a strange, crumpled, defeated sound in her throat, but she could not prevent tears from rolling down her pale cheeks. Gant flicked on the windscreen wipers. The view cleared of slush. The wipers squeaked across half-ice. "He didn't believe . . ." she repeated, but the words were submerged. She shook her head violently, as if to clear it. "He didn't . . ." Her voice was awed, and profoundly disappointed.

"And killing me makes everything right, uh?"

"Yes," she replied, staring through the windscreen at the steadily falling snow. "You are to blame. You have to be to blame. If you are to blame for everything that has happened to us, then I am not to blame and Dmitri is not to blame . . . but, especially me. I would be to blame for nothing, nothing at all . . ."

"It doesn't matter." He glanced back at Priabin's unmoving form. "We might just make it, even without Harris," he announced, switching on the engine.

* * *

With the assistance of a Norwegian radio operator, Curtin was engaged in a long, wearying, intense conversation with the senior engineering officer, the station commander, and the pilot of the Hercules Aubrey had commandeered, at Bardufoss. Aubrey himself was using the high-speed communications system to talk to Shelley in London.

Aubrey was pleased with himself, with the situation, with the progress they had made. In a little more than two hours, he had put his shoulder to the great wheel of circumstances, and had managed to move it. He was tired, but felt elated. Later, he knew he would collapse, like a cliff sliding slowly into the sea. But not yet, not while things remained to be done.

"I shall be telling Director Vitsula that Gant is required in Oslo immediately for a full debriefing. In fact, he will be brought here. You do *have* the Harrier, Peter?"

Aubrey waited while his message was transmitted via geostationary satellite to Shelley in Century House, overlooking the river. Then the tapes gathered Shelley's reply at high speed, rewound, and spoke.

There was amusement in Shelley's voice, too, as he said: "Yes, sir, we have a Harrier. It is already en route to Oslo, thence to Helsinki to collect Gant. Allied Forces, South Norway, will inform you of the aircraft's arrival. Won't Vitsula think it just a little suspicious that you had a Harrier collect Gant rather than something that *can't* land at the lake?"

There was a pause in the message, but the operator knew that Shelley had not finished.

"There's quite a bit more yet, sir," he informed Aubrey.

"Christ . . ." he heard Shelley breathe in an aside, then clear his throat. "Thank you, Bill. Yes—no, keep running the tape, man!" Then, evidently, he addressed Aubrey directly. The old man was alert, almost trembling. He understood the first drops of rain from an approaching storm. "Sir, message just received from Leningrad Station. Most urgent—the panic button, sir. Harris telephoned in with ten miles to go, and was cut off. They don't think it was the line, sir. Reception was quite good, in spite of the weather, and they swear the line was still open for some seconds after Harris stopped speaking. They even heard the pips demand more money in the slot . . ."

"My *God!*" Aubrey exclaimed, raising his hands in the air. "Oh, my God—"

Curtin was watching him from the other side of the hut. He had paused in his conversation. Aubrey absently waved him to continue, as if dismissing him from the room.

Gant—what the devil had happened to Gant?

The radio operator waited for his reply. Looking slightly bemused and a little worried, Curtin continued his conversation with Bardufoss. His technical specifications, the details of what Aubrey had called their shopping list, the ranks and areas of expertise of the men volunteered, the strength and capacity of arms of the Royal Marines—all mocked him now. Curtin's words bore in upon him in the hot, paraffin-smelling silence of the hut. Curtin was discussing Blowpipe missiles, and dismissing the idea. They had not yet decided whether there would be sufficient room on board the Hercules for more than a handful of Royal Marines and their equipment. Aubrey had been prepared to discount the idea of reinforcements because the Russians still had no idea where the Firefox was located. There was less need of defense than of extra equipment. The bales of MO-MAT occupied a great deal of space, as did the tractor tug, and both were crucial.

But now, but now, his thoughts repeated. Where was Gant? Did they have him? He had to *know*—!

He was deeply afraid. He had to talk to Vitsula, he had to have a report of Gant's arrival at the border, his crossing—*if* he arrived, *if* he crossed . . .

He had to. He needed news of Gant much as he might have needed a tranquilizer. Had to have news, had to—at once . . .

"Yes, Peter—I understand. I must talk to Helsinki. Message ends."

He turned away from the console, rubbing his cheeks vigorously with his hands. He realized his palms were damp with nervous perspiration. Curtin had moved on to the subject of air transportable fuel cells and the number required. At Bardufoss, with the Royal Norwegian Air Force's Tactical Supply Squadron, things were still happening. Everything was happening. The Hercules was already being loaded. Met reports indicated that the dawn window in the appalling weather would occur, and the drop could take place on schedule. Hydraulic and lubricating oils now, and oxygen cylinders . . .

Madness, Aubrey could not help pronouncing to himself.

He had taken leave of his senses. To have ever *conceived* of such a scheme—!

The radio operator had signaled Helsinki. Director-General Vitsula of Finnish Intelligence might already be seated before a console, awaiting his message. He must talk to him—

Aubrey knew there was nothing Vitsula could do. The Finns could not, would not cross the border. Gant was on his own until he crossed into Finland.

If he was still alive—

He must talk to Helsinki, must pretend, for his own sake, that there was something that could be done, that there were reassurances that might yet be gained. Mere talk. Filling the accusing silence.

The nose of the Firefox lowered, seemed to droop like the beak of some huge, black, drinking bird, as it moved over the crown of the slope onto the level stretch of MO-MAT. Buckholz, who had been waiting for a sign of eventual success, felt relief begin to invade his chilled body. The winches creaked. He sensed the huge weight of the aircraft as he watched the nosewheel inching forward along the portable runway, dragging the long, streaming fuselage behind it. The nylon lines quivered with strain, and he realized that the three anchor trees that held the chain-winches must be under the same strain. They seemed to protest, sounding like the amplified noises of aching muscles.

Yet he felt relieved; close to success. Moresby's head and shoulders above the cockpit sill were another sign; an imitation pilot, making the Firefox appear to be an aircraft once more. Half an hour ago, it had been different. The undercarriage had become threatened by rocks and rubble on the lake bed. Brooke and his divers had had to inflate huge black buoyancy bags beneath the aircraft's wings to lift the undercarriage clear before it suffered structural damage. Then, when the rocks had been left behind or removed, the divers had had to carefully deflate the bags once more and lower the undercarriage—main wheels first, very slowly and steadily— back to the lake bed. Though everyone had emphasized that it was no more than a hitch, it had affected Buckholz. Once winching recommenced, he had obsessively watched the nosewheel, measured its progress—waited for it to reach and surmount the crown of the slope.

He turned to look at the winching teams, at the taut ropes and the quivering trees. Then back to the fuselage of the aircraft. Then the winching teams once more; knowing that he was ignoring the real drama of the scene. Moresby was securing the ejector seat, to which any ordinary self-destruct system could be rigged. He was ensuring that no accident could trigger it. Then he would begin to search the cockpit for any other mechanical or electrical system designed to ensure the destruction of the most secret equipment aboard the aircraft. Buckholz, as a layman, could not believe in the drama of the self-destruct. For him, it was easier to imagine a rope breaking, a tree giving way, an undercarriage leg buckling, even snapping under the strain imposed by the winches. And Moresby was doing nothing; there was no atmosphere of tension generated from the cockpit. Expertise disguised danger. A bobbing head in a woolen cap, framed by the thrown-back hood of a white parka. Buckholz could not believe that the Firefox would explode.

The tree holding the winch attached to the port undercarriage leg appeared to quiver as he turned once more to look at it. The men on the winch, backs bent, suggested nothing was wrong by their continued, rhythmical movements. The Royal Engineer captain had his back to the tree, hands on his hips, watching the Firefox labor towards him. The nose of the aircraft was fully level now, the two remaining undercarriage wheels poised to roll over the crown of the slope.

The port line was quivering more exaggeratedly than the other two, its marker flag dancing. Buckholz turned his gaze to the anchor tree. One of the two winchmen had straightened and was about to turn towards his officer. The tree had begun to tilt forward. He glanced at the aircraft. Moresby's head and shoulders, the two rear undercarriage wheels poised to level the fuselage, the two other lines straining, the port line dancing, seeming to slacken . . .

He opened his mouth. His words were cut off by a riflelike crack. The anchor tree flung down its weight of snow, shuddered again, then the clearing was filled with the noise of tearing roots. Buckholz moved one pace. The engineer captain turned, raising his head as he moved to one side very slowly. The two winchmen had abandoned the winch. Pistol-like cracks. The scene consisted almost solely of sound. Hardly any movement. Monochrome—snow, trees, portable runway, the black aircraft like a creature attempting to return to the water. The roots snapped and broke in a succession of small explosions. The winchmen and the engineer captain flung themselves to either side of the tree as it lurched, then staggered as if entirely free of its roots, and began to fall.

It would miss the Firefox, miss the—

The thought became outdated in the next instant. The two remaining nylon lines began to dance and wave their marker flags as the first one had done. The aircraft was slewing to starboard, turning its nose towards Buckholz. He watched the port line slacken as the tree fell slowly into the clearing. Someone shouted, or perhaps cried out in pain. Everything was slow. Buckholz realized that the tree was moving faster than the men around it. Its dark branches enfolded a man who had hardly begun to run. Buckholz heard his muffled scream. The two lines danced wildly as the Firefox seemed to lurch backwards. He heard the winches groan, sensed the two remaining anchor trees quiver.

The nosewheel was still moving backwards, he was certain of it.

He saw Moresby's head and shoulders, then his upper torso as he stood up in the cockpit, gripping the sill with both mittened hands. Moresby's mouth opened. Some of the overhead netting, caught by the falling tree, ripped and floated downwards like part of a stage backcloth. Snow billowed and fell. Branches were dragged from neighboring trees, more netting pursued that already torn. The slack line snaked out of the winch and whipped across the clearing. One man fell, another ducked beneath the whiplash. The nylon line slithered to rest across the MO-MAT.

Moresby shouted an order. Buckholz did not hear it. He was aware of Waterford at his shoulder and then the soldier moved towards the Firefox, yelling like Moresby, waving his arms as if to increase his circulation; the two remaining anchor trees shuddered, depositing snow. The engineers were already checking the winches, the trees, the lines; moving as if under water.

Monochrome—

Then terrible color. Someone screamed, and the noise appeared to conjure up flame. On the far side of the clearing, the camouflage netting had fallen onto the stove that was supplying the relieved winching teams with hot drinks. The nose of the Firefox strained round like the head of a roped bull. The nosewheel had slid sideways, but backwards, too.

The groaning anchor trees were slowly releasing the winches, which in turn released the ropes inch by inch. The fire roared up, catching the matting and setting it alight. A man burned, then doused the flames by rolling over and over in the snow, thrashing about in agony.

Only Waterford seemed to be moving towards the scene. Then others. Other noises, other orders. The flames roared up in a fountain. Men rolled logs forward, behind the two undercarriage wheels, then behind the nosewheel. The undercarriage resisted the attempt to block its retreat to the water. The lines shuddered, their marker flags waving frenziedly. The anchor trees were almost bare of their weight of snow. Above the yelling, Buckholz listened for the first groan, the first pistol-shots of snapping roots. He knew the aircraft was destined to roll backwards into the lake.

Without realizing, he had moved forward into the chaos of the scene. Flame gouted, a tiny, ineffectual spray of extinguisher foam reached towards it. Buckholz bent and rolled a log behind the starboard wheel. The nose of the Firefox had turned through perhaps thirty degrees, seeming to fight against the restraint of the remaining lines. The tire began to mount the log—other logs were jammed against his own. The port wheel, too, was being blocked by logs.

"Get another line on the port leg!" he heard Moresby shouting somewhere above him. As he looked beneath the belly of the Firefox, he saw extinguisher foam arcing through the snowy air towards the fire. Then flame retaliated, licking upwards into the overhead netting that remained. Men ran towards the port side of the aircraft, unreeling a nylon line. He heard Moresby directing his men from the cockpit.

"Get that moved!" Waterford cried out. Buckholz could see the soldier outlined by flame, so close to the fire that he appeared to be burning himself. His body was bent, he was dragging a boxlike container. Ammunition—the ammunition supplies were stored at the edge of the clearing. Buckholz could not move. He was kneeling beneath the starboard wing, the tire trying to surmount the jammed logs acting as chocks. He stared in horrified fascination as the ammunition boxes were slowly—so slowly—dragged clear of the flames. They were doused with foam, the fire was attacked with more foam. The line just above his head quivered, its dance now a shudder, something close to climax—

He turned to look. The trees were quivering, but did not

appear to be tilting forward into the clearing. The crackling of his R/T drew his attention to the babble of orders and responses and reports. The team secured the new line to the port undercarriage leg. The aircraft seemed to sense its imminent restraint, and lurched further, skewing round, lifting the starboard wheel almost over the jam of logs beside Buckholz.

"Here—!" he called. Someone was beside him almost at once. "Hold on here!"

He stood up, gripping the makeshift wooden lever the other man had placed against the pile of logs. Together, they attempted to hold the pressure of the aircraft's weight, trying to keep the logs from rolling away from the wheel. Immediately, Buckholz was gasping for breath and his arms and back and legs ached. A third and fourth man joined them; another crude braking lever was jammed against the logs. It did not seem to ease the pressure on Buckholz's muscles. He grunted as a substitute for protest.

"Then take the bloody risk with *that* tree, Captain!" Moresby yelled in the R/T, and was acknowledged immediately. "Don't slacken the line, you stupid buggers! Pay it out ahead— yes, that's it . . . take the strain, you silly sods, or we'll all be in the bloody shit!" Beneath the language and the apparent panic, there was expertise. "Get the two remaining trees anchored before they give way!" Moresby continued. "Lash each of them to three other trees, nearest ones to them. Come on, before they uproot themselves too!"

"Come on, come *on*—" Buckholz recited, finding the words in his grunting breaths. The man beside him took up the words, like a chant. The tire squeaked in protest against the logs. "Come on, come on, come on—"

The captain ordered his men to attach the winch to the selected tree. Buckholz's leg muscles went into spasm, but they were a great distance from him. The color of the fire seemed to lessen as it was reflected on the sheen of ice already forming on the aircraft's belly. There was a scorched smell on the snowy wind—netting, canvas, clothing, and something else he did not want to identify . . . *flesh*.

The strain became worse. His mittened hands were welded to the wooden lever, his arms welded to his hands, his shoulders locked above his hurting back and buttocks.

"Come on—get on with it, Captain!" Moresby was yelling again.

"Come on, come on, come on . . ."

"Make sure that bloody fire's out! Look after—who is it, Henderson? —and get the poor sod out from under that bastard tree!" Waterford's orders bellowed over the R/T.

He heard the two remaining winches yield the nylon lines inch by inch, as the anchor trees bent. The tire that filled his gaze seemed to lift further, almost mounting the logs. Then a rapid noise in the distance, at the edge of the clearing—

"Oh, Jesus—!" he wailed. Rapid clicks, quiet pistol-shots. He was about to warn the men with him to get out of the way, to save themselves, when he realized it was the chain-winch winding the line through to take up the slack as rapidly as possible. Three lines now, almost three, three in a moment or two—

"Come on, come on, come on . . ."

"Fuck this for—"

"Come on!" Moresby yelled. "Have you finished anchoring the other trees?"

Then he saw the line on the port leg snap straight, take up the strain, quiver and become still. He heard the single winch click and click again and again. The nose of the Firefox steadied, as if the animal it had become sensed a superiority of strength in its captors. He exhaled in a great sigh.

"Is that tree holding?" Moresby shouted.

"For the moment, sir," the engineer captain replied.

"Anchor it to three secondary trees, then."

"Sir."

Someone near Buckholz grunted a cheer. In front of him, the tire had slid back behind the little barricade of logs. It just rested against them now. He raised his eyes. The port and nosewheel lines were shivering into still tension. The trees—did they still quiver and lean, or was it the cold sweat in his eyes, the effort he was making, that gave them the appearance of movement? He lowered his gaze to the star-board wheel. The tire had moved away from the logs.

The cacophony of orders and responses had become muted. Calm. He waited. His body was numb; even the tremor had gone from his muscles. He felt locked into this posture, into this effort. The captain ordered the new winch to begin once more, slowly. The Firefox protested. Its nose swung slowly round, almost balefully, the wheel protesting on the wafflelike surface of the portable runway. He saw the tension in the line from the starboard leg ease. The marker flag stopped dancing and became a rag flicked by the wind. Buckholz waited.

The port winch stopped. He could not feel his hands around the wooden lever, could hardly feel the next man's body against his.

Then he heard Moresby say: "One, Two and Three—haul away!" He groaned. Moresby added: "O.K., you lot down there—relax. And thanks. Thanks everyone . . ." Buckholz tried to unclasp his hands. The starboard wheel moved a few more inches from the heap of logs. They rolled after it from the pressure of the lever. Moresby continued talking, requesting a full damage report. Buckholz's back cried out in protest as he straightened up. His legs felt weak. He staggered a few steps, then bent painfully to chafe them back to usefulness. He groaned softly with every breath.

Then, when he could walk, when his feet began to hurt with reawakened blood, he hobbled as swiftly as he could towards the scene of the fire. A canvas sheet covered something. He glanced back into the clearing. There was something else, uncovered by the tree, being lifted and moved out of the aircraft's resumed path.

Two dead, then—

He looked into Waterford's face. It was blackened by smoke, but the man seemed uninjured, unlike the two SBS men beyond him, whose hands and faces were being salved and bandaged. Hot scraps of camouflage netting dropped like windborne flakes of ash from the trees above them. The ground was slushy, slippery with melted snow and foam. Waterford stared at him.

"Two dead?" he said.

Waterford nodded. "Two—and two injured . . . not badly burned." The man's face seemed to become chalky and vulnerable as he added: "Thank God." Then at once he was again his usual persona. "You can help me," he ordered Buckholz. "Make a full damage report. Well, come on—"

Waterford strode off. Buckholz, before following him, watched the taut lines, the inching forward along the MO-MAT of the three undercarriage wheels, all of them now on the level. Moresby was once more seated in the cockpit. Buckholz, on the point of sighing with relief and delayed shock, held his breath. The self-destruct. They were in as much danger of losing the airframe as ever. Perhaps more.

Moresby had been distracted. Time had passed—how much? Minutes . . . perhaps seven minutes. Seven—

His body was trembling from head to foot. He hurried after Waterford on weak legs, as if hurrying away from the aircraft and the danger it now represented.

The whole clearing smelt of burning.

Priabin began to realize he was cold. He seemed to be floating. At least, part of him was floating. A much smaller part, right at the back of his head, was aware that something was wrong. But, there were no answers, only images; dreams, nightmares, visions, pictures, memories. In most of them, he was apologizing to Anna.

He apologized for his work, for his colleagues, for his uniform, for his rank, and for things he knew he had never done; actions never taken, crimes not committed.

He sensed she accused him, though she did not appear in most of the pictures or memories or dreams. Not even her voice. But somehow he knew that she was accusing him, and he understood the nature of the charges. No, he had not beaten up those demonstrators in Red Square, no he had not had those people shot for black-marketeering, no he had not had those Jews interrogated and beaten and the one who died had a weak heart. No, he had not refused that writer a travel visa and passport; no he had not prevented people from leaving the Soviet Union; no, he had not ensnared those businessmen by using women to sleep with them; no, he had not operated the cameras that filmed them . . .

Some night bird moved in the bush above his head, throwing down a weight of snow onto his face. He opened his eyes. The snow was in his nose and mouth. He was aware of his entire body, and of its lowered temperature. His fingertips and toes were numb, his arms and legs cold, his torso chilled. He struggled to sit up, and looked around him.

The car had disappeared. He knew no more, for the moment, except that he had expected it to be there. It was a car he had approached, even sat in. His car—?

His car was further down the road, towards the village . . . Anna's car.

Harris's body. Harris? How did he know the man's name? He rubbed his arms with gloved hands, slapped at his upper body, then crawled out from the shelter of the bush into the snow that was now falling steadily. The wind appeared to have dropped.

Harris?

Gant—

He remembered. Remembered, too, all the images and visions; the countless apologies to Anna, who had refused to appear in his dreaming, even though she was close at hand. Anna—?

Gant—Anna.

He knew more; all of it.

He climbed to his feet, and a great weight of ballast appeared to move in his head. He groaned and clutched his temple. The bruise was numb yet tender. He could feel a tiny amount of caked blood, like frost. Anna had gone with Gant. He staggered a few steps. The faint tire tracks of the car led out of the pull-off, heading west towards the border.

He knew everything now. Gant and Anna had abandoned him in the pull-off while they made their escape. But the American had made a mistake—he had left Priabin alive. He congratulated himself on Gant's error.

He began to jog, awkwardly at first, his head beginning to pound as soon as he moved. He ran, head down, through the falling snow. Out of the pull-off, onto the deserted main road. He glanced up the road, towards the border. Empty. He bent his head again and began running, chanting over and over in ragged breaths his prayer that Gant had not sabotaged the car he had commandeered from the railway police at Kolpino.

He floundered along the road, arms pumping, chest heaving. He remembered the dreams and realized their significance. Then he slipped and went flying, skidding on his back across the road. The shock woke him as it expelled the breath from his body. He climbed to his feet, brushed down his clothes, and began running again. Not far now, only hundreds of meters, no more.

He passed the telephone box where he had killed Harris. He had intended that. Isolate Gant, he had told himself. Get Anna out then kill Gant—have him killed at the border. Turn back the clock, make it five days earlier, before all this had happened.

He could have done it, but she would not *believe* him—!

He saw one or two early lights in the village ahead. His car was only a short distance now . . . yes, there! He slid the last steps, bumping painfully against the side of the vehicle. He fumbled the keys from his pocket while he wrenched open the driver's door with his other hand. He collapsed heavily into the seat, hesitated, then thrust the key into the ignition.

And turned the key, holding his breath.

The ignition chattered. On the third attempt, the engine fired then stalled. He applied more choke. The engine caught, he revved blue smoke into the snow beyond the rear window. The engine roared healthily.

Just cold.

He eased his foot off the pedal and moved the car slowly out into the middle of the road. The studded tires bit, and he gradually accelerated. Passing the telephone box, passing the place where the snow was distressed by his skidding body, passing the pull-off. He looked at his watch, but could not estimate how long he had been unconscious. He stabbed the accelerator, and the back of the car swung wildly. He eased his foot from the pedal, turned the wheel swiftly to straighten the car, and drove on.

He had protected Anna because, in part, it preserved his own self-esteem. He was *not* a KGB officer, not *just* a policeman . . . He understood her clearly; even applauded her motives. He always had.

He would have saved her, got her away, but Gant had changed everything. Gant had placed her in danger, Gant had taken her away, she was in the car with him now. She was ready to cross the border with him—

Priabin wiped something from his eyes with the damp sleeve of his overcoat, then concentrated on the snow rushing towards the headlights. He knew he had peeled the onion a layer too deep.

He knew that he had not trusted Anna. From the moment when he had seen Gant on the train and realized how she was to help him escape, he had believed in his heart that she would go with the American. He had not trusted her to stop short of the border, or return if she did cross.

He wiped at his eyes again, savagely. *He had not trusted her!* He had believed she could, she would leave him.

Gant had held up the mirror, had shown him the vile

little heart of himself, beneath the layers of love and protection and self-esteem. He loathed his reflected image.

He had to kill Gant. More than anything, he would kill Gant.

"One, Two and Three—stop winching!"

Buckholz heard Moresby's voice over the R/T, and immediately glanced at Waterford beside him. The soldier seemed unimpressed that the Firefox had now been winched safely to the far end of the clearing. Instead, he continued to stare at the ice beneath their feet. They were fifty or sixty yards out onto the lake. The wind flung snow between them and the well-lit clearing. Fortunately, the arc lamps hadn't been brought down from the trees with the burning camouflage netting.

"Well—what is it you wanted me to see?" Buckholz asked. He wanted coffee, and he needed rest. Reaction had established itself now that their damage report was complete and his work temporarily done. Moresby's danger hardly impinged upon Buckholz's fuddled, slow thoughts. "Well?"

"Look at the bloody ice, man!" Waterford snapped in return.

"What—?"

"Snow—dammit, snow! Bloody snow!" He waved his arms above his head and kicked at the snow beneath his feet. The weather howled and flew around them in the darkness. Waterford was haloed by the lights from the clearing—where Moresby was working against time, he remembered with difficulty. As Waterford continued in a ranting tone, a break in the wind showed him the aircraft, black and safe, showed him the ragged extension of the clearing along the shore, allowed him to hear the chainsaws at work. "No bloody aircraft is going to be able to take off from this surface," Waterford was saying. "You know how long this lake is. Do you know how much runway that aircraft needs? No? Listen, then—the airspeed won't come up quick enough to give the pilot lift-off with this thickness of snow on the ice. It's as simple as that. So, what are you going to do about it?"

In the silence, which the wind filled, Buckholz heard Moresby's voice issuing from their R/Ts. "This thing is drying out rapidly, gentlemen . . ." They had no idea to whom the remark was addressed. Perhaps to all of them. "Icing up. I hope to God that whatever system they've installed, it isn't water-activated. There's nothing in the cockpit or rigged to any of the systems that looks like a self-destruct." Moresby paused, but his next words wiped away Buckholz's momentary sense of relief. "But, I'll bet there is a self-destruct, all the same. You'd all better clear the area. Gunnar—?"

"Yes?"

"Any joy?"

"I don't know. I can't find anything in the Pilot's Notes at first look. And there's nothing marked or stenciled on the fuselage so far."

The weather had removed them from Buckholz's sight, but he could envisage them clearly. Gunnar, who spoke good Russian, had been given the task of translating the Pilot's Notes which Moresby had found in the cockpit—a leaflet of fifty pages or more. At the same time, he was translating every stenciled word and instruction on the entire fuselage, searching for a clue to the nature and location of the self-destruct mechanism.

"That's it, then," Moresby continued. "Everyone clear the area. Five or six hundred feet back should do it. Go and hide in the trees—"

"Jesus," Buckholz breathed. "Is there anything we can do?" he said into the R/T, addressing Moresby.

"You're not helping the situation, Mr. Buckholz," came back the reply. "I suggest you hurry along and see a taxidermist, if you would!" Buckholz heard Gunnar's laughter, and beside him Waterford guffawed.

"Jesus—"

"Even we can walk on frozen water," Waterford said. "But planes can't take off from this thickness of snow. Even if the bloody thing survives its ordeal at Moresby's hands, it can't take off. You think we'll have a nice warm sunny day tomorrow?"

"Don't blame me—!" He was aware of the murmurs from the R/T now. Moresby and his technicians. Gunnar's translations. He knew everyone else would be listening, too. The noise of the chainsaws had stopped.

"I don't. You're just another of Aubrey's trained monkeys, just like me. That silly sod has flipped his lid this time and no mistake!"

Without conscious decision, they had begun to walk back towards the clearing. Light blazed out at them as they approached the shore. The trees along the shore had been cleared. MO-MAT would be laid, and then the tractor tug would tow the Firefox to a point where thicker ice would bear its weight before pulling the aircraft out onto the lake which would become its runway.

Which would not be usable as a runway, he reminded himself.

They trudged along the shore. The snow was blowing almost horizontally yet, in the clearing itself, there was a sense of quiet, urgent desperation. As he saw Moresby, seated in the cockpit and the technicians gathered around the fuselage, he realized he had no idea how large an explosion there would be. What would happen? Would it be small enough not to be visible until a little black flag of smoke raised itself above the cockpit? Or would it be large enough to open the nose section of the airframe like an exploded trick cigar? Enough to kill Gunnar and Moresby and the technicians . . .

And himself and Waterford, he thought as they trudged up the MO-MAT towards the aircraft.

There was a film of ice over much of the fuselage and the wing areas. There were great gaps in the camouflage netting which could not be replaced. The fallen tree lay to one side of the clearing, which was empty except for themselves, Moresby's team, and the Firefox. There might have been no chaos only a half hour earlier. It was as if everything had been no more than a dramatic prelude to the quiet desperation of Moresby's search for the self-destruct system.

The two bodies had been shrouded in their sleeping bags and removed from the clearing. They lay now like Arctic mummies, waiting for transport to their place of burial; waiting for next of kin to be informed. Buckholz shook the thoughts from his head.

Moresby saw them approach, and climbed rapidly out of the cockpit. He waved his arms as if shooing chickens in a yard.

"I told you to fuck off," he said to Buckholz.

"As a kid I used to haunt accident sites," Buckholz replied without expression. Moresby looked at him curiously, and then nodded, accepting his presence.

Buckholz looked around the clearing. Stores, the comm-pack, equipment, had all been removed. It was as if they were about to abandon the Firefox, having spent so much time and effort—and two lives—bringing her out of the lake. "What have you done so far?" he asked.

"There's no magnetic card to activate any self-destruct," Moresby snapped. "No armed micro-switches—nothing that could be set off other than by the removal of the canopy or the ejection of the bang-seat."

"But—there *has* to be something else?"

"I'd bet on it. Of course there has to be something—"

"Hell."

"Excuse me—I'm needed," Moresby said, and turned away from Buckholz and Waterford. Buckholz let the man go. He had no expertise and could not dissuade Moresby. Instead, he worried about the thickness of snow that had fallen on the ice. Gant had had snow cleared from the ice floe when he had refueled. It would have to be done here, with hot-air blowers. He would talk directly to Bardufoss, as soon—

As soon as they knew whether or not there was a clock ticking somewhere, a clock they could neither see nor hear. Was there anything?

Gunnar had covered almost the whole of the fuselage. He had worked around the airframe, reaching the fuselage below the cockpit once more. He had found nothing other than routine fueling and inspection points, catches, switches, points, bolts, panels.

"Below this small window, it reads: 'In the event of red placard, cordon off airframe and advise Senior Armaments Officer,' " Gunnar recited, then began humming and murmuring to himself over the R/T. Then he added: "Yes, that's what it says. There is a red placard showing in the window."

"Let me see," they heard Moresby say.

Involuntarily, Buckholz started forward. Waterford snorted in derision, but followed him.

"What is it?" Buckholz asked as he reached Moresby, who was craning to look through a tiny perspex window set at eye level below the cockpit.

"Approximately five millimeters of red-painted tin," Moresby answered without turning his head. "It doesn't mean a lot, does it?" He tapped the fuselage alongside the window. "Access panel—be careful, my lad, as you take it off, won't you?"

He stepped back and allowed the technician to reach the panel and gently begin to move the first of the four screws.

"Is it anything?" Buckholz insisted.

"Who knows? The instruction is pretty clear. You don't cordon off aircraft for no reason, or tell the armaments people

it's all theirs. I wonder . . . Come on, lad, get a move on!"
The technician had removed three of the flush screws, and he
pivoted the access panel. Moresby immediately moved forward,
brandishing a flashlight as if it were a weapon. He craned
towards the panel, moving the flashlight's thin beam as carefully as if he were attempting to skewer something with it.
Buckholz listened to his commentary over the R/T, having
retreated to his former position. "Mm. Two solenoids, a
relay—what's that . . . ? Wiring, a box with a tag . . . Gunnar,
what does it say on the tag—here . . ." Moresby stepped
away. Gunnar wriggled the beam of the flashlight into the
open panel.

"It says 'Battery change due on . . .' And it gives the
date. Next month."

"Useless!" Moresby snapped. "Let me have another look.
What else have we got here? Mm? Small canister, looks a bit
like—what? Old flasher unit I had on my Morris, years ago.
Top surface has a thin coating of some kind, wires from the
base which couple into the solenoids and the relay . . . and
that's it. Might be to run the pilot's model railway, I suppose
. . . Anyone else want a look?"

Moresby passed the flashlight to one of the technicians,
and turned to face Buckholz and Waterford. "Who knows?"
he announced with a shrug. "It ought to be important, but I
can't see why."

"The red placard?" Buckholz asked.

"If this is the self-destruct, then it's armed, yes."

"Thanks."

"Pleasure." He turned to his technician. "Well?"

"It doesn't remind me of a flasher unit sir," the technician offered.

"Brilliant. And what does it remind you of?"

"Looks like the automatic sprinkler device my old Dad
fitted in his greenhouses—down Evesham way . . . very
pleased with them, he was."

"Fascinating." Moresby flashed the flashlight back into
the open panel, wriggled its beam, sighed over the R/T,
glanced at the red placard in the window, then back into the
hole. "How does your father's sprinkler system work, then?"
he asked with studied casualness. They heard his muffled
voice continue: "Speak up, laddie, I'm very interested in
gardening myself."

Moresby's massive calm and expertise and exaggerated

manner had all conspired to lessen the tension which Buckholz felt was beginning to grow in him again.

"You've warned your men to stay at a safe distance?" he muttered to Waterford.

"I have." Waterford had called in nine of the eighteen SBS marines who formed his reconnaissance perimeter, to form a guard around the clearing now that the Firefox had been winched out of the lake.

Buckholz knew they should be starting to arrive within the next fifteen minutes. His concern for their safety deflected his fears for himself. The red placard must mean *something*—!

The technician was explaining his father's greenhouse sprinkler system. Buckholz could not accommodate the seeming irrelevance of the information. ". . . when it dries out it turns the sprinkler on . . . when it's wet by the right amount, it turns it off again . . ."

"Mm. Must get one for the lawn," Moresby murmured, his face still pressed to the access panel. Then he stood up, and stretched. "In the absence of anything more technical than the greenhouse sprinkler system donated by Carter and his father, I think we'll wedge the solenoids, just in case. Carry on, Carter. Let's play safe." Immediately, he walked across to Buckholz, rubbing his hands as if washing them inside his gloves. "Hurry up, Carter," he called over his shoulder, "it's getting pretty dry behind that panel."

"Do you think that's it?" Buckholz asked, his nerves and tension making him feel ridiculous.

"I should think so—*bang*," he added with a tight little smile. He flicked at his moustache, which creaked with his frozen breath. "I don't know why they wanted a water-activated system. Morbidly security-conscious, though, the Russians."

"So how did it work?" Buckholz was more and more angry. It was an anticlimax, he had been frightened for nothing.

"With the airframe's immersion, the system became operational," Moresby replied, almost with relish. "It was fully armed once it came out of the water. When it dried off completely—bang! At least, I assume that's what would have happened . . ."

He turned. The technician gave him a thumbs-up sign, and Moresby sighed with satisfaction.

"Safe?" Buckholz asked.

"Hang about for a bit and see, if you wish. I think

so—we'll get down to the real work now. I should get your chaps to cut down a few more trees, Major. It's almost three now." He nodded, and walked away towards the aircraft.

"Christ," Buckholz breathed. "Jesus H. Christ."

"No, but he's not bad for RAF," Waterford murmured, placing the R/T against his lips and turning away from the American.

Hoses, Buckholz reminded himself, masking the fears that he no longer wished to admit to. He felt himself trembling. He had been frightened, really frightened. Now, he had to find an activity, some occupation.

He wondered whether they had sufficient lengths of hose at Bardufoss to steam a runway across the ice for the Firefox, now that it was no longer in danger of being destroyed.

Then he thought of Gant.

And realized that the pilot might hang by more of a thread than the airframe had done.

The guards were bored, then impressed, then efficient. It had been simple. The barbed wire strung on crossed logs and poles was thickened, whitened and made innocent by clinging snow. It stretched away on either side into the hidden landscape. Snow covered the ploughed swath of earth that marked the border. Lights shone down on the guard post and customs office, and a lookout tower threw a shadow across the road just beyond the red-and-white pole.

Priabin had not told them, Gant thought to himself once more. He warmed himself with the knowledge. He stood with his back to the long table where Anna was now showing her papers and answering the few deferential questions offered by the Border Guard captain in command of the crossing point. Gant could see, beyond the shadow of the tower, the distant red-and-white pole on the Finnish side. Lights glowed from the windows of the huts like signals. The Finns who were to meet them would be watching the door of this customs office, waiting for their reemergence. They would get into the car, the Russian pole would swing up, they would be through. Sixty or seventy yards, and they would be in Finland.

Don't think about it, he told himself, feeling his hands quiver in the pockets of his overcoat. The snow that had gathered on his fur hat had melted, and begun to trickle down his neck and beneath the collar of his shirt. Don't think about crossing . . .

If he did dwell on it, his mask would crack in the closing seconds of his performance. It was easy, acting this officious senior diplomat or civil servant. An older man, testy with authority, dry and sharp like a fallen brown holly leaf. These people were half-afraid of him, half-afraid of his power to make telephone calls, speak to superiors, complain, condemn. They had hurried their questions, their examination of his papers. They had not wished to search his luggage. They had accepted his explanation that their Finnish companion, expected to drive them, had fallen ill—*too much drink,* he had snapped with an acid dislike—but *they* had important, vital meetings later that same day . . . planes were grounded in Leningrad, as they knew, thus the car. He was angry at losing sleep, at delay of any kind.

He paced a little now, while Anna answered the brief questions. He clicked his tongue against the roof of his mouth. Nerve, he thought. Hold on—

Act.

He glared at the captain over his half-glasses. The captain caught his look, and immediately surrendered Anna's papers, making the most of a polite bow to her.

"Thank you," Gant said with little grace. "Now, we may go?"

"Of course, sir—please . . ." He opened the door for them. Gant preceded Anna out into the snow and the lights. Stepping into the glare, he almost froze, as if he had been exposed and recognized. Then he walked on to the car. Impatiently, he held the passenger door open for Anna, and she climbed in. Then, merely nodding dismissively in the captain's direction, he rounded the bonnet to the driver's door. The captain himself held it open for him.

"A successful conclusion to your business, sir," he offered. Gant merely snorted.

"I shall be *tired,*" he complained.

He bent to climb into the driver's seat. Then he heard the approaching car. Its engine made it clear that it was moving with speed. Stifling a groan, keeping the tremor from his frame, Gant looked up. He saw headlights rounding a bend, dancing towards them. He knew it was Priabin. He hadn't found—hadn't even looked for—the man's car. He should have killed him . . .

He glanced at Anna's face. She knew, too. The captain was alarmed, then alert and decisive. He waved two guards armed with Kalashnikov rifles forward. They positioned themselves in the headlight beams. The car swayed, then skewed halfway across the road as it stopped in a skid. The door opened.

Gant realized the barrier had been raised. He slammed the door. Already, the barrier was beginning to descend. He switched on the engine, revved, put the car into gear. The captain bent to warn him, an arm raised to point at the barrier. His head flicked away as they both heard Priabin shouting. In the mirror, Gant saw Priabin running towards them, waving his ID wallet above his head, calling his rank and name and their identities—

He let out the clutch and accelerated. The barrier was coming down. He skidded, but the car slid forward before it started to swing round—the barrier bounced on the roof, shattering the rear window with its impact. He swung the wheel, grinning at Anna, and let the car accelerate as soon as he came out of the skid.

"Stop them!" Priabin yelled. "Stop *him*, stop him!" His ID was thrust under the captain's nose. The man stepped back half a pace, made to salute. The two guards had turned to follow the flight of the car. Priabin bellowed: "The tires— the tires!" The guards opened fire. "The woman is a hostage!" Priabin yelled, his words drowned by the first rounds fired from the two rifles. Horribly, one of them was on automatic. "The tires, *only the tires!*" he continued to bellow, his voice little more than a screech, hoarse and unheard. The car slid across the road, spun almost to face them, stalled. The two rifles continued firing, both now on single shot. "Stop, *stop*—!"

The Finnish barrier was up, a car was revving. Priabin could see its exhaust rising in the glare of the lights. He was running alongside the captain, who had drawn his gun.

Gant was running. He had got out of the car, hesitated for only a moment, and then had begun running towards the other barrier and the car that was moving forward to protect him.

"Shoot him, shoot him—he's the American pilot! *Kill him!*"

Gant was alone. Running alone.

PART THREE
THE AIRCRAFT

. . . the one path of my flight is direct
Through the bones of the living.
No arguments assert my right:
The sun is behind me.

—Ted Hughes
Hawk Roosting

12 / **THROUGH THE WINDOW**

She had swiveled in the passenger seat to stare back through the car's rear window at some excitement on the road behind. Just like a child—and it was as if he were gently remonstrating with that child when he turned her in her seat. Except that by turning her he could not prevent harm from coming to her. She was already dead. Gant knew that even as he moved her. He knew before he saw the neat blue hole in her forehead, just at the hairline.

He had told her to keep down, had tried to push her back into her seat; but her arm had become limp and unresponsive. Anna had turned to look back at Priabin, standing in the middle of the road, waving his arms. Gant had heard one of the two Kalashnikovs on automatic. The bellow of sound had unnerved him more than the concussions of the first bullets; the thuds against the boot and into the rear seat.

He stared at her face for only a moment. Very pale. Her eyes were open. They hardly registered shock, were without pain.

He let her body fall back against the seat and wished he had not done so. She looked very dead the moment he released her. Her head too rapidly flopped onto her shoulder, the hair spilled over her cheek, and there was a snail-track of saliva at the corner of her mouth. He withdrew his hands, holding them against his chest, afraid to touch her again. They were shaking as he bunched them into fists. He groaned.

The Vietnamese girl, burning . . .

He grabbed the door handle. His hand froze for a moment, then flung open the door. Two bullets immediately thudded into it, making the plastic of the panel bulge near his knuckles. He knelt behind the door. The two rifles ceased firing. He straightened, smelling on the freezing air the exhaust from the Finnish car moving towards him. He ran. He heard Priabin shout something; the voice sounded almost demented above the noise of Gant's breathing and heartbeat and squeaking footfalls. He hunched his body against the expected impact of rifle bullets.

Then the Finnish car, a long Mercedes saloon, swung across the road behind him, skidding to a halt. He heard the doors open. He tried to stop and turn, but slipped and fell onto the snowbound road. His buttocks and hands ached. The Vietnamese girl was incinerated in an instant beside the car he had abandoned. Two men were kneeling behind the open doors of the Mercedes, wary yet not expecting trouble. The two border guards had stopped firing, stopped running.

Another man was still moving, charging towards the abandoned car, arms flailing as if he were combating the freezing night and the falling snow. Headlights from the Mercedes glared towards the lights of the abandoned car. The brightness hid Anna; hid Priabin the moment he stopped and ducked his whole body almost frenziedly into the car's interior. Gant closed his eyes. The image of the Vietnamese girl had vanished, but he could clearly discern the blue hole in Anna's forehead. He shook his head, but her surprised, hardly shocked face would not leave him. He breathed in deeply and opened his eyes. A man was extending his hand, offering to help him to his feet.

"Major Gant?" he said.

Immediately, as if the action would help to establish his identity, or remove Anna's image from his retina, Gant tugged the hairpiece from his own closely cropped hair.

"Yes," he said.

"Quickly," the Finn instructed, clutching Gant's elbow, forcing him to his feet. Gant's legs were foal-like, awkward. "We must get you away from here—I do not think there will be trouble, but—"

"Yes," Gant repeated dully, brushing down his overcoat and trousers. The other two Finns had also stood up. One of them, the driver, had climbed into the Mercedes. The engine was still running. The incident was over. The two guards had retreated to the customs hut, where their officer stood on the wooden steps, watching through night glasses. "Yes."

He was ushered to the rear door of the Mercedes. He paused and stared into the other car's headlights. It was as if he had been trapped in a searchlight's eager beam. Beyond the lights, he saw Priabin. He was out of the car, his arms wrapped around Anna's body. Gant could see the splash of fair hair against Priabin's dark clothing. Priabin's face was white, aghast, lost.

Quickly, Gant got into the car, which reversed across the road, turned, and headed back towards the red-and-white pole on the Finnish side. Gant turned his head, wincing as he realized he was imitating Anna's last living movement, and watched the figure of Priabin diminish, the splash of blond hair against his chest no more than a trick of the light. Priabin did not move, seemed incapable of volition. He simply stared in his lost way after the receding Mercedes.

Then the Finnish border post was behind them, the glow from the overhead lights retreating behind the falling snow. Gant shivered, realizing that the car was warm, realizing that it was over.

He did not dare to close his eyes. Open, and Anna remained only a tumbled trick of the light against Priabin's chest; closed, and the white face with its blue hole would return. He stared at the back of the Finn in the front passenger seat like a nauseated drunk attempting to defeat the spinning of his head.

* * *

Waterford watched the sky. The cloud had thinned, the snow had almost stopped; desultory and innocent, as on a greeting card. The window in the weather had arrived. Out on the lake, a huge cross formed from orange marker tape indicated the dropping point. A single smoke flare betrayed the wind direction. It climbed like a plume from the ice, then bent as it reached the wind, straggled and dissipated. There was no sky above, no color except grey, but the cloudbase was high enough to allow the Hercules' first run to be at a sufficient altitude for the parachutists to jump safely. The lake was strangely silent against the slow, creeping grey dawn that revealed its far shore, the somber snowbound country and the penciled margin of trees.

Then he heard the baritone murmur of the aircraft's four engines. Other heads turned with his, towards the south. He glanced to check the smoke plume, which rose strongly before the wind distressed it like long yellow hair. He turned his face back to the clouds and saw it, at little more than fifteen hundred feet, seeming to drift up from the indistinct horizon, enlarge, then hang above them. The expectant silence around him was all but palpable. The Hercules was a plump, full shape overhead.

Then the parachuting Royal Marines appeared, dots detaching themselves like laid eggs from each side of the bulky fuselage. Parachutes opened, and the black eggs slowed and swayed. Waterford counted them, urging them to be more, wanting to go on counting. Twenty, twenty-one, two, three, four, five, six . . .

And then he reminded himself that not all of them were soldiers. There were also engineers and technicians from the RNAF Tactical Supply Squadron at Bardufoss. They and the pallets of supplies required had limited the number of marines that could be carried. The Hercules would return to Bardufoss at high speed to attempt to take on a second detachment of marines, but Waterford doubted they would be able to drop. The window in the weather would have closed once more before the Hercules could return.

Thirty-two, three . . . already, the first jumpers were drifting against the grey horizon like unseasonal dandelion down. The Hercules vanished beyond the limit of visibility at the far end of the lake. The drone of its four engines had become a mild hiss; the noise of a distant saw. The first marine landed on his feet, ran after his billowing, closing chute, wrapping it into a bundle as he moved. Then the second landed, rolled, came up grabbing the chute to himself. Three, four, five . . .

Perhaps two dozen marines, Waterford thought, assessing the degree of comfort he felt at the figure. Not much. The Hercules would have been tracked on Russian radar. Its runs would be too patternlike, too purposeful to be mistaken. They would know men and supplies had been dropped into Lapland, and they would know where. The weather window had to be slammed shut against them before they could act on the knowledge, even if its shutting did lock out a second detachment of marines.

Already, every parachutist had landed and was moving quickly off the ice. The air force experts trudged in a hunched, somehow childlike manner, the marines moved more quickly, already identifiable as a group. Everyone was wearing arctic camouflage or long grey-white parkas. They looked like members of an expedition.

Waterford returned the salute of the captain in command of the marines, then turned away from him. The last stragglers, chutes bundled untidily beneath their arms, had moved off the ice. Among marines and technicians and experts alike there was a muted, intense murmuring as they climbed the slope of the shore and confronted the Firefox, now at the rear of the clearing beneath the camouflage netting. The noise of the Hercules' return moved towards them from the northern horizon.

Then the aircraft appeared, a flattened, murky, half-real shape at the far end of the lake. The smoke flare had already bent further, like the unstable stem of a heavy-flowered plant. The wind was picking up. There would be no second drop of marines. The clouds, too, already seemed lower and heavier, and the snowflakes blew sideways into Waterford's face, as if the storm was sidling up to him in some surprise ambush. He shook his head. The Hercules moved slowly and steadily up the lake. Then the pallets emerged in turn from the cargo ramp in the rear of the aircraft. Waterford realized that Moresby was standing beside him. It was as if he had taken no interest in the men who had parachuted, only in the lifeless supplies and equipment now to be unloaded.

The tractor tug was bright yellow. Its pallet thudded

distantly onto the ice, skidded and ran to a halt. A second
pallet with tarpaulined equipment emerged, then a third.
Then the fourth, bearing great rolls of MO-MAT, a second
pallet of rolled portable runway following it. The Hercules
was almost level with them now. The smoke from the flare
streamed out horizontally, a few feet above the ground. The
trees on the far shore were shrouded in what might have
been a freezing fog. Then shapes like great, tired undercarriage wheels appeared one after the other from the gaping
cargo ramp. Waterford thought he glimpsed the figures
bundling them out, even the supervising Air Loadmaster at
the mouth of the harshly-lit tunnel that was the interior of the
Hercules. Then the aircraft was gone, lost beyond the trees
around the lake, heading south. He saw a vague, dark shape
lift into the clouds, which were lower and thicker than before.
The Hercules vanished, leaving Waterford with a momentary
sense of isolation.

The black fuel cells bounced awkwardly and rolled
strangely, like trick balls weighted with sand. Slowly, they
came to a halt. The air transportable fuel cells had been
landed safely; huge rubber containers filled with the various
oils and the vital paraffin required if the Firefox was ever to
take off from the lake.

The farthest of the pallets, with its bright yellow tractor
tug, was already almost obscured by the driving snow. A
window—? Nothing but a glimpse of something through the
storm. At least, Waterford thought, the Russians can't do
anything. They won't be able to move.

Nor will we—

He watched as men detailed by Moresby moved out
onto the ice to recover the pallets and the fuel cells. It would
take no more than half an hour to get everything stowed
under cover, camouflaged. Just in case—

"You'd better come with me," Waterford said. His voice
was pinched in his throat. He growled it clear. "Come on,
captain, we've got work to do. Your blokes aren't here to hold
spanners for these buggers."

"No, sir. But—"

Waterford turned to face him. The captain was staring at
the Firefox, stranded amid trees and beneath camouflage
netting, out of its element.

"What?"

"Hell of an aircraft, sir."

"One problem with it—it doesn't fly!"

The Russian major tugged the hood of his camouflage blouse further forward, as if to conceal completely the fur hat with its single red star in the center. He smiled at his nervous gesture, as if he really had been fearful of their being spotted through the weather from the other side of the lake.

His Border Guard reconnaissance party had heard the distant noise of the Hercules transport while they were breakfasting. He was fairly certain it was one of those big turboprop transport aircraft used by the Norwegians and the rest of NATO. His unit had made good time, even with the poor weather. The moment it cleared they had rested, hoping to make a quick, scrappy meal, then push on before the weather closed in again. Of course, once they reached the trees, the weather ceased to matter as much, inconvenient though it was. But the noise of the aircraft, muffled and distant and to the east, alerted them, created fears and prognostications and they had broken camp at once and pushed on with all possible speed. Somehow, each of his men and himself had known that the transport aircraft, even though it had not landed, had business at the two lakes.

The smaller, more westerly of the two had been empty of activity, supplies and people. The plane had made two passes, one at a reasonably high altitude as far as they could discern, the other much lower. The major had his suspicions; they were almost certain enough to report them to Moscow. But, he hesitated. He would be reporting directly to Andropov himself; his ultimate superior, his chairman. He wanted further evidence before committing himself—yet, he should alert the reconnaissance aircraft, there should be an investigation. However, the weather closed in again and he knew that no flights would now be possible to investigate the activities of the transport aircraft. But, surely it had been picked up by the border Tupolev AWACS plane and reported? Had the weather closed in too quickly?

His party of twelve men moved behind him on the long cross-country skis across the surface of the smaller lake. Out in the open, the wind was noisy again now; buffeting and yelling around them. The snow drove horizontally across the lake. The clouds were dark and heavy and seemed to hang like a great smothering cushion just above their heads. What was going on at the other lake? What had the transport aircraft been ferrying in? Men, supplies, equipment—why? The questions hurried and blustered in his thoughts, with a cold excitement like that of the wind. He felt on the verge of answers, but would not reach out to grasp them.

They moved off the ice, pausing for a short rest at the edge of the trees. Then they headed across the half mile that separated the two lakes, climbing slowly and gently through the crowding pines and spruces that were heavy with snow. Birds called from a distance. Snow dropped with dull concussions from the overweighted branches of trees. His men spread out into a curving line of advance with himself at the center, and began to move more cautiously. He could hear the slither of his skis and those of the sergeants on either side of him. The Kalashnikov rifle in its white canvas sleeve bobbed on his chest.

He crested a ridge, and the trees seemed to straggle more, with brighter snowy spaces between them. The morning was advanced, the light was pale grey. Slowly, he urged his body forward down the slope towards the unseen shore of the larger lake. He felt tense and excited, as if approaching some important promotional interview. He skirted the bole of a fir, glimpsed a stretch of snow-covered ice clear of trees, and came to a halt. He heard the slither of other stopping skis. By hand signals, he urged his men to cover. Rifles were quickly unwrapped and checked, ski poles planted like the cross poles of wigwams for rifle rests. Trees became cover, the hardware of an ambush.

The major raised his binoculars, adjusted their focus, and stared into the flying snow which swept across the lake. Disappointed, he could not see the farther shore, where he seemed to be gazing into a new and unearthly sunrise. He leaned against the bole of the tree, a sergeant on the other side of it, and waited. He knew the answers would emerge from that glow, if there was a momentary change or drop in the wind and the snow was moved aside. He was prepared to wait, even though his jumpy, tense body was little more than an impatient net of nerves.

He waited for ten minutes, perhaps twelve. He heard the muffled noises at first. Compressors, a saw, no, two saws, the cracking, thudding fall of trees. The grind and creak of machinery, the whine of drills and what he presumed might be other power tools. He was reminded of his grandfather's hut at the bottom of the garden where the old man enthusiastically concocted gadgets that never worked, or badly repaired household utensils that had been damaged or broken. The tapestry of sounds comforted and excited him, but supplied no answers to his insistent questions. The voices of men, too, were carried faintly towards him by the wind.

Then he saw it. The snow seemed to retreat across the lake like a curtain, and he fine-focused his glasses after raising them quickly to his eyes. He stretched his eyelids, cleared his throat, then saw—

It had to be the Mig-31. It had to be exactly what they had been sent to find. It left him breathless. A black shape at the back of what might have been a stage set. Men half-swallowed by the cockpit or swarming over the tail section and the main fuselage. Great trailing hoses blowing air or supplying something, lay about the aircraft. A wide snail-track of portable runway ran down to the edge of the water— yes, water, where the ice had been broken . . .

"My God," he whispered. "My God, it *was* in the lake! Do you see that, sergeant? It *was* in the lake!"

"Yes, sir. What are they doing to the aircraft, sir?"

"I don't know. They must be dismantling it. Yes, they must be taking it apart, ripping out all the secret stuff, the stuff they want . . ."

The black shape, the men, the noises and the now-visible machinery . . . he scanned along the shore. Trees being cleared, more huge rolls of portable runway, a yellow— what was that?—yellow. Small tractor . . . where had he seen those before? Towing aircraft—? Yes, at airports and airfields. One black—soccer ball?—almost hidden in the trees, certainly camouflaged from the air, and other, similar shapes behind it. Then the curtain was drawn once more just as he saw the rifles worn by a handful of the men around and in front of the aircraft. Troops, armed troops—

And then it was gone, the noises now the sole indication that they were not alone on the shore of the frozen lake.

There are too many of them, he thought. Then—do I tell Moscow what I fear?

"Sir?" the sergeant began, his voice seeming to possess a weight of insight.

The major nodded. "Yes," he said. "Get Melnik here with the radio—quickly." The sergeant turned and moved off, but the major continued speaking softly, as if answering the sergeant's unspoken question. "Yes, they're going to try to fly that plane out!"

Vladimirov stood before the tall fiber-optic map in the control gallery. His body quivered with excitement. He assessed his appearance as being like that of one of his family's hunting dogs; a luxury his rank and income had enabled him to resurrect from the family's past. The scent of the game, the dog's rippling excitement which the noise of the gun and the fall of the bird would convert to speed, to capture.

Andropov stood next to him, rubbing his spectacles heavily and repeatedly, as if to reassess the information on the map and the transmission from the reconnaissance party. Lights and indicators had been bled into the map, and the projection of Finnish Lapland had been altered. Now, an enlargement of the area of the two lakes almost filled the entire surface. The cleared site the major had seen was marked, as was the position of the major's party.

Andropov had not congratulated Vladimirov, but there had been a surprised, almost mocking respect in his pale eyes, before both of them had abandoned their coffee and hurried across the gallery to the map.

As if unable to bear the proximity of the map, the Chairman of the KGB wandered away from Vladimirov. When the general turned to look at him, he realized that Andropov, having replaced his spectacles, was simply looking through the glass down at the main floor of the underground command center. His gaze was fixed upon the huge map table surrounded by operators; a table displaying the same large-scale images of the two lakes, the position of the major and his party, the location of the Mig-31.

Eventually, as if aware of being observed, Andropov turned to Vladimirov and said: "Do you agree with the major's prognostication, General Vladimirov?" It was a complex, subtle question asked in a direct, neutral tone. It prompted Vladimirov to accept responsibility, it was genuinely undecided, it hovered on the verge of disbelief.

"Yes," Vladimirov said. "I incline to. His descriptions of equipment, of what he saw, even when I questioned him, were too detailed to be misinterpreted. Transportable fuel cells—his black soccer balls could be nothing else. Compressors and hoses."

"But, could they do it? Could they *possibly* do it?"

Vladimirov shook his head. "I would have thought their attempt likely to end in failure—"

"But not *certain* to end that way?"

"Are *you* prepared to be certain?" Vladimirov countered.

Andropov, as if suddenly made aware of the others in the room, the majority of them military personnel, seemed to scuttle across to Vladimirov's side. To create a fiction of competence, he adjusted his glasses to make a renewed study of the map. Its colors palely mottled his features. Eventually, he turned to Vladimirov and said quietly; "You realize what this means? You realize *everything*?"

"I realize."

"Very well, then. What do we do?" There was no emphasis on the plural, but it was a commitment from Andropov. Out of necessity, Vladimirov concluded. The man had no idea how to deal with the situation. He was no longer seeking a scapegoat; rather, he required a skilled, expert assistant. Vladimirov felt himself burn with purpose, what he would have mocked in a younger officer as crusading zeal. It was at once both ridiculous and gratifying.

"We can do nothing—for the moment," Vladimirov said calmly, glancing through the sheaf of papers that represented the detailed meteorological reports he had requested as soon as the major's report had been relayed to them. Andropov's face was angry, and also he seemed disappointed. "We can only prepare for action—we cannot act. Unless you wish to bomb the area from high altitude?" Vladimirov added, smiling. Andropov glowered at him.

Vladimirov pondered the map. He could, hopefully even in this foul weather, continue to assemble troops ready to move them into Lapland. In the hours after his first realization that Gant must have landed on a frozen lake, and as a preliminary to the location of the Mig by the reconnaissance party, he had ordered the Leningrad Military District to place Engineer Troops and *desant* commandos from one of their advance Airborne Divisions, on alert. Already, some units were at the assembly point, the military airfield near the town of Nikel at the meeting point of the Soviet, Finnish and Norwegian borders. The facilities at Nikel were adequate, just, for a swift helicopter assault across the border in the required numbers to guarantee success. But, the commandos mobilized and at present at Nikel, were fewer than seventy. They had been intended only as a guard for the more vital Engineer Troops who would salvage, with the assistance of a huge MiL flying crane, the Mig-31 from whichever lake contained it. Now, any salvage operation would necessitate an armed attack; a rescue by force.

Strangely, perhaps because it so closely paralleled his own embryo plan, he had recovered swiftly from the shock of discovering that he had been beaten to the site, beaten to the recovery of the aircraft. He had clenched his fist the moment he received the news, felt his nails digging into his palm until the pain became numbness. Then he realized that the weather had closed upon the lake. They were isolated. They could not be reached. They were locked in, immobile. If they intended to fly the aircraft out, they would need another break in the weather. It was a stalemate . . .

To his advantage. The British and Norwegians and Americans had done much of his work for him.

Andropov had moved to the door of the room. He was in conversation with a tall, dark-haired young man with an easy, confident manner which now seemed harassed and half-afraid. Vladimirov returned to his map and his thoughts.

To fly the aircraft to Norway, to somewhere like Bardufoss, was a distance that could be covered in minutes. The aircraft would need to be no more than half-airworthy for that short hop. Was it possible? Someone—Aubrey, perhaps?—evidently thought it was.

They needed a window in the weather. They dare not risk a takeoff with a patched-together aircraft in the kind of weather that now prevailed. It would kill the pilot, lose them the Mig.

So—

They were waiting for the break that was promised for late that afternoon. He glanced at his watch. Perhaps in seven or eight hours' time.

The site had to be occupied by Soviet troops and the secrets of the Mig protected. If they had been photographed, stripped down, examined, discovered, then—

No one could be allowed to leave with that knowledge, with those secrets. He *had* to put troops into the area, for every possible reason.

It would be close. His helicopters would move just as

the weather cleared. According to the forecasts, they would have the disadvantage. Thirty minutes delay as the weather cleared from the west.

Now his excitement was intense. He sensed the danger, the knife-edge, and welcomed it. He was combative, certain, aggressive. The prize was tangible. His troops must surround the clearing beside the lake, prevent damage to the airframe, prevent takeoff if that was feasible.

Kill—

Andropov approached him, his face grim. Vladimirov allowed a smile of triumph to appear on his lips, then said gruffly: "What is it?"

"I—I have received a report that the American has been allowed to escape. He crossed into Finland hours—*hours* ago!" Andropov was sweating. His forehead shone in the lights. He would be blamed; the KGB had failed.

Vladimirov blanched inwardly at the news. He understood fully now.

Gant.

Vladimirov knew that Gant was the intended pilot of the Mig-31, as he had been before. He could not envisage, even wildly imagine, how he could be transported to the lake. But he knew that that was the intention.

Somehow, when the first Soviet gunships drove down on that clearing, when the first commandos dropped from their transport helicopters, Gant would be there. With a lifting triumph filling his chest and stomach, Vladimirov knew that Gant would die.

The snow had turned to sleet soon after first light, sliding away from the wipers to the edges of the windscreen. The Mercedes had become a cocoon for Gant; warm, moving, self-contained. The Finnish Intelligence officers, though he sensed their curiosity, were respectfully quiet. They supplied him with vodka and coffee, had bought him breakfast at a service station restaurant—coffee, eggs, herring, cheese, rolls, jam. He had resisted at first because of the pungent unexpectedness of the fish so early in the morning, but then his hunger had insisted. Anna retreated; she was no longer present in the warmth and quiet bustle of the restaurant.

The military airfield was northeast of Helsinki. The Mercedes turned in, papers were checked at the guardroom, and then they drove directly out onto the tarmac. Through the windscreen, through the sleet and against the grey cloud scudding low across the runways and hangars, Gant saw a Harrier in RAF camouflage, standing like a fleeting visitor apart from the planes bearing Finnish markings. The aircraft surprised him, now that his next movement, the coming hours, were forced to his attention. He was reluctant to leave the Mercedes and the quiet, respectful, reassuring company of the Finns.

A drab-painted trailer was drawn up near the Harrier. It had been towed into position by a Land Rover. The arrangement of the vehicles and the aircraft disturbed him. It appeared temporary; a beginning.

"Major Gant?" the Finn next to him on the rear seat inquired politely, as if to reestablish some former identity. "Would you please leave the car now and go to the trailer?" The Mercedes drew up a matter of yards from the trailer with its blank windows and dark-grey, wet flanks. "Please, Major Gant—"

He gripped the door handle. All three of them were watching him with a patient curiosity. Already distancing themselves. "Thanks," he said.

"Our—pleasure," one of them said with an engaging smile. "Good luck, Major."

"Sure."

He got out of the car, hunching his shoulders immediately against the cold sting and splash of the driven sleet. He hurried the few yards of wet concrete to the trailer. The door opened, as if at some electronic signal from himself. He climbed the two steps, wiped his feet on a rough mat, and only then looked up as the door closed behind him.

He recognized neither man in the room. There was a smell of wetness, from the olive-green flying suit worn by one of them. He seemed to appraise Gant more quickly, but less expertly, than the one in the fur hat and the leather overcoat. A pilot's helmet lay on a plain wooden table, flanked by two cups.

"Coffee?" the man in the overcoat asked, holding out his hand. "Forgive me—my name is Vitsula. I am a—friend of Kenneth Aubrey. My men were the ones who met you at the border. Oh, this is Flight Lieutenant Thorne of the British Royal Air Force." The pilot nodded. "That is his transport parked next to us." Vitsula smiled. "Coffee?" he repeated.

"Uh—oh, yes. Sure."

Gant remained looming near the doorway, ill at ease. He was assailed by premonitions. Vitsula moved and talked with the ease of seniority. By "friend" he meant counterpart. Hence the trailer. Vitsula was helping Aubrey, but Finland was neutral. No, there wasn't anything to concern him here. No more than a covert exit from Finland in the second seat of the Harrier trainer. He moved towards the table and sat down. Vitsula, pouring from the coffeepot, nodded in approval.

As he sat down, the Finn said: "You realize, of course, Major, why we must have these precautions? I'm sorry it is cold. The heater is not working." Vitsula sipped at his coffee. "Apparently, you are required—cigarette? No? Ah—required in Oslo, at NATO Southern Norway headquarters. Your people wish to talk to you urgently. I can understand that." He smiled, exhaling the blue, acrid smoke. It filled the cramped trailer at once. "I have been in contact with Kenneth Aubrey— who is in Kirkenes at the moment. They have been trying, very unsuccessfully I gather, to rescue the aircraft."

Gant appeared shocked. "How?"

"By winching it out of the lake where you left it, Major."

"They didn't do it?"

"Yes, they did. But, they cannot get it out of the area. Their helicopter did not arrive. The weather—a breakdown."

"Shit," Gant breathed, passing from surprise to disappointment in an instant, almost without registering the implied events of the past days. "It's out, you say?"

"So I am led to believe." He shrugged, blowing a rolling cloud of smoke at the low ceiling. "Do the Russians know its location?"

Gant glanced at the pilot. He nodded.

"Not from me," Gant replied slowly.

"That will be welcome news to my minister," Vitsula sighed. "Very welcome. Excellent, in fact. Yes, excellent. Of course, we shall inform them in due course—we shall have to . . ." He held up his hand as Gant's face darkened and his lips moved. "Kenneth Aubrey and your Mr. Buckholz know all this. It is not my decision. The aircraft will be without certain systems, I imagine, by the time it is handed over. You will not quite have wasted your time, Major." Vitsula stood up. "Excuse me, now, I have arrangements to make. When you have finished your coffee, you may leave at your leisure. Do not concern yourself, Major, at the fate of a machine.

You, after all, are alive and safe. That should be enough. Good morning. Good morning, Flight Lieutenant."

Vitsula adjusted the fur hat on his head, opened the door and went out. Gant turned his head from the door towards Thorne.

"What the hell's going on?" he snapped in a tight, angry voice. "They've got the damn thing out of the lake?"

"So I'm told."

"Who's Vitsula?"

"Director-General of their intelligence service. The top man."

"Why a Harrier?" Gant snapped. "I know what they do. I've flown our AV-8A. Why a Harrier?" He looked around him, then, and added: "Is this place safe?"

"I think so. Vitsula said it was. I don't think he'd want to listen, anyway."

"To what?"

"What happens next." Thorne was smiling. The smile of a young man, his fingers dipped gently, pleasingly, into the waters of covert work. It was evident on his features that he was enjoying himself immensely.

"What happens next?"

"We take off for Oslo—"

"And when we arrive?"

"Just in case—would you like to get changed? I brought a spare suit. Your helmet in the cockpit . . ." Thorne heaved a pressure suit, folded and compressed, onto the wooden table, from the floor of the trailer. "Get into that—then we can talk in the privacy of my aircraft." It was lightly said, with an English confidence, a sense of joking, of game-playing. The tone angered Gant quite unreasonably. Anna came back. Blue hole, surprise. No anger. She should have been angry—

He leaned across the wooden table and grabbed Thorne's forearm, gripping it tightly. Thorne's narrow, dark good looks twisted, became pale with dislike.

"Before we fucking well go anywhere, Lieutenant—tell me what happens when we get there! I don't give a shit if this trailer's bugged by the Kremlin—answer the question!" He squeezed Thorne's arm. The pilot winced, tried to pull his arm away, groaned.

"All right—all right, you bloody crazy Yank! Let go of my arm, damn you!"

Gant released his grip. Thorne immediately applied himself to rubbing his forearm, beneath the suit's sleeve. He kept his face averted. Eventually, when he had ceased rubbing, he looked up.

"You're not going to Oslo. We drop off the radar as if making an approach, then I turn the Harrier north." The confusion on the American's face lessened the threat he posed. Thorne appeared to remember other superiors, more pressing priorities. "Look, I shouldn't be telling you any of this until we're airborne—" he protested.

"Why only then?" Gant snapped. "I could still pull the cord and go out on the ejector seat! Tell me now."

Thorne hesitated. Gant leaned towards him again. Thorne's arm flinched on his lap like a startled cat. Gant picked up the folded pressure suit and dropped it heavily on the floor.

"All right. But it's your fault if anything goes wrong—!"

"You don't think Vitsula's worked things out? Man, they all know everything that's going on. It's just one big game. The most dangerous game—people get killed. If Vitsula can't make the right guesses about your airplane, then he won't be in his job for long. Even I can guess . . . but I don't want to. Now, tell me."

Gant stood at one of the small, blacked-out windows. Peering through it, he could see Vitsula had taken his place in the back of the Mercedes. An old turboprop transport lurched upwards towards the cloud. He listened to Thorne's voice as if to something reiterated and already known.

"We turn north—heading up the Gulf of Bothnia into Lapland. Across the Finnmark to Kirkenes. She's almost fully fueled—we have the range to make it in one hop."

"Aubrey's at Kirkenes," Gant murmured.

"Yes, old man—"

Gant turned from the window, glaring at Thorne. "What the hell does he want me at Kirkenes for?"

Thorne shrugged, seemingly with a renewed awareness of their surroundings.

"I—look, I'm just the cab driver. Get into the suit, Major, and I can brief you fully when we're airborne. I don't know much more, anyway—"

"The hell you don't! You know and I know. How does he—how can he possibly believe that airplane can fly out of there? It's crazy."

"Maybe. But that's what they want you for." Thorne's

face was pleading. "Please, Major—get changed. We have a schedule to keep."

Gant realized that his fists were bunched at his sides. Standing, he was aware of the weariness of his body, the confusion of his thoughts. He wished idly for the movement and warmth of the Mercedes once more. Vitsula knew. Of course he knew.

"What about the Finns?"

"There's a deadline. Midnight tonight."

"For anything Aubrey might want to try?"

"I don't know. But the weather's very bad up there— there's a small window—a peephole, no more—it's expected this afternoon. Before dark. It's the one chance you have."

"They want me to break out, through a weather window? If I don't make it?"

"I don't know. They'll destroy the airframe, I imagine. You're the only chance anyone's got. I have to get you to Kirkenes. If the window doesn't open, you won't be stranded when the deadline expires. At least, Aubrey will have *you*. If it does open, I'm to drop you in at the lake. If you say you can't fly it out, then I bring you back. And a Chinook, if one can get in, will bring out the best of the stuff they can salvage. Look, Major, I was told to tell you everything. *Tell him everything*, he said. *Be honest with him. Ask him to do it. Tell him we need him*. Now, you know it all." Thorne shrugged, staring at the crumpled, stiff heap that was the pressure suit.

"Aubrey wants me to save his ass for him," Gant growled. "He's painted himself into a corner and can't get out, so he had this great idea—really great idea. Get Gant to fly the airplane out of Finland, just like he did out of Russia." Gant's tone was scathingly ironic. Thorne stared at him as if he had only just realized the identity and recent history of the other occupant of the trailer.

Gant walked to the window, looked out, then returned to the table. "All right," he said heavily. "Get me there, sonny. Get me to that asshole Aubrey!"

As the Harrier T.Mk4 lifted into the scudding, dark cloud, Vitsula slumped back from straining to look up through the windscreen, and sighed. He picked up the telephone from the central armrest compartment, and dabbed at the numbers he required. It was time for him to inform his minister of the departure of Gant. Time to suggest that the first advance units of Finnish troops should set out overland from Ivalo and Rovienimi, to rendezvous at the lake.

He would have to inform his minister of his suspicions concerning Gant's eventual destination, of course. Also, he could not avoid the suspicion that the Russians might know, might suspect, or might yet discover . . .

It was unlikely Finnish troops would arrive by midnight in any strength. If the Russians knew, if there was an attempt to fly out the Firefox—he must consult air force experts as to its feasibility—if Aubrey's people were stranded at the lake by the weather . . . ? His minister must be in full possession of the facts before any or all of those things happened.

Yes, he would tell him.

He cleared his throat and urgently requested to speak to the minister.

Gunnar rechecked the ropes lashing down the two Lynx helicopters. It was a nervous reaction, checking them again and again. But he could not abandon the tiny clearing, its snow-weighted trees, its stormswept open space, its two huddled, shrouded helicopters. The wind cracked and snapped the shrouds over the two aircraft as if trying to open two parcels with rough, greedy fingers. He worried more than ever now, as the morning wore on. The two Lynxes represented the only means of escape from the lake. They could not be flown in this weather—it would be suicide to try—and they could not fly everyone back. But Gunnar knew that Buckholz would order him, if all else failed, to remove as much as possible of the most secret equipment aboard the Firefox in the two helicopters. He might be asked to fly in impossible conditions. For the moment, he simply had to continually reassure himself that the two Lynxes were safe, lashed down and undamaged.

He let go the taut nylon rope which stretched away to the nearest tree, and thrust his mittened hand back into the pocket of his parka. Reaching the edge of the clearing, he turned back for a last glance. Two grey-white mounds, like igloos. He moved away through the trees, clumping over the snow with broad snowshoes. As he skirted the shore of the lake, he could see it was little less than a blizzard that was raging across the open ice. Snow rushed as solidly as a white wall seen from a speeding train or car. He would skirt the shore, keeping out of the worst of the storm by staying under the trees.

He settled into the slow momentum of his journey. He was cold, and becoming hungry again. Energy was being used up at a ridiculous speed. The storm thumped and cried at his hunched back as he walked with slow, exaggerated footsteps. Gunnar could not believe that a second weather window would bring the American pilot, or allow them a time for escape. They were stranded at the lake. By the time the weather improved, the Finns would have arrived and it would all have been for nothing.

There was only one advantage in the weather. Nothing could fly in it—nothing Russian. They couldn't have moved a single helicopter, a single platoon, even if they knew where the Firefox was . . .

He was colder now, and he tried to move more quickly.

A freak of the wind brought him the voices. A piece of good luck he appreciated only when he dismissed the idea that the wind had snatched the sounds from the other side of the lake and flung them in his direction. These voices were close to him. Russian voices.

Cold, he distinguished. *Fed up . . . the Major . . . balls to . . .*

Then no more. He leaned against the bole of a tree. He was shaking, almost gripping the tree for support. His hands spread inside his mittens as if to locate and tear at the bark beneath the snow. Fingers twitching—

Russian voices. Soldiers, grumbling about their location, their duties, their officer. They'd been there for some time, they had a purpose which was already beginning to bore them—surveillance without action, his mind supplied—a major was in command. There might be a dozen, two dozen, three . . .

He turned, his back pressed against the trunk. He saw his breath curdle before it was whipped away by the wind. He was emitting signals as he breathed—where were they? He studied the darkness beneath the trees around him, studied the snow for footprints . . . the big, tennis-racquet patterns of his own were already being covered. Where—?

He strained to hear, but there was only the wind. Which

direction? Over there? Near the shore. Between him and the shore—

He slid around the tree with exaggerated caution. He craned forward, staring towards the rushing white wall beyond the trees. White, white, white. He could see nothing other than the snow. Then someone moved. A white lump raised itself into a hunched back, then settled again. He could hear no words, no sound of voices. Once the lump stopped moving, it could no longer be distinguished from the ground, the trees, the white storm. Gunnar shivered.

What to do, what to do? He was unarmed. He turned his back to the tree once more. Had he already passed any of them? Was he surrounded and didn't yet know it?

It was some moments before he was able to think clearly. Then, minutes later, he moved away from the tree, scuttling as swiftly and cautiously as he could back the way he had come. He heard his own breathing, his heartbeat in his ears, the wind; imagined pursuit. He turned to his right before he reached the clearing, only then realizing that they had not discovered the two helicopters, that his trail must not lead anyone to the clearing . . .

He reached the shore. Beyond him, his original tracks had been erased. The Lynxes were safe for the moment. He felt chilled and frightened by the rushing wall of snow, which was closer now. He had crossed the lake to the clearing only an hour before, but now . . .

It was as if he had dived slowly, grotesquely out of the trees into a different and alien element. The wall enveloped him, made him blind and breathless. He pulled his hood around his face, then kept his arms about his head, as if running from a fire. He was buffeted and bullied, flung off-balance seven or eight times. Even when he fell to the ice, or onto small ridges and drifts of snow, he felt the wind dragging or pushing him; inflating his parka like a balloon in order to move him on his back or stomach across the ice. Because of the Russians, because of the distance yet to travel, because of the utter isolation he felt in that wind and flying snow, Gunnar was deeply, acutely frightened. He was lost, completely lost.

He sat on a wind-cleared patch of ice, hunched over his compass. It was only a few hundred meters, meters, hundreds of meters, hundreds—a *few* hundred meters, *only* a *few* hundred meters, to the shore. He got onto all fours, having removed his snowshoes, and began to crawl.

He met a low hard ridge of snow and climbed it until he was half-upright. With a huge effort, the wind charging against his side like an attacker, a bullying ice-hockey opponent, he stood fully upright—

And ran. Floundering, charging, slipping. Ice-hockey opponent. It reduced the wind to something he knew, something he *could* combat. He blundered on, as if skating the barrier, charged again and again by his opponents. They blundered and bulled into him, but he kept going, arms around his head, hood pulled over his numbed face, lips spread in a mirthless grin. Another and another charged him, but he kept going. Slipped, recovered, almost tripped over softer snow, skidded on cleaned ice, knowing he was being blown, like a small yacht, on a curving course across the lake.

Then the shore. He blundered onto it, and fell. He could hear the very, very distant hum of one of the chainsaws. He had made it. Quickly, before the elation deserted him, he crawled towards the trees on all fours, scampering like a dog through the snow. His hands climbed the trunk of a tree until he was standing pressed against its solidity, its unmoving, snow-coated strength. His body was shuddering with effort. Then he turned his back to it.

Jesus Christ, Jesus, Jesus, Jesus . . .

His mind chanted the word over and over until his breathing slowed and quieted. Then he listened, heard the chainsaws stop, and the crack of a falling tree followed by its dull concussion into the snow. He walked towards the sounds, nodding almost casually to the men clearing the fallen trunk. One of them—his companion pilot?—waved. Gunnar waved back. He hurried, then, along the cleared shoreline but just inside the remaining trees, towards the main clearing and Waterford. He forgot his R/T. Crossing the lake had somehow stripped him of any sense of technology, of being able to do more than speak face to face with anyone.

Waterford was talking to Buckholz. The Firefox was beyond them, as sheltered and camouflaged as it possibly could be in the circumstances. Men swarmed over it, lay upon the airframe, busied themselves beneath it. Gunnar was aware of the nakedness of the clearing, of eyes behind him. He turned to look. Nothing. Only the rushing white wall passing the clearing. Had they seen—?

Must have seen—

"Major Waterford!" he called, realizing only when he spoke how small and ridiculous his voice sounded. It was like an echo of the past minutes. He coughed. "Major Waterford!" he called more strongly, hurrying forward. Waterford turned to him, quickly alert. Even Buckholz's features mirrored the concern he evidently saw on Gunnar's face.

"What is it? What's wrong with the choppers?" Waterford snapped.

"Nothing, nothing," Gunnar blurted out. He could hear Moresby cursing something, above the noise of the wind.

"Then what is it?"

Gunnar was aware of the arm he pointed across the lake, as if it would be seen by the Russians. He snatched it back to his side, but Buckholz and Waterford were already staring into the snow, in the direction he had indicated.

"Russians—"

"*What?*"

"Russian soldiers—I don't know what unit . . . I heard only two voices, saw movement from one man—"

"Where?"

"The other side of the lake—" They had all three turned now to face towards the blind western shore of the lake. "On the shore. They must be—"

"Watching us? Yes." Waterford's face had already absorbed shock, and closed again into grim lines. "How many?"

"I don't know—"

"Did you *look?*"

"I thought I should get back as quickly—"

"Damn! Damn it!"

Buckholz said: "We have to know how many."

"We have to eliminate them," Waterford replied.

"What—"

"Work it out! If there were enough of them, they'd be sitting in our laps by now. No, there aren't very many of them. They're a recon party, keeping tabs on us."

"Where have they come from?"

"Those bloody choppers that crossed the border before the weather closed in! They've backtracked along bloody Gant's hike—and found *us*! They'll have a radio and they'll have told Moscow by now."

"Could they have seen us?"

"They must have done! Christ, don't count on them

sitting there just because it's snowing and they don't like the weather!" Waterford stared at Buckholz. "Get Moresby and his people working as fast as they can—no, faster than that. If Moscow knows, then they'll be dropping in for tea if that weather window arrives. Oh, *shit*—!"

"And you?"

"I'm going to find out who's over there. Invite them over for a quiet game of bridge. Gunnar, you come with me!"

Gunnar glanced around at the rushing snow, and then nodded silently at Waterford's back. The soldier was already speaking softly and swiftly into his R/T, summoning marines and SBS men. Gunnar hurried after his determined footsteps.

Buckholz moved towards the back of the clearing, into the false shelter of the remaining camouflage netting and the windbreaks. Like a stage, he thought. Lit, peopled, props and furniture set out. Now, they even had an audience.

Welding torches flared around that area of the fuselage which had been damaged in the dogfight with the second Firefox; beneath the ruptures in the skin, the fuel lines had been punctured, bringing the airplane here. Moresby was standing up, waist-deep in the cockpit, a conductor in a white parka directing a noiseless orchestra. His arm movements appeared like semaphore, signaling for help.

They wouldn't do it, Buckholz thought. No way would they do it now, with the Russians knowing everything.

Aubrey watched the storm through the running window. The winds, turned and channeled by the fjords and mountains, flicked the snow towards the hut and away again. For moments, the town of Kirkenes on a headland above the Langfjord which separated it from the airfield, was almost entirely visible. The roots of the peaks on Skogerøya could be seen, as could the creased grey surface of the Korsfjord. Then, for longer, gloomier periods, nothing except the snow lying heavily on the grass, and the gleam of the runway. A yellow snowplough moved across his line of sight, hurling the latest snow aside, preparing for the Harrier's attempt to land.

Aubrey was no longer even certain that Gant would arrive, would share this room with himself and Curtin and the radio operator. He turned from the window, his eye passing over the rucked sheets and blankets of the camp beds on which they had spent some of the long night. He crossed to the table and its heaps of paper. Beneath a rough-hewn paperweight, beside the maps and charts and other implements of their desperation, lay the sheaf of transcribed signals he had received since setting up his headquarters at Kirkenes. He lifted the paperweight in a gingerly fashion. The last two signals, one from Eastoe and the other from Buckholz, were little short of unbearable. Yet he was drawn to reread them, as if to punish himself for his mistakes and his pride. Mortification by coded transmission.

Eastoe reported troop movements, in extreme weather conditions, along the Soviet border with Finland, near the southern end of Lake Inari. Buckholz confirmed that a reconnaissance party had reached the lake's western shore, and had been identified as Russian. Waterford had taken a party of marines to intercept them. Now, Aubrey waited for the report of that intervention.

No, he told himself. He was not waiting for that. He already knew what would be learned. A party of Russians had discovered the location of the Firefox, had discovered that it had been retrieved from the lake—in effect, had canceled his every advantage. He and whoever controlled the operation in Moscow were now on terms. Utterly terms.

His rage of self-recrimination had passed, leaving him spent and tired. If the window in the weather appeared at all over the lake, then it would appear over those gathering Russian troops at the border no more than thirty minutes later. Thirty minutes . . .

Ridiculous. He was beaten. When Buckholz asked him to make a decision, he would accept defeat with ill-grace and snapping, waspish irony, but he would accept it nevertheless. He would instruct Buckholz to rip out the choicest pieces from the cockpit and airframe and try to get them away in the Lynx helicopters. Yes, he would do that. A Chinook would never get to the lake from Bardufoss before the Russians. His party at the lake would be outnumbered, captured, but probably not harmed. He would order them to display no resistance.

Perhaps he should tell Waterford not to engage the reconnaissance party?

Too late to interfere.

Very well. They must salvage what they could. Something of the Mig-31's secrets, at any rate.

"He's coming in—now!" Curtin announced from the other side of the room. Both he and the operator were wearing headsets. They were listening to the dialogue between Thorne, the Harrier pilot, and Kirkenes Tower. Instinctively, like a man opening his own door sensing that he has been burgled, Aubrey glanced at the window. Skogerøya, barely visible, the town almost hidden. The snow flying—

No! he wanted to say. Don't take any chances now—

But he said nothing, merely nodded at Curtin, who stared strangely at him. Watching the lead of his headset, the American moved towards the window. The radio operator, too, had turned in his seat for a better view. Aubrey put the signals back on the table and banged down the paperweight. Then he joined Curtin.

The Harrier seemed to appear suddenly, a darker dot against the wet greyness of the mountains. It was there, a moment after there had been nothing to see except a few wind-flung gulls. It seemed to rush towards the airfield and its single runway, directly towards them. Behind it, the weather seemed to hurry in pursuit, closing around the mountains and the grey water of the Korsfjord. Aubrey could hear the chatter of voices dimly from the headset clamped over Curtin's ears. He did not wish to listen, and stepped away. He felt his body tense, his hands clench.

The aircraft raced the weather in from the fjord. The dot of the Harrier became something winged, something steady— which then wobbled dangerously, as light and naked as one of the gulls being swept about.

Curtin audibly drew in his breath through his teeth. A high eerie whistling sound full of anxiety. Aubrey wanted to tell him to stop. The noise hurt his ears like fingernails drawn down a blackboard. The Harrier enlarged, racing towards them. The runway stretched out like a grey, wet finger towards the approaching aircraft and its pursuing storm. The wings waggled again, uncertain.

Again, Curtin drew in his breath. The runway lights shone feebly in the gloom. There was nothing except the Harrier, poised against the oncoming darkness. Then it dropped, almost as if falling, towards the end of the runway. It touched, seemed to bounce, then rolled across their line of sight. The weather swept over the aircraft, obscuring it, blanking out the entire scene.

"It's O.K., it's O.K.," Curtin repeated. "He's O.K. . . . he's slowing, yes, he's O.K.—*Christ!*" He was grinning.

13 / OUTSIDE THE ROCK POOL

Waterford exhaled audibly through his teeth. Brooke, lying next to him on the crest of the rise, waited for his description of what he could see through the MEL thermal imager.

He continued to traverse the area below them, his face pressed behind the curving grey box of the imager, its riflelike grip clenched in his mittened hand. Eventually, he appeared satisfied, and rolled onto his back.

"Want a look?"

"You tell me," Brooke replied.

"I count twelve of them . . . you can even see the sap in the trees with this toy. It's warmer than the bark." Brooke grinned. "Shame of it is, you can't see what weapons they're carrying."

329

They had rounded the southern end of the lake, well wide of the shore, then turned to encounter the rising ground between the two lakes. Waterford and his men were now above and behind the Russians. The surrounding trees were all but stripped of snow. The wind hurled itself between the massed trunks, flinging the snow horizontally before it. It was impossible to obtain any sighting of the Russians without the use of the thermal imager, which was capable, on its narrowest field of view, of picking up a human body's emissions of warmth at a range of a thousand meters.

"We're going to have to get closer," Waterford continued with a seeming lack of enthusiasm. "You and me. Brief your men to stay put. I'll wait for you, ducky."

Brooke slipped off into the murky, snow-blown light, crouching just below the crest of the rise as he hurried from tree to tree. The shore of the lake was two hundred yards away. Visibility was little more than fifty—yes, Brooke had already vanished, after pausing to speak to the first two-man SBS unit.

Grenade launcher, he thought. Or mortar. Even an RPG-7 rocket launcher. If they had all or any of those, and they well might, coupled with a laser rangefinder, then at the first sign of trouble they could put the Firefox on the scrapheap. Their weaponry was more important than their numbers, their knowledge, even the radio with which they had undoubtedly communicated with Moscow.

He waited for seven minutes, then saw Brooke emerge from the snow-haze between the firs, and move towards him in a crouch. He slid into a prostrate position next to Waterford.

"Well?"

"O.K. Sergeant Dawson's got our friends on the other imager. His count is thirteen, of course." Brooke smiled. His breath was still hurrying from him. "They're to give us fifteen minutes, no more. Dawson's doing some pinpointing for the others. I told them I wanted the radio operator alive, if possible. O.K.?"

Waterford nodded. "That's about it. He's more likely to talk than the officer or the sergeants. O.K., let's go."

Waterford raised his head, and closed the thermal imager to his face once more. Satisfied, he slung the device at his back and moved the Heckler & Koch caseless rifle to greater accessibility across his chest. He gripped its bulky, almost shapeless form with both hands, climbed over the crest of the rise and began to descend. Brooke moved a few paces behind and to his left. They slipped from tree to tree as quickly and silently as they could. Waterford counted the yards they gained towards the shore, waiting for the moment of visibility. Twice he stopped to check the images revealed through the MEL device. Strange, firelit, patchy ghosts, forms that danced and wavered and changed shape.

He was suspicious of a small group hunched around each other, but not around any central image. No fire, no heater brewing coffee or tea—that was fifty yards away to the left of the group on which he focused. The radio might be there. In the freezing air around each body, each patch of warmth, each heater and cigarette, produced an image. But, in the middle of the group that attracted his attention, there was nothing.

Waterford believed that a grenade launcher or mortar sat, barrel elevated, in the center of the three shifting flame-shapes he could see through the imager. If such a weapon was there, then it would have to be destroyed; its operators killed.

He motioned Brooke forward, pointing out his exact direction. Then he followed. They had covered perhaps a hundred yards of forward movement. Within another forty or fifty yards at the most, he would be able to see them. They would be able to see him. Ahead, Brooke moved with greater caution, with something almost comic in the way he lifted and placed his feet, held his rifle, hunched his shoulders. A cartoon robber. Waterford followed the same pattern of movement. Then Brooke suddenly stopped and whirled behind the trunk of a fir, rifle almost vertical, hand extended to warn Waterford. Waterford ducked behind the nearest tree.

Lower down the slope, the trees were heavy with snow. The wind was less fierce and insistent. Each time he exhaled, his breath moved upwards for almost a second before it was whipped away. He peered around the trunk. Brooke waved him forward. He scampered the few yards separating them.

"Well?"

"Laughter from the tea party," Brooke replied. "Didn't you hear it?" Waterford shook his head. "Trick of the wind. Catching the noise, I looked. Saw one figure at least. Off over there." He indicated the gloom to their left and ahead of them with the barrel of his Armalite rifle. Waterford strained to see further into the soft, shifting fuzziness caused by the light and the blowing snow. Something moved, less distinct than the flame-shapes he could see through the imager. He put the MEL against his face. Yes. Two—no, three soldiers, at a brew-up. The thermal image of the heater was clear between them. The mugs of tea or coffee moved like lumps of burning coal. Blue, red, yellow. He swung the imager. A single figure, almost directly ahead, then two more, then the group of three around a cold, empty space, then paler, more distant images. One figure moving, coming closer. Probably the officer.

"To our right," Waterford said. "See anything? There—" He pointed his arm like a sight. Brooke craned forward, then shook his head. "O.K., let me get closer with 'What the Butler Saw' here, and then you move up behind me when I give the signal." He checked on the moving man, and on the group of three, then stepped from behind the tree. Ninety yards, no more than that now. The haze would open at any moment, and he would see them. He crouched and ran, dodging from tree to tree, pausing behind each trunk to listen for noises. Snatch of laughter or jocular abuse from the tea party, a muffled cough into a mitten. He rechecked the moving man. Closer, pursuing an orderly, steady progress. The officer. Now, pausing at the group, his flame-shape bending over something—

Had to be. Had to be rocket or grenade launcher, or a mortar. Laser rangefinder. Goodbye, Mig-31. Just in case, Waterford supposed, anything intolerably wrong occurred, they would have the option of preventing the aircraft's removal. Did he hear their voices then, just as he turned to wave Brooke forward—?

No. Nothing. He pointed the MEL imager back towards the rise, scanning along it, picking up Sergeant Dawson's kneeling, burning shape, using another MEL imager. Dawson would be watching him. He would see the first shots fired. Bright, burning blobs leaving one flame-shape, entering another. Strangely, though, the change in body heat of anyone killed would not show for some time.

Brooke looked and listened. He shook his head.

"Four of them now. No more than seventy yards. Next tree should do it. Ready?" Brooke nodded. They hurried to another fir, less than ten yards ahead of them. Brooke looked once more, and nodded.

"What is it? Can you see what they've got there?"

Brooke was silent for a time, staring through the short, stubby barrel of his PPE Pocketscope. The light conditions made its use necessary, though it was most effective as a night sight. He lowered the instrument and said: "It looks like one of their AGS thirty millimeter jobs."

"Effective range, eight hundred meters. Enough. Anything else?"

"Laser rangefinder, I'm pretty sure."

"Right. Let's take them all out. Who knows, we might get the rest of them to surrender if we get the officer as well? You—work around that way. I'll outflank them on the other side. Wait until I start firing before you open up."

"O.K."

Brooke moved off immediately, working his way from tree to tree, threading his path inwards and ahead, towards the shore of the lake. When he was little more than a shadow, Waterford raised the MEL imager. Brooke's form burned in bright colors. He swung the instrument. Yes, Brooke was close enough. He moved away from the tree, working to his right for perhaps fifty yards until he was satisfied that he had chosen the optimum position. As soon as he had finished firing, he would make for the position of the radio and its operator. The man was perhaps thirty or forty yards from him. He used the MEL to check. Yes, no more than forty. A straight run. Eight or nine seconds—say ten. How many Russian words can you say in ten seconds?

He checked the group around what he, too, could now see was an AGS 30mm grenade launcher on a tripod, with its round drum, like a heavy case of film, attached to the barrel. The laser rangefinder sat on top of the barrel. Waterford had no doubt that the elevation of the barrel would direct a grenade into the clearing where the Firefox sat.

The officer stood up, addressing a last remark. Someone laughed, a noise above the wind. The officer made to move away. Waterford gripped the ribbed plastic of the rifle's barrel, and fitted the stock against his shoulder. He squinted into the optical sight. He set the selector level for three-round bursts. There were fifty caseless, polygonal rounds in the magazine. He breathed in, held his breath. The officer moved slightly, straightening like an awakened sleeper, hands on his hips. One of the others was looking up at him. It was the moment. Waterford squeezed the trigger of the G.11.

The officer leaped across the barrel of the AGS, turning

a half-somersault. Waterford felt the very slight kick of the slow recoil. The officer had taken all three rounds of the burst, fired within ninety microseconds. Waterford refocused on the man looking up from the ground, his head not yet swinging to follow the leap of his dead officer over the grenade launcher. He squeezed the trigger once more. The man's face disappeared from the optical sight. He heard Brooke's Armalite open up on automatic, turned, and began running.

The radio operator was half-upright, staring towards the man running at him. Four seconds. He was already bent once more over the radio, his fingers flicking at switches, turning knobs. Waterford skidded to a stop twenty yards from the Russian, flicked the selector switch to automatic, and raised the G.11. The remaining forty-four rounds left the rifle in a brief, enraged burst of noise. The soldier and his radio disappeared in a cloud of snow, the man lifted from his feet and flung away, the radio disintegrating.

In the ringing silence after the rifle had emptied itself, Waterford cursed. Twenty yards more, and the man would have been alive. But, he was opening a channel, about to inform Moscow.

"Damn."

Now, they needed one of the Russians alive.

Brooke's rifle had stopped firing. Already, Dawson would be moving the rest of the SBS team down the slope at the run. Waterford slipped behind a tree trunk and waited. They needed one of them alive—but only one.

"It has begun," Aubrey announced somberly as he put down the headset and turned to Gant and Curtin. "Waterford reports four taken prisoner, the rest dead. The killing has begun."

"It began days ago!" Gant snapped at him, sitting on one of the camp beds, still dressed in his flying suit. Thorne was lying on another bed, holding a paperback novel above him, reading. He seemed uninterested in Aubrey's announcement, indifferent to the surge and swell of emotion between Aubrey and Gant. "Days ago," Gant repeated. "It killed Anna, too."

Aubrey glared in exasperation. "You have already made your point most eloquently concerning Anna," he remarked acidly.

"The hell with you, Aubrey—the hell with you. Anna's death is as pointless as those poor bastards spying on your people at the lake. Just—dead. Like that." He clicked his fingers. "Just like that. And what the hell for? Why didn't you tell the poor slobs you'd given up on this idea *before* you had them shot? Just so they could know what they were getting killed for!"

"Be quiet, Gant—!"

"The hell I will!" Gant stood up, as if to menace Aubrey. Curtin watched him carefully, analytically, from the other side of the room, near the radio operator's console.

"There is nothing I can do!"

"Then there was no point at all in it."

"I—can't admit that . . ."

"Because you can't live with it."

"I have tried, dammit—I have *tried* . . ." Aubrey turned his back and walked to the window. Skogerøya's mountain roots were visible. Gulls were blown like scraps of paper over the grey water of the fjord. Kirkenes huddled on its headland. Another glimpse through the storm, but not the weather window that was still promised for later in the afternoon. Still promised, still on time. It could, they now said, last for as long as an hour. Aircraft could fly in it. "Pointless," he announced to the room without turning from the window. Then, as if called upon to explain something, he faced Gant. The table covered with signals, maps and charts lay between them.

"I—these events have been uncontrollable, Mitchell." Gant sneered at the use of his first name. "The original operation worked just as planned—yes, even to the unfortunate deaths involved. They were not planned, but they were taken into account. No one was forced to the work . . . but these events—the past days—they are happenings outside the rock pool. Do you understand? Intelligence work takes place in a rock pool. In this case, the marine creatures there, in their sealed-off world, have been disturbed, flung violently about by a storm. There is nothing I can do. I am sincerely sorry about the woman's death, but I did not cause it. Yes, yes, she was blackmailed into assisting you, but I intended— just as you promised her—that she would be safe from her own people and from ours afterwards. I would have persuaded Buckholz to set her free. She could have returned to her lover—that foolish, tragic young man who was the real instrument of her death!"

He broke off, as if he disliked the pleading tone of his own voice. He hated the confession he was making, yet it forced itself upon him not so much because of Gant's accusations but because the guilt had returned. It was filling his chest and his thoughts. There was only one justification in the rock pool—success. But, he could not control these events, he had failed to tailor them to the parameters of intelligence work. Soldiers, equipment, a timetable, weather conditions, repairs, the very location of the Firefox—all had conspired to flood the calm rock pool and fling them all into the raging water. He could now only admit defeat, pack and leave.

"I do not need lessons in guilt from you, Major," he said tightly, surprising himself.

"I wonder."

"There's nothing more to be done. Acknowledge Waterford's signal." He crossed to the charts on the table, shuffling through them. "Curtin, if you please," he said. "Now," he continued when the U.S. Navy officer had joined him, "the weather window is such as to prevent the Chinook making it all the way, in and out, from Bardufoss. Therefore, the two Lynx helicopters must be used. We must instruct Moresby to salvage what he can—a list of items from his own descriptions of the on-board systems must be drawn up. Everything must be loaded aboard and flown out the moment the weather clears. They will have perhaps less than half an hour before the first Russians arrive, probably in force . . ." His hand skimmed and dusted at the map as he spoke. It was swift, decisive, false, and he knew it. The imitation of action. The retreat. "Our people, those who can't be got on board the two helicopters, must move out to the nearest crossing point into Norway—here . . . that's northwest. Waterford can be relied upon to organize everything in that area . . ."

He looked up. Gant's shadow had fallen across the chart. His knuckles were white as he leaned on them. His face was bleak and angry; a remote anger, something Aubrey could not lessen or turn aside.

"Yes?" Aubrey asked in a voice that quavered.

"Send me in," Gant said. His eyes did not waver, nor did he blink. There was no color in his cheeks.

Aubrey shook his head, preparing a smile of quiet, grateful dissent to disarm the American. "No—" he began.

"Send me in."

"Impossible, Mitchell—quite impossible . . ." He essayed the smile. It appeared to have no effect. Thorne had put down his paperback, and was sitting up against the pillows like an interested invalid. Aubrey sensed that Curtin, beside him, was divided in his opinion.

"Send me in."

"I cannot risk *you*—"

"So now I'm valuable?"

"You always were."

"I doubt it. Send me in in the Harrier. Thorne can fly it—I'll fly it if you want to cut down on possible waste . . . if I can't get that damned airplane out of there before the Russians, then I come back in the Harrier . . . look, Aubrey, I can *tell* them which pieces to remove, which systems. I'm the only one who can!"

"The senior engineering officer is quite capable of doing—"

"The hell with you, Aubrey!" His fist banged savagely on the table. The paperweight on the sheaf of signals jumped to one side. Gant looked at his watch. "You've got less than two hours to decide. I can be on-site in five or six minutes from takeoff. That gives me twenty minutes, maybe more, before the Russians can even move. Tell them to get the airplane ready—find out if they can get it ready. Tell them I'm coming."

"If they wait, they'll have no time to dismantle—"

"Is that what you want from this—bits and pieces? Is that what anyone wants? Washington? London? They want the airplane. They want the balls that comes from pulling this thing off. They don't want bits and pieces, they want the whole damn thing!"

"I just can't risk it—"

"You try. You'll find it easier than you think. It isn't your neck. Ask them will the airplane be ready. Tell them I'm coming."

"It's no more than a machine, Mitchell."

"It always was. It's too late to remember that now." He stared into Aubrey's eyes, and lowered his voice. "Baranovich, Fenton, Semelovsky, Kreshin, Pavel—and Anna," he whispered.

Aubrey's face whitened. From the corner of his eye, he saw Curtin's quick gesture to silence Gant. Gant's face remained unmoved.

"How dare you . . ." Aubrey hissed.

"Do it, Aubrey. Give the word. You said it—we're outside your precious rock pool. Give the word. Get that airplane ready for me to fly."

Aubrey stared into Gant's eyes for a long time. Then, abruptly, he turned on his heel and snapped at the radio operator. "Get 'Fisherman,' " he said. "I want an updated report on the repairs. At once!"

"I'm afraid, Comrade Chairman, that we have to assume that your reconnaissance party was surprised and overcome. Which means, in simple terms, that they know that we know. We are each equally aware of the other." Vladimirov buttoned his greatcoat and descended the steps of the Palace of Congresses. Andropov, in a well-cut woolen overcoat made in Italy, walked beside him. "It's hard to grasp what the weather must be like up there," Vladimirov added, deflecting the conversation.

"Mm?" Andropov murmured, watching the placement of his feet; his expensive shoes were protected by galoshes. Frozen snow crunched beneath Vladimirov's boots. Andropov looked up at the general. "What did you say?"

"The weather—in Lapland," Vladimirov murmured impatiently. He was angry with Andropov, though relieved to escape the claustrophobia of that glassed-in, underground tunnel of a control room for at least a few minutes.

"Oh, yes."

Andropov's mind reached into the political future, towards failure, while his own thoughts anticipated at least a qualified success. The capture or death of the reconnaissance party was of little importance now. The weather conditions prevailing at the lake and along the border controlled everything; defined action, timetabled events.

The strategy, the tactics, did not satisfy, even interest Andropov. Already, he was attempting to anticipate how anything other than complete success might be used against him, used to thwart his ambitions within the Politburo and beyond it. For Andropov, the weather, more than a limitation, was a prison, a promise of failure.

"The weather window we are expecting in—less than two hours—" Vladimirov pulled down his sleeve over his gold watch "—will reach the forward units of the Independent Airborne Force approximately thirty-two minutes after it reaches the lake. With luck, helicopters can be airborne twenty-six or seven minutes after the weather window reaches the lake. At top speed, their flying time in the conditions would be—no more than twenty minutes." He raised his gloved hands, as if to appreciate the windy blue sky, the swiftly moving high clouds, the raw, clean air. Or the massive, crowding buildings of the Kremlin around them as they walked the concrete paths. "That means they will have less than forty-five minutes of better weather before we arrive—"

"Forty-five minutes," Andropov repeated, deep in thought.

"Gant is not on-site, he can't be. Nothing can get in or out. Probably, he is at Kirkenes—coded signals traffic suggests Aubrey is there, some kind of temporary control center, I imagine . . . Gant may take as long as fifteen minutes by helicopter or aircraft to arrive. That leaves thirty minutes or less . . . the Mig-31 cannot be ready for him the very moment he arrives . . . that lake cannot be utilized as a runway without preparation. Even if the Mig is fueled, armed and preflighted when he arrives, he will have to wait." He stopped and turned to Andropov. Behind the Chairman of the KGB, the Trinity Tower, topped by its huge red star, loomed against the sky. "Do you see? We have him. We have the pilot and the aircraft in our hands."

Andropov adjusted his spectacles. "I seem to have heard that cry all too often before," he replied sharply. "You have a second line of defense, I take it, General?"

"Defense?"

"Against failure." Andropov's narrow face was chilled white.

"I see." Vladimirov felt uncomfortable, almost guilty; as if he had joined some unscrupulous conspiracy against his friends. "Of course," he continued brusquely. "Border squadrons will be airborne. Interceptors from 'Wolfpack' squadrons on the Kola Peninsula will be in the air as soon as the weather breaks sufficiently for them to take off. As a line of defense."

"You still think you can capture the Mig-31 intact?"

"Why not? I don't believe its destruction should be our first objective."

"The Finns will try everything to arrive the moment the deadline expires," Andropov announced tiredly.

"If they get there, and find the aircraft, they will hand it over to us. As long as it remains where it is, it is ours. Obviously."

"As long as it remains where it is."

"We shall have to contrive that it does so," Vladimirov snapped. Lost sleep, concentrated thought, continual tension seemed to overtake him for a moment. He rubbed his forehead. Touching the peak of his cap made him aware of his shoulder-boards, his greatcoat, the medal ribbons he wore. They revived him, reasserted his superiority over the ambitious politician beside him. "I have computer predictions of a timetable for repairs, drying out, replacement, preparation . . . all of them suggest that, with limited equipment, they will be hours behind their self-imposed deadline. Andropov, they can't fly the Mig out. It won't be ready."

"So you hope."

"So I believe."

"Mm." Andropov turned away, like a camera scanning the walls and towers and buildings of the Kremlin. The fortified encampment in the wilderness, Vladimirov thought. His mind was filled with contempt for Andropov and what he represented. Protected by their walls, he continued to himself, afraid of the wild tribes outside the palisade. They don't belong—

"I see our revered First Secretary heading this way," Andropov murmured, smiling thinly as Vladimirov's head jerked up and his lips trembled slightly. Then anger at his own weakness darkened the soldier's features. "You can't be above it all, you see," Andropov added.

Vladimirov felt as if the Soviet leader had been watching them from his office window and had pounced, hoping to catch them at some conspiracy, or simply off balance. His trilby hat was jammed onto his head, his coat with its astrakhan collar was wrapped around him; his bodyguards hurried after him. Both men moved towards the Soviet leader, preparing their minds and faces.

"What is happening?" the First Secretary asked accusingly, looking at each of them in turn. The bodyguards loitered. "I rang the command center, only to be told that you had gone for a *walk!*"

"It is all decided—everything has been worked out," Andropov replied calmly, indicating Vladimirov. The First Secretary appeared to make an immediate pact with the

Chairman of the KGB. His face darkened when he turned to Vladimirov, ready to accuse.

"Well, General—well?"

"Comrade Chairman Andropov and myself have made our decisions, First Secretary. We were on our way to inform you privately."

Andropov's glasses caught the sun, and glinted. It was like a surrogate smile, a small signal of congratulation. "Yes," he agreed. "We differ in some essentials, however."

"I will tell you what is to happen," the Soviet leader announced, walking on down the path, careful of his footing, waiting for them to fall into step at either side of him. Vladimirov clenched his fists for a moment, then caught up with the older man. Andropov was already to his left.

"We would value your opinion, of course—" Andropov began.

"You will listen to your orders."

"First Secretary, I have to say that you are not—"

The gleam in the First Secretary's eyes silenced Vladimirov. It was more eloquent than the threats which followed. "Orders. Do you really want me to produce the Minister and Deputy Ministers, the Military Council in force, the General Staff, the Commander in Chief of Warsaw Pact Forces, members of the Politburo—more than enough to form a quorum—half the Central Committee . . . ?" The Soviet leader waved his arms in the air, as if conjuring his supporters. "All of them will tell you that I am right, even before I say anything! What is it you want, Vladimirov? What proof do you require before you realize that this business—all of it—falls under my control? I have *allowed* you to lead. Now, you will follow. Do you understand me?"

Vladimirov stared over the trilby hat, towards the Archangel Cathedral and the great bell tower of Ivan the Terrible. He fought to control his features; to prevent his lips from twisting in ugly, frightened contempt, to prevent a blush of anger and shame entering his skin. Eventually, without meeting the Soviet leader's gaze, he nodded stiffly. "I understand you, First Secretary."

"Good." Clouds moved swiftly behind the trilby hat, behind the bell tower and the cathedral's domes. Shadow for a moment or two, then cold sunlight again. "Good."

"What is it you wish to be done?" Vladimirov asked. It was evident that the First Secretary had been in consultation with members of the General Staff and the Military Council. He was certain of himself. He had a scenario prepared. A consensus had been reached.

"You have one attempt—just one—to recapture the Mig-31. If that fails, then the aircraft is to be destroyed where it stands. Do you comprehend?"

Vladimirov nodded miserably. The First Secretary had ensured his backing for such a decision. The wasted billions, the wasted high technology, the wasted lives, did not matter. Safety first. The General Staff and the Council had accepted the wisdom of erasure. Better no one than the Americans. Obviously, he had already given guarantees that the project would be continued, and that continuity of funding was assured. In exchange, the General Staff had agreed that no one be held responsible for the theft of the Mig. A fresh start would be made. The matter would be forgotten.

Vladimirov wondered who had been on his side. The Minister of Defense—Kutuzov, certainly, but who else? He still had some influential allies, otherwise he would never have been granted even one chance to recover the aircraft. Someone would have ordered a small, powerful bomb to be dropped, or a standoff missile to be fired—

And then he saw the trap, opening up at his feet. Realization raced like the clouds beyond the domes of the cathedral. He was expected to fail. He would be disgraced, and removed. The First Secretary—perhaps even Andropov, too—would be revenged upon the insubordinate soldier. A warning to others. He dropped his gaze and met the Soviet leader's eyes. And saw that his insight was a true one. This man wanted his head.

Summoning as much bravado as he could, he said: "One chance, First Secretary? Then I shall take it, gladly. We'll capture the aircraft and our friend, the American!"

The MO-MAT creaked with frozen snow as a great bale of it was slowly unrolled along the cleared shoreline. The trees there had been cut down and the bases and roots grubbed out to make an open flat area which stretched away to a point where the ice would bear the weight of the Firefox. The portable runway covered rutted mud, pockmark holes, frozen slush.

Buckholz stood on the shore, his back to the soupy,

refreezing water beneath which the aircraft had lain. He could hear the creaking of the MO-MAT, and the noise disturbed him. At that distance, he should not have been able to hear it. The wind must be dropping. He turned his face into it, and his cheeks were numbed almost instantly. But he could hear the MO-MAT, hear more distinctly the chainsaws, even hear the voices of the mechanics and engineers who swarmed over the airframe. There should be nothing else but the wind. He pulled back the cuff of his parka, and looked at his watch. According to updated reports, they had another hour.

Runway, he told himself. Runway. He would need Moresby to check that. They needed upwards of four thousand feet of clear ice, and God alone knew what lay out on the lake. He had an image of Gunnar stumbling, tripping and falling against small ridges of drift that had frozen. The aircraft could never achieve its takeoff speed, maintain its heading or preserve its undercarriage intact if the obstacles were too numerous, too solid . . .

He moved towards the aircraft. It was like entering a warm and familiar room. Cannon ammunition was being fed into the huge drum aft of the cockpit. Two AA-6 missiles had already been fitted beneath the wings. The ammunition was NATO in origin, but fitted the drum and the caliber of cannon aboard the Mig-31. The two missiles were a bonus, Buckholz admitted. Salvaged from a Mig which had crashed, killing the pilot, on the Varanger-Halvøya while trying to get back to its Kola Peninsula base with an electrical fire on board. The wreckage had been returned, together with the pilot's remains. The missiles had ended up at Bardufoss with the RNAF Tactical Supply Squadron.

Beneath the aircraft lay a crude timber support and a deflated black airbag. They had been used to lift the airframe off the ground to test the undercarriage. To one side, the hot-air blowers lay waiting for reuse. Much of the Mig's airframe was covered by temporary shrouding when operations began, and the air blown around the airframe to dry it. The shrouds remained around the engine intakes. One engineer had, only minutes before, completed his slow, patient journey around the aircraft with a smaller, more portable blower, drying off every hinge, flap, and lock on the airframe.

The fuselage had been patched where it had been torn by cannon fire. The fuel lines had been repaired. Oxygen had been loaded aboard. The aircraft looked like an expensive model, as far as Buckholz was concerned. Somehow, it no longer seemed designed to fly. Sinister yes, beautiful in a dangerous way. But—a copy. A fake. He could not believe that the avionics, the hydraulics, the instruments, the engine itself, even the flaps and rudders—would operate. More than seven hours after the drop, after work had begun on the Firefox, Buckholz could not believe.

He signaled to Moresby, who seemed reluctantly to detach himself from a conversation with two of his team leaders. Yet the Englishman hurried the short distance between them.

"What is it, Buckholz?" he snapped, glancing back towards the aircraft. "Not just a polite inquiry, I hope?"

"No." He turned to face the snow-swept lake. Visibility, he realized, was improving. He could see the ice, the patches of snow, the ridges, stretching away from the shore. "The runway," he explained.

"Ah, yes. Been thinking about that." Moresby glanced back at the aircraft, and shouted: "I don't want that radio tested until we know we're going for the real thing!" One of the two men to whom he had been talking raised his hand in acknowledgment. "Can't trust the bloody Russians not to be listening, mm? Even if they know, I don't want them knowing any more . . . that way, they might think we haven't got a hope!" His smile was like a wince. "Come on, let's have a look at this runway!"

They walked out onto the ice, hunching against the wind and the intermittent snow.

"Four thousand feet—better give him a little more . . ." Moresby murmured, studying a compass, changing direction almost mechanically. "Swings here . . . Ah, clear ice. Just a spot of paint for the moment." He drew an aerosol from his parka and sprayed red paint onto the ice, a curving arrow in shape. "There—nice touch." Then he began striding in measured steps away from Buckholz, heading north up the lake. Buckholz caught up with him, and they walked together, faces protected from the wind, goggles now in place to cover their eyes.

"How're things?" Buckholz asked eventually. Moresby appeared to be counting. Every hundred paces or so, he sprayed the snow or ice with a blotch of red paint.

"Wife's fine, thank you. Wants to go to Venice this year . . . not keen myself."

"The airplane, dammit!"

"Oh—so-so. Good and bad, yes and no."

"I see."

"It won't be ready in the next hour, nor the next two," Moresby announced. "Except by a miracle."

"Hell—what's wrong?"

Moresby sprayed a patch of clear ice. Then he bent near a ridge of snow, and poked at it. It was only fifteen inches high. "Mm," he murmured. "Some of these will have to be leveled off—hot air, and all that. The rest can be blown off with a downdraft."

"Downdraft?"

"We have two helicopters, old man. If they fly up and down this runway you want, they'll blow most of the snow clear. What's too stubborn to move, we'll have to melt! Come on, let's get on with it."

"What's wrong with the aircraft?"

"Oh . . . Look, Buckholz, let me take you through it, nose to tail, as it were—then you'll see the problem. The problem that is now increased by the fact that the Russians know where we are and what we're doing . . . I really don't think, do you, that a short slow hop into Norway is going to be enough?"

"Maybe not—I just hope . . ."

"Well, you do that, Father, and the rest of us will work. That aircraft *has* to work—it has to be capable of speed, altitude, combat tactics, firepower. Just like when it came from the factory. And that is taking a little longer to achieve!"

"Can you?"

"No. Nowhere near. Look—" He sprayed a ridge with red paint. "That's three thousand feet. The whole airframe is dry . . . the air-driven backup instruments and systems—they all work . . . hydraulics and flying controls, O.K. . . . We can't even begin to tinker with the thought-guidance or the anti-radar—we don't know how they work. We've checked the connectors, the switches, the wiring, in case of shorts or damage . . ." They paced on through the flying snow. Visibility stretched suddenly to perhaps seventy or eighty yards, then closed in again just as quickly. Moresby continued: "Patching up the battle damage was relatively easy, so was draining the water from the fuel tanks. The radar and the other avionics in the nose section—well, we've done what we can. Checked it out, replaced just about all the multi-connectors and some wiring that looked a bit dodgy . . . that's about the limit of what we can do here—without the workshop manual!" Moresby smiled, sprayed red paint, paused to kick a low ridge that extended to either side of them, then moved on. "The manual firing systems seem O.K. Your man will be able to shoot. However, down at the tail, those decoys are not what the Russians were using, but they might work. If they come off the ejector rails O.K., and if they ignite, of course, they might just give enough of a showing on infrared to fool a missile—perhaps."

He was silent, then, and eventually Buckholz said: "And yet you won't be ready?"

Moresby sprayed paint and announced: "Four thousand. Where are we?" He stared into the snow and wind. "Mm. Visibility, fifty yards. Let's have a look and see what he's got left before he hits the north shore and the trees!" They walked on for some paces, and then Moresby replied to Buckholz's question. "No, we won't be ready. She has to be fueled up, for one thing. The radio, the electrics, the engine all have to be tested. We're less than halfway through the full instrument check. I wouldn't give this aircraft clearance by the end of tomorrow." He paused. "Ah, there we are. Just a bit less than four and a half thousand feet. He'll be lucky."

"How long will it take to strip out the most important equipment from the aircraft?"

"Two hours minimum."

"Then—"

"We're committed, one way or the other. Once the weather clears, your man will have to take off, or else we blow up everything, without salvaging even the anti-radar and the thought-guidance systems. I can't put it any more kindly than that."

Buckholz stared at the trees fringing the curving shore of the lake. It was visible now, a vista that retreated into the snowy haze. The weather was improving. There was less snow, even though the wind did not seem to be dropping.

"Can we clear this runway?"

"Oh, yes—I think so. Not too much trouble, using our two Lynx helicopters. And a hot-air blower for these bloody-minded little ridges. The ice underneath is O.K. If he's any good, he could get off . . ." Moresby glanced up at the sky.

Cloud, heavy and grey, was revealed above the lessening snow. "But, now that they know, what is he going to meet up there, even if he does get off? I wouldn't give that aircraft any chance in a dogfight with a Spitfire, never mind a Mig-25!"

"Yes, Moresby, I understand that. Yes, yes, it's my decision. Thank you. I'll be in touch."

Aubrey walked away from the console towards Curtin, deliberately ignoring Gant, who was staring out of the window at the returning landscape of mountains and fjords.

"Well, sir?" Curtin asked.

Aubrey wobbled his hand, a signal of dubiousness. "Moresby is keener on salvage than on flight," he said. "What do you have from Eastoe and North Cape?"

"The traffic they've picked up at North Cape indicates at least one troop transport helicopter has crashed on landing. No details, but it happened at Nikel, which seems to be their main assembly point."

"Mm. What estimates of current strength?"

Curtin shrugged. "Now we're really into the guesswork area. Maybe upwards of one hundred commandos . . . that's predicting the time they found out, the weather then and since, the known locations of units of the Independent Airborne Force . . . just about everything. But it's still pretty vague, sir."

"A hundred—I see."

"And gunships. Our people haven't got Blowpipe or any other missile. They're sitting targets for a gunship attack—so's the Firefox."

"I know that—!" Aubrey snapped, then added: "Sorry. Go on."

"Eastoe's reporting movements all the time. It's very difficult for them . . . hence the helicopter crash. That will teach them a little caution, sir, if nothing else. There are troop movements on the ground—hard to make out, but it's safe to assume there are some . . ."

"And nothing has crossed the border as yet—nothing?"

Curtin shook his head. "We don't think so . . ."

"But, no one can be certain."

"No."

"Well?"

"It looks like they're settling for one big push—a hundred men or more, perhaps two or three gunships besides the transport helicopters . . ."

"Activity at Kola Peninsula bases?"

"Plenty. No flying—there's no weather for that—yet. The first forward base, at Pechenga, will clear soon after we do, sir. We know what will happen then." Curtin suddenly detached himself from detail, and said: "Mr. Aubrey—they know everything. They *must* know about—him," he added, nodding his head towards Gant, "and they know what we're trying to do at the lake with *Nessie* . . . it's a race, sir. One we can't win. If all they want to do is destroy the Firefox, they'll have an easy time of it."

"If that's what they want," Aubrey replied, but it was evident that his features expressed his mind's agreement with Curtin's arguments. He glanced towards Gant's back, then into Curtin's face. He shook his head as a signal of doubt rather than denial. "The weather is about to open, Curtin. I have ten minutes, little more, in which to decide. It's—difficult . . ." He pinched his lower lip between thumb and forefinger, cradling his elbow with his free hand. "So difficult," he murmured. "We would have an hour, perhaps less, of sufficiently good weather . . . after that, he could not take off anyway. Half of that time we will be safe—the Russians won't be able to move. Then perhaps another ten or fifteen minutes before their first units arrive. Three-quarters of an hour. And Moresby swears the thing won't be ready . . ." He looked up again. "It is ready, in one sense. Ready for a low-level two hundred mile flight at subsonic speed to Bardufoss. He won't guarantee anything more than that . . . Worse, he cannot tell whether or not the anti-radar is working, or will continue to work, during any sort of flight."

Curtin nodded his agreement. He dropped his voice, and said: "You could be sending him up in an airplane which might break down at any moment, which won't do what he wants, hasn't the speed to run away . . . and may be seen on every radar on the ground and in the air for hundreds of miles around him. That's the gamble, Mr. Aubrey—the *real* gamble!"

"You think I'd be killing him?"

"I do."

"Then I can't ask it of him—can I?"

"No, I don't think you can . . ."

The door of the hut opened. The wind's noise entered,

seeming to blow Thorne into the room. As he closed the door, he said: "It's just about possible—now. In two minutes, even better. What do you want, sir?"

The smell of paraffin was heavy in the air. Blue smoke rolled near the low ceiling. Gant had turned from the window. He crossed to the nearest bed and picked up his flying helmet.

"I'm afraid—" Aubrey began.

"Me, too," Gant replied, standing directly in front of Aubrey. His stance was somehow challenging.

"I meant—"

"I know what you meant. It doesn't make any difference."

"Mitchell—listen to me, please. You can't be forced to do this . . . in fact, I'm beginning to believe that you shouldn't even try. Time—time has run out for us. You couldn't survive even if you take off. You know that."

"Maybe." Gant's face was bleak. "I'm not letting them all be wasted, Aubrey. I don't care what it was all for, or whether it really matters a damn—but they're dead and I owe them." He tucked his helmet under his arm. "Wish me luck."

Aubrey nodded, but could not speak. Curtin said: "Good luck, Mitchell. Great good luck."

"Sure."

The door closed behind Gant. Aubrey remained silent. There was a clock on the wall of the hut, an old, barefaced electric clock with two thick black hands and a spider-leg, red second hand. Aubrey's gaze was drawn to it. The clock of the operation's last phase had begun running. Gant's clock. The second hand passed the figure twelve, beginning a new minute.

An hour, he thought. In an hour, it will all be over. Everything . . .

14 / **WHIRLPOOL**

The Harrier was an approaching roar which became a misty, uncertain shape against the heavy cloud; a falcon about to stoop. Waterford felt himself able to envisage the scene that confronted the pilot. Whiteness; little more than white-out. A picket fence of penciled trees fringing the lake. Contourless, featureless almost.

The shape enlarged, dropping slowly. Roundels, camouflage paint, a grey shark's belly. The undercarriage legs, almost at the wingtips like a child's approximation to their position, hung ready to contact the ice. The fuselage wobbled. Two hundred feet, a hundred and fifty . . .

Now, Gant and the pilot would see the faces; begin to

see the ridges and bumps of the ice and drifted snow. See Moresby's splashes of red paint.

Waterford saw the wings flick, the descent unsettled by a whipping reminder of the wind. Snow flurried across the ice, flew through the clearing air. Fifty feet. He wondered whether the pilot would abandon the attempt and rise again as if riding a funnel of air until he was at a safe altitude. But the Harrier continued to drop. Hovering, hesitating . . .

An image from his boyhood; the stoop of the falcon, then its violent, brute rise back up from the long grass, the rabbit beneath it kicking feebly, wounded through by the talons. The Harrier's port undercarriage touched an instant before the starboard. Then the nosewheel dropped with an audible thump. Someone—perhaps as many as half a dozen—cheered. Others ran to secure the aircraft through another flurry of snow.

"He's here," Buckholz said to Waterford, unnecessarily; merely expelling tension.

"Who? Superman?" Waterford turned to look at the Firefox, then back towards the lake. Two men were already clambering over the cockpit sill. "Yes," he added more quietly. "Poor bloody Superman. How the hell does Aubrey con them?"

"Us, you mean?" Buckholz asked, smiling. Without waiting for an answer, he moved down to the ice, raising his arm to signal to Gant, who was removing his flying helmet.

"Us," Waterford agreed.

Buckholz opened his arms to welcome Gant.

"Buckholz."

"Mitchell—am I pleased to see you, boy!"

"Later." Gant was already looking beyond Buckholz, towards the Firefox. Snow petered out against his flying suit. The wind was a thin, high whine. "Is she ready?" he asked.

"No—"

"Then get her ready, Buckholz!" Gant snapped.

"Wait a minute, Gant—"

"Later." He hurried past Buckholz and Waterford towards the aircraft. Moresby stood protectively in front of it, his technicians and engineers still clambering over the fuselage and wings, and crouching beneath its belly. An auxiliary generator hummed, providing power to test the aircraft's electronic systems. Gant hesitated in front of Moresby, as if the man demanded respect, politeness. "Moresby?" he asked.

"Yes, lad. Now, up with you into the cockpit—tell me what it looks like. You have a lot of work to do in the next half hour." The tone was light, but Gant saw that Moresby's face was grim and uncertain.

He said: "Buckholz said she isn't ready."

"Yes, sir—had a lot of cars in today."

"How unready?"

"You have to do all the final checks—we have to refuel . . . that shouldn't take long. You're not going far."

"What have you got?"

"Trolley-pump—bit slow, I'm afraid."

"Fill the tanks."

"You only need enough for a short hop to—"

Even as he prepared to climb into the cockpit, Gant pointed his thumb at the clouds. "You know what they'll have waiting up there—fill the tanks."

"You're right, Gant—but, then again, you're wrong. There's no warranty on the vehicle . . ." He paused, seeming to lean his face towards Gant, as if about to confide some secret. Then he said: "I wouldn't guarantee this aircraft for the couple of hundred miles to Bardufoss. Anything could happen—" He raised his hand as Gant appeared about to interrupt. "Listen to me, Gant—please listen carefully. Any kind or amount of damage could have occurred to any or every part of that aircraft while it was submerged. It all looks all right—it all checks out. But—under stress—*combat* conditions . . ." He paused again, calculating the effect of his next words. "*You* may not break up under combat stress, Gant— but I wouldn't say the same was bound to be true of the Firefox. Do you understand?"

Gant glared at him, then turned and mounted the pilot's steps. He swung his legs over the sill, and settled into the pilot's seat. After a moment, he looked down at Moresby, his face white and bleak.

"I understand you, Moresby," he said. "I get it, all right. She could break down, fall apart any time. You don't know for sure though, you can't say—" He broke off, seeming to stare at the instrument panel in front of him. His hands reached out towards the control column. "How long are you going to be refueling her?" he asked eventually in a clipped, professional tone.

"Thirty to forty minutes."

"Then I want her out on the ice—now."

"What—?"

Gant snapped. "If I'm not sitting there at the end of the runway when they come over, they may never give me the chance. Get her out onto the ice."

"Quite right," Moresby replied, unabashed. "O.K.—sit tight." Moresby moved away, already raising his voice, summoning and briefing his engineers and technicians.

Gant sat in the pilot's couch. The tremor in his hands subsided. It hadn't been fear. Anticipation. Moresby's warning had had no effect apart from a momentary anger. Now, all he felt was an impatience to be gone. There was an arrogance like that of a bird of prey. The activity around him was no more than the means of returning the aircraft to his control. Anna seemed to have retreated from him, down a long, narrowing perspective. Other figures followed her; the dead and the living alike.

He heard the tractor tug's engine start up. The bright yellow vehicle chugged along the shoreline towards him, creaking and grinding over the MO-MAT. It skirted him almost respectfully, and its towing bar was clamped to the undercarriage leg beneath the Firefox's nose. Gant turned up his thumb, the driver of the tug returned the signal, then exhaust fumes billowed as Gant felt a shudder through the airframe. Reluctantly at first, the Firefox began to move backwards. As the tug maneuvered him, he used the mirror almost as if he were reversing into a parking place. The Firefox rolled protestingly along the MO-MAT.

Buckholz stood watching the aircraft move. Other people, too, had paused in their tasks. Incongruously, it was moving backwards. For a moment, he had intended protesting the moving of the airplane, before he realized that camouflage was pointless, that trees did not protect against grenades and rockets. Gant would need every second, even half second of advantage.

Slowly, the aircraft reversed onto the ice, dropping down the shore, pausing, then settling level on the last yards of the portable runway. The tug continued to push her until the Firefox cleared the MO-MAT and turned a reverse half-circle on the ice so that her nose was facing north, up the lake. The snow had almost stopped now and Buckholz could see perhaps for some hundreds of yards before the chill, grey air seemed to solidify into a rough blanket hung across the scene. From the cockpit, he guessed that Gant could see no more than one-third of the total length of ice runway he would require to take off.

He hurried towards the Firefox. People returned to their work, the marines took up defensive positions beside the aircraft once more. More like a guard of honor than a force to be employed, Buckholz thought.

Around the aircraft, under the supervision of the Royal Engineer captain, men began clearing the packed and drifted snow. A gang of children clearing the front path, or the driveway from the garage to the street for their father's car.

Gant was looking down at him.

"You want the takeoff run cleared now?"

"Sooner the better."

"I'll get right on it." Buckholz turned away, then looked back at Gant. "You don't have to do this, you know. Take a risk with this, I mean." Gant did not reply. Buckholz moved back towards him, and touched the side of the fuselage below the cockpit. "Moresby must have told you about the risks involved. I'm just telling you, Mitchell—you don't have to go through with it."

Gant looked down at him. There was something uncomfortably distant and arrogant about his face. "Get those choppers aloft, Buckholz . . ." He paused, then added without grace or warmth: "And—thanks."

"O.K.—I just don't want you beefing at me when she falls out of the sky like a black brick."

"I promise."

Buckholz waved, and then unclipped his R/T from his parka.

"Come in, Gunnar—Gunnar?"

Gunnar's reply crackled in the freezing air. "I hear you, Mr. Buckholz—go ahead."

"Get the brushwork done—man here has to get to work on time," Buckholz said with a faint grin. Then he turned to watch the far shore of the lake, a misty, uneven line. The trees were emerging from the thick air like spars of an old pier. He could hear, quite clearly, the rotors of the two Lynx helicopters starting up, and waited for them to lift out of the grey, dirty haze.

Gant watched as Moresby's technicians wheeled the

trolley-pump down the shore towards him. Two of the air transportable fuel cells were clumsily rolled forward onto the ice. A hose from the first of them was dragged to the port wing and attached to the fuel filler pipe. Gant waited, almost stirring in his seat with impatience, until the noise of the pump starting up calmed him. Moresby watched the whole operation with an unchanging grimness of expression. Fuel began to flow into the port tanks.

Moresby swiftly crossed the ice to the aircraft and climbed the pilot's steps until his head was above the sill and he was looking down on Gant. He activated the stopwatch on the main instrument panel. Its second hand moved jerkily. Moresby glanced at his own stopwatch, hung around his neck.

"Right," Moresby announced. "We've been working our backsides off for nearly eight hours now, laddie. Let's see how quickly *you* can get things done, shall we?"

Gant looked into the senior engineering officer's face, and nodded. "O.K., Moresby. Let's get started."

"And don't switch on the ignition while we're pumping in fuel, will you?"

"Sure—but if I call for hot refueling . . . ?"

Moresby growled. "*Don't*—if you can avoid it." He raised his eyes, and then added: "Sixteen minutes and twelve, thirteen seconds have elapsed since you took off from Kirkenes. Let's get cracking, shall we, old man? We've been through everything we can . . . you'll know if the readouts seem different in any way." Moresby glanced down from the pilot's steps and paused in his instructions until the auxiliary power unit had been wheeled up to the aircraft's flank and reconnected to the Firefox. Then he said: "Right—run through the preflight check, taxi and pre takeoff as far as you can—I'll keep the tally."

Gant hesitated, savoring the moment. Then his hands moved. He switched on the Master Electrics, and immediately heard a whirring noise that slowly mounted in pitch.

"Good. Gyro instruments winding up," Moresby murmured. "Emergencies pressure normal—check . . . Flying controls. Normal feel and full travel . . . ?"

Gant's thumb left the throttles and depressed a spade lever. "Sixty degrees, and indicating," he announced as the flaps lowered.

As he raised the flaps again, the heel of his left hand

nudged a lever and the airbrakes extended with a mild thump which gently rocked the airframe. He waited, then. Moresby sensed his uncomfortable impatience. He looked away from Gant as the two Lynx helicopters lifted above the trees on the opposite shore and moved across the ice towards them, perhaps two hundred feet above the lake. Gant, too, had turned his head.

They curtsied and sidled as they hovered near the Firefox, before dropping slowly like fat black spiders at the ends of invisible threads. With Gunnar's helicopter in the leading position, they moved slowly away up the lake. Snow billowed around them in the downdraft, rolling like dust thrown up by a scything, horizontal wind. When it cleared there were ridges of frozen snow amid the smoother, cleaned expanse of ice.

"It's working," Moresby commented.

"Annunciator panel and warning lights—test," Gant prompted.

He pushed switches on the panel. The noise of the helicopters drummed and echoed around the lake. Royal Engineers were already using hot-air hoses and shovels to flatten and disperse the low, sword-edged dunes of frozen snow. He saw that most of them were already marked with something that might have been red paint.

The check lights on the panel glowed in the correct sequence. Eventually, Gant said: "Anti-G control—on . . . and check."

"Now the UHF," Moresby announced. "Select the Soviet Tac-channel. Then we can listen to what our friends are up to. No transmission test yet."

"O.K.—then what day is it?"

"Thursday."

Gant removed a small card from its holder on the radio control box. He required the sequencing code to lock onto the secure Soviet Tac-channel, since the pattern of frequencies was altered each day.

"Got it," he announced.

He switched on the radio, then slipped the Russian flying helmet onto his head. He plugged in the communications and thought-guidance jack at the side of the couch. Then he pressed the selector buttons, keying in the sequencing code, and almost at once the two red dots locked on, stuttering as they followed the changes of frequency. Moresby was looking at him. He concentrated on the crackling lash of voices in his ear. Activity, activity . . . he waited, hardly breathing. The stopwatch informed him that eighteen minutes had passed. Nothing was airborne. Everything was, however, fueled and ready, awaiting the order to take off. Repeated references to the location of the lake, of tactics, of the pattern of overflights, selected squadron altitudes and search areas . . .

He switched off. "It's O.K.," he announced. It wasn't. He felt a creeping numbness, a reluctance to go on. They would be waiting for him. Perhaps ten or fifteen aircraft, expecting him to be visible only on infrared, waiting in specific, clever patterns, as if they held nets between them and would cast for him the moment they saw the heat of his exhaust as he lifted from the lake.

The cloud of snow was retreating. Ridges and drifts were being smoothed and erased. The two Lynx helicopters were distant, unreal black dots at the far end of the lake.

He would have no chance.

There was no other way. He swallowed, and in a dry voice, he said: "Repeat."

"I asked you about the anti-radar and the thought-guidance. We don't know how they work so we can't reassure you as to whether they will work or not. Was there anything on the panel in connection with the anti-radar?"

Gant shook his head. "There was no electrical or mechanical action to be taken." He looked at Moresby. "I don't know—"

The Lynxes were lost again in the cloud that was now moving slowly down the lake towards them.

"Damn," Moresby muttered. Then he punched one mittened hand into the other. "Got it!" He bent his head, placing his lips close to his R/T. "Thorne—Thorne?" His voice was eager and querulous. Gant glanced across at the Harrier. He could see Thorne's hand wave in acknowledgment.

"Yes, sir," he replied punctiliously.

"Be a good chap and see if you can see us, will you?" Moresby asked with affected casualness. "On your radar, naturally."

"But—"

"No buts. Just do it, my boy."

"Sir."

"Meanwhile," Moresby said to Gant, "you can check out pressurization and air conditioning."

"O.K.," Moresby climbed down the pilot's steps as Gant closed the cockpit. He heard Moresby attach a lead to the landline socket on the fuselage, so that they could communicate. He locked the canopy. He was isolated in the Firefox. He connected his oxygen supply. The oxygen content and pressure were satisfactory. All that remained was to check the warning systems for pressurization, since cockpit pressure could only be checked at altitude. The lights all glowed comfortingly as soon as he summoned them. He could not check heating and demisting until the engines were ignited and running. Again, he checked the warning lights. They, too, glowed instantly. "All check," he said.

"Good. Now, wait a minute while we unload these missiles, then you can check the thought-guidance system. I'll give you the word . . ." Gant felt the two jolts as the AA-6 missiles were removed from their wing pylons. Then Moresby's face appeared outside the cockpit hood, his thumb erect in front of his features. Gant hesitated, then gave a mental command in Russian to fire a port wing missile. The sequence of lights stuttered across the panel. He counted them, remembered them. It appeared to work.

He opened the canopy. "O.K.," he said, removing the helmet.

"Right. Get those missiles back on their pylons," Moresby called down to his technicians. "Life-support?"

"O.K."

"Thorne here, sir," they both heard from Moresby's R/T. Gant's hand twitched on the sill of the cockpit.

"Yes?" Moresby snapped.

"It's difficult, sir—hard still object on a hard still surface against a cluttered background—"

"But?" Moresby said somberly.

"I shouldn't be able to pick up anything, should I, sir?"

"No," Gant said heavily.

"I—it's . . . I do have an image on radar, sir. Of the—Firefox. In flight, on the moving target display, I'd expect a strong reading . . . Sorry, sir."

Moresby stared at Gant. "That's it, then." Gant felt a shudder run through his body. "That's sodding it!" Moresby shouted. "The anti-radar's been damaged—it doesn't work! You'll be a sitting duck as soon as you're airborne."

"But—"

"No buts! I can't repair it—I don't know how it works!"

Aubrey turned away from the communications console. Eastoe, already supplying reports on all signs of movement along the border, especially at Nikel, and at the closest Kola Peninsula fighter bases, had relayed to Aubrey Moresby's discovery of the failure of the anti-radar system.

Curtin thought Aubrey looked ashen. He did not know what to say to the Englishman. He was relieved when Aubrey moved away towards the farthest corner of the room. It was as if he wished to hide. But the corner seemed to repulse him, for he backed away from it. When he turned, his face was determined.

"Thorne must get him out of there!" he said, coming back towards the console. He glanced up at the clock. Twenty-three minutes since the weather had begun to clear. The window must be close to the Russian units at Nikel by now. The interceptor bases on the Kola Peninsula would be free of the foul weather later than Nikel, but there, within minutes, the first helicopters would be airborne, carrying the first wave of commandos. They would take less than twenty minutes at top speed to reach the lake. Less than thirty minutes, then, before there was absolutely no possibility of rescue for Gant. What could they salvage of the aircraft in that time, prior to destroying the airframe . . . ?

And getting the people out.

Waterford would have to organize a retreat on foot, to some prearranged point where they could be picked up when the weather cleared. Vital personnel and equipment must come out aboard the two Lynx helicopters—

"He must get him out of there," he repeated, grimacing. "Get 'Fisherman' at once."

The radio operator swiveled in his chair and faced the smaller rack of radio equipment which they used to communicate with the lake. He repeated Buckholz's call sign, and was answered. Aubrey muttered and paced while Buckholz was summoned to the radio. As soon as he heard the American's voice, Aubrey snatched the microphone with a trembling hand.

" 'Fisherman,' " he said. Then realizing the futility of codes, he added: "Charles—get Gant out of there at once. Thorne is to bring him back here immediately."

"The anti-radar, you mean?" Buckholz replied. "Look, Kenneth, we have maybe twenty minutes . . . what other way do we have? He *has* to fly the plane out—!"

"Without the anti-radar, he hasn't a chance . . ."

A stray flash of sunlight lit the room. Dust motes danced, as if mirroring Aubrey's agitation. Then the sunlight disappeared.

"What about the helicopter force?" Buckholz asked.

"No movement yet. Charles, order him to get out of there. Salvage what you can. Get Waterford to organize the loading of the two Lynxes . . . and the withdrawal—Charles, do you hear me?"

Instead of Buckholz's voice, Aubrey heard Gant. His voice was distant.

"No way, Aubrey. No way."

"Mitchell, please listen to me . . ."

"I heard. The anti-radar doesn't make any difference."

"You haven't got *time*—!"

Gant was suddenly speaking to someone else—presumably Moresby. Aubrey strained to catch the words. "Hot refueling . . . the hell it does! Hot refueling—"

"Jesus!" Curtin breathed. Even the radio operator appeared abashed.

"What—?" Aubrey began.

"Refueling while the engines are running. He's going to start the engines while they're still pumping in fuel. One mistake and—"

"Charles—stop him!" Aubrey snapped.

"Why?" he heard Gant ask. "Does it matter who blows this airplane up—me, you, Buckholz, the Russians?"

"Let me speak to Moresby."

"No. There isn't time—he's busy right now."

The radio operator was scribbling busily. Curtin held one earpiece against his head, nodding as he listened. Then he said: "Three heavy transport helicopters have just taken off from Nikel. They're already across the border. Gant has less than twenty minutes."

"Charles—they're on their way."

"Three smaller helicopters—probably gunships," Curtin

reported. "One of them's moving faster than the other two. It's probably unarmed and carrying no passengers. Reconnaissance."

"Charles, give him a direct order. Tell him the mission is aborted!"

"Conditions at the Pechenga airbase should be good enough for flying in no more than seven or eight minutes."

"Charles," Aubrey said levelly, his face white, his lips thin and bloodless, "Gant may no longer have twenty minutes. It is less than one hundred miles from Pechenga to you. A Foxbat could cover that distance in—?" He glanced at Curtin.

"Maybe another seven, eight minutes, with half-fuel . . ." He wobbled his hand to indicate the degree of guesswork involved.

"Once any of those front-line airbases is clear, he has no more than seven minutes. Even if he could take off within ten minutes, he has no chance of escaping the attentions of Soviet aircraft. They will simply be waiting for him. Do you understand me? Over."

"It's all too late, Kenneth. We don't have the time to strip the airframe of even the most valuable equipment."

"We can't lose Gant—"

"This way there's a chance—"

"There's no chance!"

"I'm not prepared to have him shot in order to stop him, Kenneth."

"ETA of leading gunship at the lake—thirteen minutes."

"And when they see the aircraft on the ice," Aubrey snapped at Curtin, "and a runway strip blown free of snow—what will they do then?"

"Shoot first, talk later?"

"I would imagine so. Charles, please obey my instructions. I demand that Gant be flown out immediately in the Harrier. Then—destroy the airframe!"

"We're getting Eastoe's reports, too. The reconnaissance MiL should be with us in twelve minutes. That's the time we have—"

"No!"

"Dammit, yes! We're going to give it our best shot. Now, I'm busy, Kenneth. Out."

Aubrey was left standing with the microphone in his hand. He stared at it in disbelief, then dropped it as if it contained an electrical charge. He wandered away from the console towards the window.

The clouds were already massing again beyond the mountains, to the north and west. The light was thicker. Snowflakes drifted. The Norwegian army guard passed the window.

Aubrey knew he had failed. His final, desperate throw of the dice had, effectively, cost Gant his life. He had lost both the aircraft and the pilot. Killed people, too—Gant was just the last of his victims. There was nothing he could now do to affect the consequences of his actions. Nothing at all.

"ETA of the reconnaissance helicopter, ten minutes," Curtin recited. "Main force, eleven minutes forty. Weather continuing to clear over Pechenga. It might permit flying in four minutes, perhaps less. Eastoe's picking up infrared traces more strongly. They're on the runway, is his guess."

They would build a roof of aircraft over the lake, to keep in the Firefox. Without the anti-radar, there was no possibility of escape for Gant.

"What?" he heard Curtin exclaim like a man who has been winded. "Repeat!"

Aubrey turned from the window. "What is it?" he asked tiredly.

Curtin held up his hand for a moment, laid down the headset and looked at Aubrey. His face was lined and defeated. "Just to add to your pleasure," he said, "that was Bardufoss. Their weather is right on the margin, now. In minutes, they guess they'll have to close down. Even if he takes off, he won't be able to land."

"ETA of leading helicopter, six minutes . . . ETA main force, eight minutes."

The commpack operator was relaying the information he received to Gant via Moresby's R/T, which was still clipped to the cockpit sill. Gant shrugged, sensing the nervous tension, the urgency in his frame as he gangloaded the ignition switches, reached for the fuel valves—

And stared in disbelief at the purple light glowing on the main panel, to the left and just below the cockpit coaming.

"For Christ's sake, I thought this aircraft was *checked!*" he exploded.

Ahead of him, visibility was already decreasing. The window in the weather had lasted for less time than had been forecast. The far end of the lake was dimly visible, an irregularity of the thick air rather than a landscape. The two Lynx helicopters had completed their clearance of the ice. They waited silently now, beside the Harrier, as teams with shovels and hot air blowers completed the task.

"It was," Moresby replied grimly. He looked down at the technicians who surrounded the Firefox. "Ramp differential light's on," he called down. "Port engine intake—check it now! Come on, you buggers, the intake ramp's jammed or something! Find out what's wrong."

"How did I miss it?" Gant said, staring at the purple light. "I missed the damn light!"

"So did we all, Gant—so did we all." Moresby leaned out from the pilot's steps, clinging to the cockpit sill, straining to see what his technicians were doing. "Well?" he called. Through the open R/T, Gant listened to Waterford as he proceeded with the disposition of his forces. Brooke and his SBS men were to the south and east of the lake, while the marines who had parachuted in from the Hercules were on the opposite shore, where the Russians had been discovered.

"Nothing, sir—it's jammed all right."

"Why the hell that circuit was only routed through ignition, I don't know!" Moresby snapped in self-recrimination, staring at Gant. Frost had begun tō rime his moustache, as if the man had been breathing more heavily. Gant's heartbeat raced. His stomach felt watery, his chest hollow and shallow—as if there was insufficient space for his heart and lungs. "That bloody APU snarl-up earlier didn't help—nor the bloody rush—*come on!*"

"ETA of leading helicopter, three minutes fifty."

"Shit," Moresby breathed.

"Sir—we've found it—"

"What is it?"

"ETA—three minutes."

"Piece of sheet metal—looks scorched . . . it's folded like a bit of cardboard, sir. Wedging the door. Have to be careful with it—"

"Then be bloody careful!" He looked at Gant. "Some debris from one of your military encounters, old man," he said with forced and unfelt lightness. Gant merely nodded.

"Get me an update on the Bardufoss weather," he said into the R/T.

"Sir."

"I hope to God it gets no worse than it is," Moresby murmured. "Because, if you can't get in there, I wouldn't guarantee the vehicle for a longer distance!"

"Two hundred miles—you think I'll be safe two hundred miles away?"

"It's Norway, old man—"

"So?"

Moresby's finger flicked at his moustache. A noise of levering, and scraping, twisting metal, came from aft of them on the port side. Gant shuddered.

"Be bloody careful!" Moresby yelled.

"ETA of leading helicopter, two minutes forty," the radio operator announced.

"Where's that weather update?"

"Coming, sir—"

Gant heard Buckholz's voice over the R/T organizing the loading of the two Lynx helicopters with the Norwegian personnel who had been engaged in the operation. Women, children and allies first, he thought with bitter humor. Waterford's constant radio chatter was a muffled background, since he had left his R/T open. He had perhaps forty-five men. The three big MiLs coming behind the leading, unarmed reconnaissance helicopter and flanked by the two gunships, would be carrying perhaps forty or fifty troops each. Fewer than that only if they were bringing heavy equipment or light vehicles. Waterford dare not make the first move, even to protect the Firefox. He had to get the airplane out—! If he managed to take off, Waterford's men could melt into the landscape, avoiding all contact with Russian troops.

"I have to get her out," he repeated aloud.

"Weather, sir—"

"Yes."

"They're closing Bardufoss in five minutes, sir. Within ten, they say, no one could get in."

"O.K.," Gant replied in a small, tight voice. He closed his eyes for a moment. When he opened them, he saw Moresby staring at him.

"Where to, laddie? Mm—where will you take her when you get in the air?" It was not sarcasm; rather defeat.

"If I have to—all the way."

"What?"

"You heard me. All the fucking way, man! England or bust!" He tried to grin.

"I wouldn't advise that, Gant. Anything, *everything*—could go wrong. *Try* to get into Bardufoss—I really am serious about that . . ."

"ETA of leading helicopter—one minute."

"For Christ's sake, you buggers, hurry it up!" Moresby raged.

"Sir, we're having to be very careful to avoid more damage—it's really wedged in tight."

"Then cut the bloody thing into smaller pieces!"

"You have maybe two minutes or a little more—unless they hold back until the leading helicopter's done some spotting," Gant announced.

"Don't tell me . . ."

"Maybe we can bank on an attempt to capture the airframe more or less intact?"

"You think so?"

"It depends on one thing," Gant replied. "Who's now in command of the operation. If it's still Vladimirov, he'll think he has a chance. If it's the politicians—then kiss your asses goodbye! They'll get blown right out from under you."

"It's coming, sir—O.K.—yes, it's free, sir!"

"ETA, thirty seconds . . ."

"Change to hot refueling," Gant snapped as Moresby rammed home the circuit breaker and the light on the panel disappeared. "Thank God," he sighed.

"Hot refueling?"

"Have to now. I want to be ready to move when *I* pick the moment."

"How full do you want the tanks?"

"I've got sixty-percent capacity now." Gant shook his head. "Just keep filling them up."

Gant glanced up, his body slightly cowered in the pilot's couch, his arm half-raised as if to shield his eyes or protect his face. He could hear the noise of helicopter rotors.

Men had paused, as they crossed the ice towards the two helicopters, and were looking up. Visibility was closing in, heavy as a blanket. The far end of the lake was already obscured. It had begun to snow; big flakes pattering against the cockpit sill, on the shoulders of his pressure suit. He fitted his helmet once more, and plugged in his oxygen supply and the jack for the thought-guidance system.

The ugly MiL-24, probably unarmed to increase its speed, appeared like a squat beetle above the clearing. Gant cursed their lack of Blowpipe missiles. Even had they possessed them, he doubted whether Waterford would have opened fire first.

The MiL drifted out over the lake, over the two Lynx helicopters and the unarmed Harrier. Gant could see Thorne's helmet raised to watch it. The gunship floated above the Firefox, as if taunting her.

Moresby's voice instructed his technicians. "Hot refueling. You all know the latest drills—now's your chance to put theory into practice! Let's get one of the fuel cells close to the wing, along with the pump unit . . . I want everyone clear of the front intakes, and well clear of the tailpipes. An arc of men with extinguishers—" He glanced at Gant, but addressed no words to him. "—on either side of the aircraft. And keep alert!" Then he turned to Gant. "You listen to me over the landline. I'm staying well clear, thanks very much. Keep your engine power as low as you can, but not below generator power level . . ." Gant nodded. "Good."

Gant watched the technicians rolling one of the huge rubber fuel cells towards the aircraft and abeam of the starboard wing. He heard the connections made with the hose nozzle and the tank. Then the technicians retired. Moresby, standing perhaps a dozen yards away, signaled him to start the engines. The noise of the MiL above them pressed down upon him. The helicopter had been there for twenty seconds, perhaps half a minute. The main force was a minute behind it now. When they saw the engines ignite, having seen the fuel cell coupled, they would guess at hot refueling and know he was speeding up the preparations for takeoff. Would they still wait, when that was reported, or would they move in—?

He could not expect any more time, whoever controlled events. The Firefox was a sitting target they would not be able to resist. He switched on the master start, pressed the start button and turned on the high-pressure valve.

Behind him, halfway down the fuselage, there was the sound of a double explosion; the discharge of a shotgun's two barrels. In the mirror, he saw the two rolls of sooty smoke drift into the air. He heard the whirring of the turbines as they built up. He switched in the fuel booster pump, and eased the throttles forward. The rpm gauges mounted to twenty-eight percent. He eased the throttles back as far as he dared, and steadied them. Both huge Turmansky turbojets roared steadily. He grinned with relief. Moresby hand-signaled his team to recommence pumping.

"Thank God," Moresby said.

Waterford appeared a little distance from the Firefox, at the edge of the clearing. He raised his planklike rifle, and fired several three-shot bursts at the hovering, shifting MiL. Immediately, the gunship flicked away over the trees. Waterford spoke into Moresby's microphone. "Fucking tourists!" Then he added: "O.K., Gant—they'll be back in force in a couple of minutes at the outside . . . What they do then will depend on what you're doing. Good luck." Immediately, he walked away, rechecking the disposition of his marines.

Gant watched the fuel gauges. When should he tell them to stop? When should he end the risk of hot refueling? How much spare fuel capacity would he require?

He was oblivious of the scene around him. He scanned the instrument and systems panels, checked the center console, the left-hand console. He operated the rudder and the flaps. Stiff, sluggish by comparison with before, but they would have to do. Then he heard the commmpack operator's voice.

"Weather has cleared sufficiently at Pechenga. Two squadrons of interceptors airborne. ETA—six minutes."

He looked up. Visibility perhaps seven hundred yards, maybe seven fifty. He would be rushing towards a blanket of what might have been fog, except that it was grey-white and falling slowly. The snow was heavier. Only the wind was missing. One of the Lynxes took off, being almost immediately swallowed by cloud. The second Lynx drifted towards the Firefox, to await the rescue of Moresby's technicians.

"O.K., that's everyone except your people, Moresby," he heard Buckholz announce. Gant could see him beside the commmpack. The rotors of the Lynx died down. "We can leave our four prisoners tied up where they are. Their friends will be along any minute. So—let's go . . . ?"

Moresby nodded. "Thank you, Mr. Buckholz. We'll be aboard in a moment or two." Then he addressed Gant. "They've split into two groups—south of us and east, as Waterford suggested. But the gunships are still airborne. They're obviously awaiting orders."

Gant checked the fuel gauges. And shook his head. "Not yet," he said. "I'll tell you when to stop." Moresby's face was tired and angry; even frightened.

"Those bloody gunships," he murmured.

"Gant?" he heard in his earpiece. "Gant—this is Thorne. I've got an idea . . ."

"What?"

"A double takeoff—let me take off first . . . it might keep some of them off your back."

"What are the gunships doing?"

"Holding—agreed?"

Gant flicked on the radar. On the scope, amid the clutter from the worsening weather, he could just make out two heavy, glowing blips of light in close formation. Range perhaps two or three miles. There were paler, higher dots beyond them, at the very edge of the screen, but he disregarded them. They were still as much as five minutes away.

"Good idea—but no thanks. They know which is which. You move out now, before they get their orders. Good luck."

There were puffs of snow from beneath the Harrier which became small billows as she rose on the downward-directed thrust of her engine. The Harrier wobbled aloft, lights winking beneath her wingtips and belly; glowing as much as at dusk. The aircraft turned in the air like a clumsy dancer, then the thrust of the engine was vectored to forward flight. The aircraft slipped behind the snow and was gone.

Gunnar in the second Lynx had watched the Harrier's disappearance avidly. Now, he returned his attention to the Firefox. Gant saw the turn of his head. He was the only Norwegian remaining, waiting for the last handful of technicians. Around the lake were perhaps forty-five marines, all of them hidden except for the white-clothed figure of Waterford outside the windbreak which protected the commpack and its operator. He knew they were waiting for the aircraft to take off so that they could disappear into the forest, and make for the Norwegian border in small, quick-moving groups.

The lake was suddenly isolated and lonely. Gant wanted to stop the refueling that moment, let the technicians go, let Moresby go. Take off—

Two heavy, nearby glows on the radar; other paler dots

moving steadily closer above the clouds. In minutes, they would be above him, poised like birds of prey. The encounter was inevitable.

He watched the fuel gauges. He glanced down at Moresby. The two dots on the radar remained motionless.

"Advance units report no contact, General."

Vladimirov listened with his head cocked slightly on one side, as the reports began coming in from the airborne troops set down to the south and east of the lake. The British troops must be slowly falling back to the lake itself, with orders not to engage. A quick thrust now—a surprise outflanking movement around the tree-lined southern shore of the lake, and they might yet have the airframe intact—

The two MiL-24 gunships had been ordered to hold their position, despite the reports from the reconnaissance helicopter that Gant had started the Mig-31's engines and the Harrier and one of the Lynx helicopters had departed. There were only moments left. *They must push forward now—*!

The microphone was in his hand, to give the order. His lips had begun to frame the first words. He had summoned saliva into his dry mouth—

The First Secretary's hand fell heavily on his, startling him. He turned from the communications console. The Soviet leader was framed by the fiber-optic map. The scene upon its surface looked like an indictment.

"What are you about to do, General Vladimirov?"

"I—want our troops to push forward to the lake with all speed—" he began.

There was scorn in the heavy face of the First Secretary. "No," he said quietly. Then, more loudly: "No! Your time has run out, General Vladimirov—run out! There is no time left for you. You—are dismissed!"

The silence in the long gallery was intense, almost audible. Andropov had turned away. No one looked in Vladimirov's direction, although he knew by their stance and lack of movement that they were all listening.

"What do you mean . . . ?"

"I mean you are dismissed, Vladimirov—I mean you are to get out."

"But—"

"Go! Give me the microphone—" For a second, they struggled for possession of it like two children quarreling over a toy. Then Vladimirov wearily, defeatedly released his grip. The First Secretary cleared his throat and said simply: "Gunship commander—you will begin an attack at once. Destroy the runway, destroy the Mig! Do you understand my order? Destroy!"

Buckholz was standing next to Moresby, looking up at him. Beside him was a large briefcase. He appeared like a traveler eager to be gone.

"Mitchell!" he said through Moresby's microphone. "Let's get the hell out of here—all of us!" He waved his arms towards the east for emphasis. Gant checked the radar—

And saw that the two glowing dots, in close formation, had begun to move. At high speed.

He waved his hand in agreement. Immediately, Moresby dashed forward to the fuel cell, and switched off the pump. Then he jerked the landline free with a violent tug. As the pump's noise subsided and the first distant hum of approaching rotors reached them, Gant pulled down the cockpit canopy, checked his straps, switched on his oxygen supply, checked the anti-G device of his pressure suit, and pushed the test button. He checked the gauges. The pump was abandoned, the empty fuel cell, like a huge collapsed black aircraft tire, beside it. Then he saw Buckholz, Moresby and the technicians scurrying across the ice to the open door of Gunnar's Lynx. They climbed in hurriedly.

Gant checked the temperatures and pressures. The dots on the radar hurried through the mist of ground clutter towards the scope's center, closing on him. Runway, he thought. Runway first, airplane second. The Firefox strained against the brakes. He eased the throttles forward once more, paused, caught a glimpse of two helicopters—the Lynx lifting and sliding away towards the western shore of the lake and into the obscuring snow, and the first of the armed MiLs, a hundred yards ahead of him, at the edge of the trees. A gauntlet.

He released the brakes. The Firefox skipped forward, like a dog kept too long on its leash. It raced at the unfolding smooth runway of ice. Visibility, perhaps six hundred yards—

snow blowing across the lake once more. He switched on the wipers. He thrust the throttles fully forward, and felt the power of the Turmanskys punch him in the back. The ice rushed beneath the nose of the Firefox. Fire bloomed beneath the stubby wing of the MiL-24, and snow and ice cascaded over the fuselage of the Firefox as he raced on.

The wipers cleared the cockpit screen. In the mirror, he saw the ice open up, but the black snaking branches of the cracks caused by the rocket's impact lagged behind him, out of breath and tired.

Fierce elation. Almost delight. The airspeed indicator read 120 knots. He still could not see the far end of the lake. The airframe was shaking as the wheels careered over ridges and bumps. His teeth chattered painfully, his hand shuddered as it gripped the control column. One hundred and forty knots. The aircraft was almost skipping and bouncing as the wheels discovered every tiny indentation in the ice. One ridge that had been missed, he thought—then quashed the idea. It persisted for another moment—just one, and the undercarriage would snap—

150, 152—

He began to ease back on the column, beginning to lift the aircraft's nose. In the mirror, he saw the MiL loom up again as it pursued him. Fire billowed from its wing pods; rockets. They struck the ice behind him, around, ahead. He was showered with fire which burst into boiling snow and ice. Something clattered against the fuselage. A huge crack in the ice to starboard snaked towards him at terrible speed—then he was past it. The scene behind him was completely obscured.

160 knots.

Then he saw the second MiL, directly ahead of him, the end of the lake behind it; the trees like pencil marks against the white-grey sky. The MiL wasn't moving. Hovering. Helicopter and shore filled his vision.

It was directly in his path. He was airborne, accelerating through 165 knots. The MiL had positioned itself—it had shunted slightly a moment earlier—directly in the path of his climb-out. It enlarged, an enormous black beetle, hanging there.

He hauled back on the column, sweat bathing his body, his lips stretched back over his teeth. The nose of the Firefox rose, began to point at the clouds.

The MiL rushed forward, anticipating his action, prepared for suicide. Missiles armed. He pulled the column back almost against his chest. The Firefox seemed to stand erect on its exhaust and stagger into the air as if tearing free of a swamp rather than a frozen lake. The MiL was huge in his vision. He retracted the undercarriage as the helicopter seemed to move its nose in, so that he almost expected a shark-mouth to open and tear at the belly of the Firefox. The aircraft leaped at the low cloud. The MiL had vanished; become no more than a white dot on his scope. A missile's infrared trail pursued him for a moment, then fell away, unable to match his rate of climb. It would have been wire-guided, for use against ground targets.

He was at 10,000 feet, climbing at the rate of 500 feet a second. The airframe quivered and shuddered, like a human body that was chilled and growing rapidly colder, as the storm thrust and battered outside the aircraft. His fingers trembled on the control column. The throttles were all the way forward, through the detent and into reheat. The Mach-meter clicked rapidly upwards. Mach .8, .9, 1.0, Mach 1.2 . . .

11,000 feet. He studied the radar. Three glowing dots were moving towards the scope's center. He demanded contact time from the computer, and the readout appeared almost immediately. Twenty seconds. They were at 50,000 feet, and they could see him on radar—

He would break through the cloud ceiling at 24,000 feet, into a searing blue sky, and he would be under a roof of interceptors. Already other, paler dots were appearing at the edge of the screen. His body was still shaking from the aftermath of the almost-collision. Had he kept the Firefox beneath the MiL, he would have ploughed into the shore and the trees and exploded . . .

He tried to dismiss the past.

Don't think about it, don't think about it, his mind kept repeating. Don't think about it . . .

He pulled back on the throttles and scanned the instrument panel. No warning lights. Fuel-flow, rpm, radar, avionics, inertial navigator, armaments. The airplane functioned. It *was* an airplane again, not salvage.

Altitude, 18,000 feet and climbing. The grey cloud slid and writhed past the cockpit. The bright white blips on the screen were nearer. Ten seconds to contact.

No anti-radar. They can see you, he reminded himself. Remember that—

The Migs were too close to outclimb. Standoff missiles, heat-seeking, would overtake him even if the fighters that launched them could not. Six aircraft, all closing. All of them could see him. Already, they would have reported that fact, and would have deduced the failure of the anti-radar. The adrenalin would begin to flow, now that they knew. They would consider it easy, consider it already accomplished . . .

Hide.

Ground clutter—

Dive.

Course—Bardufoss.

21,000 feet. Contact time six seconds. Feverishly, he punched in the coordinates to the inertial navigator, and began to alter course. Hide—ground clutter. Deceive their radars. Five seconds, four-and-a-half, three.

He saw the infrared flare. A missile launched at Mach 3, then a second and a third. He banked savagely, flinging the aircraft into a steep dive, twisting into a roll so that the thicker, heavier grey cloud was now beneath his canopy. Then he completed the roll and the nose of the Firefox was driving through the cloud, the altimeter unrolling, the streaks of the missile exhausts still pursuing him across the screen. The white blips behind them had altered course and were following him down.

He banked savagely again, feeling the G-pressure build until it was painful. The suit he was wearing, not tailored for him or the aircraft, was slow to adapt to the abilities of the Firefox. His head hurt, his vision was hazy for a moment. 10,000 feet. The missiles were pursuing a different course, dropping away towards the ground, because they had lost his infrared scent. The effects of the savage turn drained away. He eased the aircraft into a steeper dive. The three closest white blips still pursued him.

5,000 feet. He began to pull out of the dive, slowly and easily. 4,000 feet. Three, and the aircraft was beginning to level out. Two-five, two, one-five, then he was flying level. He flicked on the terrain-following radar, then the autopilot. The inertial navigator altered the aircraft's course immediately, directing it towards Bardufoss. From the readout, he knew he was already in Norwegian airspace. Somewhere over the Finnmark, inland of the Porsangerfjord.

The Russians, too, were inside Norwegian airspace.

The Firefox twisted, banked, flicked like a dart through the unseen mountains. Gant felt as if he were watching a grey, blank screen ahead, through the haze of snow swept aside by the slipstream. There was nothing. Except the sense of the mountains of the Finnmark around him intruding, seeping like a gas. He could not help but feel their solidity, their massive obstruction. They were a maze through which the TFR and the autopilot flung him. He was like a runner off-balance on a treacherous surface. So long as his flight was headlong, arms flailing, he kept upright, leaping from foot to uncertain foot. TFR—autopilot. Keeping him alive. He felt, too, the constant, chilly quivering of the fuselage as it met the impact of the storm outside. It was as if his own body was growing colder and colder; shivering violently.

The three Russian interceptors followed, but they were slowly dropping back. They might have been Mig-25s, or even Mig-27s. They were not the Firefox. They were confused by ground-clutter, they had to trail him at an altitude above the mountains, they had to employ their manual skills. With each change of course, he gained upon them. He glanced at the map strapped to the thigh of his suit. His finger traced his course. Over the mountains east of the Lyngenfjord— flicking through that valley there, wings trembling as the aircraft banked and banked again through the turbulent air, following the valley's turns and twists . . .

A hundred miles from Bardufoss.

The Firefox banked steeply, almost turning into a roll, then changed course again to follow a valley before lifting over an unseen ridge and then dropping lower into another fold of the land. Rock faces on either side crowded upon the slim black fuselage. He could not avoid imagining the landscape or tracing his course on the map. He knew it was reaction; reaction to everything—the Migs that were dropping further and further behind him, the MiL helicopter that had filled the whole of his vision, the steep climb, even the hours before the takeoff.

And it was Bardufoss. If the weather had closed in, clamped down with high winds and nil visibility—a blizzard, close to white-out—he would never be able to land.

The thoughts unrolled like the images flicking upon the TFR screen; the blurs and lumps and flashing glimpses of radar-imaged mountains, rock faces, valleys—

The TFR screen went blank. Grey. Empty. The aircraft was halfway into a steep turn, following—

No time! A row of warning lights had rippled across the autopilot panel and glowed red. No time—

The Firefox seemed to hang. Grey screen, grey beyond the perspex of the cockpit. Without instructions from the autopilot, the column did not move, the engine note did not change, the angle of bank remained. The two Turmanskys were driving him towards a terrain he could not see. Into it—

He sensed the storm outside the aircraft more vividly. The fuselage seemed to shudder, as if anticipating impact. He imagined the noise of the wind, felt he would be tumbled from the cockpit when the aircraft struck and would hear the wind—before . . .

Still his hands hesitated, clenched almost into claws. *Choose*—He couldn't. The Firefox maintained the steep change of course the autopilot had initiated on the instructions of the TFR. Where—?

Valley! Lift—

He leveled the aircraft, pushed the throttles forward, canceled the autopilot by pressing the button on the column, then pulled it towards him. Grey ahead of him, nothing, nothing, nothing . . .

The nose came up, the Firefox climbed. 4,000 feet. Four-and-a-half, five-

He was above the mountains. Sweat ran from beneath his arms. His facemask was fogged. On the radar, the Migs seemed to have surged forward, away from the bottom of the screen towards its center. They could see him clearly now; a target upon which to home. Gant shuddered uncontrollably, gripping the column as he leveled the aircraft at 6,000 feet. He forced himself to look at the map on his knee, at the tiny printed heights of the peaks. Then he pulled back on the stick once more, lifting to 8,000 feet as quickly as he could. *Now* he was above them; the mountains no longer threatened him.

The Migs closed. He demanded a readout from the computer. Contact time, fourteen seconds. He pushed the throttles forward, forcing the Mach-meter past Mach 2; flying blind.

He flicked on the UHF set. He would be over Bardufoss in minutes now. He had to know.

"Bardufoss Approach—this is Firefox. Over." He listened. Checked the frequency. Listened. The UHF set was on, it should be working. "Bardufoss Approach—come in, Bardufoss. This is Firefox. Over."

The Migs seemed to have halted, dropped back to near the bottom of the screen. He knew they would be listening. It was not a high-security channel. They were waiting. He shivered. They were waiting until he made his approach, slowed down, presented himself to them helplessly as he went in to land.

The UHF set crackled. A distant voice with a Scandinavian accent spoke to him. His hands jumped on the column, as if it had been a Russian voice. But he recognized the word "Bardufoss."

"Repeat, Bardufoss. Say again your message. I wish for landing instructions. Over."

He waited, the aircraft at Mach 2. His positional readout from the inertial navigator showed him sixty miles from Bardufoss. He was aware of the turbulence outside the aircraft, almost as if it was a warning.

". . . is closed, repeat closed," he heard. "Estimated ceiling fifty feet in heavy snow. Runway visual range twenty yards with eighty degree crosswind gusting to forty-five knots." Then, in something of a more human tone: "I am sorry, Firefox, but a landing at Bardufoss is impossible. We have blizzard conditions . . ."

And they would have heard.

"Thank you, Bardufoss—"

"Good—" He cut off the hope, turning at once to the Soviet Tac-channel. Immediately, he heard the Russian chatter, the almost-glee, the agreement, the request for instructions, the decision, the tactics—

The Migs surged towards the center of the screen. He stared numbly at their advance upon him. They were at more than Mach 2, closing rapidly.

He was locked out by the storm. Already, other pursuing Soviet fighters were at the lower edge of his scope. But these three, closing so quickly—missile launch time, seven seconds—knew he was locked out. They were closing for the kill. He hesitated, expecting the leap of bright infrared dots towards him as they fired their first missiles. No—

He moved his hands slowly, almost stroking the control column. Finding, trying to find, almost finding, *finding*—

Resolve. Will. The desire to escape. He discovered it, used it; broke the spell.

He groaned aloud. As he lifted his head, he drew the column towards him and thrust the throttles forward. The nose of the Firefox lifted, wobbling in the increasing turbulence. He had ignored it, ignored the weather worsening around him, because he had not wanted to understand, had not wished to admit that Bardufoss would be closed down.

The Mach-meter passed 2, then 2.2, .3, .7 . . . The altimeter mounted through 15,000, then 17,000. The Migs below him altered course, striving to catch him. The Firefox raced upwards.

He broke out of the turbulent, snow-filled clouds at 26,000 feet, into a searing, eye-hurting blue sky. In the mirror, the cloud was massed and unbroken beneath him. The sun was low to the west. He climbed through 40,000 feet. Fifty—

The first of the Soviet fighters broke out of the cloud, a gleaming dot far below; a white blip at the lower edge of the scope. Then another gleaming spot joined it in the mirror, then a lagging third.

Gant leveled the Firefox at 70,000 feet, and accelerated. The Mach-meter passed 4.5. The gleaming dots faded from the scope. The cloud lay unbroken over the Lofoten Islands. He crossed the Arctic Circle. Almost idly, he listened to the last fading chatter from the UHF. Within minutes, he would change the frequency to the principal NATO secure Tac-channel, so that he could identify himself to RAF Strike Command and obtain clearance to land at Scampton, his original destination. He altered course in order to gain a visual sighting over Shetland, still five hundred miles to the south—eight minutes flying time. He grinned. He was a blur, a meteor, traveling a thousand miles an hour faster than any other aircraft in the world. He would have crossed the North Sea in another seven minutes; he would be over Shetland. Mach 5.1. Almost 4,000 miles an hour.

It was over. He felt exhilarated. The radio chatter faded. He heard—what was it? Rostock? Whatever that meant . . . It didn't matter. Radar clear. Empty. He was alone. The Soviet exchanges faded and were gone.

Anna—

No. He put her carefully aside. The others were paler

ghosts. They no longer troubled him. He was alive. He was in the Firefox. He had done it—

He looked down through a tear in the cloud. He was high over the North Sea. He was too high to see the flares burning off on the rigs. More gaps in the cloud. He was suspended above the flat, calm-looking sea. Elite; alone. Alone he had meant to think—alone. Not elite, alone . . .

He would be over Shetland in no more than three minutes. Time to open the Tac-channel—wouldn't be much of an ending, getting shot down . . .

Rostock? Who was Rostock . . . ?

Fuel-flow, check. Altimeter, radar, Mach-meter—

Radar—nothing . . .

He felt lightheaded. He reached forward to retune the UHF. He was alone; elitely alone. Drifting at 4,000 miles an hour.

Rostock—?

Radar—nothing . . . Glow—?

He leaned forward. He felt even more lightheaded; almost delirious. He screwed up his eyes, trying to focus. Flickering glow on the—panel—? He was floating. The nose of the Firefox dipped and the aircraft began to dive. He leaned forward against the control column, gripping the wheel but unaware of the pressure of his body pushing the column forward. He couldn't see clearly, and leaned further towards the panel. His eyesight was misty. He clutched the control column to his chest like a drunken man seeking support. As the nose of the Firefox dipped, the steepness of the dive was controlled only by his one-armed grip on the column and the straps restraining the forward movement of his body beyond a certain point.

Rostock—?

Vladimirov asked him what it meant. He was being beaten, but he felt nothing. Only numb. Warmly numb. Drugged . . . he remembered his father, shambling into that house on the, the, the—Mira Prospekt? Yes, yes, Mira Prospekt . . .

He heard voices, speaking Russian. Change channels. He did not understand—who was Rostock?

Glow on the—panel? Glow—?

He did not understand. The Firefox began to fall out of the sky. Unnoticed, the altimeter unrolled with increasing speed as he slumped towards the panel. The throttles were still set at high cruise power.

He saw dots—blips not glows. Right and left of the screen, converging on him. Rostock—? His helmet was almost against the panel, and his hanging face opposite the scope. White blips, rushing at him.

30,000 feet, twenty-five, twenty-two . . . The altimeter unrolled unnoticed.

Gant groggily lifted his head, and his hand. He felt along the panel. The Firefox bucked as he readjusted his hold on the column to gain more support. The nose came up slightly, but the stick resisted him fiercely. He believed in it as a solid, unmoving thing to which he could cling. He tried to focus. The radar was filled with closing blips which immediately became a blur. Flickering glow . . . ? Rostock, Ro—stock . . . ? What did it mean. Glow—

He touched the flicker of light, and tried to count. Tried to remember. It was important, like Rostock. But he could answer this question—he was trained to do it—

He clutched at a switch and threw it with a convulsive jerk of his body. Then he lolled wearily upright, still holding the column, aware now of the restraint of his straps. As his head came above the cockpit coaming, he could see that now the sea had huge, tossing waves. There were fires burning below and around him, flares warning of—

He saw the Vietnamese girl swallowed by fire. He saw Anna with the blue hole in her forehead. His arms ached, seemed close to being pulled from their sockets with the effort required to hold onto the control column.

The girl, Anna—himself . . .

"No—you *bastard*—!"

He fought the column, trying to heave it towards him with a fierce, sudden strength. He dragged the throttles back, then pulled further on the column. It moved more easily. His lungs gulped the emergency oxygen supply. The altimeter unrolled more slowly, the Mach-meter descended. The aircraft began to level out. He continued to fight the column, clutching it back against him. The horizon jolted, wobbled, the waves accelerated less than a thousand feet below. The flames from the oil rigs rushed beneath him. His head was filled with noises, voices speaking in Russian—

He reset the UHF feverishly. He heard it, then—

Rostock. Spoken in English, an English accent. A babble of English voices.

He raced over an oil rig, then another, then a third. Snow flurried across the stormy, tossing water, but there were bright gaps in the cloud. Shreds of it struggled to envelop him, but the Firefox kept breaking free of them . . .

His head cleared. He was traveling at less than four hundred miles an hour, at 1,200 feet, across what remained of the North Sea; towards Shetland.

He continued to gulp down the emergency oxygen supply. The airplane had tried to kill him again. Had betrayed him. The warning light had come on too late for him to recognize its signal. Lack of oxygen had already made him dizzy and lightheaded before he noticed it. His heart pounded, his pulse thudded in his ears. His helmet was filled with English voices, themselves full of congratulation. He flicked back to the Soviet channel.

Rostock—they were calling Rostock. Airbase, he remembered. It would have been the nearest front-line airbase on an interception course. East Germany. A couple of squadrons of Mig-25s had been despatched by the elite Sixteenth Frontal Aviation Army to destroy him. The RAF had reached him first. He had been a sitting target. They might even have been just sitting back, watching him dive into the sea. The Firefox had been doing their work for them.

He sat back in the couch. *Bastard*. On either side of him, aircraft appeared. They waggled their wings, coyly displaying their RAF roundels. One of the pilots, the one to starboard, signaled with his thumb. Success, congratulation—something like that. Beyond the Tornado fighter, Gant glimpsed the dark coastline of Shetland rising out of the sea.

Wearily, he retuned the UHF to the NATO secure tactical channel. The English voices gabbled for a moment, then one of them silenced the others and attempted to contact him. He glanced to starboard. The pilot of the Tornado was frantically signaling with his hand. He wanted him to answer, to use the radio—

Gant did not care. He was alive. He was safe. There was time enough to answer them. His heartbeat and pulse settled, receding in his awareness. Bastard. The airplane was a bastard.

It was over now.

"Go ahead, flight leader," he said eventually, sitting

more upright in the couch. "This is Firefox. Receiving you loud and clear. Go ahead. Over."

"Major Gant? Congratulations, Major—what happened, sir? What happened to you? Over."

"I lived," Gant replied. "Now, get me home."

At 1,200 feet and at a speed of 386 miles an hour, the Mig-31, NATO-codenamed the Firefox, drifted towards the Scottish coast, escorted by six Tornado fighters of RAF Strike Command. They were the only aircraft registering on his radar.

The grey, stormy sea flowed beneath the belly of the aircraft. A stray gleam of sunlight glowed on the cockpit. Gant, at last, allowed himself a smile of success.